ANGELS AT
TWENTY PAST

ANGELS AT TWENTY PAST

MARCHELL ABRAHAMS

Matador
9 Priory Business Park,
Wistow Road, Kibworth Beauchamp,
Leicestershire. LE8 0RX
Tel: 0116 279 2299
Email: books@troubador.co.uk
Web: www.troubador.co.uk/matador
Twitter: @matadorbooks

ISBN 978 1838594 428

British Library Cataloguing in Publication Data.
A catalogue record for this book is available from the British Library.

Printed and bound in Great Britain by 4edge Limited
Typeset in 12pt Garamond by Troubador Publishing Ltd, Leicester, UK

Matador is an imprint of Troubador Publishing Ltd

For Mary Anna, kith if not kin;
and Annie, who saw the Lancaster with me.

AUTHOR'S NOTE

It is customary, even necessary, for an author to disclaim any relationship between the inhabitants of the mortal plane and his or her created world. While I have described the exterior of the National Archives at Kew in some detail, its interior, its employees, and its visitors are entirely my own invention. In like manner, I have created both a curator for the Pozzo di San Patrizio and an unnamed college, with Dean, for Oxford. I hope I may be forgiven these lapses from good taste by all institutions concerned. Any errors remaining are my sole responsibility; and I will be glad indeed to learn that Herodotus was, once again, right.

Marchell Abrahams
Aberdeenshire, 2020

ONE

But as for him, neither hath he now sound heart, nor ever will have; thereof I deem moreover that he will reap the fruit.

Book VI, *The Iliad*, tr. Lang

IT WASN'T UNTIL we rounded the bend in the drive, just where the sun clears the trees, that we noticed anything wrong. My mother was halfway through an anecdote involving some hens belonging to the neighbour we had been visiting, when her voice trailed off and she came to an uncertain halt.

"What is it, Mummy?" I asked. Her gaze was fixed on the house in a way I didn't like. "Watch those eggs!" I made a grab for the basket and took it from her. "What's the matter?"

"The study doors are open," she said quietly.

I settled the basket on my arm, and looked. The french windows to the study, on the east side of my parents' gracious, Georgian former rectory, were standing wide. Our eyes locked on each other's.

"But you opened them this morning as usual, didn't you?" I said uncertainly. "In this heat…"

"Yes. But I shut them again before we came out."

"Did you lock them?"

"No. I didn't think it was necessary. Good gracious, you can *see* this house from Maisie's!"

I pushed the basket back at her. "I'll run and look."

"*No*, Cassie!"

I was already a pace or two away, but I turned at this, still half-running, half-walking backwards. "Why not?"

"They might be in there."

"Who? Oh, crumbs, I see what you mean." I stopped. "Are you thinking— What are you thinking?"

"Burglars," said my mother. She was pale, and her face was set. "We've been burgled. Oh, Cass."

"But there's nothing in the study to burgle," I objected, "only Daddy's fusty old research and fertility symbols."

"The drawing-room's just across the hall."

"Oh, my— Crumbs!" I said again. "What shall we do?"

"We wait, and we watch," whispered my mother, suddenly alert and steely. She melted off the drive behind a tree. After a stunned second, I joined her in the shadows. "Who do you think you are, Violette Szabo?" I hissed.

"Thank goodness we hadn't reached the sun," she said out of the corner of her mouth. "There's a good chance they won't have seen us. Now, hush, there's a good girl. Watch carefully."

We waited there under the graceful, summer-spread beech, and watched, but no one came or went; nothing stirred, except for a robin, his beak stuffed full of grubs, making for the clematis that hung its sweet-scented blossoms over our lovely old herringbone-brick wall. To one side of the creamy roundels, and half-hidden by them, was the door that led out into the lane. It ran alongside my parents' four or so acres before joining the main road at the foot of our gates. It was shut.

"Oh, come on, Mummy," I said after a bit in my normal voice. "This is silly."

"*Hush!* It's sensible to take precautions," she whispered. "They don't hesitate to bash people over the head if they're disturbed."

We waited. I was fidgeting impatiently by the time she finally spoke.

"All right, let's go. No, don't make for the study. We'll go the usual way, round the other side to the kitchen."

"Why?"

"Give them time to leave, just in case they're watching us."

Despite the warmth of the day, I shivered. "The trouble with you is you watch too many war films."

"My father taught your Uncle Will and me lots of useful tricks, darling; you never know when they mightn't come in handy. Now, come on, play up to me, do."

I felt conspicuous, even naked, as we walked out into the sun. My mother, who is a born actress, was pretending that nothing was out of the ordinary, and doing it superlatively well; but I am a creature of impulse, incapable of concealing what I'm feeling, and I felt about as natural as a clothes-horse in a ballroom. I'll confess I was grateful to reach the shelter of the house, but when my mother put down the eggs on the kitchen table, and stooped, and actually took off her shoes, I'm afraid I gave her a derisive smile. "Mummy, do grow up!" I begged.

"Hush, will you? Stay here," she said. "I'm going to listen."

"Will I hell stay here," I retorted. "I'm coming too."

"Then take your shoes off, and be as quiet as a mouse. And don't *argue!*"

I shut my mouth and took off my shoes.

Of course there was no one in the house but us.

But there had been. We stood, aghast, and looked round at the carnage that had been wrought in the study among my father's things. He was a fantastically untidy man, but not even he left books splayed open and face down on the floor with their pages crumpled anyhow. The shelves from which they had fallen—or been thrown—gaped emptily.

"This isn't normal, is it?" I asked doubtfully. My foot touched something, and I bent and picked up Walter Skeat's huge *Etymological Dictionary* (the fourth edition; published in 1910) and began straightening the leaves.

"No, it's definitely worse than usual. And there are the french windows, wide open. Don't touch a thing," warned my mother, seeing me with the Dictionary in both hands. "I'm going to call the police."

I hastily put Walter Skeat on my father's desk. "And Daddy," I reminded her.

"Yes," said my mother thoughtfully, "yes…"

The police came, asked questions, dusted for prints, covered our fingers with black ink which they forgot to tell us how to remove, took photographs, examined the french windows, and lectured my mother on alarm systems. They then locked up the study, made a desultory examination of the rest of the house and the briefest of tours round the garden, and left again.

We retreated to the kitchen, examined our inky fingers, and set to work with washing-up liquid and scouring pads. Then we poured out the rest of last night's bottle of wine and sat down.

"As if I'm going to set the alarm when I've only stepped out for half an hour to a neighbour's house," said my mother, still bristling. "And of course the french windows were unlocked; I always open all the doors first thing, especially in this weather. Most of them, anyway."

"It takes twenty minutes to go round locking up, as well," I said, heartily reassuring.

We sipped wine.

"He must have been there, watching," she said.

"He chose his moment, didn't he?"

"There we both were, and me with a basket on my arm. I expect he thought we were going to the village, or something. If I *had* left the study windows open, we would never have known he'd been here."

I know that doesn't sound funny, but I could tell my mother was thinking along the same lines as I was. In my father's presence we entered his study in peril of our lives, never mind in his absence.

"What your father's going to say, I dread to think," she added, as if in proof of this. Then: "There's no need for that expression. He'll know instantly if something's been moved, or stolen."

"Goodness knows how," I said undutifully. "Actually, I've been thinking."

"Don't hurt yourself," said my mother.

I made a face at her. "Nothing's been taken, as far as we can tell. Nothing that your common-or-garden burglar would make a beeline for."

"What, like the TV, or the DVD player?"

"Exactly. And they're not in the drawing-room anyway. And if he was slightly higher up the food chain, with more refined tastes in other people's property, tell me why he didn't pop Granny's bits of Meissen into his pocket while he was about it? There wasn't a single print in the drawing-room, and don't tell me he suddenly remembered to put gloves on as he was crossing the hall, 'cos I won't believe it."

My mother looked portentously at me over the rim of her glass. "That," she said, "is a very excellent point. I wouldn't believe it, either."

"Well, whatever he—or they—was looking for, they must have known, or thought they knew, that it was to be found in the study."

"Go on."

"The only things in the study are his books, piles of paper everywhere, lumps of meteorite, bits of old clay with gibberish on them, and photographs, and that sort of thing. There's nothing of obvious value. The walls aren't hung with Rembrandts, for example... Which means that whatever the thief was looking for, it was something to do with Daddy's work."

My mother goggled at me in owlish disbelief. "You're not seriously suggesting some sort of academic espionage? Stealing his research? *Sabotage?* Oh, really!"

I shrugged.

"Well," said my mother doubtfully, "I suppose it does happen. But since he hardly has a flourishing academic career to protect, I don't see... *And* he took his laptop with him. All his financial stuff is on it, so they can't have been after *that.*" She regarded me in mild disgust. "We've forgotten the fertility goddesses. Perhaps they're valuable."

"Not to mention the phallic symbols. People have the strangest tastes." This made us laugh, which was a relief. Then I added: "All the same, he might have trodden on somebody's intellectual toes, you know."

"Isn't that a bit far-fetched? All he does is expend a lot of ink on refuting other people's research."

"Really? Is that really all?" I asked, only mildly interested. "Still, what other explanation is there?"

"I can't think of one. And the police weren't very impressed, certainly." She grimaced. "What a very unsettling feeling it is, to know that nefarious persons have been prowling about." She brightened. "I've been wanting to redecorate, though, and this is just the excuse I need."

I shook my head at her. "Daddy still won't let you touch his study, you know he won't. It wouldn't matter how many burglars had been in there."

"I know," she sighed. "I haven't forgotten what happened the last time I tried."

We grinned at each other. I think that in the relief of finding minimal damage and nothing—nothing obvious, that is—stolen from the house, we were both a trifle light-headed.

"How long will it take Daddy to get home?"

"He was due back tomorrow anyway. Thank goodness he's only got to fly from Athens."

"Athens is in Greece," I objected. "I thought he was in Turkey."

"He was, but the island he's gone to look at is Greek."

I sighed. "Borders are *so* twentieth century. Come on, let's go and see if we can find how the thief got in. The door into the lane is always locked, so he might have climbed over the wall somehow."

"Why bother," my mother objected, "when there's the gate at the back?"

But the clematis showed no broken branches or bruised blossoms; and the shorn, velvety grass was too dry and short for footprints, although my mother, repudiating my sarcastic offer to fetch her a magnifying glass, searched minutely. We walked slowly along the wall, looking under trees and bushes, and at length came to the five-barred gate at the back of the property. This leads into the field behind, which is let to a neighbouring farmer, and was securely padlocked. At right angles to this, and abutting the lane, was another gate; and as my mother observed, anybody could have climbed over both and hidden behind some foliage to watch the house.

"In fact, I'll bet you anything you like he stood here, behind the escallonia," I said, suiting the action to the word. "He could have seen us through the branches, and we'd never have known he was there. He might even have been watching the house since you opened up this morning."

My mother straightened up from a close examination of the printless grass at my feet. "I must go and ring your father," she said. There was the faintest suggestion about her of an appointment with a firing squad, and I didn't hesitate to tell her so with a spark of malice. But all she would say, darkly, and with superb understatement, was that he would not be pleased.

*

My father came home the next day. He had been travelling without rest for twenty-four hours and had just come from the police station, answering (as he put it) a lot of damn' silly questions, and was, consequently, very far from pleased. Not until a bored young constable had come to remove the scene-of-crime tape was he allowed to enter his study (the police had relegated us to the bottom of the list; no damage to person or property), and when at last he confronted the frightful mess, with Mummy and me peeping over his shoulders, his language turned the air deep blue.

"Once a soldier, always a soldier," said my mother, blenching, and shut us both out into the hall.

We didn't see my father again until dinner, by which time he had presumably re-untidied the study to his satisfaction.

Mummy and I glanced at him, then at each other, and remained silent until the chocolate mousse when, finally, my father spoke.

"Nothing's missing," he announced in quite a normal voice. "Not so much as a Post-it note."

In case my father should come across as an old-fashioned Victorian paterfamilias and strict disciplinarian, I should say here that most of the time he is a darling: funny, annoying, reliable, *there*. The only things that enrage him are sloppy, illogical thinking (into which category his untidiness, naturally, does not come), cruelty, and injustice. Even then, his rages are like summer thunder-and-lightning: quickly over, leaving you wondering what the fuss had been about. He had covered himself with glory in the Falklands, and left the army soon after, at the end of his short-service commission. Being blessed with a large private income, which he had amassed during his second career as a venture capitalist, he had retired early when still only in his forties; bought our large rectory in a beautiful part of Surrey, not far from Farnham; and could more or less please himself. We both loved him very dearly, and now emerged from behind the chocolate mousse all smiles.

"Well, that makes it stranger than ever," said my mother, who knew better than to ask him how he could possibly tell. "I expect someone just took a chance, that's all."

My father grunted. "Even if they saw you two go out, how did they know I wasn't in the house somewhere? Tell me that, Moira."

"I can't, darling. Let's all just be very thankful that we're alive and undamaged."

And that was how it started.

*

9

I went back to work a couple of days later, the break-in all but forgotten.

When I say *work*, I must immediately confess that I am no high-flyer, and have no desire to be one. My outstanding talent being, as my mother once remarked, for choosing clothes and painting my nails, I had put some capital behind a school-friend of mine who wanted to open a beauty salon; and spent three not very arduous mornings a week as her receptionist. The salon thrived in its chic little pedestrianised street behind the King's Road, and so did my investment. My father was delighted to recognise the glimmerings of another financial brain in the family (or, at least, that's what he said); and my mother kept her own counsel.

"Mrs Burgoyne-Trench has rescheduled her appointment," I said, brushing the rubbings-out from my eraser onto the floor.

"What, again?" said Dinah, wrinkling her nose. "That's the third time in a fortnight. I think she must have taken a lover. She's never usually so indecisive."

"Oh, she's definitely got a lover," I said, scribbling in the new time. "I booked her in for that Brazilian, you remember."

"So you did. And she hasn't been back for a strim yet, has she?"

"Not yet. She must look like those paths you mow through wildflower meadows by now."

"That usually means a husband," objected Dinah, less confidently.

"We know she's got one of those," I agreed. "He came to pick her up once, don't you remember, and he was so cross when she made him come in and wait." I giggled.

"Husband trouble, then," amended Dinah, closing one eye in a significant wink.

"Lover trouble," I corrected her. "Perhaps he's playing hard-to-get. She must be well over forty. It's hard to tell what they see in her."

"Forty's nothing these days," said Dinah. "Look at Joan Collins, she's double that, and she can still dance until dawn. Wish I knew her secret: she has a complexion to die for." She returned to Mrs Burgoyne-Trench. "Lover trouble, indeed. Makes her sound as though she's got some nasty medical condition. Well, let's see who we've got next. Oh, it's the Contessa. I want to see if I can—"

"Contessa, my foot," I said roundly. "She's plain Holly Myers, from Worksop. Judith Heard told me at the last Dior show."

Dinah smiled patiently. "Whoever she is, she's a regular, and she pays. I want to persuade her not to wear her nails so square-cut. She's got hands like spades, and square-cut does not suit her at all." She glanced once again over my shoulder at the appointments book, then we both looked up as the door opened to admit a man on a wave of the distant sound of London traffic. She straightened. "Good morning, sir. May we help you?"

The man came hesitantly up to the desk. He was young, dressed in dark green moleskins and a checked shirt, and looked as though he hoped to be taken for a country gentleman. His voice, when he spoke, was a good, workmanlike imitation of the same, but the whole failed to convince me entirely. I had become quite good at spotting fakes by now, and I was nearly certain about this one.

"I'm looking for Cassie Greatrex."

"That's me," I said, surprised and intrigued. "I'm Cassie Greatrex. Oh,"—as a thought struck me—"you're not a policeman, are you?"

"Police?"

Dinah and he spoke with one voice, and turned identical looks of startled dismay on me.

"I only thought," I said, "because there was a break-in at my parents' house last weekend, and you might be C.I.D."

"I don't think so," he said, with a tinge of scorn.

"You didn't tell me," said Dinah to me, reproachfully.

"No, I forgot. Neither of us was hurt, and nothing was stolen." I surveyed the young man. "You can't be the police, come to think of it. They said there was no real case for them to work on."

"No, I'm not the police, still less C.I.D.," he said. "Did you say 'neither of us'?"

"My mother and me. My father was away at the time, in Turkey. At least, it wasn't only the mainland, it was also an island quite close. Lesbos, or something."

"Lemnos?"

"That's it, do you know it?"

Instead of answering, he came a step closer. There was an intent look in his eyes that had nothing to do with Dinah's arts. "You *are* Hector Greatrex's granddaughter?"

With the faintest feeling of alarm, I stood up. "Yes, look, what is this? What has my grandfather to do with this?" My voice sharpened. "My parents—are my parents all right?"

"I'm sure they are—that is, I don't know, I haven't come up from there." He sounded impatient. "I'm Colin Bardsey, you know." He made it sound as though that explained everything.

"Good for you," I said, mystified and beginning to be cross.

Behind him the door had opened again, and, obliged to attend to the two women who had come in, I craned to see past him. "If you'll excuse me for a moment...?"

He stepped aside with obvious reluctance. One of the women was some nails for Dinah (not the bogus Contessa from Worksop), and the other was a notorious ditherer. It was some ten minutes before I pinned her down to a facial and a back massage and got rid of her, by which time Colin Bardsey was pacing up and down by the window and looking at his watch. I eyed him thoughtfully, then approached the booth to which Dinah had taken the nails.

"Excuse me," I said politely, and in hushed tones round the pink curtain. "Dinah, it's five to twelve, do you mind if I go now? Ginny's not here yet, but I think Mr Bardsey's about to—that is, he seems to be a bit pushed for time, so if you don't mind…?"

Ginny did Mondays and Fridays, and the other three afternoons; and just in time, I remembered my professional manners in front of a customer.

"That's fine, you go," she replied blandly. "See you tomorrow."

By the tone of her voice, I knew she would want a faithful, and, if possible, a verbatim account of what passed between the impatient Mr Bardsey and me. I winked at her and let the curtain fall. Then I picked up my bag from under the reception desk and slung it over my shoulder.

"Come on," I said to him encouragingly, "I'm all yours."

We stood outside on the hot pavement and measured one another. In the bright sun, I saw that he was a bit older than me, perhaps middle twenties, with a deep tan against which the fair hair showed thick and well cut. Not precisely handsome, but with hazel eyes and a nice smile. He was smiling at me now.

"I can tell," he said, "that you have no idea who I am."

I shook my head. "Not a clue. Should I have?" Before he could answer I had added: "Tell you what, shall we go and have a civilised sit-down lunch somewhere? I've got lots of money; shall I pay?"

"I've got lots of money, too," he said with a tinge of bravado. "We'll go Dutch."

We went to an unfashionable French restaurant that Daddy had found, and he told me who he was.

Apparently, his great-uncle, John Bardsey, and my grandfather had been friends during the war, and had fallen out badly over some works of art looted from some museum in Germany.

"I don't know much more than that—and I certainly don't know the rights and wrongs of it," he said, "but this reporter friend of mine I mentioned has been commissioned to look into stories like these, and I said I'd do some digging for him. I'm ideally placed, you see."

I was intrigued. "It sounds fascinating, though I don't know how you think I can help. I don't know anything about it. How did you find out about this friendship? I don't recall ever hearing the name of Bardsey mentioned at home."

"No? Well, that's the interesting part. My great-uncle kept a diary, and your grandfather's name is in it. You see, my great-uncle didn't survive the war."

"I'm sorry," I said automatically, but sincerely. Of course it was ancient history, but he did have a nice smile. "How do you mean, you're ideally placed?"

"I'm at Oxford," he explained, "reading Linguistics. Not that that in itself means much, but it does give me access to a huge amount of resources—archives, that sort of thing. Very useful, for a would-be don."

"I see. I'm impressed," I said truthfully, but still in the dark. "But why involve me? And"—it had only just occurred to me—"how did you know to find me?"

"Oh—military records."

"I see," I said again, not entirely sure how Linguistics fitted in with military records. "What paper does your friend write for?"

"He's freelance," replied Colin. His tone was curt, though that might have been because our main course arrived just then, and we were into the business of napkins, vegetables, and pepper mills. When our waiter had bowed himself away, I began to say something about the food, but Colin forestalled me. "Tell me about this break-in."

I changed tack willingly enough. "Nothing, really, just that. I don't suppose we'd ever have guessed, the mess my father likes to work in, but he—or they—had left the french windows swinging wide open, and we saw them coming along the drive."

I thought he looked shocked, and warmed to his compassion.

"You saw them?" he echoed. "You actually *saw* them coming along the drive?"

It took me a moment, but I got it. "No—I mean, Mummy and I were coming along the drive, and we saw the windows standing open."

"Oh, I see. And was there anybody about?" The forkful of *rognons au Pernod* which he had held suspended in mid-air finally made its way to his mouth.

"Not a sausage. Mummy would have us dodging about from tree to tree, armed to the teeth like S.O.E. agents, just in case."

He had recovered himself. "Very sensible of her. What were you armed with, Mausers?"

I laughed. "No, just a couple of dozen eggs."

"And you say nothing was stolen?"

"*Nix, nade, niente*. If all those mean nothing."

"They sound as though they mean nothing."

All through this his tone was teasing, but I sensed some definite purpose to his questions under the normal dismayed concern. This increased with his next question, but still no alarm bells rang.

"And your father was away?"

"Yes, chasing Etruscan inscriptions on Lesbos. I thought the Etruscans were in Italy, but there you go."

"That's ancient history for you. And it was Lemnos."

"Is there a difference?"

"In that they're both largish islands that belong to Greece and lie close to the Turkish coast, not much. In other respects, yes."

Afraid he might start lecturing me about the other respects, I asked him to tell me something of what had led him to read Linguistics—combined with computer-programming, as I now learnt. I listened politely, but as his chosen subjects seemed to have their origins solely in how best to turn to the greatest financial advantage a natural flair for languages, it wasn't desperately interesting. He did not tell me anything of Oxford itself, which I would have enjoyed; and I wasn't much impressed by his ambition to write computer games to make as much money as fast as possible. Not, of course, that he put it quite as baldly as that. I took the first advantage I decently could of a break in the monologue to say: "Look, do you want anything else to eat?"

Neither of us did, so we split the bill and exchanged addresses. He asked me out to dinner the following week, and I accepted. We shook hands outside the restaurant, and I strolled home to More Street, not thinking much, just enjoying the sun and looking in the shop windows. I was twenty-two, summer was here, and I had a date—even if, judging by lunch, it wouldn't be a very scintillating one.

My key was in the lock when I changed my mind. I took it out, put it in my bag, skipped down the steps, and headed for Lennox Street instead.

TWO

As I was then a youth, so doth old age now beset me.
Yet even so will I abide among the horsemen…

Book IV, *ibid.*

A GYMNASIUM ISN'T perhaps the obvious place to look for
a man closer to ninety than eighty, but nevertheless that's
where I knew I would find my grandfather. He had sold his
house when Granny died and now lived in a charming flat
above the shop, as it were. He was a living advertisement for
the benefits of keeping fit: still six feet tall, upright, well-
muscled, light on his feet, and with a physique a man a third
his age would have envied. He was in his working kit of
singlet and those ski-pant things with straps under the feet,
and as soon as he saw me, he caught up a cotton jumper
from a bench, and, with a murmured word to a young thing
of no more than sixty-five, pulled it over his head and called
to me. "Go up to the office, Cassie, darling. I won't be a
moment."

He turned to address a word to the other two members
working away, one on the horse, as neat and graceful as any

Olympic athlete, and almost my grandfather's age; the other hanging like a bat from the bars and doing sort of upside down sit-ups. He was a regular, at least seventy, and made it look effortless. I gave him a thoughtful glance, and made for the stairs at a decorous pace.

While I waited, I looked at the sepia photographs of tough young men with oars, silver cups, hockey sticks, rugby footballs, cricket bats…and rifles and pace-sticks. I glanced along the names, but there was no one there called Bardsey. I wondered vaguely how many of them had come home after 1945, and whether my grandfather's survival betokened some particular toughness on his part, or whether it had been simply the fortunes of war. He was coming up the stairs now, two at a time. He shut the door behind him, kissed me warmly, and gestured to me to take a seat.

"Well, my granddaughter? You look your usual blooming self. I meant that as a compliment, by the way."

I laughed. "I'm very well, Grandpa, thank you. You're looking as fit as a fiddle too, if it comes to that."

He gave me a complacent smile that was nearly a smirk. "I still have some way to go; not ready for the grave yet. What brings you here? Everybody all right at home?"

"Everybody's fine, thanks, and send their love. And as for why I'm here—well, we're always being told to pick older people's brains, and I thought I'd come and tell you about the man I had lunch with today."

"That seems like a *non sequitur*," he observed, "but I expect it isn't. Thank heaven for a classical education."

But instead of telling him about Colin straight away, I started with another *non sequitur*. "I take it Daddy didn't tell you about the break-in at the Old Rectory."

The thick white brows began to beetle. "Break-in? No, he did not," growled my grandfather. "Recently? I thought as much. I do wish he wouldn't keep sparing my feelings in this idiotic fashion. He and your mother treat me as though I were in my dotage, and I find it intensely irritating."

I twinkled at him. "You're eighty-eight next birthday, Grandpa," I said, "even if you do look twenty years younger."

"I'll have you know that my doctor—"

I knew that one and cut smoothly across. "We all know you're a medical miracle," I said, "but you'll never stop us worrying about you."

"Stuff and nonsense. You may tell me about your young man, but first I want to know what's been going on."

So I told him, laying a good deal of stress on there having been nothing taken and nobody hurt. He was not as shocked as I thought he would be, for which I was grateful; and seemed inclined, like us, to dismiss the whole thing as an opportunity seized on the off-chance. "I'm glad to see you're not fretting over it. Now, what about this young man?"

"He's a bit older than me. His name is Colin Bardsey." I watched for some recognition, but there was none.

"Bardsey," said my grandfather, narrowing his eyes. "Yorkshire. Islands?"

"I didn't know there were any. He said that his great-uncle had been a friend of yours during the war. John Bardsey."

"Never heard of him," said my grandfather.

"Oh. He said that you and his great-uncle had fallen out big time over some looted works of art...?" I wasn't even sure that I had the terms right.

"Looted works of art? Are we talking about that business during the war? If so, looted by whom? The Germans, or the Russians?"

"I haven't the faintest idea," I replied helplessly. "He's reading Linguistics at Oxford, and a friend of his, a journalist, has been commissioned to write a series of articles about all that stuff. It's pretty hot news right now. Apparently."

"Why didn't he come to me, if he knows of me?"

"No idea, Grandpa. I'm only telling you what he told me. What happened?"

"The looting, do you mean?" He subjected me to a searching, not very grandfatherly, scrutiny. I felt somehow on trial, as though he were assessing my suitability to hear and understand. He must have been satisfied by what he saw, for the look faded. "It's a long story," he said. "Very briefly, and leaving out a good deal of it, the Germans made it their business to pillage occupied Europe—Eastern Europe, that is—of any and every work of art they could lay their hands on. That was bad enough, but when they got to Russia, they simply destroyed everything they couldn't steal: people, animals, buildings—including the churches—even the land. We took a long time to twig in this country, and eventually sent some men, graduates in History of Art mostly, to compile inventories of what had been looted. To begin with, there were only three." His eyes had gone dark with memory.

"Three dozen?" I hazarded. "Three hundred?" Suddenly I was alarmed. "Look, Grandpa, if this is too much, let's skip it, shall we?"

"I'll sweat it out," he said. "Always have done; it's why I started this place. It's the healthiest thing to do: *mens sana in corpore sano*, and all that. I'm sure you'll agree." He smiled at my expression, and went on: "No, not three hundred; not even three dozen. Just three, at least to begin with. They were armed with nothing more than a Baedeker and a few maps. Their job was to identify and protect what was left. It was an impossible job, but they managed. I had a place at Balliol to read History of Art, but of course that went by the board when I was called up." A rather grim smile. "They suggested I volunteer. It was an improvement on six inches of mud in a slit trench in Italy, so I took their advice. My job took me all round occupied Europe, and ultimately to Berlin. I was there when the Lancasters bombed it flat."

"Some improvement," I said. I must have sounded uninterested, even bored; but this was not the case. I was honestly horrified.

"Luck of the draw. I'm here to tell the tale: most of 'em aren't." He nodded at the photographs and rose lithely to his feet to examine them. "Now you mention it, there was a chap out there, attached to my regiment, but his name wasn't Bardsey. He was an art historian, too, and was detailed to Berlin with me. I seem to remember that we got on well at first because of that. Funny little fellow. He was supposed to be helping me, but I found out he was using the information to shop Jews to the Germans. Rich Jews, I mean, with collections; pictures, china, silver, that sort of thing. He was shopping his own people as well; his father was a Russian Jew. He was spared the usual fate because he was useful, and also—well, he was working for us, so we made sure he was spared. He was made to pay for it, though. The Germans used to keep him co-operating with them by tantalising him with information about his family—and we did the same by promising him protection. They—his family—were all in the camps, you see. The concentration camps."

"I know."

He nodded. "Of course, towards the end of the war, he became suddenly less useful as the Germans retreated. Then he became desperate and began to shop German looters to the Russians instead. That the fellow you mean?"

"I don't know; it could be. He might have changed his name. What happened to him?"

"We came to blows," said my grandfather shortly. "He was getting altogether too interested in some inventories of names and so forth that I'd bust several guts putting together, not all of them my own, and I found him poking around a bit too close for comfort. When I taxed him with it, he denied it. When I became a bit more insistent, he drew his revolver. So I drew mine. High Noon wasn't in it."

Now I really was shocked. My patient, humane grandfather, who had given me piggy-backs and let me pretend he was a horse, careering about the garden with me on his back and getting grass-stains on his knees? I shook my head.

"It was war, darling," he said. "So much was at stake."

"Yes," I said, pulling myself together. "Yes. I'm sorry. What happened when he— What happened then?"

"I kicked it out of his hand and closed with him. He was only a weedy little bloke, and older than me. He didn't stand a chance. He tried to duck—tripped over the leg of a chair and fell, and hit his head on the hearth. Completely freak accident, but when I checked, he was as dead as a haddock. Good thing, really. It made it all right to leave him, if you understand. The Russians were coming, and I didn't want to hang around. They might have thought I was German, and— But you don't want to hear about that."

I swallowed. Too right I didn't. "What happened to the inventories?"

"I burnt them along with a lot of other sensitive paperwork. Then I began to feel I'd seen enough of Berlin, and decided, with one or two others, to call it a day. I'd had no orders, no communication with my H.Q., even. It was rather each man for himself. But I was wounded during the bombing, and someone found me wandering around. Thank God I was repatriated just in time. I could have been taken prisoner, but the Germans knew it was all over, and they couldn't get out fast enough. I fetched up in a military hospital, and lived to tell the tale." He came back to the present abruptly. "Now, about this break-in..."

Happy to let him return to the subject, I said: "I promise you, they didn't take anything. We looked everywhere, but the only room they'd been in was Daddy's study, and they ransacked it."

"How on earth could you tell?" he protested, as tidy as my father was untidy.

I grinned affectionately at him. "That's exactly what Mummy and I said. But the police did find prints, and the french windows were left open. They couldn't have cared less, really, the police, I mean. Daddy said nothing had gone, and I suppose he must be able to find his way through his own chaos."

My grandfather frowned. "Seems a trifle careless to leave prints. Surely everybody knows about prints nowadays. Sounds to me as though he's bungled it."

I shrugged.

"What is your father working on at the moment?"

"Crumbs, I don't know. He was in Turkey when it happened, if that helps. He was not pleased about being dragged away."

"Turkey?"

"Well, an island. Lesbos. No, Lemnos."

"They're both Greek."

"I know. I learnt that today," I said proudly.

"From this Colin Bardsey?"

"Yes. No flies on you, are there, Grandpa? Look, were you in Berlin all the time? No, sorry, you said you weren't." I hadn't meant to return to the subject, except that, for some reason I couldn't identify, I rather wanted to know.

"No, indeed. To begin with, I was trudging about trying to trace stolen works of art, as I've said, but towards the end of the war, I was in Berlin guarding a great, priceless collection of treasure from Schliemann's dig at Troy," he replied. "I had been detailed to oversee its removal to the Zoo tower."

"Whose dig at *where?*" I was completely at sea.

"Heinrich Schliemann. He was a very rich German merchant who devoted his life to proving that *The Iliad* was true, and that Troy existed."

"Troy?" I echoed blankly. I had never heard of either.

"Darling… Yes, Troy. The British people are descended from Trojans. So are the Romans, but that's another story."

I was just about to laugh this to scorn when a dim memory of my grandmother fluttered into my brain. She was laughing, and telling my grandfather that he was well-named, a Trojan… It had been an expression of hers. And not just of hers, now I came to think of it; it seemed to have been an expression that people used to indicate someone of honour and probity. "Is Hector a Trojan name, then? I didn't know. I've heard of the Trojan Horse," I offered hopefully, aware for the first time of the enormous gulf that yawned between my grandfather's schooling and mine. I dredged a bit deeper. "Mazes? Though how they come into it, I have no idea."

He had gone over to a shelf of books, one of many that lined his sitting-room. "Virgil is thought to have made up the Trojan Horse," he said. "It doesn't appear anywhere in *The Iliad*. It does come into *The Odyssey*, but it's possible that the section was added later. You're right about the mazes, though. Troy Towns, they're called. You find them all over the place in the British Isles—they originated in Crete, which opens up a fascinating line of research into our remoter origins.

Bother, my Lang is still at the bookbinders." He came to sit down again. "Translator of *The Iliad,* or one of the many. Not the easiest of reads, perhaps, but a lot more faithful to the original than Rieu, for example. My favourite these days is Lattimore, but of course he wasn't around when I was at school. My grandfather gave me the Lang, I remember, for passing my School Certificate. I quite like Fitzgerald, as well, but he's a bit too colloquial for my geriatric taste. Of course, it's best of all in the original Greek."

The tone was grave, even admonitory, but his eyes were smiling. "Darling Grandpa, you lost me some sentences back. Have I got to read this Lang?"

"The bookbinders promised I should have it this week. I'll bring it round in a day or two. It's under five hundred pages."

"Five hundred pages?"

He threw his head back and laughed delightedly. "I'm not offering it to you in Greek, Cass. This is a nice, readable translation."

"Couture's about my limit," I said, dismayed, and beginning to wish I'd kept my tongue between my teeth.

"Then it's time you did some proper reading before your brain turns into nail varnish. I was intending to read it again; I haven't looked at it for years. I had it all through my time in Germany. But your need is definitely greater than mine."

"Thank you," I said doubtfully. I stepped hastily back onto safe ground. "Was your war wound bad?"

"It could have been, but I had a first-class nurse." The strong, seamed old face softened.

"Good; I'm glad. I don't suppose you know what happened to her?"

"I think so. I married her not long after the war ended. There was someone in Berlin, but—"

"*Granny?* But she never told me! She never said a thing about being your nurse! You never told me! No one told me!" I was astounded, and, it must be confessed, not very pleased.

"Well, no, darling. Much of what we all did remained classified for decades. One just didn't talk about it. Careless talk costs lives, we used to say. Oh, no, we all kept our secrets. Got into the habit of it. Apparently, I wouldn't even tell the hospital my name, rank, or regiment to begin with." He rose, and looked at his watch. "Better get going. I've got a new boy starting today. He was at Aden."

"I'll bet that's something to do with Napoleon. No, don't tell me."

"I wouldn't know how to begin. Well, sweetie, take care of it. It's about all I had on me when I got back to England, or so they told me. It was very precious to your grandmother and me."

*

He brought it round a few days later, in a parcel. He didn't stay, but kissed me, and strode off, waving. I shrugged a little, and smiled, and left it on the hall table. Then I walked to work, humming, and swinging my bag by its strap.

Dinah was agog to know about my lunch with Colin, so I told her all about it, then said that we had made another date, for dinner. She subjected this to consideration, her head on one side.

"Not sure about him," she said at last. "I mean, moleskins in a heatwave?"

"Honestly, Dinah, you are such an old stick-in-the-mud. Why shouldn't he?"

"Because it's not natural, that's why. A nice pair of chinos, now—or linen trousers would have been better still. You watch it, he'll be another Harold Shipman, and you'll never be heard of again."

"Dinah!" I protested. "For one thing, I'm twenty-two, not seventy-two, and for another, he's not a doctor!"

Dinah snorted.

We were busy that morning, so it wasn't until I got home and saw the parcel still on the hall table that I remembered the new dimension in my life. I was conscious of a faint excitement as I took its wrappings off to disclose a venerable book, quite as fat as I'd expected, and burnished in its restored Morocco leather covers.

"For goodness' sake," I said aloud, feeling its weight, and opening the front cover, "I *will* be seventy-two by the time I've finished this!" There was an inscription. It said, in a beautiful old-fashioned hand: 'To Hector, on the occasion of his passing his School Certificate, from his affect. grandfather, H. de L. Greatrex.'

For form's sake, I took it through to the sitting-room and put it by my chair. It looked jolly impressive; and there it would probably have stayed but for the fact that I found myself with nothing to do that evening, and there was nothing on television. I picked it up and opened it at random.

It was dark, and I was ravenously hungry, by the time I tore myself out of *The Iliad* and rose, stretching like a cat. The temperature had not cooled noticeably, and I stood for some while by the wide-open window, still lost in the mists of dark antiquity, and conscious that I had been communing, however ineffectually, with a rigorous, muscular, elastic intellect. I don't know what I had expected, some arid, classical work in rigid metre perhaps, full of gods and goddesses with unpronounceable names, and boring as hell; but I know only that my breath had been taken away by the intimacy and reach of it. Despite the grand, sweeping scale of it, despite the fact that many of the names and words were utterly unfamiliar to me, even the gods seemed human.

And I saw why Granny had said Grandpa was well-named. Hector the great-hearted, Hector of the flashing helmet... I was hazily aware, too, that the world had just got far bigger, and that my horizons were stretching away, dissolving, receding even as I approached them...

It was not an altogether comfortable feeling, and I shook myself, and turned away from the window. I needed grounding; and the best way to ground oneself is to eat.

I had left the book over the arm of my chair, and perhaps I hadn't properly brought myself back from the foothills of Mount Ida, but as I reached for it to put it away, I knocked it to the floor. It landed on one of its corners and flattened itself, face down. For a moment, all I could do was gaze at it, lying spatchcocked and faintly gleaming on the carpet. Then, horrified, and galvanised into action by my clumsiness, I bent to retrieve it. I was so taken up with checking the precious book that at first I hardly noticed the folded paper peeping from under the skirts of the armchair. The corner seemed undamaged; and only then was there, briefly, room in my mind to recall that I had been going through the house room by room taking measurements and jotting down ideas for redecorating. I had mislaid the bundle of notes. Thankful to have found them, as I really didn't want to have to do it all again, I grabbed them and threw them up onto a shelf before resuming my close examination of the precious *Iliad*.

Binding and corner were undamaged. I straightened out the crumpled pages (did I dare iron them, like newspapers?), and, closing the book in guilty relief, put it safely back on the table beside the armchair.

Then, sympathising with Achilles, whose knees were assailed by hollow famine, I padded hungrily off to the kitchen, poured some wine, and put something into the microwave. Next time I would start properly at the beginning.

But not tonight. I had had enough for tonight.

THREE

For hateful to me even as the gates of hell is he that hideth
one thing in his heart and uttereth another...

Book IX, *ibid.*

A FEW EVENINGS later, I was conscious of something not
quite right as I took my seat opposite Colin Bardsey at
Sammarco's.

It wasn't the normal constraint one feels on a date. Nor
was it that either of us was trying too hard, or was wrongly
dressed—even though he'd ditched the moleskins for
jeans, and I tried not to notice the pressed creases down
the front. I couldn't put my finger on it, and since I don't
have the right temperament for awkward atmospheres, I
became bright and chatty and social. The food was more
than good enough to compensate, however, and in an
effort to dispel the tension, I praised it as lavishly as if
Antonio Carluccio had invented a signature dish especially
for us. I'm not given much to insight, but as the evening
wore on, even I could sense that Colin Bardsey wanted
something badly—and it didn't seem to be me. The signals

weren't right. All in all, it was a rather sticky evening, and although I tried not to people-watch too obviously, I hailed with relief the impetuous approach to our table of a tall young man with wild, dark curls tumbling anyhow over his forehead. I'd like to say they fell romantically—even Byronically—but in fact they made him look like an Irish water spaniel.

It took only a second to see that my relief was misplaced. He loomed over us, and glowered at Colin with an expression of such rage on his face that I felt quite frightened. When he spoke, he gave the impression of an elemental force only just held in check, and his words were melodramatic in the extreme.

"So you've come out of the woodwork at last, Bardsey, have you, you thieving little leech?"

I gasped. He had kept his pitch down, but this only served to emphasise the impression of a volcano about to blow its top. Instinctively, I leant back to get out of range, and found my voice. "Do you mind? We're trying to have dinner!"

It's not easy to be impressive and authoritative when you have to look up at someone. The molten gaze shifted to me, raked me over with contempt.

"I don't suppose your name is Greatrex, by any chance?"

I was so surprised that all I could do was stare at him. My jaw must have dropped nearly to my plate.

"It is, isn't it? I knew it!" He rounded on Colin. "My God, you can move fast when you want to, can't you?" Then to me: "Ask him"—a contemptuous jerk of the untidy head at Colin—"ask him why he scraped acquaintance with you! Go on, ask him! And don't blame me if you don't like the answer! And as for you, Bardsey, or whoever else's name you're using today, from now on I shall watch you like a terrier at a rat-hole. *I know what your game is, even if she doesn't. Just you watch your back next time you decide to spend your lunch-hour eavesdropping at Blackwell's!"*

Another dagger-glance at Colin from the flaming eyes, and he flung round and strode off.

I let my pent-up breath go, dimly conscious of icy hands and feet, and a racing heart. "*Well!* Who on *earth* was that?"

Colin was pushing at the fork with quick, nervous movements, so that the tines dug deeply into the damask. "An academic rival," he said curtly.

I opened my eyes at that. "I had no idea the academic world was so dangerous. Who is he?"

"A madman. Pay no attention. What would you like for pudding?"

"What I'd like is some answers, please," I said acidly. "I *thought* you were after something! Couldn't you just ask me straight out? Just what do you want?"

He started to say something about getting to know me better, but I interrupted him without compunction.

"Oh, cut it out! I know when a man's interested in me and when he's not, and you're not! Now, spill the beans, or I'll leave you with the bill!"

A silence.

"Well?" I said challengingly.

Colin pushed the fork ill-temperedly through the damask, then dropped it. "If you must know, I'm desperate to meet your father," he said, a shade sulkily.

I gaped. "My *father*? What's with my father, for heaven's sake? Have you got some weird older-man fixation, or something?"

Colin flushed. "Of course not. He's stumbled across some...some research that impinges on my own work, that's all, and I badly want to—"

Astounded, I interrupted again. "How on earth do you know what my father gets up to?"

"I...he's well known in my field," he muttered. "I happened to be in Hissarlik at the same time. I followed him home from Turkey." He drank wine as though it were water, sunbrowned fingers tight round the glass.

"You followed..." I stopped. My brain was seething with half-formed ideas and memories: the break-in; my father's work; Mummy's and my theory of academic espionage. I finished weakly: "But why couldn't you have just written to him?"

"It's complicated. He might have got the wind up and refused to see me. I thought if I got to know you, you might invite me down to meet him."

"Got the wind up? What about, for heaven's sake?"

He hunched one shoulder; it seemed more in irritation than the embarrassment I thought he ought to be feeling.

"Well, what about?" I repeated.

He appeared to be turning something over in his mind. Whatever it was, he capitulated. "We think he might have identified another treasure trove."

"Oh, this is ridiculous," I snapped. "I don't pretend to understand what you're talking about. First my grandfather, and now you! This is not an adventure story, and you are not the Famous Five! What on earth do you mean—'another treasure trove'? A treasure trove of what? Who is 'we'?"

"Treasure trove exists, and it's not always a pirates' hoard of pearls and diamonds and pieces of eight in a chest," he said, very much the Oxford undergraduate, and not answering my questions. "Reputations are won and lost on proper identification of sites and artefacts and so forth. I happened to be interested in...in what your father's opinion might be of whatever he found on Lemnos."

"And you want to make your reputation on the back of my father's work? If you're so clever, how come you don't know what he found? You've just admitted you followed him home—I expect you trotted after him round this island, peering over his shoulder! Well?" I did not trouble to keep the derision out of my voice. I had no idea how anything my father might have found could possibly be described as treasure trove, and I didn't really believe it anyway, but by this time I was well and truly riled.

He drained his glass and reached for the bottle. It seemed to give him confidence. "I would very much like the opportunity to discuss my theories with him, yes," he replied with a touch of prim pedantry.

"But my father is an amateur," I said slowly.

"Even amateurs can make discoveries."

"Like Heinrich Schliemann?"

His turn to widen his eyes at me.

"I went to see my grandfather after we had lunch, and he lent me his copy of Lang's translation of *The Iliad*," I said, with cool confidence, and (I hoped) a precision to match his own. I shouldn't have mentioned it, on reflection, but my guard was down. And that's the understatement of the millennium.

"Your—grandfather? Your *grandfather* was talking to you—about some treasure?" He was looking intently at me, glass suspended, and once again I felt that it wasn't the right sort of intentness. I know that's clumsily put, but it's the only way of saying it. And there was an element of urgency in the question that I didn't like.

"Is he still alive?" pursued Colin. His knuckles were white. The wine was forgotten.

"Well, yes. I'd hardly be able to go and see him otherwise, would I?"

He paid no attention to this; he was following some internal course of his own, while his gaze bored into my eyes. I looked away.

"Is he your father's father? Where does he live?"

I didn't answer immediately. Dinah's words flickered through my mind, and though it was obviously ridiculous, I felt more and more uncomfortable.

He must have sensed my unease, for he brought the catechism to an abrupt end. "I'm sorry. Blame the academic's desire for information. Will you ask your father if he'll see me?" His tone was airy, less intense, but it still seemed altogether too pointed, too eager.

"I don't know," I said slowly. "I don't like the way you've gone about this."

For some reason, my guarded reaction made him relax.

"I'm extremely sorry. I'm aware it must seem rather hole-in-the-corner, but I honestly thought it was the only way. And you did enjoy having lunch with me, didn't you?"

He was smiling now. It was a charming smile; boyish, a little rueful.

"Yes," I said, melting like a snowball in the sun. I came to a sudden decision. "Leave it with me. I'll see what I can do."

I really ought to have known better.

*

The following weekend, I drove to the station to fetch him.

For some reason, I didn't give Daddy all the gen. I merely said I'd met a man called Colin Bardsey, that Grandpa had been friends with his great-uncle, and that he had been in Turkey at the same time as Daddy, and could he come to lunch because he was working in the same field of research.

Mummy looked speculative, but she always looks like that when I bring a man home, so I didn't pay any attention.

I bowled along with the top down and Andy Williams singing *Music to Watch Girls By* on the CD player. The heatwave still held, and I took the back roads to town so I could pretend I was Grace Kelly on the Grande Corniche. I was wearing a sleeveless white cotton shirt with a French collar, a blue linen skirt that stopped just above the knee, and a pair of low-heeled sandals. I had borrowed Daddy's old MGBGT (for once, with his permission); my arms and legs were long and brown and bare; and I felt good. There were enough admiring glances as I made my way to the station for me to affect to ignore them, and I turned into the station with a careless flourish, slightly marred when I scraped too close to some flaming bushes of gorse. There would be scratches in the paintwork. I gave it a second or two of vague anxiety, then I forgot about it. Daddy would know what to do.

He was there, standing in the shade. It was the moleskins again—not to mention the same checked shirt. Resolutely I pushed all thoughts of mass murderers out of my mind. Then I remembered that tinge of bravado when he told me he had lots of money. Perhaps it was true; or perhaps it was pride, just to keep his end up. I waved and pulled up at the kerb. "Hallo," I said.

He leant over and kissed my cheek. Despite the smile, my insides stayed where they were; my heart didn't miss a beat. Disappointing.

"Hop in," I said, a little too gaily.

Talk was necessarily restricted by the wind of our movement, and I wasn't sure whether to be relieved or not that we could only yell a few commonplaces at each other. I took the quicker, main route home, and was glad to turn into the drive. When at length we reached the part just before the trees give way to sunny lawn, I stopped and dragged on the handbrake. The MG sat purring.

"This is just where Mummy and I were, that day," I said.

"Yes… Yes, I can see you'd have a good view of the french windows," he said. "Which is your tree?"

"This big beech. What twits we must have looked."

"But nobody saw you," he said quickly.

"No, I suppose not. Mummy had us go into the house the other way, round to the kitchen. Give them time to hop it, she said." I shivered.

"And did they?"

"I've no idea. I've told you, we didn't see anybody." I glanced speculatively at him under cover of putting the car into gear again. He was looking relieved; and if it hadn't been absurd, I'd have said it was on his own account, not Mummy's and mine. I drove the hundred yards to the front door and pulled up.

Daddy came out to greet us, automatically glancing over the MG for damage before shaking Colin Bardsey by the hand. He shook his head over the scratches and scowled horribly at me. I made a face at him and mouthed *Glim!*

I was proud of my father. Like Grandpa, he had a good physique, even if his hair was thinning. And he held himself well. At least he wasn't wearing moleskins. I shook myself mentally. I have no objections at all to moleskins *per se*, but I did see Dinah's point.

They were talking about the journey as Daddy took Colin into the hall, and I followed slowly in their wake. Mummy came out of the drawing-room then, and amid the usual social mêlée of offering drinks, introductory chit-chat and self-consciousness, I observed him as closely as I dared. He seemed just an ordinary, nice-looking sort of chap; not particularly academic, perhaps, but then neither had the wild young man at Sammarco's. I realised that I had no idea what academics looked like anyway, so I let it go.

After lunch, which we had in the dining-room, and at which (to my relief) the conversation remained strictly general, my father swept Colin and their cups of coffee off to the study and shut the door on us.

"He seems very nice," said my mother tentatively. "Well, he must be, to be allowed into the inner sanctum."

"Hmm," I said, getting up and beginning to stack plates onto the trolley.

"Don't you think so?" She sounded startled.

"I'm not sure. I don't know."

"Why did you bring him, then?"

"Because he scra— Because he got to know me purely because he wanted to discuss a line of research with Daddy," I said baldly.

"Were you going to say 'scraped acquaintance', by any chance?" asked my mother acutely.

I stood there, a glass in each hand. I was thinking of Sammarco's. I said slowly: "Actually, yes. I *think* I've been had, but I'm not sure."

"It sounds as though you might have been. A line of research, indeed. A chat-up line, more like—and quite the most cynical I've ever come across."

"I don't know. Something odd happened, while I was having dinner with him…" I stopped, and put the glasses on the trolley. "Look, let's get this lot through to the kitchen. I'll tell you all."

While we put the plates into the machine, I told her about my conversation with Grandpa, and the angry young man at dinner. "And whatever the truth of it," I finished, "Colin certainly isn't after me. I mean, you can tell, can't you?"

"I hope so," said my mother. "You say Hector had never heard of the name of Bardsey?"

"That's right. And the wild man said, '*or whatever your name is today*,' or something like that, just as though Colin were in the habit of using aliases all over the place. Shall I do the knives?"

"Yes, please. A mystery man," mused my mother. "I don't know that I altogether like the sound of it."

"Nor did Dinah." I giggled. "She said he was definitely dodgy, and I'd probably never be seen again."

"Don't say things like that, even in jest," said my mother quite fiercely.

"Sorry, Mummy. I think she just took agin him, you know how one does sometimes."

There was a silence while I clattered about in the sink and my mother put the machine on. I was looking idly out of the window when something occurred to me, unwelcome enough to make me stop what I was doing.

"I've just remembered something," I said, in the approved hollow accents. "He said something about seeing the french windows from the drive. When we drove up and I stopped, I mean."

My mother disentangled this. "Yes? But you can't see them—not unless they're open."

"Exactly. And they weren't. *So how did he know where the french windows are?*" I swung round and stared at her, the knives in my hand dripping soapy water onto the floor.

She gave me her set look again. "Oh. Presumably you told him...didn't you?"

"No! I mean, I didn't give him an A to Z of the place! I only said you could see them open from the drive!"

"And there aren't any others," said my mother. "You're dripping."

"Sorry." I put the knives back in the sink, picked up the cloth, and bent to mop up.

She screwed up her face as though warding off something nasty, and said: "It looks as though we might have been right about the espionage, ludicrous though it is even to talk about such things. But what *can* Daddy have found that's of such importance to that young man? Heavens, I don't like to think of him in the house!"

"I don't know what he's found. All I do know is that I've felt uncomfortable about Colin Bardsey and his motives from day one."

My mother shook her head helplessly. "Why bring him here, then?"

I lifted my shoulders deprecatingly and took my lower lip between my teeth. "He has a nice smile," I said lamely.

"Give me strength," cried my mother, putting both hands to her immaculate hair-do. "And you've given him the freedom of the house! What if he's the burglar? Have you thought of that? Shall I just give him a set of keys? Then he can ransack the place at his leisure!"

I stared at her, aghast. "He said—"

"What?"

"He said he followed Daddy home."

My mother closed her eyes.

"*And...*"

"Dear heaven, now what?"

I was remembering that first conversation. Colin had said—I was practically certain—that he *hadn't come up* from my parents' house. How had he known where they lived?

"I'm going to the study," I said tersely, snatching up a towel and hastily drying my hands. I threw it down and left the kitchen on a wail of complaint from my mother.

As I crept across the hall, I heard them talking and put

my ear to the door. Something about cattle? I listened a moment longer but without making out any more. I turned the handle and went in.

"...only it appears to be far, far older than that," my father was saying. "Otherwise, how do you explain the stratification? And please don't hand me any guff about heirlooms. That explanation's got whiskers on it." He looked up from the address book which he had open in one hand, and, unhitching his hip from his desk, he said, surprised and none too pleased: "Hallo, darling. I'm sorry, I didn't hear you knock. Did you want me?"

"I didn't knock," I said, still terse. "I only wanted to know what time Colin's train was."

He was standing by the shelves behind my father's desk, with his head on one side. He was obviously checking the spines and it took a moment for him to hear what I'd said and tear his gaze away, stammering something about not having looked at the train times. But I was quivering with suspicion now, and the first thought that leapt into my head was that he was angling for an invitation to stay the night. To do what? To creep down a corridor, certainly—but not after me.

"The next one's at 5.12, which we could catch easily," I said, watching him closely. "That would give you another hour with my father, unless of course he's got something else on." I know I sounded cold.

My father said: "Perhaps Mummy could—"

"Let him stay the night?" I finished it for him in a hard, bright voice. "I'm afraid that won't be possible. Mummy says to say how sorry she is. I'm sure Colin will understand."

Some measure of understanding there was; I caught the look of chagrin. I said, still in that hard voice: "Shall I come back in an hour, then, Daddy?"

"Yes, darling, all right," said my father with a measuring look at Colin Bardsey, and a frown, slightly puzzled, at me.

"Righty-ho," I said, and went straight back to the kitchen to tell my mother the words I had put into her mouth.

We didn't speak much on the way back to the station. He climbed out and stood on the pavement, looking rather shamefaced.

"I really am sorry," he said. "Thank you for arranging things. I'm sorry, that's all."

"I'm on very friendly terms," I said, "with an archæologist. I'm going to mention your name to him. And now I'm going to go home and find out from my father exactly what you wanted to know."

Without waiting for a reply, I roared off and I didn't look back. Owing to my having forgotten to put my Grace Kelly scarf on, I had to run up to my room as soon as I got home and do something about the bird's nest that the wind had made of my hair. Then I went straight downstairs again.

The study was empty, and I ran my parents to earth in the kitchen.

It was evident from their faces that they'd been chewing it all over. I, too, had been chewing things over; and I didn't hesitate. "Okay, Daddy," I said, without giving either of my parents a chance to speak first. I shut the door behind me and came further into the room. "Just what did he want from you?"

My father considered me over his spectacles. "He wanted to know, among other things, whether I'd looked into the latest DnA findings to support certain of my assertions. I told him, no, not in any depth; I don't have access to the huge resources of professional academics. I must say, I couldn't see the point of his asking. I'm not an anthropologist."

I didn't want to expose the fact that I didn't know what

he was talking about, so I merely said: "That'll do for starters. What were the other things?"

"We discussed a book by a Dutchman which posits the theory, supported by evidence, linguistic, geographical and internal, that *The Iliad* is not set in Anatolia at all; we talked about the connections among alphabets, with particular reference to Rhaetian, Etruscan, and Coelbren; we touched—but only lightly—on the significance of the embalming procedures as practised in Egypt and exemplified by the Zagreb mummy; we mentioned—but only in passing, you understand—the plight of the Ainu; and when you skittered in all smiles and welcome, we were talking about the antiquity of Çatal Hüyük and whether it has any links with Marash."

Abandoning pretence, I protested: "Give me a break! Did you talk about the treasures of Troy in among all that stuff?"

"No, the subject was not touched on; but that was probably because you didn't give us time," said my father patiently. "Why do you want to know whether we talked about the treasures of Troy? No one knows where they are, for one thing."

Instead of answering this, I demanded to know where Uncle William was. My mother's younger brother was the archæologist I had threatened Colin Bardsey with.

"I have no idea," said my father. "Moira?"

"He went to Italy a couple of weeks ago," replied my mother. "I could look up where, if you like. He did tell me."

"Oh, he's found the treasures there, has he?" enquired my father with a tinge of sarcasm. "It'll make him for life if he has, though I feel he'd probably have more luck in Russia. Why do you want him? Are you going in for archæology? It'll ruin your nails."

I gave an impatient sigh. "He might know who this man Bardsey really is," I said. "Grandpa had never heard of his great-uncle, and he wasn't in the photographs. And that man in the restaurant said 'or whatever your name is', or something."

"Have you been bothering your grandfather with this?" demanded my mother.

"What man in what restaurant?" demanded my father in the same breath.

"That's not fair. I'd hardly call it bothering. In any case, he only lives round the corner from me, and you told me to keep an eye on him. Mummy, you tell him about the restaurant." Then, as my father still looked doubtful, I said impatiently: "Come on, Daddy, don't look like that, he's as fit as a flea, *and* he's all there, even if he is a hundred and ninety. Besides," I added loftily, "it's the other way round. He's been bothering me. He's lent me something to read. It— it seems to have started something."

"A rush of blood to the head, perhaps?"

My mother lifted her brows. "I didn't think Hector took *Couture*," she murmured provocatively. "What did he lend you, the Christmas annual?"

"Don't you start," I warned her. "If you must know, it was *The Iliad. And*," I finished impressively, "I'm a quarter of the way through it."

"Good God," exclaimed my father.

He seemed to be more concerned than impressed, and I gave him a so-there nod. "That's wiped the smile off your face," I said with satisfaction, coming to another decision. "I think that a holiday in Italy would be just the thing."

"Troy's not in Italy," said my father. I closed my eyes and sighed ostentatiously.

"What about Dinah?" asked my mother.

"Ginny'll do the extra. She always says the money's handy. Her little boy has special needs."

"You could take your father's suitcase," suggested my mother.

"Why on earth?" I looked round from the refrigerator where I was foraging.

"Because he still hasn't unpacked it properly from Turkey," she answered. "Hector, for the fortieth time, please will you? And Cassie, if you eat our supper as well as your own, we will have to go hungry tonight."

"Mummy, for heaven's sake, why don't you just defrost something, like anybody else?"

"Because," replied my mother unanswerably, and with a logic apparent only to her, "the freezer needs defrosting. Now do go away, the pair of you. Oh, and Cassie!"

I stopped in the doorway.

"I think Will said Italy—although he might have mentioned Crete. You'd better try and ring him. Do you have his number?"

"Yes, thank you. There's something in this coincidence thing, you know," I said wisely to my father as we left the kitchen. "Grandpa was telling me about mazes coming from Crete."

"Please stop," said my father faintly, "I can't take much more."

I ignored this: I had thought of something else. "Daddy, where and what is Blackwell's?"

"That does it," said my father with decision. "The universe has suspended its laws."

"Oh, don't be an idiot! Just be your age and tell me, would you?"

So he did.

FOUR

Such converse held these one with the other,
and the sun went down…and they…took supper.
And many ships from Lemnos, bearing wine, were at hand…

Book VII, *ibid.*

ON THE STRENGTH of his answer, I took a train the following day to Oxford. I had remembered what the Irish-water-spaniel man had said about eavesdropping there, and I was obeying a hunch.

It was a needle in a haystack, of course; or possibly only a bow at a venture. I found a taxi at the station, and, leaning forward, I placed my forearms on the back of the seat and addressed myself to the driver.

"Do you know if Blackwell's is the sort of place where I might, er, sort of run into someone?"

"You dunno his college?" The driver was a middle-aged man, a Sikh, with a kindly face.

"No. I forgot to ask."

He smiled indulgently at me in the rear view mirror and shook his head. "Run into anybody at Blackwell's, if you wait long enough. I got daughters," he added. "I got a daughter at Merton. You take care now."

"I will," I promised.

He concentrated on negotiating Oxford's cat's cradle of a road system, and I was glad I hadn't brought the car. I had never been to Oxford before, and I looked about me with keen interest.

"This is Broad Street," he said. "Blackwell's bookshop is on the left, about halfway up. Everybody ends up there sooner or later. Here it is. You take care, okay?"

I thanked him and paid him, and he wove his way expertly back into the stream of traffic. I made my way past the ranks of parked bicycles and pushed open the door.

I couldn't believe that people still wore those black cloak things in this day and age, and looked about me, half-disbelieving and half-entranced. They looked like so many Harry Potters milling around the bookshelves and galleries in the hushed, purposeful atmosphere.

It was a good deal more modern inside than the exterior suggested, and there were no sofas to lounge on, so I took up my position on the far side of the Geology section and peeped through the shelves. Immediately I understood the crack about eavesdropping: the place might have been designed for a spot of covert surveillance. But I saw nothing, so I cast a cursory glance over the titles. Most of them were in German, so I transferred my gaze to the door and watched the bicycles bowling past, many of them old-fashioned with wicker baskets. It could have been a film set but for that atmosphere. Feeling like a parakeet in a flock of sparrows, I caught several disapproving glances from pale-faced girls with spectacles and long, lank hair. I began to wish I hadn't come. I thought I would give it about twenty minutes, then go home and see if I could track my uncle down.

In the meantime, I would try and improve myself—though probably not with Geology. I wandered about for a bit, keeping my eye on the door and taking volumes down at random. This was even less successful: the first thing I saw (in a Welsh glossary) was something called asyndetic hendiasys. It sounded like a medical condition. Shuddering, I replaced the glossary with care, and patted it. Then my attention was caught by the title on an olive-green spine: *How to Kill a Dragon: Aspects of Indo-European Poetics*. It seemed so apposite that I drew it out, all six hundred and forty pages of it, and looked for a review that would give me a nice potted version. There were a few. One in particular, by *The Journal of the American Oriental Society*, seemed just the job. It glowed with decorous academic joy: *...a new puthmen,* it announced; *a fundamentum which must henceforth serve as the starting point and...* My head was starting to swim. I carefully replaced the volume with both hands and turned my back on the shelves, heaving a sigh.

The next moment I was suppressing a gasp of delight. The door opened and a man came in; not a sunbrowned man with a nice smile, but the angry young man with the water-spaniel hair. He was in an ancient cotton sweater with several pulled threads, and he had an unwieldy assortment of books under one arm. He didn't look angry today, so I plucked up the confidence to approach him.

"Hallo," I said.

Even though I was wearing heels, he still towered over me. And even if the anger had abated, he didn't look as though he were in the mood for a pick-up, either, so I said hurriedly that it wasn't a pick-up, but that I'd come to Oxford specially, hoping to meet him and ask him some questions about the other evening.

"The other evening?" His gaze slid past me to the History shelves, and he began to edge round me.

"Sammarco's," I said, planting myself in his path.

"Sam—" Some remembering flame lit the brooding eyes, and I saw they were a clear, cool brown, like a peaty Highland burn. He brought me properly into focus. A book slipped, and he shoved it back under his arm. "Colin Bardsey," he said through clenched teeth. "You were having dinner with him." He made it sound reprehensible, even distasteful.

"Yes, now look, don't bite my head off. Can we go somewhere and talk?"

He considered me for a moment with some disapproval, then extended a bony, well-shaped hand and looked at his watch. "I've got about an hour and a half. We could have some coffee."

At least he hadn't choked me off. "Goody. I'm Cassie Greatrex, by the way."

"I know," he replied. Then he did that classic thing called a double-take. "Did you say Cassie? Cassandra?" He pronounced it oddly.

"You can't have known my Christian name was Cassie. You can't be as clever as that! Who are you, anyway?"

"I'm Huw Trefor, Huw like Hugh, but spelt the Welsh way."

"Huh?"

"H-u-w, not H-u-g-h. And Trefor is spelt with an 'f', and pronounced with a 'v'."

"What, as in 'clever'? Well, knock me down with—I mean, I've learnt something else. Where are we going?"

"A place I know. Just let me exchange these books first."

It was strange, but over two large cups of excellent coffee, I found myself telling him everything about the break-in, my two dates with Colin, my conversation with my grandfather,

Mummy's and my theories, and Colin's subsequent visit to my parents' house.

"So now," I finished, "suppose you tell me what's wrong with Colin Bardsey, and just why you were so angry with him that evening. And I could bear to know just how everybody seems to know who I am, and why they're all so interested in my family!"

"That's easy. I'll tell you first that Colin bloody Bardsey is not only an intellectual thief, he's a con. artist. Did he tell you which college he was at? No? Well, he's at mine, more's the pity."

I said faintly: "I see. And the intellectual thief bit?"

"He lifted an article wholesale that your father wrote for *The Ready Writer* some years ago—barely changed a word, and published it under his own name in a student rag that most of us wouldn't wrap our chips in. It makes its sales on the back of provocative, politicised mischief-making between the University and Oxford itself. Unfortunately, it's just entertaining enough to keep going, and it has some very clever lawyers. Bardsey hates my guts because I turned him in to the Dean for it. There's a heck of a lot of plagiarism about these days, what with rent-an-essay off the internet and so forth, but this was different. For one thing, it was scholarly, well-researched, and beautifully written. I may be Welsh, but I'm passionate about the English language, and there's nobody of our age who could write like that. It seemed familiar as well, but it was some time before I tracked it down. When I did, I wrote a polite letter to him, to Bardsey, I mean—under the assumed name, of course—and sent it to the rag to be forwarded. You can imagine how I felt when I saw my letter, re-addressed by the paper, in his pigeonhole! I took it out, which is strictly forbidden, and I delivered it myself. Actually, I went for him."

I was staring open-mouthed. The notion that there was a magazine ready to publish my father's boring, dusty old scribbles was staggering. Ashamed, I could only stammer: "You knew my father's name?"

"Yes. You see, he happens to be interested in the same line of work as I am, and I've—"

"That's what Colin said."

"Is it? Well, I've been a subscriber to *The Ready Writer* for ages, and I've read several of his contributions. You might say I knew his style."

"So that's how you knew my name. *The Ready...Writer*, did you say?"

"Yes. It's a quarterly review. It's been around since about 1830 or thereabouts, and it's devoted to amateur hobby horses. It has some regular contributors, like your father, and some guests. It has professionally high standards but won't publish anything by anybody professional. Which is more than can be said for *Town & Gown?*. That's the cheaper-than-chips paper. What's more, I've strong suspicions that he's been selling college information for their *Gossipmonger* column. Bardsey, I mean. I need hardly tell you how amiss that would be taken. I haven't any proof, but he knows I suspect him. Well, I told him I did. He'd been earwigging already, so I didn't feel I had anything to lose."

"Crumbs, so that's what you meant by eavesdropping in his lunch hour." I put my head on one side. "Is Colin doing the same degree as you?"

"The Linguistics, yes, but not the Archæology. He goes in for Ancient History, and something to do with computers." The scorn was faint, but ineffable. "Why? Did he say something?"

I thought back. "No—at least, not in connection with you. With my father."

"Oh. But that comes to more or less the same thing. He's a perfectly ordinary student of Linguistics, all above board and…" He stopped.

"And?"

"Doesn't matter. If he tells you he's interested in what I do—or in anything at all—distrust him on principle." His brows were knit; he seemed to be on the brink of telling me something, then changed his mind at the last moment. "Look, I can't tell you everything—at least not just now—but I will tell you this. My particular line of research is not the orthodox one. Colin found out, and he made it very clear. I'll bet that he's either out to trump me somehow, or keep tabs on me so that he can use it against me in some way. Just don't fall for anything he says, that's all. Slippery isn't in it."

I regarded him for a moment, not sure what to make of this. "He said he was a don or something."

Huw snorted. "He's hardly likely to be a don at his age—or at any age. He's not likely to do better than a third class."

"Well, I'm not likely to know. These academic distinctions just aren't quite me."

He looked sceptical and rather superior, and, nettled, I spoke tartly. "We can't all have brains the size of the Albert Hall."

"I'm sure you compensate."

I looked down at my nails (they were a clear, deep amethyst: Dinah had done them herself) and smiled. Then I remembered something. "I haven't told you about the french windows," I said, and did so. "The thing is," I finished, "it looks as though he—Colin—might have had a hand in the break-in, doesn't it?"

"Increasingly," said Huw Trefor, draining his coffee. "He told you he'd followed your father back from Hissarlik?"

I nodded. It was all making me feel a bit weak. "Which is confusing, because I thought he was on that island whose name I can't remember. But Daddy told us he'd be on the mainland as well, so I suppose that's what he meant. I didn't think of Turkey, though. One doesn't, somehow. I don't, anyway."

"Hissarlik is where Troy is," said Huw. "It sounds as though your father was following up a line of thought that I..." He didn't finish this. Instead, he said: "And you're sure nothing was stolen?"

I nodded. "Quite sure."

Huw's eyes suddenly gleamed. "Perhaps something was added."

"Why would he want to add something?"

"For safe-keeping. Perhaps he was hoping to retrieve it when he came to lunch."

"Well, if that's so, he was reckoning without the hellish state of chaos that is my father's normal working conditions. Nobody could find a thing in there, even if they knew where they'd put it. Anyway, who'd he be keeping it safe from, whatever it is?"

"From me, possibly," said Huw with a wolfish grin.

"Hold on a moment," I said. "Daddy came back *after* the break-in—as a consequence of it. I mean, Mummy rang him and asked him to. Colin said he followed my father home. That means he couldn't have had anything to do with it."

"Yes, he could," said Huw. "Come on, I've got to get going. We'll talk as we walk, madam."

Before I had time to consider the implications of a man who could quote my favourite author to me, he had paid, heaved up his books, and gone ahead of me out into the sun, forgetting to hold the door open. He set off in great long strides so that I had to trot to keep up.

"How could he?" I asked.

"How could he what? Oh—sent somebody on in advance, of course." He looked surprised and vaguely disapproving. "Either that, or he lied about following your father."

"I keep telling you I haven't got an academic brain," I panted. "Do you have to gallop? I feel like a Chihuahua trying to keep pace with a Great Dane!"

"I'm sorry," he said, grinning suddenly and coming to a halt. He had a nice grin, too. We had stopped at a huge door of grey oak with bits of ironwork all over it. "I've got a lecture," he said solemnly. "Sabellic patronymics, matronymics, cognomen, and prænomina. Both masculine and feminine."

"I've never heard of any of them," I said quite crossly. "But I can tell you one thing. You really ought to use a balm, not ordinary aftershave. Your skin looks very dry. I'm surprised you haven't got spots."

I regret to say that I left him standing there. I'd had enough of feeling inadequate for one day. It wasn't until I was on the train that I remembered I hadn't told him my address in London. Tough. If he was as clever as all that, he could jolly well find out.

*

A few days later, a letter arrived. It was so seldom that I received a real letter that even the opening of it was a pleasure. He had nice writing, too, and it was written in proper ink. It was quite short.

Dear Cassie, it said…

This is just to tell you that I'm going to Italy on a field course after my exams finish, to study Etruscan funerary inscriptions, among other things. Will you have dinner with me at Sammarco's, next Tuesday? If you write back, put your telephone number, then I'll have that as well as your address. I can pick you up about 8. I promise not to talk about anything ending in —ology.

Love from Huw

Which seemed to decide against Crete, Turkey, and Greece. I had to go and buy some writing paper, which was fun; I couldn't remember when I had last written a letter.

Dear Huw, I wrote, feeling like Jane Austen…

I would love to have dinner with you. I am also thinking of going to Italy in a few weeks' time. How did you find my address?

Love from Cassie

I put both my telephone numbers on it. Before I stuck the flap down, I took the page out again and wrote a bit extra at the bottom.

Is Italy anywhere near Turkey? C

Three days later came his reply:

See you then. Electoral Roll. No, it isn't. H.

I put this with the other one.

*

"I suppose you want an introduction to my father as well."

I had made a special effort that evening (as I hadn't for Colin Bardsey). My hair was up, I had on a shift dress in black ottoman silk, and black velvet slingbacks.

Despite this, Huw gave me what Mummy calls an old-fashioned look. "I'm saying nothing," he replied. The Welsh accent was very faint, but I found myself thinking of rain-washed valleys and gleaming slate roofs.

"Do you know," I said, "I've never so much as set foot in Wales?"

"Are you really going to Italy?"

"My grandfather," I replied with dignity after a moment, "knows the name for that, when one thing doesn't follow on from another."

"*Non sequitur*. Are you?" He was in linen trousers, and his shirt was open at the neck. I can't be positive, but I think he had brushed his hair. He was grinning lazily at me.

I gave in. "My mother's brother is an archæologist. When I took Colin back to the station, I said I was on very friendly terms with him, and I was going to ask if he knew Colin's name, you know, checking him out. My mother said he was in Italy, or possibly Crete."

"Crete is a bit closer to Turkey than Italy is," offered Huw.

"And now we both know where we are on the map, can we eat?"

He was as good as his word; not an –ology or an –ism in sight, even couched in some ancient dead language so that I wouldn't spot it. I'm not sure what we did talk about, except that it was easy, even comforting. By the time he walked me home, I felt as though I had known him for ever. I rang Mummy first thing the following morning.

"What, another one?" she enquired sceptically. "You'd better talk to Daddy; we're coming up to London. He's staying at his club because he's going to a memorial service at the Guards' Chapel the next morning, but he wants to know if you can give us something to eat, and please can I stay the night?"

"Of course to both of those. I'll ask Grandpa as well, and we'll have a little dinner party. Oh, Mummy, Granny's desk isn't doing much, is it? I mean, it's just sitting there in the drawing-room looking pretty. You have your own."

"Do you want it? What on earth are you going to do with it?"

I toyed with the idea of telling her I wanted to eat off it, or use it as a nail bar, but said: "I'd just like to have it, if you can spare it."

"I don't see why not. Daddy will bring it up. What fun, a dinner party. It's just the excuse I need to get my hair done. And I can go to Peter Jones and drool over wallpaper. I've nearly talked Daddy round, by the way, so I might as well indulge myself."

I laughed, and we hung up. Then I wrote to Huw, inviting him to dinner.

*

I spent the day preparing leisurely. The food was mostly cold, to offset the unusually hot weather, and by the time I had laid the table, my father had arrived.

He brought the desk with him. It was only light, so I carried the drawers and he hefted it up the steps, along my narrow hall and into the sitting-room. I had already made a place for it, and now I put my writing paper into the top drawer, the two letters I'd had from Huw into one of the pigeonholes, and the bottle of ink I'd bought into another. Pigeonholes made me think of Colin. I wouldn't care to be on the receiving end of Huw's anger, and I rather felt for the poor man, intellectual thief or not. Perhaps he had his reasons. Even if he had, I certainly wasn't going to tell Daddy about any intellectual thievery.

"There's a chair as well," said my father, his eye going from the desk to me with far-from-flattering surprise. "I'll get it." He went, with another glance over his shoulder at me. I stuck my tongue out at him.

Then I heard my mother's voice and ran to greet her. The evening looked like being rather highbrow, and I was glad of the support. She had a chic new haircut that made the most of her delicate bone structure, and she was carrying several equally chic-looking carrier bags. She admired the position of the desk, which was veneered in burr walnut, and banded round the edges (at least, that's what she told me). Then we spent a happy half-hour or so examining her purchases. After that, we went to the kitchen and brought in the first course and arranged everything on the sideboard.

The sound of voices from the street made themselves heard, and I went to the window and looked out. I had known he would come, even though I had hardly given him time to accept, never mind answer.

"Grandpa, Huw, in here," I cried. They were already nose-deep in conversation, and ten minutes later they were still at it and I had to go and fetch them in.

In point of fact, the evening was quite a success, even though I talked little and understood less. Huw seemed to be hanging on to every word uttered by my male relations, and I was suddenly attacked by doubt; not an emotion I was very familiar with. I wondered whether I was somehow missing out on something important in life, a life which had until now been both satisfying and undemanding. I looked from one to another of the three men, observing their concentration, their interested, gravely happy expressions. They were all talking about something that obviously fascinated them, cuneiform jostling for position with Linear A (or was it B?); and when Huw contributed an observation about a language called (I think) Luvian, with particular reference to inscriptions recently found at some sanctuary on Lemnos, it made my grandfather goggle at him, while my father, eyes sparkling, pounced on this and began to hold forth.

All I could do was watch while Mummy dipped in and out, trying, with limited success, to weld the five of us together, and you could see everybody's good manners struggling wildly with academic absorption. I couldn't lay claim to half her social expertise, and I felt isolated. I had not bargained for this. It was a curiously forlorn sensation, and I think my mother must have seen something of it in my face because she leant across the table and said with a twinkle that she knew exactly how I was feeling, and now did I understand why she was so keen on interior design.

"But I was listening to you, Mummy," I said. "It sounded as though you were more than holding your own."

"Bluff, darling, pure bluff. I pick up a book of your father's from time to time, learn a few words, and bring them out when he least expects it. It keeps him on his toes."

This reminded me of what Huw had said.

"Did you know that Daddy has been writing articles for a magazine called *The* something *Writer*?" I asked her.

"Goodness, yes," said my mother. She made her cat-at-the-cream face. "I've even read some of them."

"*Have* you?"

"Well, yes. It's quite a sensible ploy for married people to take an interest in each other's hobbies." She glanced fondly at my father, and then naughtily at me. "I don't tell him that I hardly understand a word." Her eye rested momentarily on Huw with a speculative glint that I affected to ignore. "I'll teach you a few shortcuts to sounding academic, if you like. It looks as though you might need them."

At this point, some belated sense of social obligation seemed to descend on the three men, and the conversation lapsed suddenly.

"Angels," I said into the silence. "It's either twenty past or twenty to."

All three of them shot wrists out of sleeves and examined watches, which made Mummy and me laugh.

My grandfather said soberly: "A friend of mine in the R.A.F., fellow called Johnny Selborne, he always used to say that if the angels came for him it would be at twenty past."

This somehow united the five of us as none of Mummy's valiant efforts had. After a moment, I said: "And did the angels come for him?"

"I'm afraid they did. He was shot down over Pas de Calais. Left a young widow, too." He brightened a little. "She married again, though. Very nice chap; Lancaster pilot. Dropped one of Wallis's bouncing bombs on the Möhne Dam and survived to tell the tale. Which is more than can be said for the dam. So that was all right."

A real, live Dambuster! I had even seen the film.

"Did your friend fly Lancasters as well?" asked Huw.

"Johnny? No. He was fighter escort. A beastly, thankless, heartbreaking job. Like the escorts on the Western Approaches."

Nobody found anything to say to this, which seemed to bring the evening to a natural close. My clever mother left exactly the right amount of time before pushing back her chair and getting up. "Hector, let's walk your father home, shall we? It's a lovely night, and I'd like a stroll."

"Now, look, Moira," began my grandfather with an edge in his voice, "I've had just about enough of this coddling, d'you hear? The child's just as bad!"

"Nonsense, Pa," said my father. "Of course Cassie keeps an eye on you. That's why we bought her this house, so you could be nice and close to each other. That's a very good idea, Moira, darling. Come on, old boy."

"I can rise unaided," said my grandfather irascibly, shaking off the helpful arm my father extended to him, and poking a long forefinger into his son's barely perceptible paunch. "I'm probably a good deal fitter than you are. Well, Huw, it has been a great pleasure. I should very much like to hear how you get on. Don't forget the Carthage inscriptions, will you?"

"Indeed I won't, sir. Thank you very much for alerting me to that particular aspect of them."

They shook hands. Huw grinned at me. "I'll do the washing-up," he said obligingly.

"Machine," I said, "but thank you."

"Clearing up, then."

"Accepted. Where or what is Carthage? Is it in Italy?"

"Tell you in a moment."

It took the usual length of time to get the leave-takings out of the room and down the hall. Even then, Daddy and Grandpa dawdled down the steps, and would have remained on the pavement lost in conversation had not my mother linked arms with both of them and steered them away in the direction of Lennox Street.

"Goodness," said Huw, into the silence, "what an illuminating evening. I can't thank you enough." He looked deeply satisfied with life.

I was reflecting on the difference between this evening and the awkward dinner-date with Colin. "Well," I sighed, "it's a jolly good thing that I have oodles of common sense, isn't it?"

"By way of compensation," he agreed. "You've got quite a family. I know plenty of people who turn up their noses at amateurs, which is idiotic. I said to your father that an intelligent amateur should be looked on as God's gift to any discipline."

"I heard you say that. He looked awfully pleased. But why?"

"An unbiased approach, for one thing. For another, no professional greasy pole to push your rivals off, so no need for professional jealousy and damaging bouts of mud-slinging."

"Will you have to do any of that?"

"I don't know. Your father was telling me about being a venture capitalist, but I don't think I've got much talent for making money. I'll try not to push anybody's face in, that's about the best I can say."

"Except Colin Bardsey's."

"That's different. I loathe intellectual deceit and dishonesty."

There was a silence, not quite awkward. I said: "What does your field course entail? And where will you be entailing it?"

"I'm not sure yet. I'll let you know." He had given me an automatic response, as it were, and now came, visibly, to a point. "Cassie, I ought to tell you something."

"Such as your unorthodox line of research?"

He looked relieved. "That's it. Some of my researches could get me—and others—into trouble."

"You mean this is what Colin knows, and is threatening you with?"

"He's found out too much for comfort, yes."

"I see. What does he gain?"

"A hold over me—a way of causing trouble for me."

"Why does he want to do that? Apart from sheer mischief-making, I mean? What on earth have you been up to, anyway?"

He saw my look. "I haven't been stealing other people's intellectual property, don't worry. No, my crime has been to follow my nose instead of the party line."

"You make it sound like the corridors of power!"

"It's not much better." His tone was sober.

I said doubtfully: "I'm very out of my depth, you know."

"Are you? I wonder. Doubts and difficulties and obstacles and no-go areas are common to every area of human existence, don't you think?"

"What a lovely thing to say. All right: own up. What have you done to annoy the academic thought police?"

"I have consulted—and, worse, cited—a body of records that is not recognised by my college—or, indeed, by anybody else."

"Gosh. What records?"

"British records, both Welsh and English."

I was mystified. "But—that's all in the history books, isn't it?"

"No. Much of what's in the history books, especially if it concerns anything pre-Roman, is so garbled, distorted, bowdlerised, and plain invented as to be to all intents and purposes worthless. I have been putting a few records straight—*with* irrefutable proof—and in the process I've ruffled a few feathers."

I said: "Look here, can you tell me while we clear the things? Like most women, I can do about five things at once, and I promise to give you my full attention, for what it's worth."

"Of course. It's a long and rather dreadful story, but I'll give you the gist. Happily the Dean of my college is a decent bloke, and pretends not to know what I'm up to. He says he's gone grey overnight keeping me afloat. At least, that's what he says. He hasn't got much hair, so I don't know how he can tell."

He turned to me, and I thought for one electrifying moment that he was going to kiss me, but he didn't. He was close, though, and there was what you might call a speaking silence, charged with meaning. The lamplight threw sharply defined shadows across the craggy young face. I had not thought him handsome, but now I saw him more clearly, there was an untamed, mountainous beauty to him. We looked at each other for a bit.

"Come on then, Mr Mop," I said, deliberately breaking the spell. "Tell me about this eavesdropping. I take it that was how Colin 'found out'?"

He grimaced. "Spot on. I was at Blackwell's to request some books, and Colin was behind me in the queue. I didn't even see him. I didn't know, then, that some areas of research are academic poison, and that the titles I'd requested were—well, it sounds dramatic, but the only way to put it is to call them forbidden. The bloke behind the counter reacted as though I'd asked for dark net stuff."

"How ridiculous!" I protested. "What is this, Galileo and the Vatican?"

I was expecting him to laugh, I think, but he said seriously: "Pretty much just that." The fine mouth twisted. "Blackwell's said they were very sorry, but they couldn't supply them." He shrugged.

I studied him in the lamplight. "What about the internet?"

"I looked, of course. They started at about £600."

"Oh. And don't tell me, Colin knew they were a no-no, and—then what?"

"It was after *The Ready Writer* business. He told me to keep quiet about it, or he'd go to the Dean about me. Thing is,"—he grinned—"I'd already told the Dean myself, so that was a damp squib. The Dean," he added, choosing his words, "was hired for his financial acumen. He...er...he doesn't approve of prohibitions."

"Well, that's brilliant—but in that case, how could Colin make trouble for you?"

"By making trouble for the Dean. Colin has contacts in journalism, as we know."

I said nothing for a moment. Then, in a small voice: "But that's—blackmail."

"As you say. Look, I know all this sounds very unlikely, but it is as true as I stand here; and academic witch-hunts have not gone out of fashion: they've only gone underground."

I came to a decision. "I think I'd better know a bit more, don't you?"

So while we cleared the table and took things through to the kitchen, he told me of the comet which had devastated the British Isles in A.D. 562, with a consequent loss of national memory which would, in time, lead to the quite erroneous (but politically correct) belief that British history began with the Romans. He told me of the suppression of all things Welsh from the time of (French) Edward I to a German-dominated England after the Hanoverians assumed the throne in 1714. He told me of the brutal and unrelenting campaign of detraction waged against the antique history of the British Isles, and the defamation of their Trojan heritage. He told me that among the worst detractors were Welsh academics, a shameful state of affairs to the reparation of which he intended to devote his career. He told me of the Royal Roads of Britain; of the Marcelline laws (hijacked by Alfred the Great); of the freedom of women to rule, or to bear arms—in short, to please themselves. "And don't get me started," he said with an air of finality, "on the theft of early Christianity and the sadistic rape and suppression of the British Apostolic Church by the Roman Catholics—or the shameful involvement of the British Government over the last three hundred years in this suffocating cover-up, or we'll be here all night."

I had listened with as much attention as I could, but it was like *The Iliad* all over again. These were huge subjects, out of my experience, and vastly out of my reach. Also like *The Iliad*, I found it both tantalising and exhausting.

However, it was late. "I don't think I could," I said weakly, and put on the washing-up machine without a tablet.

FIVE

So…the Dream…departed and left him there, deeming in
his mind things that were not to be fulfilled.

Book II, *ibid.*

I WOULD LOVE to say that I romped through *The Iliad* taking in
every word from first Book to last, and then joyously turned
back to the beginning, but the afternoon Colin Bardsey called,
I was curled up with a magazine and looking at shoes. When
the doorbell went, I sighed, uncurled, and stood up. Obedient
to some insistent inner prompting, I went to the window first.

When I saw who it was I shrank back instinctively,
thanking God for woman's intuition, or whatever its new,
politically correct name is. Everything Huw had told me
about him flooded back as I stood with my back to the
curtain looking from side to side as though for a means of
escape. I took a few deep breaths to compose myself. Then
I went to open the door.

"Colin!" I said, assuming a social smile and forgetting
that we had parted in none too friendly a fashion. "How
lovely! How are you?"

"I thought I'd look you up," he said. He was already practically over the threshold.

"How lovely. I mean, how thoughtful of you. Are you coming in? That is, for a few minutes? I've got—um, I've got a doctor's appointment. You're lucky to have found me in."

This was a bare-faced lie, and I think I've already said that I'm a rotten actress. I'm also a hopeless liar. I felt the too-ready colour surging into my face and hastily turned away.

It was the moleskins again. He followed me into the sitting-room and sat where Huw had sat, and I felt quite unreasonably that he shouldn't be sitting there. I shook myself mentally before that appeared on my face as well.

"I've caught you at a bad time. I'm sorry." He stared at me for a moment, as though at last seeing me in focus. "You look rather startled. Is everything all right?"

"Oh—nonsense! Do I? I'm awfully sorry, but yes. That is, you have caught me at a bad time. I wonder where I've put my bag."

Through my inane little titter, I saw that this rubbish seemed to satisfy him. He looked round with unabashed interest, and once again I had the strong impression that he wanted something.

"Did you contact your archæologist?"

This fairly took my breath away, but I had myself well enough in hand. "Yes," I said baldly.

"Oh. Are you going to see him?"

"Yes, I am."

"Oh. Where is he?"

"On a dig," I replied, as laconically as any Spartan.

"Oh."

A short and awkward silence ensued, which I was determined not to break. Colin gave in first.

"I enjoyed dinner," he said after a bit. One heel was tap-tapping on the floor, the knee jigging up and down infuriatingly. "Would you like to have lunch with me? We could try the pub on the corner. I've been there before."

This flung me onto the horns of a dilemma. Did I grab my bag and leave the house, leaving myself open to the danger that he would decide to accompany me and I'd never get rid of him, or did I come out into the open and confront him, as Hector confronted Achilles (or was it Agamemnon?)? Whichever it had been, I decided to confront him.

"I haven't time today, thank you. And talking of which," I said, challenge edging my voice, "and since you've turned up unexpectedly, isn't it about time you did some explaining?"

He said nothing, so I tried again. "You know, I was in Oxford not long after we had dinner, with...with my father, and we ran into your academic rival in Blackwell's. We had a most illuminating conversation." *Now let's see what you do with that.*

His face was a study. I nearly laughed aloud as chagrin joined battle with an intense desire to know more—such as whether Huw had told us anything that Colin would find embarrassing. I think I'd decided to make him sweat a bit, and even let the silence lengthen while I tried to think of something clever to say that would take the wind out of his sails, when I saw that his gaze, dropping furtively from mine, had fallen on *The Iliad*. I might not even have noticed if he hadn't made a movement towards it of such bursting emotion that I was startled, and more than that.

"Have you read it?" I asked the question warily.

He didn't answer, and I could see that he hadn't even heard me. He had opened the front cover briefly as though to check the title, and now lifted the volume into his lap and spread both his hands on the gleaming leather, palms flat and fingers splayed. For a second, I thought I had yet another Homer-mad male in the house, and then I saw that the hands were not those of a lover of antiquity, or even an ordinary bookworm or antiquarian. They were, rather, staking a claim. The hazel eyes were blazing, his colour had risen, and the corners of his mouth were trembling—I'm almost sure it was in triumph. The strong sense of possession that came off him in hot waves filled me with disquiet, and when he opened the book at the back and seemed to jump where he sat, I got hastily to my feet and went over to him. Without giving either of us time to think, I took my grandfather's book from under those hands—he was actually trying to pluck at it with his fingernails—and caught it close to me protectively.

"It doesn't belong to me," I said, gently cold.

It seemed as though something momentous hung in a precarious balance, or that some weighty Damoclean sword glittered over his head. When he spoke, it seemed to cost him an effort to maintain the civilities.

"Whose is it?" He tried for an airy unconcern but succeeded only in sounding too interested for my comfort.

"A friend's," I replied. I left the gentleness out of my tone this time.

"Perhaps I might borrow it," he said. He hadn't taken his eyes off it. I saw possession again, and some other strong emotion that I couldn't identify but found even more disquieting.

"I don't think so. It's not mine to lend. I'm sure you can get it out of the library, or you could buy it in Blackwell's." I watched his colour intensify as this went home. "I shall have to get ready to go now," I said, holding the book close.

"I'll walk you," said Colin Bardsey. He got up with evident reluctance, his eyes firmly fixed on the book in my arms.

"No, thank you," I said, and stayed where I was.

Even then he just stood there.

I jerked my chin. "The hall's that way. Show yourself out, please."

He caught his breath on some muttered curse which I—thankfully—didn't hear, and with one final, longing, covetous look, left the room.

As soon as the front door slammed, I ran to the window. He was striding away. He looked as though he could hardly contain himself. I leant against the curtain on a wave of relief that shook me physically. A few moments later, I made myself look again, very carefully. Even while one half of me thought my caution laughable, the other half didn't; and that was the half I was going with, thank you very much.

Hell, he was waiting on the corner, by the pub. Waiting for me, to see if I really was going out? There was a stillness to him which the idle lifting of the fair hair in the London breeze only served to emphasise. The fixity of purpose was almost tangible, even at this distance; and the stillness was the stillness of a coiled spring. If he'd been waving a banner with *I shall be back* on it, his intention couldn't have been plainer.

Then, as though he knew I might be watching, and wasn't prepared to risk it again, he turned with deliberation and disappeared up the King's Road.

I was—almost—frightened.

In the dining-room there is a safe built into the disused fireplace. Designed by my father, it was concealed behind a moveable front of plasterboard, wallpapered to match the room. Its edges had been cleverly disguised, and our ingenious electrician had managed to secure a radiator to it. The false front was on concealed casters, and easy to move.

After this second visit, I put my grandfather's book into the safe with my jewellery.

*

Colin Bardsey made no further effort to contact me, but this didn't reassure me as much as it should have done. I had as much experience as I wanted of his underhand methods, and I said as much to Huw.

"I don't think he's got you in his sights at the moment, Cassie," he said. Not even the tinny little speaker could disguise the warmth in his voice.

"Good, I'm so relieved." I said it sarcastically, to conceal—perhaps even from myself—how ridiculously this pleased me. Then my attention sharpened. "What do you mean? Has he got *you* in his sights?"

"Not by name, but there's a rather snide article by *Gossipmonger* in this week's *Town & Gown?*—that's the rag Colin's friend-the-journalist writes for."

"I remember. What is the article about?"

"It's difficult to tell through the mangled grammar and other infelicities, but, mainly, it's a diatribe against irresponsible Linguistics undergraduates wasting money on the discredited discipline—sorry, so-called discipline—of comparative etymology between Etruscan and the Indo-European languages."

I picked this apart as intelligently as I could. "But that's not what you do, is it? I remember the comparative bit, but the other doesn't sound familiar. Mind you, that's not surprising."

I heard him laugh. "No, I'm Comparative Philology. Just to confuse you still further, most of the colleges call it Comparative Linguistics these days, but ours hasn't got round to it yet. I suppose because we do a lot more literature for its own sake. But that's neither here nor there. The point is, the people who read *Gossipmonger* aren't going to ask them to cite their sources—or mind about their grammar. Sling mud, and some of it will stick."

"Don't tell me he's put his name to this article!"

"No, of course not. And in case you're worried, he hasn't put your father's name to it, either. But it has got his stamp all over it, don't ask me how I know."

"You're the linguist," I said. "I suppose what people write gives off a fingerprint, so to speak, or—or vibrations. Would that be it?"

"Yes, you're right: it just smells like him. I'll send you a copy. I'd be interested to know what you think."

I wanted, very much, to believe this, but I had been struck by a sudden thought. I said: "Have any articles about wartime looting appeared yet?"

"Not yet. I'd imagine they involve a good deal of research. Why don't you have a good look through, and see? Only, wear gloves—or wash your hands thoroughly after reading. It leaves a very nasty aftertaste. By the way, I've been doing a bit of sleuthing. I rang *Town & Gown?* and asked to speak to the freelance hack who knows Colin Bardsey. I said someone had some information for him which they didn't want to be associated with. I was put through to a mobile voicemail belonging to one Kevin Dunston. I've made a note of the number."

"Clever old you," I said admiringly. "One way and another, your fish-and-chips paper seems to have Colin Bardsey in their pocket. I suppose this *Gossipmonger* column pays well for its dirt?"

"I should say so: the dirtier, the more lucrative seems to be the general rule. I'd better go, guess why."

"More patronymics?" I asked cleverly.

He chuckled. "Good try, but no: it's matronymics this time. I'm meeting my mother for lunch."

This conversation made me preen myself for the rest of the afternoon. Despite my lack of academic attainment, here was an undergraduate of an ancient university with a world-wide reputation casually treating me like an equal. I felt ten feet high.

The parcel that arrived from Huw included not only the *Town and Gown?* but also a bar of soap. It wasn't the bath-time variety, either, but industrial strength household soap. I smiled at it, and put it in the kitchen, under the sink. Heaven knew what my daily would say. Then I made myself comfortable in Huw's armchair and looked at the cover carefully.

It was outlined in boxing-ring ropes, and in the top right-hand corner there was a cruel caricature of a gowned and donnish figure. In the bottom left-hand corner was a downtrodden and abject-looking townsman, cap in hand. The print was blurred, the paper cheap, and the title rendered contentious and provocative by the question mark. I found the article and read it in increasing anger and disgust. Then I read it again, and this time I noticed the rider. It was at the bottom in tiny italics. It said, merely: *To be continued...*

I settled back properly then, and read the nasty thing with close attention from cover to cover. Not only was there no article about wartime looting, but the subject was nowhere mentioned. I rang Huw straight away, and it was just as well I did.

"I missed that," he said. After a short silence, he added: "I think I'd better go and spill some more beans to the Dean."

"Would you like me to send the soap back? You might need it."

"I don't think so, thank you. It won't be soft enough."

As usual, he had got the better of me. I put the telephone down with something of a snap.

*

"How are you getting on with Homer?" asked my grandfather.

He had come over to have a bit of lunch with me, as he did quite often. I love my grandfather, so I told him the truth.

"I won't pretend I've learnt every word by heart, Grandpa—or read every word. I'll even confess that there are bits of it that go utterly over my head. And I can't tell my Argives from my Eubœans, but..." I fell silent.

"But...?" he prompted me gently.

I groped for words. "It's the atmosphere of it. Just when you think you can't stand yet another medically accurate and minutely detailed wound, or another gory death, or some other ghastly battle—Grandpa, some of the *descriptions!* honestly!—it suddenly goes all personal and immediate, and gets you right *there*. I don't mind telling you that the bit with Hector and... Hector and..."

"Andromache," supplied my grandfather.

"That's her. The scene on the battlements before he goes to his death, and she's got their small son in her arms, well, it made me cry."

"Got you under the cuirasses, did it?" He said it with a private smile.

"I've no idea what they are, but—yes. Yes." I sighed, and shook off the mood. "I must say, they didn't go in for armour, much, did they? Greaves—even if they are well-fitting—and a linen chiton, if that's how you pronounce it, are all very well, but they're not what you'd call generous, and they don't seem to stop the spears in their tracks very effectively." I considered this. "How do I find out what a chiton looks like? I might try and start a fashion. I must ask Dinah."

My grandfather laughed. "I think Homer might be a bit bemused to find himself on the catwalk. Have you finished it?"

"Nowhere near, are you serious? But—can I hang on to it for a bit?"

"For as long as you like."

After that last telephone conversation, I didn't hear from Huw for a bit, but then I didn't expect to. He had told me about his exams, but I realised that I didn't even know when his term finished. No doubt he would let me know. The thing was, if Huw had exams, so too did Colin Bardsey. Perhaps they would keep him away from me for a bit.

Some days later, I took *The Iliad* out of its hiding-place again. I stood there, just looking at it, and remembering those spread, acquisitive hands and the fire of possession in the hazel eyes. With no real purpose in mind, I flipped through the last few pages, as he had done, just to have a look. In doing so, I found his treasure trove.

It had been stuck onto the inside of the back cover, behind one of the endpapers. The endpaper was coming away—had it been plucked away by those eager, questing nails?—and a folded corner of paper was showing. Whether I had been infected by Colin's intense interest, I don't know, but I was aware all at once that my heartbeat had quickened. With the greatest care, I freed the paper and eased it out.

It was a leaf torn out of some notebook, the paper furry and the ink blotched and faded. Despite my care, it tore a little, along one of the folds. It was in my grandfather's hand. The writing was young, vigorous, and hasty:

Then the sound began. A sound so deep, so profound, that it was as though the deepest organ-stop on the mightiest organ in the grandest and most awe-inspiring cathedral on the face of the earth had opened; a sensation more than a sound; an earthquake in the very soul of Earth. And the Lancasters came, wave after wave of them, squadron succeeding squadron, until the skies were filled from horizon to horizon and the face of heaven was obscured by the mighty, rushing sound of them. It was as though God Himself had opened His mouth to speak; and His words were the thunder of thousands upon thousands of pounds of high explosive packed tight into brass shell casings and primed to detonate upon impact.

In all, four hundred and forty-three Lancasters dropped their payloads on Berlin that day, 25th November 1944. I was there, and I survived.

It was signed in full:

Hector de Lisle Greatrex, 2nd Lieutenant, 1st Bttn. Royal Regiment of Rifles, on secondment to M. F. A. & A.

He can't have been more than twenty, if as much. I had no idea what M. F. A. & A. stood for. Was this what Colin sought so greedily? And if so, whatever for?

I looked at it for a long time, but no answers came to the myriad questions buzzing in my brain. Eventually, slowly, I put it back behind its endpaper and closed the covers on it.

I don't remember what I did then. But I do recall a queer feeling that even if I placed it right at the back of the safe, it still wouldn't be quite deep enough.

All in all, I was glad to have the salon. My horizons had expanded too far and too fast, and I went to ground, burrowing with relief among important matters like serums and the newest colours for lips and nails. I know Ginny needed the money and I didn't, but my three mornings were offering me something I needed quite badly.

Which was a good thing, because after that period of uneasy peace, Colin Bardsey came—irrupted—back into my life. He didn't ring the doorbell, either.

I had popped next door to deliver a letter to my elderly neighbour, which had come to my address by mistake. We stayed chatting on the doorstep for a few minutes, and she had just invited me in when I saw she was looking over my shoulder. Something about the twinkle in her eye made me turn in sudden hope. When I saw the tense figure on the pavement, my heart sank, and it was with the utmost reluctance that I made my excuses to Mrs Mitchell and came down the steps. I decided on attack to bolster my wavering courage.

"Don't you ever give up?" I demanded, feet apart and hands on hips, like Henry VIII. "What on earth have you come back for? What do you want now? Haven't you got exams to go to?"

His answer staggered me. It came without preamble; without any of the circumlocution I had come to expect from him.

"Sod all that. I want the Homer, and specifically, I want the lists."

"Homer? Lists?" I echoed blankly.

"Yes, the *lists*. I want those bloody *lists*."

My arms dropped to my sides, and I stood there, staring open-mouthed at him for what seemed like for ever. He made a movement of such suppressed violence then that I did the only possible thing, and gave in. Lightning-fast, and too late, it flashed across my mind that I had not, after all, put *The Iliad* away after finding Grandpa's piece about the Lancasters, and it was still lying on the dining-table. Call me careless, and I suppose I was, but I suddenly thought I knew why he wanted it so badly, and it seemed that honesty might now be a better defence than belligerence.

"I don't know about any lists," I said. "But you may come in for a few minutes and look at it since you've made such a nuisance of yourself. But any funny business and I'll whack you over the head with it, and don't think I won't."

He wasn't listening. Nor did he wait for me to do the polite hostess act. He took the steps—my steps—two at a time ahead of me and made straight for the sitting-room.

"Where is it?"

I felt like asking him rather where his manners were, but I didn't. Frankly, I was frightened by the change in him. The fair hair was dirty, he was unshaven and his face haggard, the eyes bloodshot and shifty.

"Over there," I said, jerking my chin at it. I picked up the door-stop and stood by the door, holding it as though it were a lacrosse stick, but he had seen the book before I'd finished speaking. He went straight for it, turning immediately to the back, where he found and removed the folded page. I could have kicked myself for not putting it back in the safe. I said sharply: "Be careful of that!"

He paid me not the slightest attention, but unfolded it with dirty, unsteady fingers that were nevertheless careful enough, and stared at it, devouring it. Then, on a long, shaky breath, he refolded it and put it back.

I was trying anxiously to recall what the passage about the Lancasters had said, and I believe I had some idea of wartime codes whirling about in my head. Was there a code concealed in that poetic paragraph? The thought made me tighten my grip on the door-stop. The smell of him, unwashed and foul, came to my nostrils.

The hazel eyes flicked, cold and purposeful, to my face. He didn't lift his head. The effect was chilling.

"Where are they?"

I stared warily back. "Where are what?"

His jaws clamped shut. He turned the book spine up and shook it. Then he jabbed his finger at it. "They're not here. That stuff was not them. Where are they? What have you done with them?"

I took a firmer hold on my weapon and spoke angrily and clearly. "I don't know what you're talking about. You've seen everything you wanted to see. You have overstayed your welcome and I would like you to leave—and do not come back!"

He was white, and the nostrils flared. I could hear the breaths, heavy, and even, but in the wrong way. For a few stretching seconds, I wondered if I'd been the rankest kind of idiot to let him in, then he slapped the book shut, threw it onto the sofa beside him, rose and came towards me, all in one compact and ugly movement that spoke not of trained muscles but of unconcealed, driving need.

I hefted the door-stop. "Don't come a step closer! I'll use this!"

He thrust his unshaven face at me, and I recoiled.

"I think you've made a fool of me. If you have, you'll pay," he said through clenched teeth.

Frightened as I was, I registered that they hadn't seen a toothbrush for far too long. I registered something else as well. Grandpa's Lancasters were not, after all, what he had been looking for. I hissed: *"Get out, will you?"*

My mouth was opening on a rising scream. He thrust out a hand and pushed me roughly against the wall. Momentarily winded, the scream died abruptly, but my ears were on stalks to catch the sound of his retreating, hasty footsteps. For some seconds after they disappeared, I remained there, listening. Even after they had gone, I stayed there for quite some time before sliding down the wall to the carpet.

When the doorbell rang, I was on my feet again as though lifted to them by Hera herself. Backed flat against the wall, I stood there, unable to move, my heart pounding.

"Cassie? Are you there, dear?"

I drew a shaky breath of the utmost relief. It was Mrs Mitchell. I ran—stumbled—out into the hall.

She was standing on the doorstep, one immaculate Gucci-shod foot already on the threshold. As soon as she saw me, she came forward hastily.

"Are you all right, my dear? I'm sure I don't mean to be nosy, but I was watching you both from my window, and I saw him go into the house the way he did, so rude to push past, and then when he came out again, you didn't come to see him off. Which was odd, I thought, and I could tell you weren't all that pleased to see him, so here I am."

"Mrs Mitchell—" I had no idea how to proceed, but she forestalled me.

"Let's go and sit down, and you can tell me all about it. I'd quite like to know which of you frightened the other more."

"Frightened the…? I…I don't understand." Bewildered, I gestured to her to precede me into the sitting-room.

"You didn't see his face as he ran past my window. He looked frightened to death. Hunted, is the word. And I can't say I'm surprised."

"*He?* But he was… Oh." I followed the quizzical gaze to my hand, and realised I was still holding the door-stop. I put it down carefully. The smell of him was still there, faintly in the room, sharp under the unwashed sourness. I knew what it was now. Fear.

"He wants something from me, and I don't know what it is," I said in a rush. My voice was wobbly, and, close to tears, I longed to confide in her yet didn't dare. *The Iliad* was between us on the sofa, the corner digging into my thigh. I compromised. "There was a break-in at my parents' house some weeks ago."

Mrs Mitchell patted me. "Hence the door-stop. I quite understand. Was he making a nuisance of himself?"

I seized on this. "Something like that, yes."

This was evidently something she understood and could cope with. She was kind and comforting, and full of good advice, and I listened and took in very little. She stayed about twenty minutes, which at least gave me time to compose myself, but when I showed her out at last, with renewed promises to call on her whenever I needed to, I could hardly wait to shut the door behind her. There was only one person whom I could confide in, and now I had a legitimate excuse for disturbing him. But I would send him a text first; it might not be convenient for him to speak.

Two hours later, and with no reply, I threw consideration to the winds and rang him.

"Huw? It's Cassie again."

"Yes?" His voice sounded tired and harassed, and even unfriendly, and I felt as though he had thrown cold water over me. Exams, I thought hurriedly. Remember he has important exams.

"Did you get my message?"

"Yes."

"Then why— Huw, what *is* it?"

"Surely you shouldn't be ringing me? What will your boyfriend say?"

So that was it. I made the face that is popularly supposed to be that of a bulldog chewing a wasp. "It sounds," I said, indignation rapidly dispelling the alarm that had thrilled through me, "as though my *boyfriend*, as you quite mistakenly call him, has already been saying far too much. Come on, Huw, get a grip. Don't you know me better than that?"

"I hardly know you at all," he said, but his voice was warmer.

I said something basic in reply to this, and he laughed.

"I feel I know you a lot better now! I'm sorry. I've had my head down, and the little bastard keeps hinting how he's seen you, and been invited to your parents' house—and all the rest of it. I was tempted to try a right hook when I found where he was going today."

"He said he'd seen me? Is that how he put it? Hounding me would be more accurate."

"Indeed? And just how has he been hounding you?"

I told him. Just in case he thought it was one-sided, I also told him about the door-stop. He didn't laugh.

"He wants the book, Huw. I thought I'd signed my death warrant for a moment or two. Perhaps I shouldn't ask, but could you…could you come? You see, I've found something, and there's no one I can tell but you. I don't know if your exams—"

"My last one's on Friday. I'll come straight up on Saturday morning."

"*Will* you?"

"Of course. You can't know how I've lo…how I've wanted to get up to London to see you."

"*Have* you? Have you *really*?"

"Yes. I'm very sorry to be such an idiot, Cassie, really I am. I minded a lot—and I wasn't sure if I had the right to mind."

The last wisps of alarm vanished. "If you haven't," I said, "no one has."

SIX

Hard it is for me…alone to break through,
and make a path…

Book XII, *ibid.*

THREE DAYS TO get through. I went back to work resolved to
put behind me Colin Bardsey and the frightening experience
I had gone through at his hands, but it proved impossible. I
kept seeing those calculating hazel eyes—and as if that were
not enough, I kept worrying about the Lancasters, and, more
vaguely, the wartime looting of precious artefacts. Eventually,
after a more than ordinarily complicated morning at Dinah's
during which I found that I had double-booked clients not
once but twice, she let me go early.

Deep in thought, I meandered along the pavement until,
looking up briefly, I realised that I had reached the pretty
house on the corner (where Mummy had once worked for
Monet Europe) without remembering how I had got there.
The high sun struck glinting brass into my eye with enough
force to make me wince. I moved on a step, out of reach
of the reflection, and squinted. The library. I don't think I'd

been in since my mother last took me. My reverie punctured, I was up the steps and pushing my way through the heavy doors like any academic bookworm.

Before I'd even reached the shelves to start browsing along them, my eye was drawn to the stands used for returned books before they are put back. There were several, but I saw only one. It was on the top shelf. It had a golden jar on the cover, and it was called *The Lost Treasures of Troy.*

I pounced on it, and found to my astonishment that not only did it cover those legendary treasures, but it also delved into the subject of wartime looting in detail. I could barely let go of it for long enough for the librarian to do his thing.

Once home, I flung my bag onto one end of the sofa and myself onto the other, and settled down with my trophy in pleased anticipation of tales of gold and priceless jewels. These abounded; but instead of being enthralled by them, my horror grew at instance after instance of ruthless and terrifyingly methodical despoliation of culture by Germany, who, having ransacked every country she occupied, laid Russia waste from Leningrad to the Urals with particular brutality and thoroughness. I could barely do more than skim over this part with one eye shut, but when I reached the tales of treasure, somehow the anticipation and excitement had evaporated.

The three men and a bicycle wasn't funny any more. It was tragic, pathetic, splendid, utterly noble, entirely British— and ultimately effective. Their efforts to track down works already looted; to itemise both them and what had been left; to protect buildings, libraries, churches; and to gather evidence and information subsequently presented at the Nüremburg Trials were nothing short of heroic. In fact, it was Trojan; and it made me grimly determined to thwart Colin Bardsey, whatever he was after—and whatever that grand-sounding resolve might entail.

Not even serums and a delicious new black-and-white theme in fashion helped to lift this mood. I won't say I was exactly a changed woman, but Dinah shook her head and said something mysterious about love. I refuted this hotly, but she only said that if it wasn't love, it looked a lot like it. I expect she was right: it seemed an infinity before Saturday finally dawdled along, and at last brought Huw with it.

I could hardly believe how much joy surged through me at the sight of the tall, slim figure. I went headlong down the steps to meet him, and we came face to face about two feet apart, grinning broadly at each other.

"Hallo," I said.

"Hallo."

I pulled myself together. "You don't know how glad I am to see you."

"I'm profoundly glad to see you, too."

For some reason, I found this absurdly touching. "Really? Really profoundly?"

He nodded slowly. The grin faded, and the peat-burn eyes began to glow. I think something might have happened then but for the gaggle of Japanese tourists making for the achingly smart second-hand shop just up the road, who forced us off the pavement and onto the bottom step. It brought us very close. We hadn't taken our eyes off each other.

"I've finished my exams."

"I rather thought you might have. How were they?"

"Grim."

"Of course."

Another pulsing silence. He flushed a little and looked at the ground. "I am really sorry I was such an ass on the telephone. I couldn't bear the thought of him—"

"It's forgotten."

"Thank you. At this rate," he went on after a moment, "which I calculate at about three minutes per step, it'll take us twenty minutes just to get inside."

This brought me out of my trance. "At least you've waited for an invitation," I said darkly. "Come on. I've been chewing my own feet in desperation to talk to you properly. Dinah had to give me a pedicure specially."

This time, I did shut the front door.

Huw picked up *The Iliad* and held it while I rambled through an explanation. It was as full as I could make it, even if I did have to backtrack a few times to fill the gaps. "So ever since then, it's been in the safe. No—" at his slightly startled expression "—it really has been. I only took it out because I knew you were coming. I suppose it must be an incredibly rare edition, or something. I can't account for his weird attitude otherwise. When I went to take it from him, he kept his hands on it. Do you know, I had to pull it away? It was rather beastly. He found Grandpa's thing about Berlin, and I thought that was what he was after, but it can't have been after all, because he... Oh, of course, you don't know about that. Have a look—it's at the back."

Huw's expression as he read the piece was a picture of awe and professional interest. "Well, well, well. This is fascinating. Talk about the horse's mouth."

"The Trojan horse's mouth, at that. 'Treasure trove', that's what he said. 'We think your father has found another treasure trove'—and that was before I found this! Oh, and he kept going on about some lists. 'I want the bloody lists.' Of course, I hadn't the faintest idea what he was talking about, and so I told him, but I might have saved my breath for all the notice he took. Do you know, he looked so unkempt? He was dirty. And he smelt."

Huw glanced up, interested. "Aha, so you noticed, too. He's been missing lectures."

"Has he?" I was momentarily diverted. "I thought you all did that. High jinks, and debagging in the quad. Oh, yes, I've read Dorothy L. Sayers."

He gave me his warm grin and shook the curls out of his eyes. "To begin with, yes, maybe, but no high jinks in your Trinity term, if you've got any sense. And these days, you'd probably be sent down if you debagged anybody."

I made a face. "Don't tell me."

"I know: jolly, harmless fun—for some. He didn't say lists of what?"

"No, he seemed to think I'd know what he meant. As if. Is there some kind of code concealed in the Lancasters, perhaps? Every fifth letter makes a word? I can't stop thinking about it. Or, I know, it's marked with pencil dots, or something. I can't say I saw any, but then this sort of thing hasn't come my way before. Will we have to do a Harriet Vane and Lord Peter Wimsey and work it all out backwards?"

"You are a fan! This is wonderful!"

Homer and his secrets receded rapidly as we drank in this further evidence of divine synchronicity. Huw said: "You're thinking of the code in *Have His Carcase*, aren't you? I know how to do that. Come to think of it, if this particular plot thickens any further, we might need it. *Busman's Honeymoon* is my favourite."

"I didn't think detective stories were approved of at Oxford."

"*Gaudy Night* is set at Oxford," he said. "They get engaged at the end. Have you read it?"

This seemed to me to be so full of promise, so replete with possibility and the not-yet-broached, that I blushed hotly.

"No. Is it a plot?" I asked idiotically, then moved on in a hurry. "I mean, what could he have meant by lists?"

"As it happens, there are lists in *The Iliad*. They're usually called the ship lists."

I had flopped down on the sofa opposite him, with Homer on the table between us, but at this I sat up and stared. "That's it! It must be! Tell me all about them!"

"Well, it's a catalogue of Achæan commanders, ships, forces, their lands and dominions, that sort of thing. It comes in Book Two, I think. Let's have a look. It sits a tad uncomfortably in the narrative—it's thought to be a later addition. Perhaps that's got something to do with it. Here we are. No,"—he scanned the pages rapidly—"not a pencil mark in sight here, either."

"Not even an underlined word?"

"Not one. Not an acrostic in sight. The mystery deepens. Cassie?"

"Yes?"

"I'm going to Italy in a couple of days. The twenty-first."

Instantly Homer was forgotten again.

"The twenty-first," I repeated, as though it were a magical password.

"Is there any chance you might be…?"

"Oh, *yes*," I breathed. "Mummy told me that Uncle Will is in Italy. I still want to ask him if he knows anything about Colin, and I can kill two birds with one stone. What are you looking for?"

He was patting his pockets. "My diary. How about if we—"

"Oh!" I said suddenly.

"What?"

"Something you said… Diary! That's *it*! He said his great-uncle had been keeping a diary! I'd completely forgotten!"

I had his attention now, and no mistake. He tossed the little notebook onto the table and gazed eagerly at me. "Can you remember exactly what he said?"

"Wait!" I said, biting the back of my hand. "It was over so quickly… Grandfathers… No, that's not it… *His* great-uncle had been keeping a diary—*and my grandfather was mentioned in it*! Oh, Huw! That was it! That's how he knew! No wonder he got in such a flap when he found another Greatrex poking around on Lemnos! Greatrex is a very uncommon name, and ours is an even more uncommon spelling…" I trailed off again.

"What?" asked Huw. His gaze was fixed on my face.

"Grandpa said he didn't know anybody by the name of Bardsey, but—"

"Well? Come on, Cassie, this is killing me."

"It might be a clue. The weedy little chap was in his regiment," I said slowly. "No, 'attached', that was it. 'A weedy little chap, older than me…'" I could almost hear my grandfather's voice. "'He didn't stand a chance…'"

"What was your grandfather's regiment?" The clear brown eyes were sparkling.

"I don't know. Yes, I do!" I pulled Grandpa's long-suffering *Iliad* round, flipped open the back cover, and shoved the book across the table again. I pointed. "There, at the bottom."

Huw read it, then said: "Goodness me, I was so intent on the text, I didn't even notice that. Not very scholarly."

"Is 'on secondment' the same as 'attached'?"

"Not quite. 'Attached' is usually used of journalists. 'On secondment', or 'seconded to', means you're in one regiment, or service, and you're sent to another because you've got some skills or experience they need."

"You said it with the stress on the second syllable." I said it with a hint of provocation, but it was wasted on the linguist in him.

"Yes, it's se*con*ded, not *sec*onded, as though it were a proposal at a committee meeting. Come and take my degree for me."

"I don't think so. What does M. F. A. & A. mean?"

"'Monuments, Fine Arts and Archives'," said Huw absently. He was scrutinising my grandfather's piece again.

"Was that the three men and a bicycle? No, a typewriter?"

"Just exactly that—and a bicycle as well. There's a book about it. It's a grisly tale. I'll have to look at it again."

I said excitedly: "I know the exact one you mean! *The Lost Treasures of Troy*. It's here somewhere; I got it out of the library. It must have been meant: I was barely through the door, and there it was. It's hardly cosy fireside reading, I must say. Here."

"That's the one." Huw took it and began to leaf through it. He was pulling meditatively at the top of one ear, and wore the deeply thoughtful expression that I was beginning to know. I had a sudden vision of him at work on an essay, covered with cobwebs and consulting dusty, forbidden volumes, with the Dean on guard outside like Elizabeth I's giant doorkeeper. He closed it with a snap and placed it beside Homer. "Cassie, you realise that Colin must somehow have got hold of his great-uncle's diary. Inherited it, or something."

"Yes, I suppose so. It makes sense. In fact, it's the only explanation that does. Even if he didn't survive the war, his diary did."

"But if your grandfather left Colin's great-uncle dead-by-accident on that office floor, how did the diary get back to this country for Colin to inherit it?"

I shook my head. "Not a clue. Somebody brought it back, I suppose. I expect Grandpa searched the body and found it, and took it, intending to try and return it to his family. You wouldn't want something like that falling into enemy hands. I can't imagine anybody just politely forwarding it, can you? Not with all those thousands of bombs dropping."

"And the Russians coming."

I wrinkled my forehead. "Would you call inventories lists?"

"Certainly. Why?"

"Because Grandpa mentioned he'd been compiling some inventories, I can't recall what of, I suppose it must have been art treasures and their rightful owners, that sort of thing." This seemed for a moment to be promising, but only for a moment, and I subsided again. "It can't be that, though, because he said he burnt them. Oh, well. Why did you want to know his regiment?"

"Because the military records will—now what?"

"Military records! That's how Colin said he'd found us! If he's got access to military records, and he's the weedy little chap's great-nephew—"

"...he'll have gone straight to the Royal Regiment of Rifles Museum and put in a request for family artefacts—and found the diary! Never mind for the moment how it got there!"

We gazed at each other, for perhaps rather longer than this revelation warranted.

"Hold on a moment," I objected. "How do we know it's in a museum?" His eyes crinkled most attractively at the corners, I decided.

"We don't, really, but it's the most likely place. What I mean is, if it was in somebody's private collection, Colin probably wouldn't know whose, and therefore wouldn't have had access to it."

"Oh, no, of course not. How did it get to a museum, though?"

"*Viva voce*," said Huw. "Sorry. This feels like my aural exam. That was a pig, if you like," he added reflectively.

"Never mind your exams," I said. "You're the man with the answers, and I want the answer to this one: how did it get into a museum?"

"Not this time, I'm not. I expect it was willed there by whoever brought it back. That's what usually happens."

"Oh. That's a lot less exciting than I was hoping for. You know," I said after a moment's thought, "if my grandfather was in that regiment, whatever you said, presumably they'll give me access to the records as well. And if Colin has seen that diary, which mentions my grandfather...and perhaps it mentions *The Iliad* too—though why it should I can't imagine—well, it means there really is some mystery attached to Grandpa's book, doesn't it? Huw, we have to see that diary."

"Yes, indeed. That's something I can organise."

"Can you? As long as it won't be another needle in a haystack," I said doubtfully.

"There can't be many Royal Regiment of Rifles officers on secondment in Berlin at the right time. 'Another' needle?"

"Ah." I had the grace to blush. "Blackwell's. I can see I shall have to come clean."

"Was I the needle? Did you really come looking for me?" He looked both astonished and gratified.

"I think so. I'm not sure. I know I said I did. No, really, I'm not sure whether I was looking for Colin or not, to try and get some answers out of him...but then you walked in, and I sort of knew it was you I'd wanted to see all along. I just remembered something you'd said about eavesdropping at Blackwell's, and I went on a whim. And my taxi driver told me to be careful, too. He was most insistent." I shook my head sadly.

"I noticed you instantly, that first evening I saw you," he said. It was his wolfish grin again, but kinder.

I lifted my lip at him. "I noticed you, too. You glared through that tangle of curls like an Irish water spaniel."

"Welsh water spaniel. One of the reasons I was so angry was that I couldn't believe he'd managed to get someone like you to have dinner with him. You looked as though you ought to know better."

"And lunch," I said provocatively, "though that was my idea. Anyway, dinner was grim until you turned up breathing fire and brimstone. Incidentally, if we're still playing detectives, how did you know where to find him?"

"I didn't. I was walking past and I looked in and saw him. I was thinking of happier times. My parents used to bring me up to London to go to the galleries and museums, and they'd take me to Sammarco's in the days when we had a little money, before my father died. I was on my way back to Oxford; I'd been talking to a philologist friend of my tutor's, and I nearly blew a gasket when I saw Bardsey's smug mug in there. He'd been avoiding me. I'm afraid I saw red and just barged in. It's...er...it's a habit of mine."

"But how did you know who I was?"

"I didn't know that, either, but I was already very suspicious of his underhand methods, and I didn't put it past him to oil up to someone in your family to cadge an introduction to your father. You seemed the most obvious, and the most likely."

I must have looked puzzled, because he explained: "Contributors to *The Ready Writer* are invited to provide a short biography. His says among other things that he's married, with a grown-up daughter. You know, you ought to read it. I'll send you a copy."

I blushed, embarrassed. "I'd like that. But I still don't understand. Colin said he'd gone all round the houses because he was afraid to approach my father directly. And that doesn't make sense, either! Why should he want an introduction so badly on the one hand, and yet be afraid to contact my father himself on the other? Unless he was afraid Daddy would find out about the article he'd lifted?"

"Highly unlikely that your father would ever know. I don't expect he reads student rags. It was probably a risk that Bardsey was prepared to take. He badly wanted to know certain things, and I should think he felt he had more of a chance if he got on terms with you first. If he came down to your parents' house on your arm, he'd bypass all sorts of barriers."

"What certain things?"

"There you have me."

I said slowly, and with growing conviction: "Certain things that required his presence in my father's study."

"Why do you say that?"

"Because when I went in after lunch and more or less told him to his face he wasn't wanted, he was standing by the bookshelves."

"And?"

"He was searching them. Oh, I don't mean obviously going through them under my father's nose, but it took me a moment to get his attention, and when I did, all I could see on his face was annoyance at my interrupting him."

Huw patted the leather-bound book between us. "Would he have found this in your father's study?"

"No. It's my grandfather's. My father has a copy, but it doesn't look anything like this one."

"And yet when he sees this particular one, he behaves as though he's found the Holy Grail. Which would seem to indicate that it is specifically this *Iliad* that interests him, for whatever reason, and not just any old edition."

I said rather helplessly: "But how do the treasures of Troy come into it? Where are they, anyway? Daddy didn't seem to know."

"That's just it: nobody knows. Heinrich Schliemann bequeathed them to a museum in Berlin, which was looted."

"I remember that: it's in the book. By the Russians?"

"Definitely by the Russians."

"If Grandpa was guarding the treasures from Troy, you don't think that these lists that Colin wants so badly include the treasures?"

"I don't know. Your grandfather was working for M.F.A. & A., so lists in that context imply those inventories he mentioned, but I haven't a clue if the artefacts in the Berlin museums would qualify. If we're right about the ship lists, though, there's some sort of a clue, in code, perhaps to the intended destination of the treasures themselves, that Bardsey badly needs. I know. How about this, Miss Vane? Your grandfather's inventories include the Trojan treasures. He wants to keep a secret record of the names and addresses just in case they're useful after the war ends, so he uses the ship lists somehow to record them."

"Elementary, Lord Peter. Or it's somehow recorded in among all the Lancasters. Invisible ink? Is that why Colin didn't see anything? No, don't laugh at me! You should hear my grandfather's tales about dead rats with sticks of dynamite in them, and maps on silk handkerchiefs. Honestly!"

"I don't doubt it. We can check very carefully for codes," he said more seriously, "but I daren't check for invisible ink."

"Why not?"

"Because you have to heat the paper, and I wouldn't dream of doing that even with permission. That's for the experts."

"No, all right. Gosh, the things you know. Isn't this exciting? But what I don't understand is why Colin wants them. I mean, a spot of plagiarism to boost one's academic reputation is one thing; I get that. Though I think it's a jolly risky way to go about it, but that's not the point. What's in it for him? I mean, suppose he somehow found the treasures of Troy. He couldn't possibly gain from them—I mean, if he were stupid enough to try and flog them, he'd be caught in two seconds."

"Good point. Family reasons, perhaps? Unless..."

"Go on."

"Well, there's a rumour on my stairs that he's in debt. I expect there'd be a big price paid by either Russia or Germany to get their hands on any information relating to the whereabouts of the treasures of Troy."

"Crumbs, aren't *Town & Gown?* paying him enough?"

"They can't be."

I was dismayed. "He must be desperate. He's really playing with fire. I wouldn't care to have anything in my possession that the Russians wanted badly, would you?"

"No, I wouldn't. Though I think you could just about trust Germany to play by the book these days, even though it'll be an E.U.-prescribed script rather than a national book. That's always a danger now."

I hunched my shoulders. "That means two more lots of people after Grandpa's wretched *Iliad*, as well as Colin."

"Three: don't forget the journalist. He's the one who started all this."

I had completely forgotten the journalist. I said suddenly, anxiously: "I don't want my grandfather involved."

"He might have to be, Cassie: it's his book; his war. It's my bet he'd be fine, you know. Don't worry about him. In the meantime, I'll do some asking around and see if I can find out anything more concrete about Colin's financial circumstances."

"In debt, you said. Drugs? No, he was verging on desperation, and nasty with it, but he wasn't showing any signs of the addict. It wasn't drink, either: he stank, but not of drink. What else is there? Loans?"

"Very possibly. Most of us are in hock to the bank to pay tuition fees and so forth, and for some people it becomes unmanageable. What else gets people into debt?"

"Living the high life if you haven't got the income to support it," I said soberly. Rich I might be, but I'm not conscienceless. "The horses?"

"I don't think so… though you may be on to something: it could be another sort of gambling. You know, hours spent stewing over fruit machines. Either real ones in arcades, or the internet variety. The latter's more dangerous; you can't just whip out a credit card in an arcade. At least, I don't think you can. I've never been in one."

"That's sad," I said. "It would explain why he felt the need to steal my father's work and sell it to someone else, wouldn't it? And it would explain why he's so keen to sell stuff to *Gossipmonger*."

"Yes, it would." He sat back and stretched luxuriously. "And it would also explain why he's so keen to help a journalist who's writing articles—or says he's writing articles—about such an explosive subject as looted works of art. Well, we can't do anything more until we see this diary. I shall have to go back to Oxford anyway, to pack, and I can make some telephone calls."

"How can we find out if the diary is at the regimental museum?"

"We could just ring them, but the National Archives will tell us not only that but also a lot of other useful information."

"Such as?"

"I don't know," he replied with a vagueness that made me look twice at him. "I'll know it when I see it."

This sounded rather unsatisfactory, but I'd heard this sort of thing from my father, so I said only: "Where're the National Archives?"

"Kew, mainly."

"Have we got time to go to both Kew and the Regimental Museum before you leave for Italy? Where is the museum, by the way?"

He picked up the little green diary and consulted it. "It's in Hythe. And we have time, if we do both in one day."

"'We'?"

He looked up, as though surprised I'd asked. "Well, of course, if you'd like to come. It's not that I exactly need your permission for either, but it'd do my street cred. a lot of good if I waltzed in with a real live Greatrex in tow."

"Beautifully put," I said. "I'll be your passport."

"Would your grandfather let you bring this to Italy?" He indicated *The Iliad.*

"Probably. I'll ask him. I haven't finished it yet, and I'm sure it'll make brilliant holiday reading. That's a joke. Just at the moment, I feel like chucking it in the Thames."

"Tell you what; I'll bring my own edition as well. Then I can scribble anagrams all over it in pencil if I feel like it." He stood up. "How do you feel about staying here tonight?"

Are you offering to stay with me? Just in time I bit the hasty words back and subjected them to some radical on-the-spot editing. "On my own, do you mean? I'm not sure. Not over-keen, I suppose, but he's hardly likely to come back so soon.

I've got Mrs Mitchell next door keeping an eye on me—and I can always put a note on the door saying *Homer has left the building* or something."

He put out both hands to me. I put mine in his and he lifted me to my feet.

"Do you know yet where you're going to be?" I asked a little shyly. "I wish I could fly out with you, but I must give Dinah some notice at the salon."

"I'll ring, or text. There are two possible places I might be sent to: either Arezzo, or Orvieto. There's another linguist who's keen to get to Arezzo, and I'm not fussy, so I expect it'll be Orvieto. There's a dig not long opened near there, and the man in charge lectures at my college sometimes."

"Goody, that means I can go to Assisi. I haven't been there for ages, and I seem to remember it's about midway between the two."

"Where's your uncle working?"

"Haven't a clue. I'll track him down when I get there, if I don't manage to before I leave."

"Friends in high places, eh?" He was still holding my hands, and he looked down at them. Just for a second his mouth twisted, and the thick brows drew together. "I wish I hadn't got to get straight back. You've got my number if you need me. Just you stick that note on the door."

"I will," I said. "In neon orange. He'll see it all the way from his gambling den. Thank you for coming at all."

"Nuts. I'll see you on Monday. Can you be ready by half past eight?"

"Yuck. Of course."

As I watched the tall figure vanish into the London crowds, I frowned. "Hythe," I said to myself. "That sounds familiar."

But I couldn't place it. All the same, I went to bed that night with a light step and a song in my heart that not even thoughts of Colin Bardsey could dispel.

*

"I got you a pass," whispered Huw. "You're my research assistant, vouched for by my college."

"Wow, how thrilling. I wish I'd known; I'd've dressed in sackcloth for the part."

Huw slanted an approving eye at my three-quarter-length-sleeved dress, which was of cream-coloured wool (the heatwave had vanished) with interlocking circles of tangerine and lime-green. Dinah had done my nails alternately in the same colours.

"Have you brought a notebook?"

"Whoops." I clapped a guilty hand to my mouth. "But I've got my smartphone. I'm sure they're the latest thing for research assistants. Talking of smart, you look as though you've spent the last two years behind a mahogany desk raking in vast bonuses and living entirely on Champagne."

"If I had been, we'd be sweeping down to Kew in a chauffeur-driven BMW instead of sitting on a bus."

"It can be arranged," I said hopefully.

"Another time."

"Actually, now seems a good moment to confess that I've ordered a taxi to meet us at Kew. Buses in the rush-hour... Well, you know what I mean. And you did say we might be going to Hythe. Tell me about the suit."

"It was my godfather's. He gave it to me when I got my place at Oxford. I think he knew perfectly well that the only clothes my father ever wore were the sort you might find useful for gardening. I don't think my mother kept much for me beyond that tatty old sweater I was wearing when I saw you at Blackwell's. Dad always wore it to write." He smoothed one pinstriped sleeve. "The second time this term I've worn this suit. I had another early interview before I left for London."

I looked at him. "Is that good or bad?"

"I'm not sure. It wasn't for a job, and nor was I precisely *sur le tapis*. I was invited by the Dean to explain the bad feeling between Colin Bardsey and me."

"Oh. What did you say?"

"Very little, since it involved you, and I hadn't discussed it with you first. I merely said that we'd got across each other, the way it happens sometimes. He was very nice about it. In fact, he was so nice about it that I plucked up the courage to ask him a question or two. He told me they've had their eye on him for some time, but it was the blind leading the blind: I couldn't help the Dean, and the Dean either couldn't or wouldn't help me. It might have been quite funny, the pair of us pussyfooting round each other without a clue what to ask."

By the process of association, I said: "Homer's in the safe. And Grandpa's so thrilled I'm finally improving myself that he agreed to let me bring it to Italy."

"That's good. He'll enjoy being taken among Etruscans again."

"I thought Homer was Greek," I objected.

"Don't start."

"Perhaps he was Turkish. Why is that funny?"

"I'll tell you one day."

"Make sure you do. What is your Dean like? I don't mean as compared with other deans; I wouldn't know a dean from a duke."

Huw gave this a little thought. "I don't think you could compare him with other deans. He doesn't look at all like a scholar, even if he does have a first-class brain. He's very good at the financial side of things, and that's all-important these days. Too important, and all in the wrong ways."

Call me banal, but this was interesting. "Such as?"

"Oh...cheeseparing when they should be backing initiative and not spending far too much on unimportant rubbish like logos and letterheads and politicising. I don't mean him personally, but it's the way they all think nowadays."

"Rebranding," I nodded.

"Exactly. Suffocating, sticking-plaster-over-a-torn-artery approach. Don't get me started."

"All right," I said pacifically. "That's the second time you've choked me off. We won't go there, either."

SEVEN

Tell me now, ye Muses,
that dwell in the mansions of Olympus…

Book XIV, *ibid.*

THE NATIONAL ARCHIVES building was spanking modern, with three low, flat roofs which made it look like a multi-story car park, plate-glass doors, air conditioning, and a glimpse of a somewhat barren expanse of water, its grey surface ruffled under a sharp wind and a solitary waterfowl. We swished in, and immediately attracted varying looks of disapproval, presumably for being too smart. A dried herring of a woman behind the reception desk looked me up and down and audibly tut-tutted.

"Next time, sackcloth for the pair of us," I whispered.

"I'll bring the ashes."

The woman checked our tickets and admitted us, casting my dress and nails one disgusted glance. She transferred the disgust to my arm.

"You can't bring that in here," she said, as though I'd come in coiled from elbow to wrist with a black mamba.

"My bag? What do you suggest I do with it?"

"Put it in a locker, of course!" Her tone was acid, and implied that she would like to see it disposed of altogether, preferably burnt at the stake while I was still carrying it.

"Could I have a key?" I asked, deceptively meek.

"When I've signed you in."

Her face was the colour of porridge, with a cyclamen-pink gash of a mouth, and what I recognised immediately as a provincial attempt at a Sassy & Jo signature scissor-cut. She looked like one of Mummy's dahlias gone over. I resisted the strong temptation to tell her so, and fished out my smartphone. "Can I bring this with me? It's only for—"

"Certainly not! It might be wired! In the locker with the rest, please." With a gesture of outraged repudiation, she pushed the key across the desk to me. I took it, found my locker, and put my bag in.

"I'm so sorry, Professor Trefor," I said clearly. "It's just as well I have a photographic memory, isn't it? One wonders when the academic world is ever going to embrace technology fully and finally."

Huw was looking preternaturally solemn, but his eyes were dancing as he hustled me ahead of him. "I'll give you Professor! Have you really got a photographic memory?"

"No, of course I haven't. What did she mean, wired?"

"For a bomb," he replied drily.

I let out a crack of delighted laughter. "I wish I had been!"

This elicited an angry *"Quiet, please!"* from someone, which did silence me, but only because I put both hands firmly over my mouth.

We were in a huge room, lit, it seemed, entirely by glow-worms in the ceiling. Like Blackwell's, there was rank upon rank of shelves stretching away into the far corners, but as well as those with books on them, some of them supported dozens of brown cardboard boxes, while yet others held tiers of small wooden drawers with brass handles, the sort that look like a tortoise's upper jaw.

I looked round in dismay, reminded of the hangar at the end of *Raiders of the Lost Ark*. "Oh, dear! Whatever do we do now?"

"When I booked, I had to tell them what I wanted to look at. Don't look so worried! I was given some references…" He strode off, hunting along the shelves, and I hurried after him.

"Here's something." He pulled out one of the little drawers. The spotlights, in themselves not bright, were cleverly angled so as to shine right in, and even though the room was sepulchrally dim, we could see the card indices perfectly.

"Will that tell us where the diary is?" I was craning on tiptoe over his shoulder at the slip of card. "I can't read that, it's in Syllabic. What does it say? Or don't you have the faintest idea, either?"

"It doesn't matter anyway, it's not the right one. And don't you mean Sabellic?"

"Of course I do. How silly of me. Patronymics, anyway." I touched the card with one lime-green nail. "Is this in Patronymics?"

"Idiot. It's only the system they use for cataloguing. I know, it looks like nothing on earth."

"Another alphabet for you."

"I cracked this years ago. It's an alphabet isolate. Next one, please… Aha." He took out another slip of card, and a thoroughly satisfied grin dawned. "Here we are. This is more like it. That didn't take long, did it? We were right. One diary, custody of the Royal Regiment of Rifles Museum. That means a trip to Hythe, just as we thought." He turned over the card, and the grin faded abruptly. "Well, how absolutely astounding. Over to you, Miss Greatrex. Can you shed any light?"

"I very much doubt it, Professor, but I'll have a go. What is it? Oh, crumbs, will you look at this!" I read it in a stage whisper. *"Deposited at Somerset House by the executors of the estate of the Lady Aileen Philippa Greatrex, deceased 17th September, 1953...* But that's my great-grandmother!" I met his eyes in astonishment. "What on *earth* is going on? How does she come to be mixed up in all this?"

"Heaven knows. What do you know of her?"

"Well, the only thing I can call to mind at the moment is how she hated people mispronouncing her name as Eileen. Oh, and she had a canary, if that's any help."

"Not hugely. It's all good solid social history, though. Somerset House... I wonder."

"I know where that is, but I didn't know it had records there."

"It hasn't anymore. That's what must have happened. When Somerset House came to Kew, Birnam Wood to Dunsinnan, ubiquitously and inanely mispronounced Dunsinayne, the diary must have been sent to Hythe. Ergo."

I followed this with some difficulty. "By my great-grandmother? Don't tell me she was in Berlin as well."

"It seems a little unlikely. No, the diary will have been sent on by whoever it was who had the lovely job of packing up hundreds of years'-worth of records and overseeing the move to this place. I don't envy them." He turned to face me. "Cassie, hasn't it struck you as odd that your grandfather should have lent his precious *Iliad* to you at all?"

"Not until you came to mention it, no, unless you mean he doesn't rate my intellect very highly, either? He did say he was concerned that my brain was turning into nail varnish. Oh… I get you, he doesn't know how important it is? Important to Colin, do you mean? That's not very well put, since we don't yet know why it's important—I'm getting in a muddle."

Huw was pursuing a line of his own. "It's almost as though he doesn't know. And yet he *must* do." He frowned, thinking. "Did he say where he was wounded—I mean, whereabouts on his body? In the head, for example?"

"You mean, he might have lost his memory?" I stared blankly at the card in my hand, and then at the open drawer for a moment. "Wait a moment. Wounded… No, I don't think I ever heard him say where he'd been hit. He would never willingly have handed me a live coal if he'd had the faintest idea, I know he wouldn't. He did tell me he'd married his nurse, who became my grandmother, and I didn't know a thing about that, either. Nobody ever said a word to me."

"Was she Queen Alexandra's?"

"I don't know who she belonged to," I said, it has to be confessed a trifle pettishly.

"If she was Queen Alexandra's Royal Army Nursing Corps, which is probable, she'll be here somewhere."

I heaved a sigh. "Haven't you got enough members of my family to be going on with? You're beginning to sound like Colin. Why do you want Granny as well?" I caught at myself. "Sorry, I know I'm behaving badly, but I'm right out of my depth. And I don't like the way that woman spoke to me. She wouldn't last a second in my job."

He put his hands to my shoulders and gripped them. "She doesn't deserve to last a second in hers." He hugged me to him briefly. "Cassie, if your grandmother was his 'special', as they used to call them, it will have been her duty to itemise everything that came into hospital with him."

All I was conscious of just then was an uneasy combination of my shame and the comfort of him, but then I was with him. "Supposing he only *assumed* he burnt those inventories! He said he burnt other papers; he might well have thought he'd burnt them as well! But what if he brought them home with him?"

"And the diary as well, just as you said."

"Oh, Huw! He must have done! He said he'd toted old Homer all round Germany with him!"

"We are getting very slightly warmer. Permit me, Miss Greatrex, to bring my superb intellect to bear upon the matter. How old was your grandfather in 1945?"

I screwed my eyes shut. "He was born in November of 1925… I think."

"So, in April or May of 1945, he'd have been nineteen, going on twenty."

"I suppose so. I'm not brilliant at maths, either. Why?"

"Because in which case he was under age—which was still a full twenty-one in those days—and all his effects would have gone to his named next of kin, who was—"

"My great-grandmother!" I was still holding the card, and with one accord we put our heads together over it. "She must have taken the diary from his 'special', not knowing it wasn't his—and probably his *Iliad* as well— *and* not knowing that the 'special' would one day be her daughter-in-law… Ooh!" I executed a hop from sheer excitement. "He said it was practically all he had on him…'*or so I'm told*'! Yes, told by my great-grandmother! He *must* have lost his memory! And I'll bet that my great-grandmother was warned not to mention anything and stir it all up…"

"…and once he'd got out of hospital and gone home to recuperate, it was gradually forgotten about…"

"…and she'll have put the diary away somewhere safely, perhaps still thinking it was his. No, that won't do. She must have looked at it and seen by the writing that it wasn't."

"She might well have assumed that it was a keepsake from a brother officer who hadn't survived."

"Yes, that's probably it. Which means there's no name or address on it, otherwise she'd have returned it to his family. How's that for a brilliant piece of deduction! But we're no nearer to discovering the name of this great-uncle of Colin's." I thrust the card at Huw. "We'd better put this back."

He replaced it and shut the little drawer. "We'll probably never know just what happened—unless she told your father?"

"No. She died before Daddy was born."

"She must have had some conception of the diary's importance, though, to have willed it to Somerset House. I wonder why she didn't will it directly to the museum."

"Perhaps it didn't exist then. Daddy's regiment wasn't disbanded until after the Falklands. Part of Tom King's 'Options for Change', whoever Tom King was. Mummy and Daddy were invited to the museum's opening, that I do remember. Oh, of course! That's how I knew the name of Hythe! I was thinking only the day you came that I'd heard it before. Yes, I suppose I must have been about eight. He went scarlet with rage about 'Options for Change', that I do remember. He used to say that options didn't come into it. 'Bloody weaselly euphemism from a bloody weaselly administration. Margaret Thatcher's the only man in the whole bloody Cabinet.'" I chuckled. "Gosh, I haven't thought of that for ages."

He was still looking at the drawer. "You know, if you're right, and I think you are, we still don't know whose diary to ask for."

I considered this. "How about if we just give the name of Greatrex, and see what happens?"

"We might at that. It does seem to be something of an open sesame. Of course, all we have to do is say it was deposited by your great-grandmother's executors at Somerset House, and they'll know exactly how to lay hands on it. Do you think," said Huw, "and now I do sound like Bardsey, I could cadge another meeting with your grandfather?"

"I'm sorry I said that. It was cheap. Yes, of course, I'll be glad to arrange it. Why?"

"I'd like to look at the photographs. You never know, I might recognise someone under a different name."

I was doubtful. "It's a bit of a long shot, isn't it?"

"Possibly. Family likenesses can be very strong, though."

"Don't look at me. I look like my mother."

"There you are, then."

I sighed. "Last word," I said softly.

Somebody hissed "*Hush!*" just then, so close by that I jumped. I whispered: "Have we finished?"

"I'll just quickly look… No, that's it."

"Then please let's get out of here," I begged. "The atmosphere's getting to me; I can feel a fit of the giggles coming on. I'll be dancing on the tables next."

I retrieved my bag and returned the key, and Huw signed us out. The porridge-coloured woman accorded Huw a thin smile, but she ignored me altogether. I said sorrowfully (and loudly) as we walked past and out into the fresh air: "A clear case of asyndetic hendiasys, Professor, don't you think? Or could it—after all—be merely a hyrax? So sad…"

Our driver hurriedly stubbed out a surreptitious cigarette and swooped to open the door for us. I slipped in, settling myself into my seat, just as the porridge-coloured woman came out of a side entrance in excellent time to see our driver usher Huw in beside me and shut the door on us with a movement that looked very like a bow. Her expression of sour disapproval was too much for me, and I'm afraid to say that I waved to her as we moved off. Then we gave way at last to gusts of laughter.

"Oh, Cassie, Cassie, I shall never be able to show my face there again! You and your hyraxes—you mean hapax, and she knew it! It's no good, I shall have to take up hedonism as a career and call it anthropology. I'm obviously cut out for it. My father would have a fit if he could see me now."

The taxi took us to the station, and we bought sandwiches to eat on the train. At Folkestone, we hailed another cab, which took us along the seafront the short distance to Hythe. We peeled off from the centre of the little town, hugging the sea, and finally swept under an arch of some pinkish stone and came to a halt on what I recognised immediately as a parade ground. A sign in dark green and yellow proclaimed us to have arrived at the museum.

This couldn't have been more different from Kew's air-conditioned modernity. The Georgian buildings ran round all four sides of the enormous square, and the sash windows (they looked original) were glossed white and newly washed. The door was standing hospitably open, giving us a glimpse of a low-ceilinged room filled with militarily themed merchandise. We climbed out and asked the taxi to wait.

The curator of the museum was a Major Reg Simmons. A spare, upright man of no more than middle height, what remained of his white hair was as disciplined as the rest of him, and he came out of the office behind the reception desk to greet us and take us upstairs. He was kindness itself, and obviously delighted to have a daughter of the regiment under his roof. He asked after my parents, and listened attentively to the story we had concocted on the way down. This was that I was helping my grandfather compile a Greatrex family history, and we had only just learnt of this bequest of my great-grandmother's. Huw? Oh, he was a friend of mine; just finished his exams, and was helping me negotiate my way round unfamiliar archives. When I finished, Major Simmons told us that there were only two artefacts in the bequest: a cap badge dating from the Crimea, and a diary.

"But there's no name, which is only to be expected," he warned as we came to an archway that led into a large room hung with pictures of officers and decorated from floor to ceiling with weaponry. "It is part of Lady Aileen Greatrex's bequest, however, so I think you'd be on the right track. *This* way!" He ducked under ragged swathes of faded scarlet colours embroidered with battle honours and embrowned with the blood of the fallen. We hurried after him, threading our way among glass cases of battles re-enacted in miniature, and followed him at the quick march into a private office at the back.

This, surprisingly, was in much the same state of chaos as my father's study. I gazed round wide-eyed at drums (one with a bullet hole punched through it) stacked up next to piles of books, boots, rusty rifles, empty holsters, shell casings, canteens, helmets, headless mannequins incompletely dressed in uniforms from all eras, and piles and piles of dusty, tattered and bulging folders. Behind what looked like—but surely couldn't be—an oversized Ali Baba laundry basket dribbling earth and pebbles over the floor, peeped a safe. The Ali Baba basket ("a genuine Peninsular gabion, from Orthez," said Major Simmons proudly, if—to me—incomprehensibly) had a rusty bayonet embedded in its guts; and the door of the palpably Edwardian safe was standing wide. Major Simmons dived at this, seeming to know exactly where to lay his hand on the diary. He brought it out and regarded it.

"Strange how things go in clusters. Like buses."

"Clusters?" I repeated, rather blankly.

"Yes. You're the third person interested in this bequest."

I jumped, but he was examining the cap-badge, in his other palm. He went on thoughtfully: "There was a bloke here some weeks ago. Grandson, I think he said. And there was someone else a few months back. Don't know about him: I was away then. I can check. Think he was a researcher. Not sure."

"It wouldn't be my cousin Paul Greatrex, by any chance?" I asked, innocently mendacious. "Not that he's interested in family history."

Major Simmons shook his head positively. "No, that wasn't it."

"I've only one male cousin."

"Ah. I might have got the grandson bit wrong."

"Are your records online?" asked Huw politely.

"Not item by item, nor even page by page; we haven't the resources. But there is an inventory available on the museum's website, with photographs. Come and take a pew."

We took a pew side by side, and he put two pairs of white cotton gloves on the table in front of us with something of a flourish. "You'll need these, if you don't object. I'll leave you to it." He strode away, leaving us alone with the precious little artefact. It sat mutely in front of us, and we eyed it cautiously.

"It's an address book!" I whispered.

"Got your phone?"

"Of course—what had you in mind?"

"If there's anything worth reading, I want it recorded. I'll make notes by hand as well."

The diary was tiny, far smaller than I had expected: only about two inches by three, and the dark blue leather cover was rubbed and cracked. We put on the gloves and bent eagerly over it. The smartphone lay on the table in front of us, ready to record every word.

"Give a description," he said.

"What—out loud? All right." I picked it up with reverent care, and, rather self-consciously, described it minutely. Huw made notes with practised fluency, and held his hand out for it.

"It's only about a third full," he observed.

"At least it's in English. Why so small?"

"Easier to conceal, I suppose. It was a heinous offence, to keep a diary in wartime." He turned the pages with the utmost care, scanning the tiny writing. "Here we are," he said quietly. "Damn these gloves. The entry's under 'I'. I wonder why?"

"'I' is for *Iliad*," I said without thinking.

Huw seemed to leap in his seat. "*Yes*," he said, his eyes kindling. "Listen to this!" He began to read, keeping his voice low. "...*time is getting very short. The Russians are getting closer and closer, and the bombing has been frightful. Told today that Dada and Misha are still alive; they have moved them to Sobibor. No idea if it's true. No news of Mama or Olga. I am in HELL. At long bloody last, Greatrex left the ruddy book on his desk for a moment while he was out of the office and I managed to find those lists he's been...*" His voice petered out.

I said urgently: "Go on. 'He's been...' 'He's been' what?"

"It ends there."

"It can't do! Let me see!"

But he was right. Infuriatingly and inevitably right. I slumped in my seat, savagely disappointed, but he was leafing gently through it again.

"Just let me check and see if there's any clue to this fellow's true name... No, as we thought: nothing. He wouldn't have been such an idiot: keeping diaries was strictly forbidden anyway, never mind writing your name all over the place." He tugged thoughtfully at his nose. "'Misha' is short for Michael in both Russian and Polish, and probably other languages as well, which is a sort of clue, at any rate. Does that ring any bells?"

I thought back. "Grandpa might have said something about a Russian Jew... In fact, I'm sure he did. You can ask him yourself when you see him again."

"Well, I will."

He returned to the entry, and it was a moment before he spoke again.

"That's odd." He checked each virgin page through to the last one, and was now examining the final entry again closely.

I pulled myself together. "What?"

"Does that or does it not look as though a page has been torn out?"

He indicated the place to me. The page had been removed so carefully that the bookbinder's long stitches camouflaged the excision from all but the minutest inspection. Disappointment vanished, replaced in an instant by a surge of renewed hope.

"You're absolutely right—though it's a very neat tear. It would explain why the entry finishes so abruptly, in the middle of a sentence, wouldn't it?"

"It would indeed," he said, with satisfaction.

We looked at each other.

"Colin? Or the so-called grandson?"

"Or Major Simmons's unidentified researcher?"

"*The journalist?*" We said it together.

"*He's been...*" I read it again. "Obviously the rest of the entry tells us what Grandpa was doing with the lists."

"Yes, and if it was the researcher—the journalist—who tore it out, it would have given him a hold over Colin, who was his key to finding them."

"Why does he want a hold over Colin?"

Huw shrugged. "Journalistic coup? It would be worth thousands in increased circulation, not to mention deals done behind the scenes. He'd want to make sure of Colin's close—and continued—co-operation."

He closed the precious little book and folded a careful hand over it. "At least now we know why *The Iliad* is so important."

"Hold on a second."

"What?"

"It doesn't mention *The Iliad* by name."

"N…no, that's true. But he wouldn't, would he? And it is entered under 'I'. I expect that's as definite as he felt comfortable being."

I let it go.

"However, I could also bear to know why Kevin Dunston is writing about wartime theft of art, and who commissioned him."

"If anybody did. Perhaps he just saw an opportunity."

"If so, it's not an opportunity *Town & Gown?* have yet availed themselves of."

"No." I shivered. "Thank God I put the book in the safe. Although…"

"What?"

"Well… Colin actually shook the poor thing, upside down, and nothing fell out. What's the betting the lists were lost years ago?"

"More than likely."

I touched the little diary with one gentle finger. "Do you suppose Major Simmons knows about the torn-out page?"

"I've no idea. And I don't know if I've got the courage to mention it to him. But we can at least make sure of one thing."

"What's that?"

"We can make sure we're right, and it is the journalist who's the likeliest culprit. I think that's him coming back."

When Major Simmons returned, my smartphone was safely back in my bag, and we were examining the cap badge. Huw said it was exactly what we had been looking for, and that we'd made some notes.

"Excellent, excellent. I've found one of the blokes, by the way. Dunston, his name was. Kevin Dunston. Not a researcher; a hack. That was it. I'm sorry, but I can't put my finger on the other one. My records aren't what they should be—my secretary's on sick-leave."

"Then it's not my cousin," I said.

"Do your records say which paper?" asked Huw idly, and as though expecting the Major to return a negative answer. He got one, with a decisive shake of the head.

"No paper: freelance."

"Any address?"

"Just says *Oxford*. If you're done..." He swept up the diary, jiggling it in one hand. "Glad you found what you wanted. Did I say, no photocopying, but if you're willing to stump up, you can have a microfiche. You are? I'll thread the roll through for you. Give me a shout when you're done. Cheers."

"The military mind," said Huw to me, "is very direct."

"Don't tell me," I said with some feeling. "I was brought up by one. How do you suppose this Kevin Dunston knew about Colin's relationship to this diarist? After all, there's no name."

"I expect he found out the other end. You know, corresponding German or Russian records. If more than one person is researching the same subject, it's odds on that they run into each other, and usually more than once. Come on—I want a microfiche copy of this entry."

I was dying to ask what a microfish was, but I was getting tired, so I just followed him and watched him go to a sort of antique-looking television screen and sit down. He manipulated a lever, and the diary began to slide past, like on an old video tape. It was miniscule; I certainly couldn't read any of the entries. These were few and far between; most of the book was empty. Huw scrolled to the end and gave it the command to print. The silent white filing-cabinet I was leaning on suddenly sprang into life, which made me jump, and spewed out some blueprints.

"Modern magic," I said.

"Most places use the internet now, but these are incredibly useful still. We're all done here."

We paid, and thanked Major Simmons, and bade him goodbye.

On the train home I said idly: "I wonder why the bookbinders didn't take out Grandpa's Lancasters. After all, it's not part of the book."

"Conservation techniques, I suppose. The thing is to do as little as possible. Mend, not meddle, you might say. And since it's been there since the end of the war, I expect they decided it had become part of the book by then."

"Like extensions on a house. You know, Victorian orangeries stuck onto Georgian houses. I know that," I added smugly, "because we've got one."

"Exactly like that." He flashed me an affectionate grin. "Oh, by the way..."

"Yes?"

"Can you put that recording safely onto your laptop somewhere, and expunge it from your phone?"

"Yes—but why?"

"Not sensible to cart it around with you."

"No?"

"No."

"Oh. All right," I said equably, but with a touch of scepticism. "What about your microfish?"

"Send it to my mother's house for safekeeping. I don't particularly want to be found with that on me, either."

"Oh."

I digested the implications of this with considerably less scepticism.

About fifteen miles later, I said: "Okay. Just suppose they're not lost. If they're not in *The Iliad*, where are they? After all that, we're still no closer to finding the wretched things."

"I am not, alas, a haruspex," said Huw. His eyes were shut.

I looked at him for a moment, then got out my smartphone. "Sounds as though it's first cousin to a hapax— if I heard you aright. How do you spell it, anyway?"

He told me, and I typed it into the search engine.

"Well, do you know, I'm glad to hear you say so," I said when I had finished reading. "Myself, I think I'd rather use a nice crystal ball, much cleaner, but there you are."

"No accounting for tastes," said Huw. He opened one eye at me and shut it again.

I regarded him straitly. "None. None whatsoever."

EIGHT

...he sent him to Lykia, and gave him tokens of woe,
graving in a folded tablet many deadly things...

Book VI, *ibid.*

WHEN MY FATHER knew he was going to be a very rich man,
he taught me a valuable lesson. Like many people, I had a lot
of half-baked and ill-informed ideas that it was somehow
wrong to be rich, and I will never forget what he said.

"You can have a lot of fun with money," he told me. "You
can enjoy spending it on yourself, you can enjoy spending it
on your friends and family, and you can enjoy doing your
duty with it. Just make sure you do all three, and don't listen
to the killjoys."

Which was why, when I turned twenty-one and came
into possession of the income from an extremely large and
interestingly varied trust fund, I bought a healthy tranche of
JetWorld hours. This purchase came into the first category,
by my reasoning; and it was with unabashed pleasure that I
now crossed the tarmac at the little aerodrome and stepped
up into the Hawker. Quite often there are other passengers,

and I always enjoy meeting new people, but this time I had the aeroplane to myself and I could pretend it was my own, and that I was Catherine Zeta Jones with a diamond the size of a quail's egg on my finger.

For some while after we had lifted gently into the air, I thought idly over all the activity since Huw and I got back to London. Ginny had been glad to do more time, and Dinah had promised, rather grimly, to choke Colin off if he came looking for me. I smiled to myself as I recalled the conversation over the telephone with my uncle. Once we had ascertained that I was not my mother, I told him of my intention to come out and see him on his dig. My heart leapt when he told me he was actually near Orvieto, and digging up chunks of ancient Umbria, where (he said, employing what was presumably the correct archæological term) they had found a spanking great villa. I wondered if it were the same villa that Huw had mentioned, then reflected that the area was probably stiff with them. I kicked off my shoes, pulled out a magazine, and wriggled luxuriously back in the squashy leather seat.

One of the many joys of this mode of travel is that you can choose your airport. The nice woman at JetWorld had asked me whether I preferred Rome, with a much larger choice of hired car, or Perugia, which was far closer to Assisi. I had chosen Perugia, even though I was travelling at such short notice that no car was available until the following morning, and I would have to take a taxi to the Hotel Soliano, in Assisi.

This was a stone's throw from the famous Basilica, and I had chosen it on two counts; the first being that I already knew it, and the second being that I was right in thinking Assisi was roughly equidistant between Orvieto and Arezzo, just in case. Anyway, I like driving.

I looked lazily out of the window, pleasurably lost in thoughts as fluffy as the clouds below. My uncle, in a rare burst of family feeling, had said he would drive over from the dig and give me dinner at the Soliano. When I told Mummy, she had warned me that I wasn't to offer to go Dutch: it might be taken amiss. I had accepted this without question: my uncle was not only very poor, but also fiercely proud. And finally, Huw and I had arranged that he would ring me when he arrived. I hugged myself, then began to turn over the pages, but none of the male models was a patch on Huw, so I dozed off.

My driver was waiting by the arrivals gate with a board emblazoned with my name, or a version of it. He had little English, and I even less Italian, so after an exchange of uncomprehending smiles that nevertheless conveyed the utmost and mutual goodwill, I settled myself in the back and turned my attention to the exciting difference in my surroundings.

I opened the window to let in the warm air and scents and sounds, and soon discovered that there was another topic of which I was woefully ignorant. I could identify none of the shrubs studding the flat (and not desperately interesting) plain of Perugia; and only one of the trees, which was the cypress. And although the air smelt deliciously the same as when you open a jar of Italian seasoning, only more so, the only herb I could put a name to was basil. At this rate, I'd have to go back to school, or put in an afternoon or two at the Chelsea Physic Garden. I am quite a lot better at birds, probably because of the plumage, Daddy says—except that Grandpa usually laughs to scorn any notion that I can tell a blackbird from a peacock. I didn't expect to enlarge my knowledge much while I was here, since the average Italian man regards as sacrosanct his right to shoot at anything he sees on the wing. However, thanks to the people of Assisi, who had once risen in revolt against the slaughter, the population was beginning to recover. In any case, any improvement in my scholastic attainment seemed likely to be of the linguistic variety, about which it has already been seen that I know practically nothing either. I would content myself with that.

It was a short journey, consisting mostly of roundabouts and hairpin bends, and before long my taxi had swept round in front of the Basilica's magnificent west door and into the narrow confines of the Via Frate Elia, and I was standing outside the Hotel Soliano with my suitcase beside me. A waiter came out and picked it up, and I followed him into the foyer and stood looking round me with pleasure and interest.

The Hotel Soliano is not a boutique hotel. It is solidly, decorously comfortable, with dark wood, a cool, marble floor and pink-washed walls from which hang well-chosen oils in heavy gilt frames that should swamp the delicate *fin de siècle* fashions of the sitters, but somehow don't. There are flowers; climbing plants spread their green and delicate fronds against the pink; and the magnificent majolica-ware dish behind the reception desk would not have been out of place at the Villa Borgese. Nothing had changed here since my last visit; and this was a comfort.

The manager came out of his office and was pleased to pretend he recognised me. Perhaps he did. Perhaps a too-close association with Colin Bardsey had made me cynical. I resolved not to be.

"I'm very happy to be back," I said. "Thank you, yes, my parents are both well. Has... are there any messages for me?"

There were not. I sat resolutely on both the cynicism and the upsurge of disappointment, asked for a SIM card, and followed my suitcase into the lift.

My room was gorgeous: duck's-egg blue, and airy, with curly, white-painted and gilded furniture that Marc Chagall would have recognised—and with *what* a view. I permitted myself one sweeping, rapturous glance, then, with some more of that resolution, turned my back on it and quickly unpacked. After that, I rang Huw, but there was no answer, so I went out.

I crossed the Piazza and slowly climbed the hairpin bend. We had often eaten at the restaurant at the top, the one that looks down on the Basilica, so I chose a table. The delicate-looking chair of worked iron was comfortably cushioned, and I ordered coffee. A warm breeze patted playfully at the fringes of the biscuit-coloured umbrellas shading the tables, and I sipped my coffee and watched the crowds gathering.

Nuns in blue habits and grey veils walked and talked earnestly with black-soutaned priests; pilgrims with shining eyes and tired, rapt faces stood in drab-clothed little groups; the backpackers planted themselves in everyone's way and consulted maps; while tourists, determined and unstoppable as tankers, carried chic carrier bags and flowed round the brightly coloured cumbersome packs like water round rocks in a stream. Doves fluttered and cooed on the red-shingled roofs and at my feet; and I remembered that this was the best-preserved mediæval city in all Umbria. You can blame it on the luxuriant, spicy air, or the elevated view of the Basilica, perhaps, but when my waiter brought the bill and a plateful of chocolate kisses, I asked him what time the next service was.

"The bells will tell you, *signorina*," he said kindly. "There is plenty of time for some shopping."

I thanked him, and paid. Then, feeling that he had summed me up a little too easily, I went shopping with the suspicion of defiance, and the salve to my conscience that I intended to do penance later. I am one of those who rarely go to church except at Christmas, and perhaps Easter, and for friends' weddings, so it was with a sense of virtue that I took my purchases up to my room just as the bells were beginning, threw a wrap shawl-wise over my head and round my disgracefully bare arms, and went back out into the late afternoon light.

The sinking sun had begun to wash the walls with rose, and peach, and cinnamon, and burnt umber; the ravishing colours of evening in Assisi. I hadn't remembered how beautiful it was, and realised, as I swelled the ranks of the faithful streaming into the Basilica, that I was deeply glad to be here.

I slipped onto one of the benches next to a blue-habited nun and automatically looked for a hassock. Of course, there weren't any, so for a few moments I adopted the posture that Mummy calls the Anglican Crouch, then sat back and allowed my gaze to wander at will. The service was in Latin, and naturally I couldn't follow it, so I let the chanting and the incense-laden atmosphere flow over me, and stood when the nun stood, and sat when she did, and drank in the stories displayed on the frescoes. I had read about the shattering earthquake in 1997 and the subsequent restoration, and even though there were bare patches of plaster in the scenes from St. Francis's life and miraculous doings, they did not detract from the general riot of colour that infuses the Upper Church of the Basilica. I gazed at the blue ceilings studded with gold stars, disturbingly Egyptian-seeming, and wondered what Huw's Latin was like.

There was no message when I went back to the hotel.

I am aware that, Colin Bardsey notwithstanding, I seem to do little beyond eat out and generally live the life of Riley, so I shall say little about the delicious dinner on the terrace of the Soliano, high enough up the hillside to be mosquito-free, except to mention that Uncle William wasn't the easiest companion. He arrived late, for one thing, and even though he had evidently bathed and changed, he still bore about him the faintest suggestion of red dust and antiquity. One nail was bruised dark blue, and there was a bad cut across the back of the same hand. His mind was obviously running on the day's doings at the villa; and his efforts to make civilised conversation with a niece he hadn't seen for some years reminded me strongly of my dinner party—as did most of our somewhat stilted conversation. He seemed to think I was still about sixteen, asking me what subjects I'd chosen for my A-Levels, and recommending Geology, while single-mindedly despatching his share of a carafe of Umbrian *vino bianco* and pike baked in herbs and served with asparagus as though he didn't know when—or perhaps whether—he would eat again. But he gave me exact instructions for finding his dig the following day, called me Moira, and left after bestowing a touchingly awkward hug upon me which I was too surprised to return. I waved as the dusty figure strode away down the Via Frate Elia. He was half a head shorter than Huw, more compact, and a good deal less volatile, but I thought they had plenty in common for all that.

I went back to the terrace to finish my wine and have some coffee.

Later, as I was making for the lift, I heard someone call my name.

"*Signorina?*" It was the receptionist. "I have a message for you."

"Yes?" I hadn't realised I could move so quickly.

His smile broadened as he pushed the pad across for me to see. There was an address in Orvieto, and Huw's mobile number. He reached beneath the desk. "And your SIM card, signorina." His smile seemed to suggest that now at last I and my lover could be together again.

Who was I to argue? "Thank you," I said with real gratitude. Ignoring the lift, I went slowly up the stairs dialling his number. He answered almost immediately.

"I'm here," I said.

"And I'm here too."

"That's tremendous. What kept you? Did you swim?"

"I beg your pardon?"

"You've taken ages to call. I was beginning to imagine all sorts."

"I'm at the airport bus stop. I had to wait for hours for a stand-by seat."

I stopped dead, there and then in the corridor. For a moment, I couldn't speak for the hot wave of shame that flooded my entire body. "I'm sorry," I said humbly. "I didn't think of that. I'm really embarrassed."

"Don't be. I really don't mind. Next time you can come with me."

"You are a very nice person," I said gratefully, "and I promise to stand the whole way if I have to. Where and when shall we meet?"

"Can you do the day after tomorrow, say, midday? I'd better knuckle down on my first day. You can? That's good. Find your way to the Duomo, and my museum's bang next door. We'll have lunch. Here's my bus; I'd better go. On second thoughts, I could walk—it might be quicker."

"Don't push it," I returned, as casually as I could. "'Bye 'til then."

"'Bye," he replied, equally laconic.

The whole conversation couldn't have taken a minute. We could have been going out for years. It was a nice feeling.

*

I slept soundly and woke to a glorious morning. Sliding out of bed, I padded over to the glass doors, pulled them wide, and went out onto the wrought-iron balcony to drink in the view.

This was simply breathtaking. A patchwork of greens, almost English in its rich, sleepy, domestic tidiness, punctuated by the dark green spires of the cypress trees, and seamed like corduroy with vines. Even in this unromantic electric age one or two chimneys were smoking; and although the road was modern, and the cars on it, they crept unobtrusively enough through the antique landscape, somehow reduced by it. Soon a pattern emerged: the vines, the road, even the boundaries of the fields, all combined to draw the eye to a modest domed building set down in the middle of the Umbrian plain. This was Santa Maria degli Angeli, within the protecting womb of whose four walls nestled the little chapel where St Francis had wrestled with the devil for the soul of man. Here were my misty, expanding horizons.

And nowhere at all, the dead hand of town planners with their brutal concrete prisons. The only square building in sight was a water tower, already untold hundreds of years old. I remembered something Huw had told me; that the Trojans were the people of the towers. It made me feel somehow humbled and exalted all at once.

It must have been an overdose of *Iliad*, but I watched the view while I dressed, and I drank it in during breakfast on the terrace where Uncle Will and I had sat last night, where fronds of ivy tumbled, a few birds flitted, and the rich, burned scents of the plains rose in the lifting sun. And over all, the sound of bells through the clear, cobalt promise of morning.

"*Prego, signorina,*" said the manager as I passed the reception desk. "Your Panda has arrived."

My mind was wreathed in herbs and cypresses and fruits of the vine. I know I stared blankly at him. "My...panda?" I repeated at last.

"Yes. I am to convey apologies."

I resisted the temptation to tell him I'd requested a polar bear. "I'm so sorry, but I wasn't aware I'd asked for a panda."

"It is not in the group you specified, no, but it is all there was available at short notice. Here is the key. It is in the Piazza. *Buon viaggio.*"

I had everything I needed in my slouchy shoulder-bag. This included not only the picnic lunch Uncle William had told me to bring, and a bottle of water, but also a large-scale map on which he had marked the location. I had tried to find the route in 'maps' on my smartphone, but for some infuriating reason it refused to acknowledge the country road off which the dig lay, and wouldn't take me past Todi. I was wearing a sleeveless linen dress the colour of the Umbrian earth (specially chosen), and I started up the slope and across the Piazza with a swing in my step and a sense of adventure fizzing in my veins.

This sustained a slight check when it occurred to me that I had no idea what a Panda looked like. After a bit, I located it by the simple expedient of pointing the key in the general direction of the several vehicles parked under the narrow corrugated roof, and pressing the 'unlock' button. A small square car flashed its indicators at me. I was deeply and simply pleased, not only with my ingenuity, but also to find that it was white, and that in the covered shade the headlights looked like black eyes.

The adventurous feeling waned again once I was in the driver's seat. I regarded, with dismay, the plethora of black buttons on the plastic dashboard, and realised that I had no idea what any of them were for. I had passed my test in a modern car, it's true, but my driving thereafter had been behind the wheel of my father's 1960s MG, all walnut and chrome and pounds per square inch. Still, there's nothing like learning on the hoof. I found the ignition without the least difficulty; and I knew perfectly well how to fasten a seatbelt.

Pushing my sunglasses firmly into place, I nosed carefully onto the Piazza and made my careful way up past the Basilica and its inviting stretch of lawn, past the restaurant and so down from the hairpin heights of Assisi. I remembered to take the right-hand side of the road, but it took me several kilometres to stop scrabbling at the door for the gear lever. At least the foot pedals were in the right order; and once I had located the indicators, the change to left-hand drive grew easier. My confidence began to grow again, and after I had negotiated without mishap the several roundabouts spotted across the plain like a join-the-dots puzzle, and filtered (in the right direction) onto the main road at the bottom for Perugia, I was feeling fine.

After about twenty-five moderately hair-raising kilometres, we had to filter once again, this time onto the main route south for Terni.

And this time, I realised to the full what I'd let myself in for. My father complains—a lot—about the lack of manners on British roads, and I always roll my eyes at him, but the Italian traffic made our home-grown variety look like very models of correct conduct on the highway. Somehow I got the Panda onto the road in one piece, and cautiously picked up a little speed on the inside lane. Sweat pricked out all over my body, and I wanted to open the sunroof, but I gave it at least ten minutes before I nerved myself to take my eye off the hectic, noisy, shimmering road and glance at the dashboard. I pushed experimentally at a button. The hazard warning lights came on. Someone hooted angrily at me and overtook far too fast, making a rude Italian gesture. This was swiftly altered to loud cheers of appreciation and an even ruder gesture as the car swept past. I ignored him, switched the warning lights off in a hurry, and clamped my gaze firmly ahead. Some kilometres further on, I tried again. This time I succeeded, but not before I'd opened a few windows by mistake, and somehow activated a green light that said, mysteriously, but in a spirit of pure altruism, *CITTÀ*. This being Greek and Double Dutch to me, I sniffed cautiously. Nothing seemed to be on fire, so I shrugged and forgot about it.

The sun was on my left shoulder, and climbing. The wind of our passing was deliciously cool. I had allowed a couple of hours for the journey, which was about fifty miles, and I settled down to a comfortable speed that the speedometer told me was ninety in kilometres. Several more cars hooted at me as they flashed past, but I was used to that and looked straight ahead. Perhaps it was normal practice, or even required by Italian law, to hoot as one overtook.

For much of the way, we were kept company by a river that snaked along, glittering, beside us, but it was some time before I could appreciate such snatches of the view as I allowed myself. The fields through which it meandered looked like an English water-meadow on a hot summer's day, and with a little shock of excitement tinged with awe I realised that it was the Tiber.

The sense of confidence grew, staying with me until we approached Todi. Here I turned, preening myself rather, off the main road, but it deserted me utterly when I reached the turning for Orvieto. Within a hundred yards, I knew I had made the wrong choice. On the map, this road more nearly resembled somebody's small intestine than a navigable man-made structure, and, stupidly, I had chosen it for its scenic qualities and interest value instead of taking the longer, easier way round. I took the first of many swooping bends at a cautious thirty, wishing savagely that I had stuck to the main route. Committed now, I concentrated hard—too hard to think of admiring the scenery. This was sparsely inhabited, and seemed to be little more than vines, and olives, and the occasional spear-thrust of a cypress. At least it was easy enough driving—and I refused to acknowledge the difficulties I might encounter as I approached my journey's end.

I had begun to feel like Sisyphus as, shoulders set and hands tight on the wheel, we approached yet another wide left-hand bend. My eyes were sore with sun and concentration, and although I wasn't exactly panicking, the sense that I had bitten off more than I could chew was a barb beneath the surface calm. Then there, miraculously, was the farm track winding up into the gentle hills; and there the scattered figures, some spotted with bright yellow hard hats, that proclaimed my destination and that my uncle had told me to watch for. In one of those strange twists of fortune, I had found the dig without even trying.

Thankfully, I turned off the road and crept a few hundred yards up the appalling track to join the rear of a line of dusty vehicles parked on the sparse verge. I switched off.

The silence rushed at me, and for some moments I could do nothing beyond sit quietly, let the absence of sound wash over me, and congratulate myself on having arrived in one piece. Then I got out and stretched, and, reaching for my bag, hoisted it over my shoulder.

I looked about me.

The track, a rutted, stony way of rich, red earth, curved over a small stone bridge. Beneath this, and round to a pretty cluster of farm buildings, burbled a small stream, its watery music cool and refreshing. Above the buildings, the hillside was dotted with groves of the slender cypresses and clumps of holm oaks, and on the other side of the road from the dig were vines, more vines, and the silver-green olives.

The silence was wonderful, and complete—unless you counted the everlasting scraping of the cicadas, the high, sweet cries of some birds of prey wheeling and banking in slow turns so far above that they looked as small as larks, and—now that I heard it—the murmur of desultory conversation, interspersed with musical tinkling noises, tiny and random, from the excavation. Someone laughed. I looked the other way, down the slope.

Here the hard hats crouched, gaudy as toadstools, behind low stretches of newly disinterred wall; or pushed wheelbarrows of spoil to the tents thrown up where, presumably, delicate sieving operations were in progress. All the while, the gentle clinking fell on my ears; the age-old sound of metal on stone, bringing antiquity back to life for the present's sake. A yellow-hatted student was standing not far from me, and talking earnestly to someone. He bent over his barrow and took something out of it, and I saw that the back of his tee shirt said—in bright blue on what had been white—*Dig Archæology!*. For some moments, the two discussed whatever it was he had found. Then he put it back, picked up the handles of his barrow and trundled it away; and there, notebook in hand, was Huw.

"*Oh!*"

The exclamation was startled out of me, and he looked up. The craggy face split into a wide, startled grin of pure pleasure, and he started towards me.

He was, if anything, even dustier than Uncle Will had given me the impression of being, and considerably untidier, as there was a tear in his shirt under one collarbone, and a twig, two dead leaves, and a caterpillar in his dark curls. The thought flitted across my mind that he and my father would either make fast friends, or drive each other to drink.

"Hallo," I said with a grin as wide as his own. "What are you doing here? I thought you were knuckling down. Has the museum let you out on parole?"

"Yes, can't you see my chains? I'm here on loan, as you might say. It was arranged in a hurry. The resident expert here has gone down with the Umbrian equivalent of Delhi belly. I'm fluent in Etruscan, d'you see, all two hundred and fifty words of it, so as soon as I'd put my nose through the museum's doors this morning, I was despatched up here. I only hope I can justify my existence. There's an inscription— But what are *you* doing here? I thought I was expecting you at the museum tomorrow. You didn't know I was here anyway! Or did you? Are we telepathic?"

"I don't know which to answer first," I protested laughingly. "William Maskell's my uncle. Didn't I say?"

"You didn't tell me his name, but I should have guessed it when you said he was an archæologist. I expect my mind was on other things."

"More synchronicity?"

He laughed. "Possibly. It could be beginner's luck. You look absolutely gorgeous."

"Thank you. So do you."

It was true: he did, despite the leaves. Our eyes were locked. "I did wonder if you'd have anything to do with this dig," I added, "but it seemed too much of a good thing. I didn't even know that my uncle was involved to begin with. Nobody tells me anything."

"Somebody's looking after us."

Averting my gaze from him with an effort, I gestured round. "Who lived here, and when?"

Immediately, the academic mercury rose. "That's just it. Your Uncle William has found this inscription, and he sent off a frantic SOS to the Archæological Museum in Orvieto. The hugely exciting thing is, we don't think it's a funerary inscription— and just about everything we know about the Etruscans is from what you might term their gravestones."

"That's rather a coup for you, isn't it?"

"If I can translate it, it will be. Thing is, it's a bit like using a vocabulary that consists of names and 'Here lies so-and-so' to translate…oh, crumbs, a family motto or something. It's rather damaged, of course; probably by locals breaking up the stones to repair their houses. That chap I was talking to, he thought he might have found a chunk of it, but sad to say they were only chisel marks." He half-turned and waved a comprehensive arm. "I couldn't wait to get up here. I've been champing at the bit ever since they found it."

"I don't blame you."

He looked absorbed, and grave; alight. "You see," he went on, "there's something about the construction—I mean, the way the sentence is worded—that makes your uncle think it's pre-Roman, which would be very special. And the fact that we've found it in the villa proper and not among the rubble of the family mausoleum is even more astounding. We're trying very hard not to get too excited about it just in case."

I laughed. "Without much success, if I may say so. You're shimmering round the edges."

"Oh? Oh,"—in quite another tone—"that's got very little to do with the dig."

I looked at my feet. After a moment, I said: "If it's as thrilling as that, couldn't you apply to come here, or something?"

"I would give my eye teeth to. But I don't know if it'll be possible. It's all a bit…" He looked round vaguely.

I waited, but he didn't enlighten me. I said: "Where is your dig, then, if not here?"

"I'm not on a dig. Archæology is only a secondary field of study for my degree. I'm stuck in the museum half the time. The rest of it I spend with a lot of dead bodies, and that's just the tourists. Come and see the villa, and meet the gang."

"I'd love to—but three's a crowd. May I?" I reached up and gently removed the caterpillar, the leaves, and the twig from the thick curls. I put the caterpillar on a nearby shrub.

"I had to lie down to examine the inscription," he said, and I think he was blushing, but it was hard to tell under the dust.

'The gang' were mostly students, about our age and dressed in shorts or jeans and tee shirts. They were making the tiny chinking noises I had heard, with tools no bigger than table knives, and dabbing gently at barely visible stones with what appeared to be paintbrushes, the narrow ones that you use for glossing window-frames. One or two looked up at our approach, and we exchanged smiles and murmurs of greeting that didn't need a specific language.

I looked round eagerly, but despite my best efforts saw little beyond the ruin of tumbled, stony earth and scrub, and the jumble of stone. I couldn't prevent myself from saying: "Er, where is the villa, so to speak?"

He looked doubtfully at me. "I know, it's rather difficult. We're only just uncovering the perimeter walls now. There's a corner there, just by that cypress, see?"

"*I* see," I said, seeing no more than before. "Well, it's a gorgeous position for it." I nodded down the hill, where the little stream chuckled on its lazy way to a river, some kilometres this side of the autostrade. "It's even got running water."

"That's the Chiani."

"The what? Chianti?"

It came out involuntarily, and I coloured under his look of disbelief. "Well, I'm sorry, that's what it sounded like," I said defensively.

"No 't'."

I said: "It's not a wine-dark river, then," and gave him a smug so-there look.

"You've been at *The Iliad* again. Come on, walk round with me."

The words sparked off an unpleasant memory, and it was a moment before I ran it to earth and shook myself clear of it. Colin Bardsey and his preoccupations could have no place in this enchanted spot.

We strolled round the gradually appearing boundaries of what I now at last saw was indeed a spanking great villa. The gardens (Huw told me) had been laid out in terraces, and I could just make out undulations in the earth's surface falling gently away down the slope. He did his best to describe the layout to me, and explained, in detail, that as yet they couldn't tell whether the villa had met its end during the Punic War, or whether it had been abandoned as a consequence of the famine some four hundred years later. As I didn't know the first thing about the Punic War, I made polite noises and tried hard to recreate the villa in my mind's eye. Perhaps in time I would see it the way he did.

I shaded my eyes and looked down the hill at the glinting, silky reaches of the dark river. From beyond rose just the faintest hum of traffic from the autostrade that runs the length of Italy's Tyrrhenian coast, but what breeze there was came from the east, and took the worst of the noise with it across the plains. But it looked the same as motorway traffic everywhere, and just for a moment the comforting sense that Colin Bardsey had no idea where I was vanished again. I hunched my shoulders.

"All right?"

I nodded with an absentness that had, all at once, nothing whatever to do with Colin. My attention had been filled completely.

Out of the haze of the plain below, and beyond the ugly slash of the autostrade, rose a town of shingled red roofs snug in the oval embrace of its ancient walls. It seemed unsullied by development, a mediæval picture map; and from this distance it glittered like diamonds. Oh, I know it was only the sun flashing on a myriad windscreens and windows, but the spell was a powerful one, and it held.

"Is—*that*—Orvieto?"

"Yes. Isn't it beautiful? Welcome to Velzna."

"Is that its Etruscan name? I'll remember."

I won't pretend—since I am not a haruspex either—that I had any foreknowledge of what was going to happen, but I was dimly aware, as we stood side by side looking down at the rose-red oval town on its defensive plâteau, safe inside its high walls, that something important had taken place; was taking place. Orvieto was both the full stop at the end of the previous chapter and the capital letter that begins the next. Tomorrow I would be inside those walls, with Huw. The morning's sense of adventure was taking on a strangely mystic aspect that brought the hairs furring up on my arms.

Then the spell fractured into a million glittering sparks as a faint *chug-chug-pop* made itself heard. Huw, listening, said with satisfaction: "That's your uncle. He's been to Prodo to find some more spades for the new contingent of students who started this morning. Let's go and meet him."

The burble was growing stronger, and resolved itself into a very old Vespa scooter, belching a protest of blue smoke with each pop. My uncle, with three spades looped over his back on a doubled length of rope, wobbled off the road and parked behind my Panda, and the Vespa's labouring engine died with a wheezy cough. I suddenly felt very glad to be here, and greeted him with a hug the equal to his own.

"Hallo, Uncle Will, it's lovely to see you again."

"Good, er...you made it," he replied, looking as though the hug had startled him into forgetting who I was. He clanked as he moved. "Have you met Huw?"

Huw was right beside me, so close that I felt rather than saw him smile. My mother would have got it immediately; and not for the first time, I wondered at the sheer difference between brother and sister. "Yes, thank you," I said solemnly.

"Good, good!" His tone was vague as he hefted the spades over one shoulder. With his free hand, he wrestled the helmet off his head. "Any luck yet?"

Since this was obviously not addressed to me, I kept quiet and listened to Huw's answer as we walked back to the emerging walls. Delighted though I was to see my uncle, that was my last chance of understanding much of what was said, particularly since when we reached the working party, the *Dig Archæology!* man clambered lithely out of his trench and fell into animated discussion with my uncle in rapid Italian. I said as much to Huw the first chance I got, and he replied that I could think myself lucky they weren't speaking in Umbrian.

The look I gave him was rather old-fashioned. I had begun to feel I'd like to get out of the sun and have something to eat.

NINE

...he...followed...the fairest...
Kassandra, without gifts of wooing...

Book XIII, *ibid.*

TO MY RELIEF, I wasn't alone. The chinking noises stopped and the noise level rose as picnics were unwrapped in shady spots and bottles were uncorked. Huw handed me a plastic tumbler of a dark red wine, and told me it was Chianti. We exchanged one of those brief wordless glances that somehow say more than words ever can, and made me blush to the roots of my hair. My uncle, more relaxed now, attempted (between mouthfuls) to instruct me in Etruscan history, while lamenting the utter lack of anything approaching interdisciplinary study, such as was—at last—beginning to catch on in Britain. He brought his discourse to an end with the sorrowful reflection that Italy remained, at heart, an agglomeration of separate city states, do what you will.

"Boxes," agreed Huw. "But look at all the British potters who flock to this part of Italy."

"Potters?" I echoed. Any moment now, I'd be floundering in another marish bog of academia.

"Majolica ware," explained my uncle. He saw my expression of apprehension and said: "You know! That beautiful dish in the foyer of the Soliano: that's Majolica. The British potters come out here and study it, and work with the local people. It's an extremely important link between the two countries."

Huw said under his breath, as though musing privately: "It's not the only one."

My uncle looked sharply at him, and I thought I detected a trace of disapproval and even alarm. For the first time, I sensed that the area of studies that Huw had voluntarily chosen to excavate, so to speak, was indeed an academic minefield. I wondered whether they had perhaps argued about this before—had Huw contested some assertion or other of my uncle's to do with the Etruscans? Or perhaps he had quoted from one of those forbidden texts of his in an essay. I thought I knew him well enough now to be sure it was a distinct possibility. Short of asking point-blank, there was no way of discovering; but one thing I was increasingly sure of: this was no misty horizon. These were uncharted ocean depths, with shoals and treacherous mud banks. Here be dragons...

A natural silence had fallen, as though by tacit mutual consent. My thoughts drifted from dragons to angels.

"Uncle Will," I said, accepting a thermos mug of coffee along with the challenge that the angels had not offered the previous evening, "have you ever heard of the name of Bardsey, Colin Bardsey?"

"No, never. What's his discipline?"

I thought Huw said something beneath his breath. "I'm not sure," I said tactfully, over him. "Something to do with linguistics. He knows something about Daddy's work."

My uncle snorted, and too late I remembered that he regarded my father's facility for making money with the deepest distrust, and his amateur researches with ill-disguised contempt.

"Mr Greatrex has quite a reputation for comparative linguistics," put in Huw. "I know of one or two professionals who respect his work."

"Facts," said Uncle William, sounding like Mr Gradgrind, "are more convincing than theories."

"Indeed yes," said Huw. "But an intelligent theory that takes proper account of the likelihood of the thing can help stick together seemingly unrelated facts. I've known a case—"

"Speculation is seldom helpful," declared my uncle with an air of finality. "You linguists seem to exist in a bath of it."

"It is a good deal more fluid a discipline than archæology, certainly," replied Huw with a good-natured smile. He seemed to be taking an inordinate amount of trouble to placate my uncle, and I didn't know why. My eyes went from one to the other of them in some consternation.

"Don't bring that approach—or any of your hobby horses—to my lectures, please, Huw," advised my uncle shortly. "You make me nervous enough as it is. Let's get on." He scrambled to his feet and strode off, scattering crumbs.

"What's his problem?" I enquired.

"Well, he hasn't said anything definite," replied Huw, shovelling picnic things into his and my uncle's haversacks regardless while I tidied my own away, "but I think it's money. And pride."

"Pride!" I stopped tidying, a plastic plate in one hand. I was thinking of what Mummy had told me. "Money?"

"That's what I wanted to tell you."

I waited, but he remained silent. He even looked a little embarrassed.

"Shoot!" I recommended after a few seconds. "You needn't worry. I can tell the difference between a try-on and genuine need."

He gave me a grateful glance. "You see quite a lot. Here it is. This dig only has six more weeks before it runs out of money. There's at the very least six seasons' work here, and he must find it unbearable. I know I would. He badly wants it to be pre-Roman, you see, and all the early signs are encouraging. The less the Roman influence, the more important the discovery becomes to Etruscan studies—and the greater the kudos for him. Not that he's concerned about that aspect of it, unlike some of his colleagues." He hefted the rucksack over one shoulder. "I shouldn't say that to you—you're his niece. But his lectures are popular, believe it or not, and we don't pay much attention to the bark. I'd like this place to be pre-Roman for his sake."

"That's very nice of you." I put the plate in the carrier and squashed the whole thing into my bag. I thought I began to see. My father, the rich amateur who didn't need to work; my uncle, the impoverished professional who did, and to whom proper funding was critical. No wonder he scorned my father's efforts. "I could help," I ventured. Then, seeing his face: "No: I know that wasn't your intention. You don't even have to say it."

"All right. How?"

I told him about the trust fund and my father's three categories. "Don't you think this comes into the category of helping family and friends?" I demanded. "I do."

"He'd never accept it," objected Huw.

"I know he wouldn't. Mummy warned me I wasn't even to offer to go Dutch for dinner last night." I shook my head impatiently. I wasn't sure why, but it had suddenly become of the first importance that this dig should go ahead and my clever, difficult uncle have the glory and credit for it. It was then that I had my clever idea of the day. "What if," I said, and I'm sure my eyes were shining, "what if I made an anonymous donation?"

Huw didn't, as so many people would, accuse me of thinking I could make everything right by chucking money at it. He considered it carefully, and identified an objection. "We don't know how it's funded. It could be through a lump sum left to your uncle's discretion, or a grant, or a loan, or some sort of sponsorship." His turn to look impatient. "I'm only a raw undergraduate," he said with endearing candour. "I haven't a clue how these things are funded. I've never given it a single thought!"

Perhaps it was the Chianti, or something altogether headier, but this struck both of us as exquisitely funny, and we went off into fits of laughter.

I might not be academic, but I do have my fair share of that rare commodity, common sense. Still smiling, I stroked the tassels bordering the tartan rug we had been sitting on, and which now hung over my arm. "I know from something my father once told me that digs like this need a licence from the local authority. Presumably, they also put up the funds."

"Oof," said Huw in patent dismay.

"Why oof?"

He was glancing round melodramatically. "You've forgotten which country we're in. This is Italy."

"Well done." My response was mildly sarcastic.

He bared his teeth. "Mafia land," he said with sinister meaning.

"Oh, golly, yes. I hadn't thought. Well, it'll have to be a pillowcase full of gold sovereigns, that's all. Or, I've got it, I'll ask my father on the QT. He'll know. And he knows how to be discreet. That's the answer. I'll do it the second I get back to the hotel."

"I wish you luck. Did you bring the Homer, by the way?"

"I did—but I haven't got it with me today. Do you want to look at it again?"

"Yes, please. I'd like to see if I can tease anything out of the Lancasters."

"Well, can you get to Assisi somehow, by any chance, and have dinner with me tonight? My treat. I could pay for the petrol, if you promise not to turn into my uncle about it."

"I'd love to. I have a car, courtesy of my mother, and money for petrol, courtesy of months of hard work in a bar, and a clean shirt, also courtesy of my mother."

I smiled at him and let it go. "All right: you win. Just don't bring the caterpillar."

"No? Do you think he might be a bit out of his depth?"

"No more so than I am. Well, I suppose I'd better push off and leave you to your chiselled lumps of rock."

"It's a long way to come just for lunch."

"I like driving," I replied, with only a little less conviction than I had felt yesterday.

"You could have a look at Orvieto," he suggested.

I considered this. "N…no. I think I'd rather wait and do that together."

We located my uncle in one of the tents. He was talking to a wiry little woman, thin, and somewhat stringy. Her hair was still dark, with a fine streak of grey over one temple. She could have been anywhere between forty-five and seventy-five. There was a table between them supporting several unidentifiable objects over which they were bent in close conference.

"Oh," said my uncle, straightening up with some reluctance. "Are you going already?"

I grinned at him. "Yes, Uncle Will. It's been lovely to see you again, and I've hugely enjoyed seeing round the dig, and what you do, and everything, but I know you've got lots of work to get through."

"Yes," he said. He seemed to shake himself. "Julia, this is my niece—my, er, my sister's daughter. This is Dr Julia Upjohn. She's our gemmologist."

"Retired," said Dr Upjohn, with a pleasant, eager smile. "I don't cost anything."

Uncle Will said something under his breath and squinted beyond the confines of the tent. I introduced myself to Dr Upjohn, and we shook hands.

"You're a gemmologist?" I knew perfectly well what that meant. "What is there to find here? Sorry—I don't mean to sound sceptical."

"Look at this." She picked something up from the table and held it out to me. I received it as gently as if it were a new-hatched chick. It was a ring, simple, solid, rich, and plain. The shanks were each encircled by a snake, and supported an exquisite cabochon-cut tiger's-eye. The design was timeless; I would happily have worn it myself.

"But—it's absolutely beautiful! You really found that here?"

"Among other things. This was the first to be cleaned. Isn't it gorgeous?"

I tilted it this way and that, watching it flame hot gold and tiger's stripes in my palm. "What will happen to it?"

"It'll probably go to the Faina Foundation."

"Never while there's breath in my body. British Museum," interpolated my uncle vehemently.

Dr Upjohn smiled. Was this, too, an old bone of contention? I slid the beautiful thing onto the ring finger. It fitted perfectly. It could have been made for me. "How old is it?"

"We'll know better once I've done the tests, but the only other remotely resembling it is approximately eighth century."

I knew that was the eighth century B.C. I looked up from it to my uncle. He was frowning down at the objects on the table and turning them over with a not-so-idle forefinger. He looked miles away. I said: "Does that make it pre-Roman, Uncle Will?"

He started, a sombre light kindling. "Certainly it does. Latin was no more than a crude dialect at that time, and Rome was a cluster of wattle-and-daub huts on the Palatine Hill."

"I take it that's a good thing?"

"It might be, if it's not an heirloom," he replied a touch repressively. "We can't date the villa from it, if that's what you're driving at."

I won't say I gave it up as a bad job, exactly, but I didn't know how to put heart into him. So I handed the ring back to Dr Upjohn, kissed my uncommunicative relation and thanked him again for last night. Then I told him not to get sunstroke and (quite fiercely) reminded him that he knew where I was if he wanted some family solidarity. I wanted to give him another hug, but didn't quite dare.

"Don't forget now, Uncle Will. If you get bored with your crumbly old Etruscans, come and talk English with your favourite niece."

"I've only got one," he said, relenting, and with a slow and singularly charming smile that made him look startlingly like my mother.

"Then you'd better make the best of her, hadn't you? I'll see you soon."

And I left him to his life's passion.

Huw came with me to the car, but I flatly refused to say goodbye, on the grounds that I didn't approve of it, and I'd see him in a few hours anyway. Then I stood there, looking at the ground. Tears were not far away. I swallowed.

"What is it?" he asked kindly.

The Panda's white wing was hot under my restless stroking.

"I don't like—I don't like the way money never seems to go to people who need it, and deserve it," I said eventually, and with some difficulty.

His hand came down over mine; warm, firm, and immensely comforting, stilling the unquiet fingers.

"It's an unsatisfactory state of affairs, certainly. You speak to your father. See if you can't alter it a bit."

"Well, I will. Watch this space."

"I'll watch a good deal more than the space. You drive safely."

I didn't mind the bends on the way home. In fact, I don't think I noticed them. Possibly I flew.

*

He sat where Uncle Will had sat. I had on a vintage Pucci print jumpsuit and strappy gold sandals, and my hair fell in soft curls. I had spent ages getting ready, and I wanted to appear as though I had tossed the look together in twenty minutes. Yes, I know, more hedonism and idle riches, and I'm sorry, but it's one of those things. I can't help who I am.

We must have presented a puzzling picture. I had Homer by my side plate, dignified in his burnished leather, and Huw had planted something in a fetching lime green by his. We ordered a bottle of Chianti, and settled down for what looked like being a thoroughly educational evening. He took the scrap of paper from war-torn Berlin from me, and read it through carefully a few times, peering closely in the dim, intimate

151

lighting on the terrace, before shaking his head and handing it back. Then he picked up the lime green book, which was called *The Etruscan Language: an Introduction*, by several people called Bonfante, and showed me a line drawing of a warrior with a spear, who looked exactly like my father: it was the same pure length of nose and forehead, and the same finely moulded mouth. He told me that in addition to a Trojan Christian name, I was blessed with a surname that was pure pre-Roman British. Then he told me not only why, but also how.

I listened, rapt, soaking it up. He told me about his father, a fiery Welsh poet, and the devastating effect his death had had on the younger Huw and his mother, Glesni. They had lived in a cottage on the Welsh-Herefordshire border until his father's death, when she had moved to Cambridgeshire to be near her sister. Here, Huw said, his face softening as he spoke of her, she designed patterns for knitters. He told me, quite matter-of-factly, how he had deferred taking up his place at his college for two years until he was sure she would cope; and I wondered whether in helping his mother come to terms with the tragedy, he had also arrived at some degree of peace himself.

I have no recollection of what we ate, or of how many hours we sat there talking it all over in the violet, falling dusk. I do know that by the time we at last fell companionably silent, it was dark, and we were the only diners left on the terrace. The waiters had gathered the way waiters do when they want to clear up and go home, and were watching us, not quite idly.

Becoming conscious at last of their collective gaze, we looked round with apologetic smiles. I realised, with a little shiver, that we hadn't once mentioned Colin Bardsey. The unwelcome thought made me clumsy: as I rose, my elbow swept *The Iliad* to the floor.

"Oh, good God, not again!"

I stooped hurriedly to pick it up, and examined it as carefully as possible in the dim light. "Hell, Grandpa's precious book, he's had it practically since the dawn of time," I said in some distress. "That's twice I've dropped it. Look, I can't see a thing."

"If I suggest that we go to your room," said Huw, carefully casual, "it's only because the light there is probably better than it is here, and we can see if it's all right."

"It could hardly be worse. And if I say that that brings cold reality back with a rush," I replied with a rather tight smile, "please do not misunderstand me."

"It's just as well we speak the same language, isn't it?"

I laughed at that and relaxed a little. "Just as long as we're using the same alphabet, too."

We ran the gauntlet of the waiters' knowing grins and winks, and stood at least two feet apart while we waited for the lift, trying not to laugh. Once in my room we sat down side by side on my bed, and I plumped Homer down on our collective knee. Huw switched on the bedside light and angled the shade.

"It looks all right, except— When did this come apart?"

"What?"

I peered over his elbow. He had a careful finger under the corner of an endpaper. "That must have been just now," I said, dismayed. "If I've done it any damage—"

"You haven't. This was stuck down, and not by any bookbinder, either. And it looks as though there was something behind it."

"Yes, the Lancasters."

"No. Something else."

"*The lists?*"

I looked eagerly. Between the back cover and the last endpaper there had definitely been something.

"Your grandfather must have done it when he stuck his bit in between the next two endpapers. See how this last one has been glued both sides? He must have stuck the Lancasters in over the top of the lists as camouflage."

I gaped. "You mean a…a sort of decoy? They really were there after all? My! No wonder Colin was so angry! Are you sure there's no damage to the book itself?"

Huw was checking carefully, but I thought suddenly that I had spoken Colin's name without thinking. His ghost was there in the room with us, breathing cold on our necks, but for some reason it didn't matter anymore.

"It looks all right." He ran a gentle finger round the edge, feeling how the old glue had dried over the decades.

"But no lists."

"No."

"I wish I hadn't brought it," I said discontentedly. I put Homer safely out of harm's way, then leant against Huw with a sigh of relief. His arm came round me and we sat looking at our reflections in the black windows. I saw his lips curve. I was going to offer him a penny for them, but he beat me to it.

"If I stay here any longer," he said, "those waiters are going to think they were justified in thinking what they obviously were thinking. And we can't have that."

I chuckled. "Can't we? You sweet, old-fashioned thing."

"Yes, and not ashamed of it." He stood up and pulled me to my feet, and cast a glance at the Homer where it lay on my bed. "It's a good thing I've brought my own copy. I'll have another look at those ship lists. You never know, I might have missed something. I must have done."

I sighed. "It's mind-boggling. We've examined that book from cover to cover dozens of times and found nothing, but *something* has been there, I'd be ready to swear, even if the lists themselves are long gone. Why else would Colin behave so oddly about it? He was so determined. Then the way he pushed me, he was so desperate, Huw. It was frightening."

"Whatever it is, if we find it we'll make sure that it ends up in the right quarters, then there'll be no reason for him to bother you ever again."

He was right, of course. I achieved a smile. "Sounds lovely. Ring me and let me know when you've cracked the fiendish code. And I'll see you tomorrow."

We went downstairs hand in hand.

He kissed me chastely on the cheek under the interested gaze of the concierge, and walked away into the soft dark.

I hung onto the door, watching his diminishing figure until I could see it no more, then traipsed back into the foyer with a sideways glance at the concierge that the *Mona Lisa* would have recognised.

I lay awake for a little, listening to the air-conditioning and wondering what I would find within Orvieto's encircling walls. A coronet of towers, like Ilium; high Troy, holy Troy…

I lulled myself to sleep by murmuring 'Cassie Trefor' several times to see how it sounded.

*

The first thing I did the following morning was to ring my father. His opening salutation (I nearly put salvo) was entirely characteristic.

"Don't tell me you've run out of money, because I refuse to believe it."

"That's all right," I said, "because I haven't. I don't think I could."

"Why are you ringing, then?"

"*Daddy!* Why shouldn't I?"

"All right, what do you want?" came my father's voice, bristling with suspicion.

"Well, as it happens," I said, crossing my fingers, "I do want some money, but..." Flinching, I held the telephone away from my ear and counted to ten. "No, wait! Before you go off the deep end, I don't want yours, and I don't want it for myself."

There was a disbelieving grunt. "Well?"

I said it in a rush. "I went to Orvieto yesterday, well, not actually into it, and I had lunch with Uncle Will at his dig. Daddy, he's in an awful fix. He badly needs money for his villa, and they've only got a few weeks left before the money and the licence run out, and Huw says it's all stitched up by the Mafia. Couldn't you do something? What I mean is, I want to make a donation, but it's got to be anonymous, you know what he's like about us having pots of money. It'll come out of my capital, I suppose, unless there's enough income to cover it, but I don't have the first idea how to set about it. Please, Daddy? It'd mean such a lot to him, and he need never know."

"I don't know how you suppose I could set about it," said my father much more mildly. I think I've already said his bark is worse than his bite.

I said in disbelief: "Oh, come, who's supposed to be the venture capitalist round here? There's that friend of yours in Rome, the one you helped start up in some business or other, *I* don't remember, he'll know, surely? Even if he doesn't, he'll know who will know. I'm only asking you to organise it, Daddy, it's my pigeon."

"All right," he said. "Leave it with me. I'll see what I can do."

"Thank you, oh, *thank* you," I said. "It's Category Two."

I heard him laugh. "I'll contact you. Don't get into trouble."

"I won't. Lots and *lots* of love, and to Mummy."

"Creampot love, my child," quoted my father, and hung up.

Two hours later, and with only three wrong turnings, the Panda and I swept into the Piazza Marconi car park with a careless flourish worthy (I hoped) of any Orvietan. After I had bought a parking ticket and made sure I was in a visitors' blue bay, I located Huw's museum in the guidebook. There it was, the Palazzo San Martino; a square, rather forbidding building.

The plate-glass doors swished open, and the air conditioning breathed cool and welcome over me. It made me think of Kew and pink lipstick, and I know I was smiling as I halted just inside for a moment to allow my eyes to adjust to the dimness.

Here the clean, bare lines of mediæval stonework were seamlessly married, with effortless, specifically Italian *panache*, to the modern minimalism of the illuminated glass cases housing every sort of Etruscan artefact. My eye went straight to a magnificent jug in the shape of a farmyard cock, standing proudly on his own shelf. I just had time to take in the glossy black of the background, against which the colours glowed, before my gaze went straight through the case and focussed some distance beyond.

He wasn't covered in dust today. In fact, he was looking almost housetrained in jeans and a short-sleeved shirt. He was standing at a case and drawing something with quick, economical strokes of the pencil. I watched the play of muscles in his forearm, entranced, and aware somehow that one of those expanded horizons of mine had just become a lot more defined.

Perhaps we were telepathic, as he had suggested. He

looked up, not startled, but as though he had arrived at the right moment for looking up and seeing me. He flipped the sketchbook shut and pushed it into a back pocket. We met halfway.

I said the first thing that came into my head. "What, no caterpillar?"

"No, you told me not to bring him. I washed my hair too, just to make sure."

Whether this tugged at the beauty salon-owner in me, I can't say, but the back of my hand went of its own accord to his cheek. "Much less dry," I said, my voice soft.

"I took your advice."

Our eyes had not left each other's, and I'm not sure what might have happened next if it had not been for our hushed and civilised surroundings. I remembered to drop my hand, and it was several seconds before he turned away.

"Come and look at this."

He gestured to me to follow him to the case where he'd been drawing. In it, among other artefacts, was a hand mirror, an exquisite thing of worked and polished bronze.

"It's beautiful," I said in hushed tones, and deliberately not looking at him. I was very conscious of how near he was. I could feel the heat from his body, and there was a pulse going in the crook of his elbow as he pointed.

"It's got your name. See? It's engraved round the top. The legend has it translated."

With a little help, I made out the letters CASNTRA. I tried it. "Cass'ntra. But—"

"I know. You're thinking that it should be pronounced with the stress on the second syllable."

"Possibly," I replied, with caution. "If that means what I think it does, it's how I say it anyway. It's how everybody says it."

"It's a Trojan name, however, and they pronounced it with the stress on the first syllable. If ever I have to call you by your full name, that's how I shall pronounce it, too."

"You already have, the first time we met. I thought it sounded—different."

"It was the second time."

So he'd remembered. "You're quite right; it was. At Blackwell's." It was odd how the necessity of keeping our voices down seemed to intensify the electricity crackling between us. I gave the mirror another look, then turned my gaze to him. "However does Troy fit in with your studies here?"

"Aha. One of the odd things about Etruscan is that it has no known relations. Like Basque, it's called a language isolate—or at least it was thought to be, until recently. A lot of people, both professional and amateur, have spilt gallons of ink trying to link it to other Indo-European languages, such as Greek, and Sanskrit, and all that happened was that they got nowhere, Etruscan remains largely a mystery, and comparative etymology got a completely undeserved bad name."

"Is that what my father's been up to?"

"No. His speciality is related alphabets. Now, just off the coast of Turkey, within sight of Troy, is the island belonging to Greece called Lemnos. But you know that." There was a glint in his eye.

"I learnt it 'specially," I said demurely. "Here's my old friend comparative etymology again. What exactly is it?"

"It's simply seeing how languages resemble one another, like French and Italian. You remember the line drawing I showed you that you said looked like your father? That's on the Lemnos stele."

"The...the what?"

"It's a fancy term for a lump of stone with writing on it. You sound as though you're trying to catch me out."

"That should make you happy: another inscription for you. And of course I'm not trying to catch you out, it's just that you've used more new words since I met you than I've come across in all my life. I think I shall have to recommend a deep-action conditioner, just to keep my end up. Your hair looks as though it could do with it. Honey and beeswax, that's what you need."

His smile was wide and warm and tender. "That should keep away all known species of insect—except, perhaps, bees. Didn't we talk about this last night?"

"Chianti got to you too, huh? It was mentioned in passing. Go on, surprise me and stick all that to Troy. I'll tell you when the cogs begin to creak."

"I remember, we decided that the warrior must be the first Greatrex. Well, that lump of stone is engraved in a language called, strangely enough, Lemnian. It's cognate with Etruscan, which is cognate with what they spoke at Troy. That's called Luvian, and is an Indo-European language, which Etruscan definitely is not. However, recent research has shown—"

A light dawned. "*That's* what you were talking about to my father and my grandfather at dinner!" I exclaimed. "And you think the people who spoke Luvian have something to do with the Etruscans, despite the difficulties? What does it prove if they had?"

"It proves that the Etruscans and the Trojans were ultimately the same people, exactly as the—"

"—exactly as the Welsh and British records say they were," I finished for him in a voice that didn't seem to be mine. I shook myself. "I'm sorry: I interrupted you. What were you going to say?"

"Only that Etruscan is now known to be connected to Rhaetian, which is what they spoke in the area now covered by northern Italy, Switzerland, and Austria. The thing is, Rhaetian is one of those alphabets your father's keen on. And Rhaetian is—ultimately—the same as Coelbren. Coelbren, before you ask, is a discredited forgery dreamed up in the nineteenth century by a Welsh con. artist and drug addict."

"*What?* It can't possibly be!"

"Dead right: it isn't. Coelbren—literally 'holy wood'—is the Welsh granddaddy of them all. It is attested as far back as fifteen hundred and something."

"And they say it's a forgery? I don't get it!" I studied his face. "Don't tell me—academic reputations at stake? I'm right? It's disgusting. You mean…that Welsh is the source of writing?"

"Just that. Etruscan is also related to some Anatolian languages, though that's less conclusively proved."

"Go on, then," I said, relieved to see he was smiling at me. "Hit me. What's Anatolian?"

"Anatolia is an old name for Turkey," he said.

"Oh, help," I protested. "What did they speak there?"

"Among other languages, Luvian."

It took a moment for this to wind along the neural pathways; my brain was feeling as though it had been put through a mangle. "But you said they spoke Luvian at Troy…" I made a face of impatience at my own slowness. "It's all right, I'm with you." I looked at the mirror. "But I was able to make that out even if it is back to front," I objected. "I can't read or speak Greek, but I know what the alphabet looks like."

"They used the Greek alphabet to embody, or reveal, their own singular language, if I can put it like that. It's a bit as though the Russians were to use our alphabet instead of their own; you'd be able to read it even if you didn't understand a word."

"Where did the Greeks get it from, then?"

"It's thought the Phœnicians…who got it from Egypt."

"*Egypt?* Look, I'm doing my best, but enough is enough."

"Bear with me: you'll live. Phœnician script is a sort of shorthand of Egyptian hieroglyphs. It's much more efficient and powerful, which is why it caught on and hieroglyphs didn't, much. Hieroglyphs are like Mandarin. Instead of our twenty-six letters, there are over two thousand pictograms to learn."

"Gosh, no wonder chaps like you get into such stews about this sort of thing," I said. "I'm not surprised that academics fight like ferrets in a sack to prove their theories!"

Huw said shortly: "They can't have it both ways, that's all."

"Who can't? Academics?"

"Yes. Either Luvian is related to the language they spoke in Lydia, which is where Herodotus says the Etruscans come from, or it's not. If it's related to Lemnian, which the linguists now state it is, then it's related somehow to Etruscan; and you cannot, in all conscience, then deny a connection between Troy and the Etruscans. But they do."

I said mildly: "Simply because they haven't found the connection, they say it doesn't exist?"

He nodded, shrugging.

"What a potty attitude—and dangerous. It quite shakes my faith. I had no idea academics were as illogical as the rest of us. All I can say is, I don't have to understand your discipline in all its detail to recognise common sense and logic when I hear it."

"Well, that's something. And we've agreed, have we not, that you have oodles of common sense."

"Bags. Huw, what's a puthmen?"

He looked startled, as well he might. "I haven't the faintest idea. Where did you find it?"

"In Blackwell's." I told him about the dragon-killing book and the review, which made him laugh. I said it was as bad as the hendetic whateveritwas, "*which* you hadn't heard of either," I pointed out, "and I found *that* in a Welsh glossary, so now!"

"Quite so. Some linguist I'm proving to be. My only hope is to make my name known by proving the impossible."

"Oh, you'll do that all right," I said.

TEN

...let us twain also take thought of impetuous valour.

Book V, *ibid.*

A SILENCE FELL, of the variety known as companionable, and wrapped us round. There were other people in the museum, of course, but we might have had the place to ourselves. I gave the gorgeous bronze mirror a last long gaze.

"Oh, well," I said, "I expect if you turned the language the right way round, you'd be able to understand it perfectly well, and connect it to all those others you mentioned."

He frowned. "Say that again."

"Well, look at the alphabet, they write that back to front. You can see that by comparing it with the Greek. And they write from right to left, unless they've done that on the mirror just because it's a mirror, so perhaps their language is back to front, too. I expect that's why they like mirrors so much. I mean, look at them all, and this is just one museum. I bet you'll find it's Anatolian back to front, or something."

He made no response, and I eyed him with increasing curiosity. He was looking at the mirror. His expression was hard to read, but a half-smile hovered on his lips, and his brows twitched as though he were working something out.

"'Trojan or Crooked Greek'... *Is* it arsy-versy?" His eyes began to blaze, and he gripped the sides of the cabinet. "But that even gives me the clue—*arse-uerse*! To turn away from fire! For God's sake, what if she's right? I thought it referred to the evaporation of seawater, but what if it's really a process of spiritual refining—a...a sort of Etruscan version of alchemy? After all, who knows better than the individual soul when it's ready to walk through the flames? On the other hand, it could be that they knew they as a people weren't ready, so they went in the opposite direction..."

I couldn't make anything of that, backwards or forwards, but he didn't seem to need a contribution from me. I said a little warily: "It's just a thought."

He was still gazing into the case, but this seemed to shift the main beam of his focus back to me. Whatever it was I had said to rivet his attention had gone onto the back burner. He straightened, and dropped his arms. He looked as though he had been through some sort of spiritual experience himself, but his voice was quite normal when he spoke again.

"I know your father went to Efestia, because he told me at your dinner party, but I'm just wondering if Colin was there too, trying his damnedest to get near enough to your father to crib his findings."

I sighed. "What or where is Efestia? Is that in Anatolia? Has it anything to do with caterpillars?"

"Idiot. No, it's a sanctuary on Lemnos. I didn't tell you, did I, that the original stele found on Lemnos is now in the museum in Athens? But a few years ago, another was discovered on the island, at a place called Efestia, which proves the theory that the languages are connected."

"Etruscan comes in from the cold?"

"Exactly. Though knowing the academic world as I do, we'll grow beards waiting for them to accept the fact. I told you that Herodotus talks about the Etruscans coming from Lydia—that's the old name for part of western Turkey—but because there's no archæological evidence for it, all the scholars say it isn't true, even while they're praising his exceptional accuracy in most other aspects. The usual thing. It's a very depressing way to think, very limiting, and as you say, distressingly lacking in logic. Why the blazes don't they get off their flat bums and go and look? Absence of evidence," he finished sternly, "is not evidence of absence. Still, I have great hopes of the DnA testing. Herodotus one, academia nil."

He reminded me of my grandfather. "I've heard of Herodotus," I confided proudly. "Daddy's always dipping in and out of his Histories and leaving him about and losing him."

He was still on his private path. "I would be more impressed if people said, All right, here is a theory posited by one Herodotus, whose word we know we can usually trust. Let's go and see if he's right about the Etruscans as well. But they deny it, without thinking, without foundation. As you say, potty."

"Why don't you do a Heinrich Schliemann," I said, "and set off with nothing but your trusty Herodotus and several dozen servants, and prove him right, and them all wrong? Grandpa told me about him. That'd be something!"

"I intend to," he said, "only I expect I shall have to do without the servants."

As I had, he gave the mirror a last look and turned away. "What I would like to know is whether Colin is going to use my more—occult—researches against me. He's given no sign, but that's nothing."

"'Occult'?" I repeated, with a tinge of alarm. I had a sudden vision of Blackwell's; all bats, flying cloaks and wizards.

"Sorry. It simply means 'hidden'," he said. "He's been doing some snooping round me too, don't forget."

I remembered the eavesdropping taunt, and was silent.

He looked at his watch. "How about some lunch? My treat. You paid last night."

"Right you are. You can buy me a pizza."

"You're on." He led the way back out into the blinding, shimmering sunlight. "There's a good family-run place not far. I don't think I've told you about Carthage yet, have I?"

"Now that," I said, "is seriously chic."

We had emerged from the side street where we had bought a couple of pizzas and a bag of fat, furry peaches, and I stopped to gaze at the Duomo. The frescoes on the west front were startlingly vivid and colourful, but it was the body of the building that caught my eye. It was striped in cream and a soft, greyish blue, unlike anything I had seen before, at least in a building. I put my head on one side. "Very clever. If they'd been vertical it would have looked like mattress ticking."

"My mother always says that horizontal stripes are a lot more slimming than vertical ones."

"Your mother is a sensible woman, and knows exactly what she's talking about. Come on, let's go and be proper tourists."

We crossed the Piazza and went to sit on the shallow steps of the shady north side of the stripy Duomo, and spread the pizzas' rough grey paper across our knees.

"Have we got any forrader?" I asked, I regret to say through a mouthful of creamy, buffalo mozzarella and melt-on-the-tongue anchovies.

He didn't pretend not to know what I meant. "The only lists in *The Iliad* are the ship lists, and despite my spending a good deal of last night immersed in mind-bending anagrams and acrostics, they remain unfathomed. How apt."

"I expect that was the Chianti, too."

We ate in silence for a bit.

"Are they actually lists?" I asked.

"Itemised by number and area, that sort of list? No. It's a bit like the genealogies in the Bible. *Diomedes of the loud war-cry was lord over all. And with them eighty black ships followed.* That sort of thing."

"'Them all' being the commanders of the eighty ships?"

"Exactly that. We know there are no pencil marks, or pinholes, or anything of that nature in your grandfather's copy, and that's the important one. So unless it's the missing inventories, it must be something else. I mean, perhaps there really is a hidden code. I don't pretend to be a cryptographer, mark you."

"I know we've decided that it is, but let's suppose for a moment," I said, "that it's not the Homer at all. Let's... what's the word?"

"Hypothesise?"

"That's is. What else might there be for my father to find on Lemnos that made Colin so mighty interested?"

"Apart from the stele at Efestia, you mean? Well, the people of Lemnos claimed descent from the Argonauts. With that in mind I'd give anything to say he'd found some proof, but it's not going to happen. And what Argonauts have to do with these lists of Colin's is anybody's guess." He gave me a speculative glance from under his lashes, as if to gauge how much more information I could take before I revolted. "The Argonauts still exist, you know. Only you'd have to go to Africa if you want to meet them: they fled there and became absorbed into the Dogon tribe. And here's a *non sequitur* for your collection: did you know that Todi's Etruscan name was Tuder, just like the Welsh?"

"Blimey, no, I did not," I replied in dismay. "Are you sure you haven't let your brains go to your head?"

He acknowledged this shot with a grin, but said, as though I hadn't spoken: "Or that Narnia actually existed?"

"Oh, *what* ? Come on, this is getting ridiculous!"

"No, really. There was an Etruscan town called Narni, and the Romans latinised it into Narnia. C. S. Lewis certainly knew a thing or two. So did T. H. White, for that matter. *The Once and Future King* is possibly—"

I interrupted him firmly. "Carry on like that and I'm off, here and now, for a facial, and probably a full body massage." Then I relented. "Argonauts...that's Jason. I've heard about him. Well, I've seen the film." I brightened. "It's not another name for the Argives, is it?"

"No, it isn't. I'm sorry," he said penitently. "It's desperately confusing, even for people who are supposed to know what they're talking about. The names change every two seconds, and from author to author, and from country to country. How are the cogs?"

"Squeaking a bit but still grinding on, can't you see the rust? Just supposing it existed, this proof, what would it say? Would it be on a third stele somewhere?" I tried to bring the word out as though I used it every day.

"Probably; they made their records to last in the ancient days. Goodness knows what it would say, though. *We, the people of Lemnos and descendents of Argonauts, hereby attest for the sake of posterity that we are first cousins to the Etruscans.* In our dreams. In any case, every inch of Lemnos has been examined minutely, not to mention invaded, and its population replaced more times than either of us has had hot dinners."

"I can imagine how minutely that is, too." I was thinking of my uncle's villa, and the paintbrushes. "Well, it can't be that. So it must be something to do with my family after all, and, specifically, the Homer. Have a peach."

"Thank you. Do I dare to eat a peach? Eliot. Sorry: I'll stop. All right. If we're assuming, and I think we are, that Colin was your burglar, and given that he's after your grandfather's *Iliad* for some strange, Wimsey-cal reason of his own, I expect he thought he might find it in your father's study. It's the obvious place. I say, did you hear that? Wimsey-cal! I'm rather pleased with that."

"You have no right to be. Tell me this, Lord Peter, how did he know where the study is?"

"Easy. Tiptoe round the house and look for a room with books in it."

"Clever clogs. All right, crack this one. Why should Colin think he'd find Grandpa's *Iliad* there? He lives in London."

"Heaven knows. Your father might have inherited it."

"He'd have a job: my grandfather would need to have kicked the bucket for that, and he's always telling us he's nowhere near ready for the grave." I nearly choked on a bit of peach. "Huw!"

"Yes?"

"Listen to this! Colin was jolly keen to know about my grandfather! He even asked if he was my paternal grandfather. It *is* something to do with my family! You know, this is getting as bad as your alphabets: there are far too many grandfathers involved."

"Like so many Alexanders," said Huw. "Except that that's fathers, but who's counting. Have you a handkerchief, or something? I've forgotten mine."

I fished in my bag for a tissue and handed it to him. "I'll tell you something else: he was surprised to learn that my grandfather was still alive."

"Was he? Was he, indeed!"

He sprinkled our crumbs for the birds, then crumpled up the sheets of paper and stuffed them into my bag. He shifted a little so he could see me.

"Okay, how about this for some brass tacks hypothesising? We're right, in that it's not something your father has found on Lemnos, or in the museum in Athens. It's not even your family, except insofar as they have something Colin wants. It's Colin himself, trotting round the sites like a good little linguistics undergraduate and running, all unsuspecting, into your father. He gets talking to him, finds out his name, and feeling guilty as hell and excited at the same time, thoroughly gets the wind up—"

I said brilliantly: "Troy, the windy city! Oh, that's *far* better than your miserable effort!"

"Mere flourishing. Where was I?"

"Full of hot air."

"Peace, froth. He gets into a flap, streaks home, turns over your father's study—"

"How does he know where my parents live?"

"Search engine, like your haruspex. He turns over—"

"I bet you he searched for my grandfather and thought he was dead."

"Why should he think he was dead if he isn't? I know they make mistakes, but that's going too far."

I slewed round on my warm marble step, and our knees touched. "No, listen! This is genius thinking! What if he got my great-grandfather instead, who really is dead?"

"Why would he want to do that?"

"I don't say he wanted to. It's possible, that's all. If he just put in Hector Greatrex, Royal Regiment of Rifles, he could have got him, or Grandpa, *or* Daddy! It's a family name, see, and they were all in the same regiment! Now then!"

Huw opened his mouth to object, then shut it again. "Do you know, I really think you've got something there. If he got your great-grandfather by mistake and thought he was your grandfather, who was dead (except that he's not), he might well have thought your father had inherited the Homer...and *that's* why he ransacked the study! Cassie mine, he was hunting for it!" He added in parenthetical disapproval: "He ought to have checked. Very sloppy. Always check your sources."

"He was out of luck, then," I said with some satisfaction.

"Well, yes, but why, particularly?"

"You haven't seen the chaos that my father likes to work in."

"I sympathise utterly. Let us now praise untidy men. We'd better do a bit of checking of our own. When did your great-grandfather die?"

"Ages ago. 1965, or something like that. They've all got the same middle names, too. It causes no end of confusion. Lawyers hate us."

"Why lawyers?"

"Oh... Trusts."

"I see. Cassie, my Trojan heroine, I think we're getting somewhere. Where is the contentious tome, by the way? Have you dropped it again?"

"Certainly not. I left it at the hotel. You wanted me to bring it out with me, and I thought it might give me a bit of kudos, but I'm ashamed to say I haven't even opened it."

"I see—suddenly it's all my fault. I'm..." He broke off abruptly, uttering an exclamation, and clutched his head. "It's Lang's translation, isn't it?"

"Yes," I said lugubriously.

"I'd have thought... Well, perhaps the style is a bit heavy going. Lattimore would probably suit you better, or Fitzgerald."

"That's what Grandpa said. Why, particularly?"

"Here's something to make you laugh. I'm supposed to be graduating in a year's time. Guess what I've overlooked?"

"What?"

"My translation's by Fitzgerald."

"Meaning? Oh! Meaning a code based on Lang's translation is not going to work in somebody else's?"

"Just exactly that." He drove his long fingers into his thick curls. "All those anagrams! I could weep!"

I began to laugh. "Do you know, that makes me feel so much better? But surely the names are the same? You could—"

"Don't even suggest it," said Huw with some feeling. "I don't care if there are fifty hidden codes and the security of the western world depends upon my cracking them all before breakfast. I haven't the remotest intention of going through that again."

Afterwards, I gave Huw a lift to his other place of business. This was the Crocefisso di Tufo, the Etruscan city of the dead. The only culturally significant comment I made was to observe that the little square buildings below us, greened over with some vegetation or other, looked exactly like the padded silk boxes you sometimes find on dressing-tables. I was a bit punch-drunk on a cocktail of culture and academia by that time, so I took in little of the remains—which were, indeed, magnificent. I did manage to nod politely as we traversed the grid-pattern, so modern-seeming; and I had lots and lots of Etruscan funerary customs explained to me, but after a bit Huw saw me wilting and took pity on me.

"I'm really sorry—I'd properly got going again, hadn't I?"

I nodded, and ostentatiously stifled a yawn. He laughed.

"I'd better get on, anyway. There's an—"

"I know. There's an inscription. We must do this again one day." I said it in tones of bored, bright insincerity.

"Double-tongued Southerner. I hope you drown in your own moisturiser. I'll come with you to the car."

"*Hasta la vista*," I said darkly. "I can see it from here."

"You might be mugged."

It was a steep climb back to the little car park. I unlocked and opened the door, and a gush of oven-hot air spilled out.

Huw said: "Thank goodness for air-conditioning."

I stared at him in disbelief. "In a car? Come on!"

"Yes—where have you been for the last twenty years?"

"In a 1960s MG, that's where," I retorted, "an open-topped one at that. This," I added proudly, "has a sun-roof. I know that, because I made it work."

"By mistake?"

"Very funny."

"You need hardly get out to do some sightseeing. Aren't you going to do any sightseeing?"

I shaded my eyes to take in the towering, defensive walls rearing up not far away, straight out of the rock. They were furred with summer-green, starred with bright splashes of oleander, and studded here and there with domestic dwellings where washing danced in the sun to dry. It looked deliciously inviting, but I was thinking of the small-intestine road. It was either that, or a wholly unknown route back to Assisi.

"I don't think I will today," I said eventually. "After all, there's plenty of time, isn't there? I can always come back and make a proper day of it."

"Good notion. *A presto.*"

He hovered for a moment, as though he wanted to say something else, then turned and walked back to his tombs. I watched his slim, muscular back and broad shoulders recede; then he was gone among the crowds.

When I got back to Assisi, the clerk on duty at the Soliano asked me apologetically if I would mind parking my car elsewhere as there was a special Mass on at the Basilica for a local feast day. There was another car park at the bottom of the hill, she told me, just round the sharp corner to the right.

When I had found the place and trudged back up the hill, I went straight up to my room and changed, then went to spend a lazy couple of hours by the pool. For pride's sake, I took Homer with me, but he didn't make it out of my bag. When I woke, I dragged him back upstairs, wishing for the fifteenth time that I hadn't brought him, and had a shower.

My telephone went as I was lolling on my bed, reading a magazine, and still wrapped in a towel. I was feeling pleasantly hungry and content, waving my feet about, and looking forward to dinner.

I rolled onto my back. It was Huw's number, as I had known it would be.

"Hallo. Don't tell me you've cracked it already."

"No, Cassie. It's something else."

Instantly, I was on the alert. I sat up and swung my feet to the floor. "What's wrong?" I was aware that my hands had gone cold.

"You need to listen to me. You-know-who's here."

"*No!* Here, in Italy? How?"

"He asked my tutor where I was. He told him I was in Orvieto, gave him my address, and out he came."

Too simple, really.

"Are you there, Cassie?"

"Yes," I whispered. I cleared my throat. There were little tremors running up and down my spine.

"He knows you're here, too."

"Oh, God—"

I jammed my fist against my mouth, then snatched it away again. "How? How on earth does he know that? No, never mind, it doesn't matter. Are you all right, Huw? He didn't try and beat it out of you?"

"I'm fine. I'd like to see him try. Thing is, Cassie, the bastard's pinched my wallet and my car. My mother gave me the money to hire it, too. He came here on the train and came straight to where I'm staying. I've only just discovered that he got into my room by a ruse. He got everything out of Giovanna—that's my landlady—where the dig was, your uncle's name, the fact that I'd gone up there early, that you'd been there—everything."

"How did she know?"

I could almost hear him shrug. "I'd told her."

The rest of me was cold, too. "Oh. Well, it can't be helped. Don't tell me: he's after the Homer again."

"It looks like it. I rather think he was looking for me, and for you by association. He's made rather a mess here. Your hotel address was on the pad by my bed, and the top sheet of paper has gone. I've got enough change in my pocket—I could get on the train, but by the time I reach you—"

"I'm coming," I said immediately.

"I didn't like to ask. Cassie, sweetheart, I'm not sure how to say this without frightening you, but I'm asking you to get out of there for your sake, not mine. He only has to ask for your room number. Not that I think he'd try anything on when you're safe in the hotel, but—"

"I'm frightened already," I said. A certainty shivered over me in a sudden douche of ice-water. "You think he might be here in Assisi already, don't you?"

He waited just a second too long before answering. "Giovanna said he was here about an hour and a half ago, asking if I was alone or accompanied, so yes. He must have been eavesdropping on us, you know."

"Mr Bardsey's special talent," I said grimly. "But how? When? I didn't see a thing. Did you?"

"No. It was probably at the Duomo. All those people milling about... And we were sitting with our backs to it. We wouldn't even have known he was there. Darling..." He sounded both angry and helpless.

I said: "You know where we had lunch?"

"I'll be waiting."

"I'll be as quick as I can."

ELEVEN

...the bright-eyed goddess Athene disregarded not;
but went darting down from the peaks...

Book II, *ibid.*

MY HANDS WERE trembling as I ripped off the towel and
flung it on the bed. I hauled a pair of slacks out of the
wardrobe and hopped about, dragging them on over my
still-damp body and swearing lamentably. I pulled a cotton
tee shirt over my head and scuffled my way into my driving
shoes, the flat ones with rubber studs in the soles; and I
had to snatch twice at my bag before I could get a grip on
it. Dropping in the telephone, I grabbed my cardigan and
was still trying to get my other arm in as I left my room
and ran clumsily down the stairs. As I ran I fumbled in my
bag for my car keys, and shoved them into the pocket of
my slacks.

The concierge looked up as I came breathlessly up to the
desk.

"My friend is in trouble, my friend from dinner yesterday."
My voice was shaking, and consternation grew in the man's

face. "He's in trouble. He's been…he's been robbed. Car—money—stolen. I'm going to Orvieto now."

Automatically, he opened his notepad, but I took it from him, and the biro out of his fingers. "My number. I don't know when I'll be back." Then I pushed the notepad at him, tugged my cardigan on anyhow and ran out of the hotel.

The warm dark baffled me for a moment, but then the lamplight in the Piazza seemed to brighten and show the way. There were plenty of people about; the boutiques were doing a roaring trade, and tables outside the *trattoria* had their full complement of diners. I barely heard the cosy, domestic noises of knives and forks on plates, or the laughter and the conversation; or saw the holiday-makers leisurely mounting the hill, arm in arm, heads together, silhouetted against the lights. They were laughing too, and chatting animatedly; carefree.

It was just my wretched luck, I thought savagely as I hurried down the hill, away from the warmth and lamp-lit intimacy, and dodging between the holiday-makers, that for once the car was not immediately to hand. And—it sent my heart suffocatingly into my mouth—I would have to take the same tortuous route down to Orvieto. I didn't dare risk getting lost on the longer but easier road and having to attempt a motorway in the dark. After all, I had already taken the way twice now, and recently. I would have to hurry, but it should be all right…

My night vision was coming—but not before a cat streaked across the narrow street almost under my feet. My heavy bag swung round my body and sent me stumbling off balance, just as Colin Bardsey stepped out of the slow-moving current of people and caught me hard by the upper arms.

There was no smile now. "What a piece of luck," he said.

I was too surprised to scream. "Goodness, how you startled me!" I stammered, retaining just enough wit to try for a tone of friendly astonishment. "What on earth are you doing here?"

"Looking for you."

"What, again?" I wriggled futilely in the hard grip. "I can't imagine why my family seems to exercise such a fascination over you, but I can't stay now, I'm afraid. Will you please let me go!"

"Oh, I think you can stay for a moment," he said, and, releasing me, stepped back as though to observe me better. "I shan't keep you long, you see."

He was barring my way. If I tried to push past him, he would simply grab me again. My involuntary glance round verged on the panic-stricken, but none of the holiday-makers gave us a second glance.

"Now, let me guess where you were off to in such a hurry. Of course. My rival managed to ring you, and you're tearing off to rescue him. Just give me the Homer, Cassie, and I'll let you go. No harm done, eh?"

I hardly know how I prevented myself from laughing in his face. And if that sounds an odd thing to say, it was because I had just remembered why my bag was heavier than usual. All the pent-up fear and anxiety I had suffered at Colin Bardsey's hands surged up on a jet of anger, and I gave way to it without a second's hesitation. "You can have it!" I cried. "Here you are!" And, shrugging the bag swiftly off my shoulder, I took the neck of it in a double-handed grip, like a tennis racquet, and swung it at his head with as much force as I could put behind it. It connected with a most satisfactory thud, and I'm not ashamed to say I was delighted to hear it.

It took him off guard, and he slipped and half-fell against the wall. I staggered too, a little, with the momentum, then recovered and sprinted past him and on down the hill. Thanking God for London-bred forethought I scrabbled—with some difficulty—in my pocket for the key and pulled it out.

Of course he followed me. His running feet behind me were an echo of my own. I increased speed, grabbing at a drainpipe to swing myself round the corner into the street at the bottom. He shouted something, but I didn't hear. As I ran towards the little car park I pointed the keys at the Panda and pressed. Nothing happened. I tried again, wasting precious seconds before I realised that I was pressing the wrong button. Colin burst round the corner just as the indicators winked orange, and I dragged at the door and flung myself in, throwing my bag onto the other seat.

I had barely assimilated the appalling fact that the steering wheel was missing when it came to me—broke over me—that I was on the passenger's side. Half-sobbing with urgent haste, I slammed the door and locked it, and, sweeping my bag into the back, struggled into the driver's seat just as Colin reached me and began pounding with his fists on the windows, the roof, the bonnet. I screamed something futile and desperate at him as I flicked the key out and jammed it anyhow into the ignition. The engine started immediately. I slammed the car into gear, shooting out of the bay backwards and round in a tight curve.

But he was there, foursquare in front of me and yelling something, beating the bonnet with his fists. I engaged third gear and stalled the engine. I screamed again, and tears sprang, blinding me. The engine coughed back into life. I got the thing into first and began to roll forward regardless. A twist of what I prayed was the right stalk, and the lights flared on, the figure in front of me suddenly far too close and far too easy to see. The contorted face slid by, fists pounding harmlessly on the roof, as I gathered speed and threw the Panda at the road.

Smearing the tears away with the back of my hand I thanked my lucky stars and anything else keeping a benevolent eye on me that I had already driven this route. But hardly had I negotiated the left-hand corner than headlights stabbed through the rear window on full beam, blinding me in earnest this time. I had forgotten he had Huw's car. I found the switch under the rear view mirror and flipped it up, but I couldn't spare the time to find how to alter the wing mirrors, so I had to deflect that cold, bright glare with an upflung hand. This I had to drop straight back onto the wheel, however: we were into another sharp bend, and another.

I drove as fast as I dared, chewing at my lip and sitting hunched over the wheel like a jockey riding a neck-and-neck finish. At least the little Panda was nippy on its feet. Compared with the MG it stuck to the road like gorilla glue.

It needed to. We took the first roundabout too fast, itself on a hairpin bend, and I skidded a little in the dust and gravel at the side of the road before the power steering hauled me back onto the tarmac. The ice-blue halogen lights of Huw's car poured at an angle over the road in front of me, then swung, and dazzled, lighting up the inside of the Panda again. One of his sidelights was out.

I made myself concentrate ruthlessly on the road. I did not dare think how close he was. He had the bigger engine, but I had the lighter car, and just managed to gain on him round the corners.

The road straightened out as we reached the plain, and I was heading at speed for yet another roundabout when I saw lights coming fast from the left.

Not just headlights, either. There were four sets of subsidiary glows poised—or so it seemed—in mid-air.

Something large, perhaps an articulated lorry... and I couldn't remember the road ahead. The huge dark bulk roared closer at what seemed like a wicked speed, pinning me to the road in its glare as we converged on the roundabout.

I put my foot down and shot across in front of him, right under his bumper. My hair whipped into my eyes, and a noise like the foghorn in the Bristol Channel split the dark. An oil tanker.

The Panda lit up like the broad of the day as the driver angrily flashed his main beam at me. The tanker was sickeningly close behind me and it seemed to take a teeth-gritting age before we began to draw away and its glare faded out of the car.

We were approaching a built-up area of undistinguished modern houses, and I slowed, and followed the signs, trying to keep the hair out of my eyes. More roundabouts...and here at last was the slip road onto the Perugia road, blessedly traffic-free just when I needed it to be. Barely checking my speed, I hauled the little car round the long right-handed turn, slowing down just in time for the sharp left onto the main road.

I was still crouched over the wheel. I made myself drop my shoulders, sit back, and take five deliberate deep breaths. Then I dared a look in the rear view mirror.

The tanker was lost in the traffic, but the next but one vehicle behind me was missing a sidelight. I gave a little sob and put my foot down.

I got a round ton out of the Panda on the long, straight stretch to Todi. Colin was never far behind, lights dipped now, then agleam again at the edge of my vision. Never did I think I would be grateful for the way the Italians drive: time and time again he was obliterated by a vehicle's reckless overtaking, and more than once a horn blared—whether his or someone else's I neither knew nor cared.

I had long since become conscious that there was far too much night air in the car, and in trying to shut the sunroof, which I had left wide open that afternoon, I managed to switch on the radio. Naturally, I couldn't find how to switch it off, so the rest of that hideous journey was made to the accompaniment of Italian pop, which, mercifully, I could barely hear above the rush of the night wind.

A gleam showed, rushing upon me. The sign for Todi, looming incandescently out of the dark. It plunged me into an agony of indecision, and my careful plan evaporated. Should I try to lose him just beyond Todi on the tortuous road I'd taken yesterday, or stay, after all, on the longer, main road that runs to the south of the Lago di Corbara, and risk a road I didn't know? Then the decision was made for me. A big, black four-by-four overtook, far too close, and I automatically swerved to the right. With the minimum of indication, and to the accompaniment of several impatient blares of the horn, I found myself on the road I knew.

I spared a hunted glance over my shoulder, and saw the big car with the missing sidelight speeding past, towards Terni.

He would have seen straight away that I had turned off, and he wouldn't waste time trying to follow me. He would go immediately to the car park nearest the Duomo, and Huw and I would run straight into him.

There was nothing but black night behind me now, but with each sickening bend in that dreadful, endless road, I became more certain that he would be waiting for me.

I can't say how awful that part of the journey was. We shot past the farm track to the dig as though I knew this road like the back of my hand; and the only conscious thought in my head was that there at last was the motorway, and this bat-out-of-hell flight through the dark would at last be over.

This brief respite soon evaporated. I peered desperately at the signs, trying to concentrate. Did I want *Orvieto est* or *ovest*? Which way was I facing, anyway? Brake, check to the left, indicate… and for God's sweet sake, don't get onto the motorway itself…

Under the motorway now, with a silent prayer of thanks, and round a wide curve to the left. This doubled back on itself, so that Orvieto was now on my right hand. I wove my way onto and off several more roundabouts, becoming more and more baffled as the mediæval walls slipped tantalisingly by, until it dawned on me that despite my brave efforts, I was coming into the town by a completely different route from yesterday. I had no idea where I was, and now, no idea how to get to the Duomo.

My hands tightened on the steering-wheel until the knuckles cracked, and I think I had almost given up to the point of just following the car in front when somehow we had done almost a whole circuit of the town, and were there. My lights picked out a road sign: *il centro*. Town centre.

I sagged in my seat with relief. There was even a shop front I recognised from yesterday. It was shuttered now, but with a new surge of hope I turned right as though by instinct, and my headlights flashed momentarily on a street sign. The Via Manente. That meant that just along here somewhere was the Via del Duomo… Thank God; I would find him after all.

I felt frighteningly conspicuous in this small, human-scale town, and longed for the anonymity of London. Worse, I was increasingly worried that I was in a non-driving zone. At least the icy, three-cornered glare was nowhere to be seen. I could have picked him out from a dozen others now, even though the cold lights, far too bright, were everywhere...but I was worrying unnecessarily about one thing, at least. Ahead of me, and to my right, the luminous skyline showed a dark, domed silhouette that I recognised with passionate relief.

I had originally intended to find yesterday's car park, but now I remembered that where we had sat with our pizzas, there had been cars. Where there were cars, there was a car park... Damn, there *was* the Via del Duomo. Braking abruptly, I turned into the narrow street with more speed than judgement, shooting out and across the square towards the north side of the Duomo like a torpedo out of a tube. There was a space at the far end. I threw the car at it like a heat-seeking missile, not giving a tinker's cuss whether it was reserved for visitors, residents, or the Doge of Venice. The lights, which I had left on, obligingly cut at the same time as I switched the engine off, but the radio instantly lit up with the information *1 ora* in bright green, and continued to sing loudly. I banged at it. This ramped up the volume by quite a lot, so I offered it the rudest valediction I could think of and grabbed my bag. As I scrambled out, the interior light came on and stayed on. I gave it a glare which might have given Medusa pause for thought, but it had no immediate effect. Abandoning the Panda to its fate, I slammed the door and ran for the shadows.

Lapped round by the dark, I made myself stand quiet, and listen, and look. The warm night breathed round me. I heard no racing, gaining footsteps, but from the Cathedral came a hum of voices in worship. And there, in counterpoint, my little Panda was singing away to itself, lit up like a fairground attraction; instantly visible, immediately recognisable. I hissed desperately, vainly: "Shut up, won't you? Please, please *just shut up!*"

"Cassie!"

I spun round.

"Cassie?"

There was someone a few feet away. My heart jumped, painfully, then the tall figure was hastening towards me, a stray beam of light from a street lamp gleaming on the dark curls. I gasped: "Huw!" and flung myself into his arms.

"Cassie, Cassie, thank God."

For a moment, we clung to each other speechlessly, his hand unsteady as he smoothed the wind-tangled hair back from my forehead. "Did he hurt you? Did he?"

I shook my head.

"Sure?"

I nodded vigorously and found my voice, my eyes filling again. "No, I promise you he didn't, it was the fright he gave me. He just appeared, and grabbed me, and then that drive helter-skelter on that *ghastly* road—the *endless* bloody roundabouts, of all the hellish devices to disfigure a road with—and I couldn't find how to shut the sunroof, and—well, everything. I left the radio on." I wiped my eyes on the nearest available material, which happened to be his cotton sweater, and sniffed loudly. Later, I would see that I'd left streaks of mascara.

"You don't say. How do you think I knew it was you? I heard you coming." He gave a little laugh and cocked his head. "What were you listening to?"

"Heaven knows. It wasn't exactly Linguists' Question Time. And as for his hurting me, if anything, I hurt him." I sniffed again, defiantly.

"Why, what did you do?"

"He told me to give him Grandpa's Homer, so I did: right across the side of his head. It was in my bag, you see, I'd been reading it by the pool. Actually, that's utter rubbish: I'd taken it down, just to show off, but I fell asleep instead."

He caught me to him in a fierce hug, and his cheek came down on my hair. "Cassie Greatrex, you are indeed a Trojan, through and through. What a girl!"

I took him by the sweater, fistfuls of it. "That's all very well, but what on earth do we do now?"

"We get out of here," he said. "That's what we do. It's too damn close to my bed and breakfast for comfort."

"Wait!" I twisted in his arms, looking this way and that across the ranked metal roofs. "What do you think Colin will have done? Will he have gone there to look for you? I swear I lost him—at least when I was trying to find this place, he wasn't behind me—and do you know that one of your sidelights isn't working?"

"I expect he smashed it, or something. He won't be able to park anywhere near there. This is the only place—and this is reserved for Cathedral staff. Unless he's dumped my car somewhere, he'll have to leave it here."

I buried my face in his shoulder. "Oh, Huw, you don't know; it was like having a tiger sitting on my rear bumper. And I got into the passenger's seat by mistake, and he was banging anyhow on the roof, and then I nearly ran him over, and there was a *huge* oil tanker—*Huw*—"

"Steady, sweetie, it's all right." He hugged me again, hard, but I had heard something, and twisted round again.

"*Look!* That's him! He's here! He's found us!"

A gleam showed. Lights swelled, piercing the dark of the car park. There was a sidelight missing.

"Okay, let's get out of here."

My heart was pounding fit to choke me. As we turned to run, the tiger's dazzling, ice-cold eyes swept into the square and skewered us for a flying second in their glare. He stood on the brakes, and his car—Huw's car—bunched to a tyre-stripping halt full in the right of way. In another second, he had the door open and was running towards us. He had left the headlights on, undimmed. I almost expected the anti-aircraft guns to open up.

We linked hands and ran for it on cats' feet.

Our run was short-lived. To reach the Panda, we had to cross in front of him, and we didn't stand a chance. Before I had time to do anything useful, Colin went in low and dirty with a headbutt to Huw's midriff. My hand was ripped from his and with a grunted expletive he went sprawling onto the ground, Colin flinging himself on top. Just in time, Huw drew his legs up, and I think I was going to scream for help, but he can't have done it in pain for he put both feet to Colin's chest, thrust him up and aside, and rolled over and up in one quick movement. Colin, recovering quickly, lunged across, caught him by the ankle, and brought him down in an awkward, twisting fall right over the bonnet of an Alfa Romeo, which instantly split the night apart with a screaming alarm like an air raid siren gone mad. At the same time, the Cathedral burst into joyful song, all organ stops out. Even if I did scream, nobody would hear.

Huw slid off the bonnet and fell heavily on his back. Colin plunged down, straddling him. Clenching both fists together, he brought them down in a powerful arc, aiming for Huw's face, but Huw twisted just in time to avoid them, and Colin, literally pulling his punches, hit the patterned, flattened cobblestones a harmless enough blow. He uttered something ugly and bunched a fist again.

I started forward, shouting something, hardly knowing what I was doing. Colin, seeing me, flung himself off Huw, and, catching at my bag, pulled me towards him down onto the ground with a crash that winded me. He actually had hold of the Homer through the suede, and was tugging at it and cursing it, cursing me, when Huw, already on his feet, seized him round the middle in a bear-hug that drove the breath out of him, and dragged him off me. I scrambled up and stood there, helplessly trying to gulp air back into my lungs as both men crashed to the ground once more. Somehow Huw had one knee on Colin's chest.

"Run, Cassie! Get to the car!"

Before I could move, Colin had writhed round like a snake and aimed a wicked punch at Huw's midriff. It connected. Huw fell heavily onto his side and lay there, curled round his hurt.

Colin scrambled up unsteadily and aimed a kick at Huw. It went awry, and he staggered a little. Then he shook the thick fair hair away from his face and started towards me.

He was between me and the car. For one endless second, we stared at each other, then I veered sharply out of his reach and ran for it. Behind me I heard Huw shout: "*Got you!*" and Colin's yelp of pain.

"Oh, God, God, come on, *come on*," I muttered in frantic little gasps, once more dragging the key out of my pocket and pointing it in one shaking hand. I pressed the button, grabbed the door-handle, and pulled hard. Nothing happened. The interior light had gone out—just when I needed it—and once again I had to feel with useless fingers for the right bloody button. From behind me I could hear ugly grunts as the men struggled. The Alfa Romeo's eldritch scream went on spearing intolerably through the night, and more orange lights started flashing a warning as Huw and Colin hurtled into another parked car. My own indicators winked as yet another alarm joined in, and at last I yanked the door open and flung myself in.

I made myself feel for the ignition and insert the key carefully so as not to waste a second, and fired the engine. Then I backed out and round, and while we were still moving, I shoved the gear lever into first and put my foot down.

The Panda leapt forward, and I twisted the lights on. Radio singing, headlamps blazing, and bearing down fast on the two men, I leant over and got the passenger door open, then jammed on the brakes and halted about six feet away from them with my foot hard on the pedal and my leg jumping convulsively.

Both were in light-coloured tops and for a ghastly moment I couldn't see which was which. Then Huw landed a pile-driven punch on Colin's jaw that snapped the fair head back, and followed it up with the other fist under his ribcage. Colin fell to the ground, winded and bleeding, and Huw went staggering back a few paces to bend double, hands on knees, snatching ragged breaths through distended nostrils.

"*Huw!*" I screamed over the dreadful pop music. "*Get in! Hurry!*"

He straightened painfully, and saw me just behind him. He fell against the car and into it, cramming his long limbs in anyhow. He reached for the door just as Colin put a hand on the bull-bars of the four-by-four nearest him, hauled himself upright, and spat blood disgustingly on the cobbles.

The interior light had come on again as though a well-trained butler had thrown a switch, and by its little glow I saw Huw's hand. It was bloodstained, and shaking violently. He missed the handle, groped again, caught it, and pulled the door shut. I put the car into reverse and shot backwards a few yards. Into first, then second, and we twisted round the panting Colin and were away, plunging into the suffocatingly narrow Via del Duomo.

The screams of the alarms, and Colin's shouts, faded behind us.

Huw had to work hard to get his breathing under control. "Cassie, we've got to get back to Assisi…put that bloody book under lock and key. This has gone quite far enough."

The thought of driving all the way back was appalling, but he was quite right. "I agree," I said, barely able to remember which side of the road I was supposed to be on. "Too far has definitely been gone."

"Yes—damn, my *hand*." He was nursing it. "I don't know about you, but I think the sooner we turn this safely over to the police, the better. Turn right at the chemist's here."

I was squinting. "Are you sure? This says"—I attempted it—"'Quartiere del Corsica'."

"Quite sure. This is the Corso Cavour."

The street—if one could call it that—that I had come in by. I said: "Police? What can they do?"

"The police at home, I mean. They'll take it seriously. And I'll have to tell the Dean." He felt his face cautiously, then, flexing the fingers, leant forward and turned the radio off. "Do you mind?"

"I've been trying to do that since I left Assisi," I said. "Are you feeling better?"

"I'm fine," said Huw shortly. He rearranged his legs more comfortably and winced. "Dirty little brute. My God, I wanted to kill him."

"I thought you were going to."

"Nothing would give me greater pleasure. If he gives me any more gutter-fighting, I will, and take the consequences."

"I must ask Daddy," I said, trying to follow his lead, "which of his categories bail comes into. Where are we going, anyway?"

"The Corso Cavour leads all the way to the eastern edge of Orvieto, to the Piazzale Cahen. If you bypass that and bear left onto the Via Postierla, where the *funicolare* stops, we can take the Perugia road from there."

"I am glad," I said, "that one of us knows what we're doing."

"I wouldn't say that, exactly. Never come to blows with anybody before—at least not outside the boxing-ring."

I spared him a glance. "Nature red in tooth and thingummybob? I know a bit about that myself. I wouldn't have minded in the least if I'd cracked his head open when I hit him. Shocking."

"Hmm. It's quite frightening," said Huw more calmly, "how bestial and primitive one can be, given the provocation. I quite see how people become addicted to the feeling. Watch out for that woman. Why isn't she riding that bicycle instead of pushing it? Why, she's all over the place!"

"Adrenaline," I said obscurely.

He grunted, and I was content to be quiet. My elbow was throbbing and sore where I'd hit the ground, and a graze stung raw on the side of my hand and wrist.

In any other circumstances, I would have enjoyed the drive. The Corso Cavour is lined with achingly smart boutiques that—in any other circumstances—I would immediately have dived into, hardly knowing which to choose first. The busy restaurants spill out into the street, already in places no more than a car's width; the banks ply their usurious trade on into the evening from buildings half a millennium old, and I suddenly remembered that it was the Romans who had invented banking, bringing it, courtesy of the Lombards, to London with such success that they had a street named for them. I suppose I was trying not to think of Colin and what he had done to us, but when a taxi hooted angrily at me for obliging it to draw aside as we approached, it brought me abruptly back to the present. I tried to focus what remained of my concentration on not hitting the pedestrians who wandered along in front of the car, bringing us to a nail-biting crawl, and stepped straight into the road without looking and regarded us with offended disdain as we crept after them, asking politely to be past.

We had almost reached the pleasantly open and tree-lined expanse of the Piazzale Cahen when the engine faltered. I registered it and forgot about it. My gaze was flicking back and forth between the road ahead and the rear view mirror, while my mind wandered off to the nightmares I'd had occasionally about being chased in the dark. How on earth I would get us safely back to Assisi—and what would we do if he followed us, as he undoubtedly would? Could we rely on the hotel for help? Surely, yes: I had told the concierge myself that my friend had been robbed. Could I count on him not to ask why my friend was being so comprehensively followed by the presumed robber—who—oddly—was just as battered as Huw? I opened my mouth to say something of this when the engine coughed again and we lost way. I put my foot down. Nothing—no response at all.

"What is it?"

"I don't know."

But even as I spoke, I saw. I hadn't even noticed the warning light on the dashboard. We had run out of petrol.

Huw saw it too. "See if you can get us onto the Piazzale Cahen, at least. We might be in time to catch the last *funicolare* of the day."

"When is it?"

"Eight-thirty." He checked his watch. "It's nearly that now."

His tone was expressionless, and I couldn't have answered if I'd tried. And I didn't need to check the rear view mirror, either; the Panda had filled with cold light like the inside of an Antarctic iceberg. He must have driven like a demon to catch us up.

Why I passed the handy parking space under the trees I will never know. I did see it, and it might have saved us a lot of trouble, but like an automaton I kept my road. We jerked along, the engine alternately coughing and firing, and I somehow nursed the little car out into the open.

Here the engine died completely. We coasted silently along on my wrong side for a few more yards, and came whispering to a standstill.

TWELVE

...like wolves leapt they one at another,
and man lashed at man.

Book IV, *ibid.*

We had stopped at a zebra crossing, mercifully without
hitting any of the pedestrians trooping slope-shouldered
past the bonnet like so many Beatles. It was a moment or
two before I saw the bus waiting patiently behind them. In
fact, I heard it before I saw it: the driver gave vent to an ear-
splitting and indignant blast on his horn that nearly blew me
out of my seat.

I flapped madly in response as the last pedestrian stepped
off the crossing and disappeared under a canopy of red-
framed glass gables. "*Senza gaz!*" I cried idiotically, in the
intervals of craning vainly round for a petrol station. "*Senza
gaz!*" Even if there had been one, we would have had to get
out and push the car onto the forecourt, and Colin would
catch us, and then Huw would have to fight him again...

I was trying not to cry, so I didn't see Colin take the
parking space I had missed; didn't see him hurl himself out

of Huw's car; didn't see his hectic, stumbling run towards us until the last second, when the face I had learned to loathe was suddenly there, horribly close, and looming at the window. One hand starfished itself with a thump against the glass, smearing blood; the other was fumbling at the door. I screamed, flinching away violently, but Huw was already out.

"I'll deal with him! Get that book away safely—anywhere! Forget the bus! I'll call you!"

Then with a light step up onto the tyre, he flung himself bodily across the Panda's bonnet, and Colin vanished, floored by the rugby tackle from hell.

The bus driver, not to be outdone, banged angrily on his windscreen. Eyes popping, he mouthed something, then shook the meaty fist at me. His thumb was between the first two fingers in a gesture which even I knew to be vulgar in the extreme. Then he flashed his lights up and down, blinding me; and, when that didn't work, accelerated to within a foot of the Panda's defenceless radiator grille and sat there, blocking access to the zebra crossing, alternately blowing his horn and revving aggressively.

The two men were struggling again; they banged against my door. Then, ricocheting off, they cannoned into a parked car, which immediately began to scream.

It was too much. I let my upflung arm fall and scrambled anyhow out of the other side. I stumbled, but only a little way, as though I too had run out of fuel. The very last thing I wanted to do was leave Huw to 'deal with' a desperate thug. On the other hand, the Homer was—evidently—the repository of some vital secret. But without the car I was helpless. It was all very well to tell me to get it away, but where to? Where could I go in this strange town in a foreign country, where we had already caused enough trouble for one evening? Would they help me at the *funicolare* terminal?

Possibly—but I didn't speak Italian. And where was the bloody thing, anyway?

Then I forgot about it. Huw had dragged Colin up and laid tight hold on him in a ruthless armlock. Frogmarching him back to the Panda, he forcibly bent him double over the bonnet so that he yelled in pain. Huw shouted at him to shut up, then again to me to get away; and now the renewed fracas, augmented by the shrieks of the alarm and the klaxon's din, was attracting attention. The driver sprang down from his bus and strode towards us. I dithered uselessly as he berated me and gesticulated at Huw. All I could do was clutch at my bag and smile appeasement at him and stammer *"Sorry... sorry...sorry..."* in English over and over again. Now a couple of men approached purposefully from the ranks of parked vehicles; passers-by who, presumably, wished to try and break up the fight. At least I hoped it was that—God knows what I would do if they wanted to join in. Perhaps they were off-duty police...anonymously dressed, they looked tough and competent. One of them spoke, in Italian. I made myself blank out everything else so I could hear. Even the bus driver stopped shouting to listen.

Huw looked up, but he did not loosen his cruel grip. He said something to them in English—I barely caught it—about an argument going wrong. The other man had engaged the angry bus driver in excited conversation; the first was gesturing to the Panda, to Colin, with a query that even I, with no command whatsoever of Italian, could understand. They paid no attention to me at all, and it was several moments before I realised they thought I was just another interested onlooker. If they detained Huw and Colin for a little longer, I might be able to get away. I tried to edge backwards a pace or two, but there were people there, close. Huw was speaking again, this time in a mixture of English and tolerable Italian. No need to worry…a college friend…silly prank…drunk too much… *"Ma si, molto vino"*… He looked wilder even than usual, but considering everything, his face was relatively undamaged, and he sounded remarkably calm and convincing. Colin had gone limp; all fight seemingly punched out of him and bloodied mouth turned away from the men's scrutiny. I hovered indecisively, suspicious and distrustful, but whatever his reason, it lent much-needed weight to Huw's explanation. It seemed to do the trick. The men lifted their shoulders, and, with a final word to the driver, disappeared among the parked cars, leaving Huw and Colin to it. The driver seemed to take the hint as well: he went back to his bus, reversed, and simply drove round us in a wide, overtaking arc.

So he didn't want strangers involved? I could understand that. Perhaps Colin had seen sense after all… The little crowd which had gathered, as crowds do, shrugged with disappointment and began to disperse, and I started towards the car, hope leaping, just as Colin, taking advantage of Huw's momentarily slackened hold, kicked him savagely on the shin and wrenched himself free. He looked round quickly, and saw me straight away.

I would love to be able to say that at this point I remembered I was a soldier's daughter and acted in some courageous and heroic fashion—that I even went for help before saving my own skin. But I didn't. I had been badly frightened and manhandled, I had driven some sixty miles at high speed in unfamiliar conditions, I had borne witness to some nasty, dirty fighting, and all my instincts were now concentrated on one thing: flight. Huw had said I was to get to safety, hadn't he? That seemed good enough for me.

So much for altruism. I didn't stop to think; couldn't have summoned up a coherent thought if I'd tried. I only knew that I must get away. I gripped my bag tightly to me and flung round wildly. Where was the funicular? Where the hell was it?

It seemed like a lifetime, but could only have been a second, before I realised it was staring me in the face. Its glass doors, red-framed like the gables, were standing wide, and between them, the legend in block capitals: *FUNICOLARE.*

Before Colin had had time to wriggle round the front of the silent Panda, I had leapt for the pavement and dived through the nearest. Here were human beings. Safety in numbers...

I found myself in a concourse, far smaller than one might have expected. Just inside, and between the two sets of doors—I was only peripherally conscious of it—was a control block in the same framed plate glass. In front of this yawned a kind of railed inspection pit that sloped down and away, its edges striped wasp-like in yellow-and-black warning against the rotating twin pulley-wheels. These were strung with steel hawsers as thick as my wrist; one to let the outgoing car down at a controlled speed, the other to haul up the incoming. All round were barriers, and people gathering. I fetched up against one of the barriers and hung over it, and there was the same rush of air in the face one gets on the Underground when a train is approaching. I leant further, until a woman next to me nudged me back with a kindly, imperative elbow. But I had seen it; the square, red driving-end of the *funicolare* heaving ponderously up the hill towards us. It filled the tunnel deafeningly, surged onto the concourse, and came to a clanging halt. The doors swished back to discharge its load of home-coming and hungry tourists onto the concourse. As they disembarked from one side, the waiting passengers embarked from the other.

I was at the front, and so found myself obliged, as it were, to embark with them. I believe I had some thought of taking the train back to Assisi, but I cannot be sure, for just then I looked through the smeared glass across the Via Postierla.

He was coming fast, the pale blue top showing discoloured and stained even at this distance; and Huw after him at a fast limp. They met the outgoing passengers head on; were swallowed up by them.

I will never know why I changed my mind, but I simply stepped out of the opposite side, slipping past in their wake and into the shadows as Colin was fighting free. A musical beep of alarm sounded, accompanied by the kind of incomprehensible announcement one usually associates with railway stations, and an official stepped out of the control block. He had keys in his hand. Waving Colin away, he locked the doors in his face just as he came up against the plate glass with a shock that could be felt.

He was fifteen feet from me; and he hadn't seen me. I shrank back. True to form, he pounded both fists on the glass and yelled. Then he saw the other doors and went impetuously to try them, but they had already been locked. These he kicked; and when they remained closed, kicked them again, and then the others for good measure.

I shrank. Beside me, in the concourse, the lights dimmed, and the *funicolare* sank gracefully out of sight, like the demon king through the trapdoor in a pantomime. The last one of the day.

The crowds were thinning, and he was still there. He seemed once more to have been detained by someone. Someone tall—not Huw—who was standing in his way, and who, oddly, seemed to be arguing with him.

Here came Huw now, shouldering his way past the stragglers. He was looking extremely angry, and also rather puzzled, like a large dog when the rabbit escapes him at the last minute. For a disbelieving moment, I watched the three of them in heated discussion. Then Colin, with an abruptly dismissive gesture, turned and tried to push the tall man aside.

The tall man stood his ground. Huw reached out a long arm to grasp Colin by the collar and drag him back, and that was when everything turned very ugly indeed. Colin shouted something aggressive and vulgar at the top of his voice, then smacked Huw's arm away viciously, spun round, and brought his knee up into Huw's groin.

I screamed "*No!*" as Huw folded in two over the pain that depth-charged through him. He crashed to the ground like a felled tree with a horrid noise halfway between a cough and a moan of pain, and writhed there. For a moment Colin stood over him, fists clenched, while the tall man seemed to be torn between a desire to detain Colin and the need to help Huw. Huw's need proved greater, and the tall man went down on one knee beside him.

I could do nothing but obey Huw and get the hell out of there. At least he had help of a sort. I looked wildly round. There were people coming out of some sort of entrance next to the *funicolare*, and I saw now that this was a lane going at an angle off to my right, lightless and dark with trees.

The nightmare at my heels again, I clutched my bag to me as though it were my first-born, burst out of the shadows, dodged round the knot of holiday-makers, and ran like a coursed hare towards the lane, just as Colin, casting round swiftly like an attack-dog, found me.

I must have run a couple of hundred yards along the dark tunnel before I came to an untidy halt, legs flailing, and unable all at once to fathom why this was a sensible thing to do. Whether it was because (as I later discovered) we were at the edge of the plateau here, I don't know; but the wind seemed to have got up, and was moving restlessly in the tops of the trees. These were in full leaf; there was, momentarily, nobody else about; and all at once the only footsteps I could hear were my own. These sounded unnaturally loud and even menacing, and seemed to drown any noise of pursuit, but I had to see if he was following me. My only comfort was the darkness. It was black enough to hide anybody.

I looked fearfully over my shoulder. The Piazzale Cahen was a glow-worm. Perhaps it was the rustling leaves, or perhaps it was my fear, but I could hear nothing above the sobbing rasps of my own breathing. I could see nothing, but he might have hidden, hoping to gull me into thinking it was safe to go back. Back to Huw.

A shadow moved at the far end. It made no sound. He must be on the grass.

I melted into the still blacker shelter of a large tree and tried to quieten my breathing. Nothing. After a bit, I dared a look round the trunk.

He had vanished; subsumed into the dark. But then the restless sighing of the upper boughs lulled a little, and I heard him panting hard. He was still on my tail: perhaps he tripped over a root then—or was favouring his injuries—for I caught a muttered curse.

Then, wonderfully, running feet, after him. The darkness was disorientating, and I couldn't even see the road surface. From where I was standing—cowering—a little light showed the other way, at the far end. Light meant people, and people meant safety. For a second, I wondered whether I could double back behind the trees, back to Huw, but rejected the idea almost immediately. If Colin did not see me straight away, he would certainly hear me scrambling along the banks that bordered the lane. And I could not count on its being Huw behind him: I knew that a man did not easily recover from the sort of cad's blow that Colin had dealt him. No, I dared not retrace my tracks.

The panting breaths were not far behind, and I think I heard, in a shout that sounded thoroughly winded, someone calling my name. In sudden desperation, I broke cover, peeling myself away from the trunk. I hit the metalled surface and ran towards the little light. A flurry of footsteps followed me, and there was another shout. I ignored it.

At the end of the lane was a small building, a round hut of a thing, where the light was. I burst from the cover of the trees before I realised that if I had been visible before, I would now be floodlit. A sitting duck.

I was perhaps twenty feet from the building, and light spilt out in a welcome glow from the arched entrance. My spirits soared suddenly. I don't know what made me think of public lavatories, but if that's what it was, no Italian matron on earth was going to allow Colin Bardsey in after me. I whirled round to face the dark mouth of the avenue.

Colin, wheezing hard, had stopped a few yards away. He put a shaking hand out to me as though in supplication, and called to me.

"Cassie, just…give me…the book." He put the other hand onto his knee, bending double with exertion. His sides were heaving, and his face a bloodied mess. "I don't want… to hurt you, but I will if I…have to. I just need the book. There's…nowhere to run to." He straightened and came forward a step, his hands—with Huw's blood on them—on his hips as his overcharged lungs strove for air.

But I hardly heard. Approaching up the avenue were two figures, the nearer slowing to a jogtrot even as I watched—

and, thank God, Huw, instantly recognisable, and walking rather carefully. Perhaps, like me, Colin wouldn't hear them over the noise his lungs were making. Perhaps. And perhaps I could keep Colin's attention on me, so the men behind him would have a chance to catch up, to catch him before he caught me. I went a pace or two towards the light. I let him see me hesitate; let him see my hand go protectively to my bag.

"What are you going to do with it?"

My voice was genuinely unsteady, but I lifted it as well as I could so that Huw would hear me.

"That's my business. Come on, Cassie…be sensible." He gasped out the last two words, then turned sharply. He had heard them too. I managed not to call Huw's name.

I was fifteen feet from safety now…ten feet. Surely I could leave Colin to them to deal with, while I slipped from his grasp again.

"Sensible?" I repeated. The jogging figure had caught up, was walking now; had stopped. It was the tall man. Some way behind was Huw, fighting mad, and also very out of breath. I had to fight the urge to run to him—in any case, I hadn't a chance of getting to him past Colin. It was a locked cubicle and an Italian matron or nothing. I didn't want to think of what I would do if it proved to be empty.

Colin called out, with desperation in his voice: "You really don't want to be mixed up in this. Just…just give me the book. For God's sake, Cassie, give me the bloody book!" He was recovering his breath; he took a couple more steps towards me. Huw had caught up at last; silent now, but at this angle the light caught him, showed him clearly, leaning against a tree, head back, white face turned to me, chest heaving. Even from where I stood I could see the marks of battle.

Colin saw him, too—and the tall figure standing quietly. Something seemed to go out of him, and his shoulders sagged. At the sight of it, the coward impulse which had sent me down this dead end yielded to something else rather less ignoble.

"In your dreams, mate," I shouted, loud enough for Huw to hear. George Ezra's Cassy had known what to do, hadn't she? And so did I. I tensed, ready to bolt.

For a second, none of us moved. I think I was waiting to see if Colin would give up. I had completely forgotten that he had played this trick once before. Gripping my bag to myself as though I were carrying the heir to a violently disputed kingdom, I watched him; wary, desperate, defiant, defeated, piggy in the middle; and Huw and the other man, whoever he was, both of them unsure of their next move, and all of us knowing only that it depended on what Colin did. He was glancing from one to the other of us, his head moving in uncontrolled jerks. I thought: *If he attacks me now, they're close enough to overpower him...*

I don't know how much longer we might have remained like that, four atoms in a highly volatile molecule, when voices sounded behind me and some people emerged from the small round building. I froze, and tried to look normal, whatever that means.

They passed me, not looking at me; a little knot of well-dressed and well-oiled businessmen. They seemed to be enjoying a group joke that involved much slapping of thighs and backs. I stood rooted to the spot, smiling like an idiot and hugging my bag—and I think I even gave them a murmured "*Buona noces.*" Then they were between Colin and the other two men, just as someone else came out behind them, it seemed in proof of my deduction. And Colin, taking instant advantage, lunged at me.

I whirled and ran.

Dimly, I was aware of someone shouting angrily. I paid no attention.

I was inside before I realised it wasn't public lavatories. It was a spiral staircase.

I was in St Patrick's Well.

THIRTEEN

...a fountain of dark water...

Book II, *ibid.*

MY MOMENTUM HAD carried me down several of the shallow steps before I allowed myself to realise what I'd done. I had been reading about this place—I had even thought I might like to visit it. I was in the mediæval Pozzo di San Patrizio. So called because, like St Patrick's Purgatory, it was very, very deep.

My headlong pace slowed abruptly on the shiny-smooth and treacherous surfaces. Thank heavens they were adequately lit—if you can call an oval glow-worm every tenth step adequate—and thank heavens for my rubber-studded driving shoes.

"Cassie! Stop!"

I knew the voice before it had even registered. Galvanised afresh, and heedless now of the slippery surface, I plunged on down. I didn't dare think of Huw. But I did curse myself for my stupidity as some facts came back to haunt me. The guide book had stated that there were two staircases, each of two hundred and forty-eight steps. One was for the journey down to the water, and one back up. This was for the donkeys, said the guide book in approval of this humanitarian gesture, so they wouldn't meet on the way. And each staircase (added the guidebook proudly) had its own entrance. Which meant that since I couldn't turn round and run back up to freedom, I would have to go all the way down to the bottom and up the other side.

Two hundred and forty-eight steps down was one thing, but two hundred and forty-eight back up again was another. I would be winded and spent, easy prey, before I had got a quarter of the way back up. And Huw, damaged and battered as he had been, might not reach me in time... Ten to one he didn't even know about the other staircase—and nor would the other man, in which case... But I didn't pursue this, admitting to myself at last that Colin was desperate enough to hurt me badly to get what he wanted.

Savagely, I told myself to shut up. There would be somewhere, some cranny where I could hide and let them catch up with him before he did me any serious damage. There would be places to rest, surely? If not... I stamped on it ruthlessly. If I kept close to the wall, and tried not to think how narrow was the way... At the very least, I could thank my lucky stars I didn't suffer from claustrophobia. Oh, added my memory obligingly, and there were some seventy windows let straight into the well-shaft. If all else failed, I told myself with a gallows humour I had not known I was capable of, I could throw myself into the water, then the bloody Homer would be ruined, and there would be no point in Colin's continuing this grim pursuit.

Dear God, the water. This was a well—and, whispered the guidebook helpfully in my ear, still in use. Water; deep, deep at the bottom. I might run straight into it. I slithered to a halt on a step and steadied myself with both hands against the rough surface of the wall, and tried to listen over the frantic beating of my heart and ragged breathing.

Shouts, more shouts, some way above me. Would Huw and the other man risk cornering Colin with no way of knowing if they could reach me in time? But they would have to follow him—they would have to.

If only there were somewhere to hide. But there was no sign of a niche, or doorway. I looked the other way, down the staircase. There might be one, just round the next spiral. I could let Colin get safely past, let Huw deal with him... get the Homer away to safety... And he wasn't coming fast; Huw must have damaged him quite badly.

Fiercely glad of this, I looked in front of me, my head spinning gently. There was one of those seventy-odd windows right there, with two slender iron bars across. I had no idea how far down I was. With another fruitless glance back the way I'd come, I jumped for the window and peered cautiously down.

The water was there, black and gleaming, and strangely striped across the middle. My head swam sickeningly, but it was easy enough to see that I was about half-way down. And he was coming, faster now; the footsteps were loud, and louder. The window was no sheltering niche after all: there was no hiding-place there. I abandoned the idea of staying and hoping that he would run past me, and took to the steps again.

On and on, down and down, deep down... My head was whirling with vertigo, and my hand gingerly out to the coarse, jagged surface of the wall to guide me seemed my last hold on reality.

Surely I must be near the bottom now. I had had dreams like this, this flying on down, down, down...but in my dreams there was no water at the bottom, never any water...

Then the lights went out.

The sudden dark was a living, suffocating, blinding thing; an enemy leaping out of nowhere and bringing me flailing to a dead stop. I put both hands to the wall again and pressed close as if I might melt into it and be safe from him. The world spun nauseatingly, and I bent my forehead until it touched cold stone. It steadied me. I listened.

Yes, there they were, the footsteps, hurried yet halting. And behind them were others; it sounded like more than one set, though perhaps that was only the echo off the water. I prayed that it wasn't only the echo. Trying to control my breathing, I turned carefully and backed flat. There was another window opposite me, but at this depth, and without light, it was more a lifting of the black than a definite shape. Coming away from the wall, my lifebelt, my one frame of reference, was one of the most difficult things I have ever done, but I had to see where the water was.

I forced myself away, forced myself to shuffle to the window. As I neared it, my left foot slipped off the narrowed angle of the step, and the next, hurting my ankle bone unbearably and scraping the skin. I cried out as I stumbled forward and onto the flat surface of the window ledge.

"Cassie? Cassie!"

He wasn't bothering to keep his voice down. I could hear him panting, like a bloodhound closing in for the kill.

Then from somewhere, wonderfully loud and close, Huw's voice, echoing, angry and urgent: "Colin! If you so much as touch her, I swear I'll kill you!"

I had to thrust my fist to my mouth to keep from crying out to him. At least he seemed to have recovered from that cad's blow up there, outside the *funicolare*. But where was he that he should sound so blessedly near? Did he know about the other staircase after all? I dared a glance across the well shaft and saw nothing. But I could smell the water. No light, nothing from the moon, nothing from the stars. Black and impenetrable; the tiny disc of sky a pewter coin. I looked back to where the stairs were, still blacker. I didn't dare call to him in case Colin...

A footstep, another; closer still...almost confident. If I stayed any longer he would walk right into me. I leant my head against a jag of stone and squeezed my eyes shut for a second against the tears. The stone was damp and cold beneath my cold palms.

But only for a second. A glimmer of light pricked at the edge of my vision, and vanished. Heedless of my hurt ankle, I whipped back to the bars. There it was again, bobbing bright and dimming to a glow on the far wall. A torch. Someone was coming down the other staircase. The light gleamed again; was extinguished. It must be Huw. He did know about the other staircase after all. He was coming down the other way. Oh, thank God, thank God. I would meet him head on, and then...

"*Huw*! I'm here, just across the water!" I shrieked it, and leant over the railing as far as I dared, waving frantically, but in this blackout I could see nothing beyond that blessed light. He was there, though—and his answering call was drowned by Colin's.

"Cassie, where are you?"

He sounded horrifyingly close behind me. As though it were broad daylight, I jumped for the steps, found the guiding outside wall by the simple expedient of hitting it with my face, and ran on.

I only knew I had reached the bottom when the curve of the wall vanished from under my hand. My knees jarred on the level ground, and I smashed shoulder-first into the unyielding stone. I hardly had time to register this when with a rush and a slither a body cannoned into me.

I screamed, whether from surprise or fright or pain, or a combination of all three, I can't tell. Colin gripped me tightly, Homer and all, and tugged violently at my bag. His breath was rank and hot on the back of my neck, and I screamed again and tried to wrench myself free.

"Shut up!" he hissed in a driven, desperate undervoice. "Just shut up and give me the bloody bag!"

I screamed again, more of a choking gurgle against his stranglehold, and he took one hand off my bag and hit me across the side of the head.

This display of violence should have quenched me but instead it made me angry. Even though I didn't have access to whatever rampant emotion was driving Colin, when the lights stabbed on again with a suddenness that hurt the eyes, and his grip loosened for a second, I twisted round in his arm and brought my knee up as hard as I could into his groin. Then I shoved him away from me, said, pantingly, that that was to pay him back, and ran for the steps.

And stopped before I had got as far as the third one. There was someone else coming down—and coming fast. It was the stranger—the tall man. He stopped just above us, breathing hard. Unable (as I supposed) to speak, he put out a hand to me, it seemed in invitation.

My thoughts were thrown into turmoil. I got a confused impression of a fair man, older than I. He seemed harmless enough, and I had seen him bending solicitously over Huw; had seen him trying to reason with Colin. But I couldn't bring myself to run to him. I didn't pretend to understand what was so deadly important about the burden I was lugging about with me, but without absolute proof of this man's trustworthiness, I wasn't going to run to anybody except Huw. I whipped round again.

My aim had not been true. Colin was standing at the bottom rubbing the inside of his thigh, his face ugly with pain and frustrated rage. I glanced past him, to where an archway led to the water. There was only that one way to go, but at least I had that. For a long second, we stared at one another, then I jumped the last three steps as though they had been one.

"You bitch!" he gasped, and grabbed for me. I swatted his hand aside and fled past him out over the water.

My panicked flight had carried me halfway across before I remembered it again. It wasn't that I couldn't swim; I could. But I was terrified of water if I couldn't see the bottom. You couldn't see a fraction of an inch through the obsidian gleam of the water in St Patrick's horrible well. The ramp was suddenly too narrow and too high, and the lights made spider's-silk of the solid railings.

I stopped, paralysed by fright. I had completely forgotten Colin; was barely aware of a commotion breaking out behind me. If I'd been able to move at all, I'd have seen another figure appear on the opposite side, but I just stood there, a stiff hand on each fragile railing and my terrified gaze glued to my feet. Despite this, all I could see was the black water grinning below and to either side of me, like the mouth of Hades where the sad shadows are.

The ramp was vibrating; my jarred, quivering knees gave suddenly and I sank down and tried not to think about the water, how deep down, how black was the water. Fathom-drowned...

Hands on me; a known, beloved voice; a mirage; a miracle. I clutched them, clung to him. "The water," I gasped. "I can't. It's the bottom—I can't see the bottom..."

Huw bent, lifted me, supported me. I had my face turned into his shoulder and he kept my head there with one gentle hand. I let him guide me to solid stone, to safety, away from the waiting water, away from Colin. Here, he sat me down on the steps and held me until the trembling began to quieten. He rested his cheek on my head and murmured to me, gentling me the way you gentle a frightened animal.

"All right, darling, it's all right. You're safe now."

"You came. You came. I couldn't get past him to you." I had him by the sweater again.

"Of course. I came down the other way. I thought I might reach you first. And how right I was."

I gave a little spurt of laughter, half hysterical. "Academics! Huw, there's someone else—he's down here too. He came down behind Colin. Is he—he's not—"

"It's okay, sweetheart. I gathered—rather on the hoof, as you might say—that he's on our side. There wasn't time for more." His hand came over mine. "Cassie?"

"Yes."

"Listen. I'm going to leave you here for a moment—only for a moment. I have to help him deal with Colin."

"Yes, of course. Huw, the lights went out. They won't go out again, will they? I don't think I could manage it, not so close to the water—I can smell it—I'm no good if I can't see the bottom…" My voice cracked and I was silent. I buried my face in his shoulder again, and he rocked me gently.

"No, my love, not again. That was the curator. Let me go, and I'll tell you, okay?"

I couldn't speak for a second, so I nodded and made my fingers release their grip on him. "Just tell me you're all right? I saw…what he did. I did it back to him just now, only I missed."

He laughed out loud. "Trojan, didn't I say? It hurt like hell, but it wears off. I still feel a bit sick. If I do throw up,

I'll contrive to throw up over him, okay?" He dropped a kiss on my upturned lips and stood up, rather carefully.

For a while, I kept my eyes shut and rested my cheek against the dank wall, while round my ears rolled Huw's voice, and Colin's, angry and defensive; and another, unknown to me: the other man, the tall one, who was on our side after all. I hugged my bag to me and took deep breaths of the cold air and began to recover.

As soon as I felt my legs would hold me, I stood up cautiously and assessed the damage. My left shoulder and ankle were throbbing painfully, and there were runnels of blood down my shin, drying now. But I was alive, and I still had the Homer safe.

I made myself turn to face the ramp to see what was happening. It was all right, as long as I kept myself pressed safely back, and looked at the three men and not at the water.

Colin was arguing with the stranger. It didn't occur to me to wonder who he was and how he fitted in: all that registered with me was that he represented no threat to us. Indeed, his whole stance seemed to be one of conciliation. His low, reasonable tones contrasted starkly with Colin's hectic, intemperate voice. My hurts forgotten, I strained to make out words.

"...no danger from me, I assure you," the stranger was saying calmly. His hands were stretched out, palms down, as though to soothe. There was a slight accent, and I wondered if he were Swiss, perhaps; the Swiss are proverbially even-tempered people.

"So you say," shouted Colin. He was shifting from foot to foot as though the ramp were too hot for him, then backed away a restless pace or two. "That's what you say! You were at Kevin's flat—I saw you leave! Ah, you didn't know that, did you? You might have murdered him, but you're not going to murder me! Do you hear? Do you?"

I heard Huw say something; he sounded startled and made some movement towards the two. Colin rounded on him, a fist clenched and raised.

"You stay put! This is all your fault, you stupid, interfering bastard! You have no idea of the damage you've done, sticking your sanctimonious nose into what doesn't concern you!"

Huw started to say something angry and heated, but the stranger intervened. I listened in disbelief and growing dismay.

"Mr Bardsey, the questions your journalist friend had been asking signed his death warrant. It is true that I want to question you, but I can assure you once again that you are in no danger from me. Indeed, I have come here expressly to make sure that you are in no danger from anybody. Mr Dunston's death is deeply regrettable, deeply, but my government had no hand in it. Indeed, all my government wishes is to see justice done and reparation made."

There was something about the calm way the tall man spoke that reminded me of Dinah with poor Lady Bartlett, scarlet with rage at some perceived omission or mistake, and Dinah agreeing with everything, not just for form's sake, or for a quiet life, but because she really cared. But a death warrant? I shivered. Huw had been right: this had gone far beyond what we could deal with.

Colin had fastened on something. "Reparation!" he was saying angrily. "You—a German!—to talk of reparation! What about my great-uncle? His family, eh? What reparation has *your government* made for them? His whole sodding family! Well?"

A dull scarlet flush coloured the stranger's face, and his jaw worked. "What happened to your family, and untold others like them, will forever be a stain on Germany's conscience. All we can do is forgive ourselves and work tirelessly to make amends that others might forgive us too. That is what I have been instructed to do in this case, Mr Bardsey, only you do not help either me or yourself."

Germany. He's German. I shrank back against the wall, renewed horror and fear pouring over me in cold waves. *And the Homer—is he after that too?*

"Well, you can stick that," shouted Colin. "Are you mad? Me, trust you? In a pig's eye! All I care about is not letting the filthiness of war and what it does to people be a *stain* on my great-uncle's reputation. He was forced into spying for you lot, and then for the Russians—his own people!—and if it had got out, *my* reputation would be up the creek and no mistake!"

"You already paddled your canoe up that particular creek," struck in Huw forcefully, "when you stole somebody else's work and put your name to it. I don't think your great-uncle should have to bear the responsibility for that, do you?"

"As if that matters," said Colin with a kind of nervous impatience. "Who cares what some half-baked amateur thinks?"

"Evidently you did, since you went to the trouble of publishing that half-baked amateur's article under your name without a word changed," replied Huw with an edge of steel to his voice, "not to mention sucking up to that same half-baked amateur's family so you could finish off what you started when you turned over his house!"

That went home; I saw the fear register, like a flicker of lightning, in Colin's eyes.

"Oh, all this is so much balls," he shouted after a moment. "Where are those bloody papers? Tell me that! Find those bloody papers, and nobody's going to care about some pathetic article! By the way you two have been nursing that sodding book, and carrying it about with you like the Holy bloody Grail, they've got to be in it somewhere, in the spine, probably, or under the bindings! They've *got* to be!"

His hot gaze slid past Huw to where I was standing by the doorway. "You *bitch*," he said again, through set teeth, and started towards me.

"Oh, no, you don't!" Huw stood square-shouldered between him and me.

So might Hector and Achilles have looked, grimed and bloody with battle.

Colin, thwarted, glared at him, then jerked his head over his shoulder. "You, Mr squeaky-clean Landeck, or whatever your stupid name is, you ask her about the lists. She's got them, I'll swear she has. I was only going to photocopy them and sell them to him—he didn't even want the originals— she'd have got them back... "

He stopped then and took his head in both hands and bent almost double. He had turned away, but not before I had seen the torment on his bruised face. We were silent. All at once he straightened, dropped his hands to the railing, and spoke, quite conversationally, to the water. "I have to have them. Without them I'm ruined."

I could stand it no longer. I lifted my cheek away from the cold damp and called to him. "*What* lists, Colin? What *is* all this about lists?"

My voice bounced off the walls, queerly distorted. It acted like a bolt of electricity on Colin. He seemed to jump where he stood.

"Inventories!" he shouted, flinging round so we were eye to eye. "The lists of names and addresses your granddad stuck into that bloody *book*! That's what bloody lists! Oh, for God's sake!"

"Listen to me," I called. I couldn't look at him any more. I backed up against the wall once more, cradling my bag. Trying not to let the futility appear in my voice, I spoke more calmly. "Huw and I, and you, for that matter—have searched that book from cover to cover. If ever they were there, they've long since vanished. It was seventy years ago, for heaven's sake! *There are no lists.* Unless you mean the ship lists? Is there some sort of code? Are the inventories coded in the ship lists? Is that what you mean?" I turned my head. He was still facing me. "Why don't you help yourself and help us find out what all this is about? Can't you see you can't possibly carry on like this? We'll see you don't suffer for it. My father—"

Colin began to laugh, high and uncontrolled. I can't say how horrible it sounded at the bottom of that deep shaft.

"Ship lists! Code! Listen to her! Talk about the Famous Five! 'My father'! Daddy's little girl! You're all the same, you rich people, you think you can cure everything by chucking money at it! Oh, get the hell off me, will you?" He smacked Huw's hand off his shoulder, but Huw caught him by the arm and twisted it behind his back, hard. Colin tried without success to free himself, and snapped: "Sod you, let me go! I'm not going near her!"

Mr Landeck said something then, and I saw Huw's eyes flick to him, then back to Colin.

"Very well," he said, sounding almost as calm as Mr Landeck, and released him. "But I'll break your arm if you lay a finger on her again."

Colin flushed angrily, and jerked himself out of Huw's grasp, but his voice, when he called to me again, was more reasonable. "Listen, Cassie! Kevin and I were going to use those lists to shame Germany into returning stolen property to its rightful owners—my family among them. That's all, I promise! Yes, I had agreed to sell them—and sell them hard; it…it doesn't matter why. Kevin was going to print them as a…as a sort of challenge. He was going to black most of the information out, obviously, but he would have left enough to get people moving."

"Moving?" Mr Landeck asked.

"Yes, moving! In our direction!"

Even at this distance, I saw the puzzled expression on Mr Landeck's face. Colin suddenly lost patience again.

"Financially, you thickhead! God, do I have to spell it out? All right, then: *blackmail*! Got it, at last? Blackmail! I'm sorry, but I don't know what that is in German, but I expect you do." As suddenly, the passion spent itself, leaving him weary and beaten-looking. "I know you think I'm completely unscrupulous, but I wanted to make up to those families for what my great-uncle was forced to do. I didn't want a scandal like that to come out! Would you? Well, would you?"

This sounded a false note somehow, and Huw heard it as well. He gave a disbelieving snort. "What you really mean, you shifty little sod, is that Kevin Dunston somehow found the connection between you and Cassie's grandfather, and suckered you into doing his dirty work with promises of big money from Mother Russia. *That's* the truth, isn't it? I know you're up to your snotty nose in debt, so you can stuff all that sanctimonious guff—I'd sooner believe that you're capable of graduating *cum laude* without stealing other people's work. And as for shaming Germany, by God, at least she's trying to make amends, even if she is making the same old mistakes! 'Make up to those families', indeed! You—you're just a thief, and a thug, and the only reason you're here at all is because whoever bumped off Kevin Dunston frightened you so badly that you arrived here wetting yourself practically before you'd left!"

Colin had wilted long before this molten torrent of words ceased, and I received the impression that this last accusation particularly had struck home. I didn't look at the German, standing silent and still.

Colin hunched a pettish shoulder and said sullenly: "I've told you the truth. That's all, and I don't care a flying...I don't care whether you believe me or not."

Mr Landeck said mildly: "The lists are not as important as that, Mr Bardsey. We are making good progress in reconstructing them from our end, you know."

Colin flared up briefly. "They are sodding important to me, however. They have their price. And God knows I need the money."

I called to him: "Are you going to tell us what for?"

I wanted to reiterate that I might be able to help him, but for some reason I didn't. There was altruism, and then there was sheer stupidity. To be honest, I didn't expect an answer, and was surprised when he spoke.

"To get a loan shark off my back. To pay my debts. All *right*! To keep my name out of it! There, satisfied? To try and salvage something. Kevin was going to change my great-uncle's name in the articles, 'to protect my sources', he said. To... Oh, what's the use! I'm a dead man walking!"

"With the protection of my government—" began Mr Landeck, but Colin turned on him fiercely.

"Could you protect me from the Russians? If you didn't murder Kevin, you realise that they probably did? Does the name of Yuri Saratov mean anything to you? Yes, I see it does! He let me believe that you'd killed Kevin, but it's a hell of a lot more likely that he did. Yes, now I come to think of it, he's exactly the sort of hired heavy who would kill as a matter of course, and not bother to ask questions! What do you think will happen to me if I go home without them?

Can you protect me from Yuri Saratov, *Mr* bloody German Landeck? Can you?"

"Of course we can," said Mr Landeck. "If you are sensible and place yourself under protection. Saratov will not be able to come near you."

He still spoke in that calm, deep voice, but his eyes were watchful. Now I saw them flicker across the well-shaft and up towards the windows on my side. His gaze went straight back to Colin's face, but instantly Colin was suspicious.

"What is it?"

I peered up the steps. I had heard what Mr Landeck had heard: the clatter of descending feet, far up. There was a moment of complete silence, even stillness, into which the sound intruded quite clearly.

I wasn't watching the three on the ramp, so I don't quite know what happened next, except that all at once there was a bustle, a bitten-off exclamation, and a flurry which brought my attention back to them with a snap. Colin, with sudden terror plainly visible in his face, sent Huw staggering, shoved past Mr Landeck, scrambled somehow onto the topmost railing, and jumped in an untidy, impossible sprawl for the nearest window.

FOURTEEN

I will make amends and give a recompense beyond telling…

Book IX, *ibid.*

His FOOT MUST have slipped, because even as he groped for the sill, his head hit the stone with a sickening crack. For a split second he seemed to stick to the wall like a salamander, then slowly, almost lazily, the clawing hand opened, and he slid down the dank, mossy wall into the water. It swallowed him whole with a splash so muted and idle as to be insulting.

The second splash was much louder, and followed so closely behind as to seem part of the first.

"*No!*"

I screamed it, and ran onto the ramp, all fear of the water forgotten. Mr Landeck's jacket lay in a heap where he had flung it, and his spectacles anyhow on top, and he had dived straight in over the railing as neatly as a kingfisher after a minnow.

For a second the black, disturbed water showed a pale blue patch, darkening rapidly as it sank beneath the surface…showed white and greenish-white as Mr Landeck, in his shirtsleeves, felt for and found Colin...paled again as the German brought up the unconscious man. Both heads broke the surface, water-dark hair plastered to their skulls, and streaming. Colin's chin rested in the crook of Mr Landeck's right elbow in the life-saving position, the left temple showing gashed and bleeding. His eyes were shut, and his skin had a grey tinge against which the cuts and bruises from his fights with Huw showed starkly. The black ripples slapped hungrily against the sides of the well shaft.

"He's breathing!" gasped the German, shaking his head and spitting water. "No, don't even try to reach us: we're too far down! I can tread water for a bit. Go and get help!"

This was to Huw, who had flung himself flat on the landing and was stretching down an arm. He realised immediately that this was useless and stood up with a muttered curse of infuriated impotence.

"You stay, Huw. You're stronger, you might be able to... to do something," I said foolishly. "I'll go and tell them we need help—tell them to hurry up. They're...they're closer to the top."

Without waiting for a reply, I turned and ran for the steps.

I didn't think about saving my strength; I just went at them. The noise of my rush helped to deaden the sound of splashing, anyway.

I can't have managed more than fifteen or twenty at that headlong pace before my legs began to fail me. I slowed to a jogtrot—a walk—a crawl—and tried not to remember how far down we were...

Even with both hands on my burning thighs, I wasn't going to make it. I went on anyway, towards the approaching, hurrying footsteps, tears of pain, shock, fright, and exertion slipping down my face. I know I was praying to God, to Hera, to whomever might have ears to hear, to send help...

a doctor...the police... I pressed each leg down on each alternate step and crawled up, up, up towards the footsteps, towards help...and bumped straight into a blue-uniformed figure, who gripped me, and shouted at me in Italian.

My whole being had been so concentrated on those horrible steps, and on my prayer, that to have it answered in this spectacular fashion was like the whole Olympian pantheon coming to Hector's aid. Heaven knows what he thought I was on: I know my face was shining with joy, transfigured through my tears. I clutched eagerly at the gripping arms. I nearly flung my arms round him and hugged him.

"Thank God, you're here, you've got here!" The words wouldn't come out. My knees were jumping and I could hardly keep my balance. I pointed. "Down there! They need help! Please go, oh, please go *now*—there are two men in the water, *hombre in agua*, no, that's Spanish, and one of them's unconscious, he's had a bad crack on the head..."

"*Non parlo Inglese*," he said curtly. He was groping for something in the formidable and pipeclayed armoury at his belt; handcuffs, possibly, or perhaps it was only his truncheon, when a succession of yells for help from the bottom of the well volleyed up to us and caught his attention.

"It's all right, they're coming!"

I tried to shout it, but my voice sounded so feeble that I don't suppose it reached them. The policeman put me aside with a suddenness that took from me any remaining power to stand on my own two feet, and, with a curt order to the men behind him, ran on down. His rapid Italian faded.

I had been so determined not to count the steps on my way up that now I seemed incapable of thinking at all. I merely slid down onto the worn stones and stretched my legs out anyhow, and pressed myself against the wall while the rest of the keen-eyed and fierce-faced police detachment passed me at a businesslike jog-trot. The rearguard, a stout, tough-looking man who was not in uniform, spat something in Italian at me as he trotted past. Unintelligible it might have been, but it was unmistakeably idiomatic, and probably extremely rude. I tried a smile and invited him to go and play in the traffic. Just before he disappeared, I saw that he had what looked like leaf mould in his hair. This was unlikely, but it made me think of Huw, and just then I heard him shouting my name. I couldn't have got to my feet for love or money, so I just shouted back, not caring how desperate I sounded.

"Here! I'm here! Huw!"

Then he rounded the curve and all but fell on top of me. I think he had even started to apologise for this, but I only know that my arms were round him, pulling him to me. Whatever he had been about to say went unsaid as his mouth found mine in a kiss both tender and demanding; possessive, yet somehow freeing. We kissed as though neither of us had eaten or drunk for a month.

"Wow," I said shakily, as soon as my power of speech had been restored. "Suddenly it's a whole lot warmer down here."

He said something else, I think it was in Etruscan, and kissed me again. I don't know how much longer it was before we fell apart and searched each other's faces in wonder through the gloom.

"Thank God," he said. "I've been longing to do that for ages. In fact, I rather think I'd better do it again, just to make sure I've got it right..."

After some time, I surfaced for long enough to assure him that he had got it exactly right.

"Are you sure? Hadn't I better just—what's this I'm lying on? It doesn't feel like you."

"It's not: it's Homer," I replied, on a bubble of laughter.

He said something extremely basic about Homer, and rolled off me and sat up. "Talk about coming down to earth with a thud. How do you feel about trying to stand up again? I think I rather scuppered your last attempt."

"You could put it like that. I'll try if you will."

He stood up and helped me to my feet. We held hands tightly and made our way to the bottom step, where I sank down again to rest against the wall. I had come up far further than I had imagined. I shut my eyes against the thought.

"Stay there!" he commanded.

Only too happy to obey, I watched his tall figure stride out onto the ramp and exchange a word with the policeman who had first grabbed me. There was one of the oval lights just next to me, and by its little glow, I saw what I could already feel: my thigh muscles contracting in long muscular spasms, like the tide going out. I had managed more than a hundred steps. That was quite something. But if they hadn't come when they did...

I heard more descending footsteps then, but I didn't bother even to lift my head. The sound expanded and died, and grew and swelled as it passed each window. Whoever the newcomers were, they were coming in a hurry.

Huw made his way back to me and sat down. His warmth and solidity were wonderful, a miracle, a benison. I cuddled up to him as closely as Homer and my bad shoulder would allow.

"Listen to that," I said. My teeth were chattering, only partly with cold.

"They sound like castanets," agreed Huw. "Or the coconut shells that they use on the radio as horses' hooves. Studio horse. That's what my father always used to say."

"I don't mean my teeth, you twit! There's somebody else coming down. Will they be able to do something? They won't last much longer in there, will they?—the water must be icy—"

Huw said gently: "Believe it or not, darling, they've only been in there about ten minutes, if that. And that'll be the police divers, probably. And lifting gear, and stretchers. They were radio-ing for them. The police station's just behind the Piazzale Cahen."

That was what the policeman had been groping for: his radio. I repeated stupidly: "Lifting gear?"

"He's still alive, Cassie."

I burst into tears.

They lifted Colin first. I didn't watch, and Huw didn't tell me the details at the time. I listened anxiously to the clanging of metal as the lifting gear was assembled in an astonishingly short space of time. Two more loud splashes sounded from what seemed like (and indeed was) the bottom of the well, and some curt commands. More splashing, and a tremendous sucking noise, with water running; then a sodden sort of thump, and more quick-fired commands.

I waited, without wanting to hear any of it, while the performance was repeated. Then footsteps squelched towards us. Huw hugged me.

"That's both of them up safely," was all he said.

Mr Landeck appeared, looking like a dignified and senior *Star Trek* extra in a silver blanket which had been cast round his shoulders cloak-fashion. "Good," he said, with calm satisfaction, "you are both all right. That is excellent." A dark puddle of water was spreading over the ground beneath the rustling silver skirts.

I would have stood to greet him if I could, and not just to get out of the way of the growing puddle, but my knees were not yet my own. I gaped up at him. "*We?*" I repeated incredulously. "We're just fine—but what about you?"

"I've swum in rivers colder than that," he said. "I think the Mediterraneans find that quite difficult to grasp about us northerners. I understand you went to get help. Thank you."

"I didn't get very far," I muttered.

"At least you made the effort. The police were already on their way, I gather, *Gott sei dank*, but considering everything you have already been through this evening, the effort alone is praiseworthy."

There was nothing I could find to say in response to this, so I said nothing. The heat washed up into my face, and I was glad of the dim and cool. It didn't occur to me to wonder how he had come by his information.

I don't know how we would have fared without Mr Landeck. Even soaked to the skin and rustling like a Christmas turkey in his blanket of tin foil, he remained calm, even authoritative, when the police came to question him. He answered their sharp questions in perfect Italian, and when he produced some sort of identification or authorisation from a pocket in his—mercifully dry—jacket, all the police immediately became far more respectful and polite. A lot of excited and much less official conversation then ensued, and, after a while officialdom, in the person of the officer whom I had met on the stairs, turned its attention to Huw and me. He spoke good English, so Mr Landeck went back to the others, and he took our statements there and then, sitting down on the steps beside us. It seemed to take an age, and my attention kept wandering back to the ramp. Colin was already lashed safely onto his stretcher, and I saw Mr Landeck look down at the still figure with a kind of disinterested protectiveness that I hadn't come across before.

The policeman had to repeat his question to me twice before I heard him and made some sort of answer.

The stretcher party began to make its way off the ramp then, taking the opposite staircase. I just had time to see the professional bandage round Colin's head, and the neck brace, before the police started the arduous climb. Mr Landeck came with us. He had disdained a stretcher, he said, explaining that the exercise would warm him up.

They had been alerted by the curator, of course. Huw told me that the man had been showing a group of V.I.P.s round the Pozzo di San Patrizio by special arrangement. He had gone out to answer a call of nature after the party had gone, and just before he closed down for the night. He had seen me dart through the doorway. Unable at just that moment to remonstrate, he found himself obliged to stay put behind his bush and watch helplessly as Colin followed me. Hot on Colin's heels came Mr Landeck, by which time the curator was dancing with rage behind his bush and yelling his head off.

"...so by the time I hurtled along a few seconds later," finished Huw, "having seen the whole thing beautifully floodlit at the end of the lane, and heading—as previously arranged with our obliging German friend, who is acquainted with this hellhole—as fast as I could for the other staircase, the curator was frantically making himself decent again and was out for blood—preferably mine. If I hadn't put a hand to his face and pushed him into the bush, he probably wouldn't have called the police, but in the event it's just as well he did, don't you think?"

I was chuckling weakly, but at this I laughed aloud. "I thought I saw leaf mould in his hair! And then I told him to go and play in the traffic! I expect he speaks fluent English, too."

"How to make friends and influence people in a foreign country. Ah, here *is* the curator. He's offered to escort us up. He does this several times a day, you know."

I shuddered.

It took a little while to placate the indignant man, but when he learnt that both Mr Landeck and Huw had been intent on nothing more than rescuing me from Colin, he became very much more affable, and, with the two policemen detailed to escort us, he took us up the other staircase to the top.

I won't begin to describe that ghastly climb, other than to say that with Mr Landeck bringing up the rear with one policeman, and the curator and the other policeman going ahead of me while Huw supported me, we took the steps in batches of ten, the three of us counting carefully, and with rests in between. Huw declined to count in Etruscan on the score that nobody yet knew the difference between four and six, and apart from ten they hadn't got beyond six (or four) anyway. One of the policemen thought this was a very good game, and by the time we were halfway up that muscle-torturing, endless, purgatorial, God-forsaken well-shaft I could count fluently from one to ten in both Italian and German. I felt for the donkeys, and could cheerfully have murdered both St Patrick and the curator, whose thighs of iron powered him effortlessly up, and whose notion of encouragement was to make copious and obviously stock jokes over his shoulder about the unfitness of tourists.

I'm ashamed to say that it was the smell and sound of dry land, as it were, that drained the last of my resolve from me and saw me collapse in a weeping and pathetic heap not five steps from the top, declaring that I would not move another inch. My assorted escorts were wonderful; indeed, they all seemed glad of another rest. Except for the curator, who cast an indulgent glance at me, and a scornful one at the men, and skipped on up, fresh as a daisy.

When I did finally pull myself together, it was to find a welcome-party of Orvietani and tourists waiting for us, and a policewoman on guard at the door. She was armed, and managed to be both businesslike and glamorous. She and the curator were occupied in frustrating the desire of one or two trippers to make an after-hours tour of the well without paying, and I hid behind Huw and slunk past her on leaden and quivering limbs, passionately glad of the police car we were ushered to.

When I gave my temporary address as the Hotel Soliano, in Assisi, however, smiles vanished and mouths were pulled down, but Huw's stock soared when he disclosed the address of his bed and breakfast.

"*Ecco, va bene*, Giovanna Giffone is my aunt!" said the young officer who spoke English. He had evidently constituted himself our special guide. "I myself take you! She will find you a couch, *signorina*, and we will ring the Soliano and tell them you are safe."

"Perhaps you'd better warn her first," I said. "She'll think we're Orvieto's Most Wanted otherwise, arriving home with a police escort—even if you are her nephew."

We were halfway along the Corso Cavour when I remembered.

"The Panda!" I exclaimed. "We left it in the Piazzale, and I've run out of petrol! How am I to get back to Assisi? What am I going to do? Officer..."

"Is a white one, lights on, sunroof open, doors open? Everything open?" enquired the police driver coldly over his shoulder.

I bit my lip and nodded. "That's the one." I could tell that this was not popular. I tried a placatory smile. "We managed to turn off the radio," I said hopefully.

"It is in the pound," he said, unplacated. "It was on the wrong side of the road, and was causing an obstruction. It has been towed away—and yours too, sir," he added, throwing Huw a cold stare as though it were his fault. "You may fetch them tomorrow when we have finished with you. There will be a fine." At least, that's what Mr Landeck, jammed between us in the back, told me he said.

"I'm awfully sorry," I said humbly. "I couldn't find how to turn anything off, or…or shut them. I'm sorry," I said again, "but my friend was in trouble. I had to rescue him."

"È allora," said Luigi, surprised, from the passenger's seat. He turned and peered at us round the head-rest. "In his statement, he say he come to rescue you!"

"That's also true," said Huw. "Er, the man in the well…"

"Yes?"

"He pinched my wallet and my car. I don't suppose there's any chance of getting my wallet back from him at any point, is there?"

Luigi looked puzzled. "So that is why you were chasing him, yes?"

"Not entirely," confessed Huw. "You see, I know him well from college in England. I'm afraid he's none too scrupulous about how he gets his degree. My friend here happens to be something else he's not over-scrupulous about."

Luigi gave me a speculative, rather doubtful glance that yet contrived to hold a good deal of understanding, and said positively: "This is not in your statements."

"Well, no," I said, following Huw's lead. "You didn't ask, for one thing, and for another—well, it didn't seem… I mean, it's not something you just… I'm awfully sorry if I've…" I let my voice peter out.

The young policeman shrugged, then gave me a dazzling smile. With a commendable grasp of essentials, he said: "*Va bene.* Boys will be boys, eh? My aunt will look after you both. She is famous in all Orvieto."

In the event, Giovanna Giffone provided more than a couch. She produced not only a profuse apology to Huw for being the unwitting cause of our trouble, but also a sumptuous lamb stew and two bottles of wine, all of which Huw and I despatched gratefully and at record speed. While we ate, Luigi told her the story. Not that I understood a word of the conversation flowing over our heads, but the body language was unmistakeable, as were the broad smiles and mock grimaces of pain on the faces of both aunt and nephew, and the occasional droll glance in my direction. I smiled back, and ate and drank steadily, deliberately not catching Huw's eye.

After her nephew had left, Giovanna escorted me to a spotless bathroom in peach enamel, and lent me an impossibly glamorous nightgown in peach satin, which made me feel, if anything, rather worse. She made me undress, and tended my ankle and my shoulder, then she showed me to a bedroom, also spotless, and just as glamorous, and bore away every last stitch of my clothing, including my shoes.

The police had promised to come back in the morning. Huw was somewhere under the same roof. Mr Landeck had vanished, presumably to his own hotel. The Panda was safe, even if it was in the police pound. I hoped somebody had managed to shut the sunroof. I took one look at the bath, and shook my head. Then I fell into bed and was asleep in a second.

FIFTEEN

Zeus doth stablish peace between the foes, even he that is
men's dispenser of battle.

Book IV, *ibid.*

I WOKE LATE the next morning, and lay for a bit wondering
sleepily why my room had changed its décor overnight and
where Assisi had gone to. Then realisation broke through,
and I tried to sit up, yelping as my assorted aches and pains
bit. The sight of the peach satin brought everything back,
and I looked round the room rather wildly. My clothes were
on a chair, neatly folded; the blessed woman had washed
and dried and ironed everything, and brushed mud and grass
from my shoes.

I washed and dressed as well as I could with a stiff ankle,
a badly bruised shoulder, and thigh muscles that seemed to
have turned into concrete, then sat down on the bed and
pulled my bag towards me for a comb.

The first thing I saw was the Homer, one corner peeping
coyly at me, and the bookmark in the page where the ship-
lists were. I made a bulldog-and-wasp face at it, found the

comb and tried to make something of what remained of my hair-do, then slung the bag over my undamaged shoulder and stood up. Vaguely surprised and pleased to find myself able to walk, I turned into the corridor and examined the doors on either side.

I had gone a few steps before I realised I didn't know which was Huw's room. Feeling rather a fool, I stood there looking up and down as though I could conjure him out of thin air, when a door opened, and he came out. I limped towards him eagerly and a little shyly. "Thank heavens, I didn't know where your room was. Are you okay? Did you sleep?"

One cheek was bruised and cut, and there was a plaster on his forehead, but he looked clean and pressed, and somehow brand-new. We surveyed each other. There was a little constraint this morning, almost as though the rest of us needed time to catch up with that sudden lifting of the barriers on the stairs last night.

"Like a log," he said. "And I'm fine, just rather sore in quite a few unusual places. What about you?"

"I'm jolly sore as well, and a bit subdued, what with everything, but I slept well, and hey, I'm alive." I caught at myself. "I shouldn't have said that."

"Why not? We're all alive, and thank God for that. Let's see if Giovanna will run to breakfast."

"Do you mind if we don't? Run, that is? I don't think I could. Oh, dear, I'd forgotten about these stair things. Why will people have them? How did I get up them last night?"

"On all fours. Luigi and I offered to carry you, but for some reason you didn't fancy it."

This made me laugh, and constraint vanished. I took his hand. "Now, don't rush me," I told him sternly.

"Think of the coffee."

Indeed, the rich scents wafting up were seductive enough to tempt a hermit out of his cave. We put our noses in the air like the Bisto Kids and followed them, taking the stairs very, very slowly.

No terrace here, and no richly domestic landscape to refresh the soul. But we could see Orvieto's roofscape, which was romantic enough, and made me think of *A Room with a View*. I took my place opposite him, suddenly conscious of the domestic setting of Giovanna's dining-room, and consequently suffused once again with shyness. But Huw, eating, rather like my Uncle Will, as though he wouldn't see food again for a fortnight, seemed to be unaffected by anything except hunger, and I soon lost my shyness. We were still sitting over coffee when Mr Landeck arrived with Luigi.

The daylight revealed Mr Landeck to be an inch or two over six feet and slimly built, with straight, light-brown hair thinning at the temples. His spectacles were of the unrimmed sort which at a distance seem to disappear against the face. This was of a clerkly pallor proper to a government employee, but there was an elastic toughness to him that belied his calm manner. I remembered the way in which he had handled Colin; that unhesitating dive into the inky waters. If Colin was still alive this morning, he owed it to Mr Landeck. At Giovanna's invitation, he sat down and accepted some coffee, and we surveyed each other a little awkwardly.

"Please call me Helmut," he said. "Since we were thrown together last night in such frightening circumstances, it would be absurd to insist on formalities."

I accepted this with an increasing interest in him, since although he was in jeans, the rest of him was formally dressed in shirt and tie, and the same blazer as last night. A covert glance at the tie revealed it to be patterned with rabbits. It has never been a favourite get-up of mine for a man: it so often looks awkward, as though the man had changed his mind halfway through dressing, but on this man it somehow didn't.

"And now we talk. Since you made your statements last night, you will not mind Luigi's taking notes: he is doing so at the behest of my government."

We glanced at Luigi, who smiled widely. He had laid down his white helmet, in shape so like those of our own policemen, and also the radio which he wore slung over his left shoulder. As he sat down, I saw for the first time, and with a vague sense of alarm, the white holster at his left hip. He adjusted this comfortably, saw me looking, patted it, and winked solemnly at me.

Helmut said: "I must first of all tell you that Colin has survived the night, and is expected to make a recovery. There is, however, the danger of some damage to the brain. It will be some time before the hospital can assess whether this is the case, and if so, how much. He has a bad concussion."

"Which hospital?" asked Huw.

"Santa Maria Stella Maris. It is in the Via San Domenico."

"You saved his life," I said. "The speed at which you reacted—well, it was amazing."

I hadn't meant it to sound faintly questioning, but he smiled at us.

"You will be wanting to know how I come into all this, I have no doubt."

"I did wonder," I said.

"Very well, then. I am retained by the German government to negotiate in all matters relating to works of art misappropriated during the last war. I was sent over to England to talk to a young man who was doing some research for a local paper, who unfortunately had made himself unpopular in certain quarters."

"Kevin Dunston," nodded Huw, in a satisfied tone.

"That's the man Colin accused you of—who Colin said had been murdered," I hurriedly amended.

"He was certainly murdered, but not by me. The Oxford police had been authorised to let me search his flat, however, and I found—this." He put a hand inside his jacket and pulled out a pocket-book. From it, he extracted a bit of paper, which looked familiar.

"*Oh…*" I breathed, on a long sigh. "The missing page from the diary!"

"Just so." Mr Landeck carefully spread it out on the table, and we craned over it. It said:

…so assiduously compiling. I nipped in and had a look, and he's pasted them into the back of the Homer, I could feel them. I can't get at them, and if I try, he'll know it's me. I am at my wits' end; I have to have those papers. The Breughel arrived safely, so my mole tells me, but it hardly seems to matter now. God knows what the Russians will do to me—if they find me before the Germans do. This will probably be my last entry. Shalom.

Huw and I exchanged a glance of triumph tinged with sadness. I said: "We saw that a leaf had been torn out, and guessed that it must have been either Kevin or Colin. I'm so glad you've got it. Will you be able to return it to the museum?"

"Eventually, of course. But just for the time being, it is classed as evidence."

"Of course. Why are you showing us this?" I asked. "Isn't it classified, or something?"

"This? Not exactly. I had already ascertained from the curator that you paid a visit to Hythe and had seen the diary.

There was no harm in showing you this page. But alas it gets us no closer to the inventories."

"Have you really been reconstructing them?" asked Huw.

"Only partially," he replied. "I said that to take some of the tension out of the situation, in the hope that Colin might be induced to relax a little and trust me. Oh, some things we know, but not nearly enough. Truly, I presented no threat to him—quite the contrary—but when a man is desperate, the only safe person to trust is nobody." He drank some coffee, and Giovanna silently refilled all three cups.

For a moment, I was embarrassed, and looked at the table. Then I said: "Go on. You seemed to appear from nowhere. How did you get on to us so quickly? And how on earth did you know where to find us?"

He twinkled at me. "I had orders to keep an eye on Colin. I was on the same flight out."

"But all the same, you couldn't have known where to find us," I protested.

"I had someone follow Colin when I got here. I had a little essential business to execute in the meantime. It was unrelated to this, but you will remember that Italy was Germany's ally during the war...? Very well, I need say nothing more." He smiled at my expression. "My running into you all like that was not such a great stroke of luck as it might have appeared. The colleague tailing Colin simply followed him to Assisi, and your progress all the way back to Orvieto, and rang me to say that if I came up by the *funicolare* and waited for a little, I would, er, bag all three of you in the Piazzale Cahen. This I did. I had descriptions. It was easy."

I said blankly: "Good God."

"And we hadn't even got round to wondering about that, had we?" said Huw in admiration. "One up to you, Helmut."

He twinkled at us. "Would you, Huw, now be so kind as to tell me about this article you mentioned yesterday while we were waiting for the police to finish their fishing expedition and take their catch away?"

I smiled to myself. This had been said with the straightest of faces.

"It's how I got involved with Colin in the first place. You seem to know so much, it's probably redundant my telling you that this lady is Cassie Greatrex, and her father writes for a magazine called *The Ready Writer*."

"That I did not know," said Helmut. "I was aware of the lady's identity, however. But please."

So Huw told him everything, and Giovanna went to make another pot of coffee, and Luigi sat in the corner taking notes.

"And we still have no clue about the lists he kept on about. We'd worked it out about the inventories, but he kept trying to get hold of the Homer, and we thought then that they might have been encoded, you know, in the ship lists in Book Two, but what you've just shown us puts the kibosh on that. And there's definitely nothing behind that pasted page: we've searched the book from end to end."

"Where is the book, Cassie?"

"It's here. I shall have to have it surgically removed: we have become too attached." I dragged poor old Homer out and laid him on the table. He looked as gleaming and undamaged as ever, despite his exciting experiences, and I breathed a sigh of relief. Helmut patted a pocket and brought out a magnifying glass and a torch. He examined the page with the bookmark, then turned to the inside back cover.

"Ah, yes, I see this has been pasted down at some point in the past. But no papers."

"No," I agreed, with feeling. "My grandfather brought it round for me when it got back from the bookbinders, and surely if they had unstuck that page and found something, they would have at least mentioned it to him?"

"Most certainly; and returned anything that was not part of the book; flowers, perhaps, or love letters… most certainly inventories of persons concerned in war crimes." This, too, with the utmost solemnity, as well as the twinkle. He was gently feeling round the edges. "No, nothing under there but the leather binding. Would you be so kind?"

"Of course." I took the torch and held it for him.

"Thank you. Now then, this is most interesting. If you would care to look very closely at the underside of this page, you will perhaps be able to see that the ink has become transferred to it."

We bent, and peered. The torchlight showed the faintest brown markings.

"That must mean they were there for some time, surely?" I hazarded.

"Not necessarily. It could be that your grandfather stuck them straight in and the endpaper blotted the ink. However—"

"If that were the case," remarked Huw, "there'd be little or no marking at the top, would there? I mean, ink dries as you go along." He studied the page. "This is uniformly marked all the way down, which would seem to indicate that Cassie is right."

"Indeed, yes. This is my own opinion also."

"Can you make anything of it?" asked Huw with professional interest.

"Inscriptions…" I murmured, and realised with a slight shock that I sounded exactly like my mother.

"There are photographic techniques we can employ, certainly," replied Helmut. "These will prove that the papers, the lists, were here as the diary entry says they were."

"But where are they now?" I asked rather hopelessly, as I had done before so many times.

"Probably long since lost," said Helmut, turning down the corners of his mouth, and shrugging. "It is too much to expect that they would still be *in situ* after all this time. Well, but no matter. We will write to your grandfather, Cassie, and ask for permission to examine the book thoroughly and do some tests. There will be much to gain even from a partial inventory. And we will ask him," he added, smiling, "whether he encoded the inventories as well."

"My grandfather knows nothing about this," I said quickly.

"Really? But this is his book," said Helmut in surprise.

"Yes, but he's never said a thing about them, and if he knew they were there, he would never in a million years have lent me his *Iliad* so casually, never mind let me bring it to Italy with me. Huw and I had already decided that. He was wounded during the—he was wounded in Berlin, and we think he must have lost his memory. Besides, he can only have pasted them into the Homer to get them safely out of the country. He'd have handed them to the right quarters long ago, wouldn't he? It would be difficult, if not impossible, to broach this with him without stirring up a whole lot of... you know..."

"I quite understand. Well, we will think of a way. Do you happen to know where in Berlin he was stationed?"

I thought back. "No. Not in so many words. He did say he'd been guarding Heinrich Schliemann's treasures from Troy, not that that's much help. That's how he came to lend me the—" I got no further.

"*Ach, du lieber Gott!*" exclaimed Helmut Landeck. He seemed to expand where he sat. "The Zoo tower itself! *Was für ein Glücksfall! Um Gottes willen!*" He struck himself on the forehead, quite hard. "I beg your pardon. Your grandfather is alive, yes, you have said, but is he—*es tut mir leid*, I am so excited, I forget my English…"

"I expect you mean, is he *compos mentis*," offered Huw, throwing another language into the melting pot.

"Oh, he's all there," I said. "I mean—"

"I am familiar with the idiom," said Helmut, subsiding again and all at once very correct. "*Also gut.* The Zoo tower was a target for the Allies—it was surrounded by flak towers, you see, and these were badly bombed."

"Was the Zoo tower hit?"

"No, but the gardens were, and the animal houses."

I looked at the table. For some reason, I can just about stand what man does to man, but not what he does to animals. Not that I'd ever given it much thought, but I realised now that it's because man, however disenfranchised, always has a voice, even if nobody listens, even if he doesn't dare raise it. Animals have none.

"And the Troy treasures?" asked Huw.

"After this bombing Major Greatrex writes of, the Russians came," said Helmut, "and again Berlin was bombed. This time the Pre- and Early History Museum was razed. We know that the boxes with the Troy treasures were removed to the Zoo tower, but this was in the closing weeks of the war and—well, when I tell you that in under three months, the Russians had advanced over two hundred miles, you will understand that there was confusion, and haste."

Huw gave a crack of laughter, somewhat to Helmut's surprise, and I grinned. "That must be the understatement of the century," I said. "No, don't mind us; that's just English irony. Grandpa told me he hadn't wanted to hang about in case the Russians found him and thought he was German." Too late I heard what I had said, and blushed hotly. "I'm so sorry, that was unforgivably clumsy of me."

He smiled charmingly. "*Es mach' nichts*. It doesn't matter at all. For all of us in this room, it is past. We are not obliged to fight. We can be friends, for our grandfathers' sakes. *Naja*, then their sacrifice is not wasted, eh?"

I saw Luigi lift his head and give Helmut a long, considering look in which I thought I saw grave approval. Then his eyes dropped to his notebook again.

I said slowly: "You could argue that people are not altogether responsible for what they do under a dangerous and corrupting influence."

"The dangerous and corrupting influence being the rhetoric of the little Austrian? Well, maybe you're right. Nevertheless, we must still clear up the mess we make, while we work out what lay behind the dangerous and corrupting influence."

"I won't argue with that," I said slowly, not fully understanding.

"I don't suppose," said Huw, "that there's any way of finding out what happened to the treasures of Troy?"

I smiled, and wondered what my father would say if he could have been privy to this conversation.

Helmut made a fist, turned it over, and examined the nails. He said, and I could tell he was choosing his words: "Some are found, and safe; others are not. I should say it is highly unlikely that they will ever be together again. For some time, the climate has been, shall we say, less friendly than hitherto. There is less co-operation than there should be between Germany and Russia. You will understand why I say this."

"Hence this Russian Colin was so afraid of?" asked Huw.

"Yes, Yuri Saratov. My Russian counterpart—or at least that is the official version." He saw our questioning expressions, and elaborated: "Remember, I am a professional negotiator. It was Saratov's job to mediate, if you like, as it is mine."

"I wondered last night if you were," I said, pleased. "You had the feel of it."

"You are familiar with what I do?" He looked interested, but there was no disbelief or scorn. I warmed further to him, but disclaimed.

"Gosh, no, not at all, nothing as grown-up as that. It's just that you were so utterly rock-like and unflappable with poor Colin, and I was reminded of Dinah, and the way she handles difficult clients. The ruder and the more demanding they are, the calmer she becomes. They always end up purring."

"Dinah?"

I said awkwardly: "A school friend of mine. She runs a beauty salon in Chelsea. I put up the money for it and work there three mornings a week. Some of our clients have tremendous psychological problems, and she's just brilliant at handling them. She listens, and draws it all out of them, and it gets thrown away with the cotton wool. At least until the next time." I stopped, feeling an utter fool. "I'm sorry, it's hardly relevant."

"But they come back?" asked Helmut.

"Yes," I said. "Yes, they do."

"That is the test," he nodded. "You will have then also some good idea of what I am trying to do, but on perhaps a larger scale."

He reminded me of the way Huw had accepted my widely different experience of life as being on a par with his own. I won't say I felt myself to be their equal, suddenly, either in intellect or in training—that would be ridiculous; but perhaps it was only a question of degree after all. An animal is an animal, whether it's an elephant or a mouse.

"It is regrettable—so much is regrettable—that Yuri Saratov had a different approach to the recovery of those lists," Helmut was saying. "Under Russia's present governance, it has become acceptable to shoot first and ask questions later—if at all."

Huw sat up at this. "Kevin Dunston was *shot?*"

"That is so. In the back. The Russian calling-card."

"He sounds more like a contract killer than a professional negotiator!"

"Just so. Saratov searched the flat and found nothing. My training is perhaps superior, however." A reminiscent smile that gave him, fleetingly, the look of a satisfied polar bear. "These ineffable, priceless treasures that Major Greatrex was guarding as a young officer were removed by the Russian troops. Nothing more was heard of them, and the fact that the Russians were interested enough in Kevin Dunston to send a man after him to silence him would seem to suggest that when they left Berlin, the Troy treasures went with them. But you understand, we have no proof. This is why Major Greatrex's testimony is so very valuable. It is as you say a long shot, but there might be a clue, a hint as to their destination."

"Major?" I repeated. "He signs himself Lieutenant in that piece." I jerked my chin dismissively at the Homer. I hated the very sight of it.

"Ah, yes," said Helmut. "But he came out of the Royal Regiment of Rifles as major, in 1964, at the end of his regular commission."

I stared open-mouthed. I felt as I had when Huw had told me about *The Ready Writer* and my father's contributions.

"I didn't know," I said humbly. "I'm horrified by how little I seem to know about my own family. Everyone seems to know more than I do."

"You are young. This is natural." Helmut took out his notecase and put the sad little diary entry carefully away, and stood up. "I must go and make a report. This is my card. I shall be here for a little while longer. Please contact me if you need to." He put the slip of pasteboard down on the table. Then he frowned. "You say—he *signed* himself Lieutenant? In the Homer, somewhere, perhaps?"

I felt Huw's eyes on me. I said: "There was something stuck between the last two endpapers." I added in a hurry: "But it wasn't the inventories."

SIXTEEN

Headstrong man and violent of deed,
that recked not of his evil doings…!

Book V, *ibid.*

IMMEDIATELY I HAD his full attention. It was like standing under a spotlight. Behind him, Luigi quickly looked up again.

"Oh? This is the piece of which you speak? You have it with you?"

"Yes," I answered unhappily. "It's just that—you might find it distressing. I'm sorry I didn't tell you before, but you'll see why. It's about Berlin. It's just something my grandfather wrote. It's nothing to do with treasures, or…or anything. It was stuck over the top of where the inventories were. We decided it must have been to camouflage them." I took it out of the notebook I kept in my bag and rather hesitantly gave it to him.

He read it through carefully, and his face changed, but all he said was: "A remarkable piece of writing. Quite poetic. May I ask how you found it?"

I screwed up my mouth. "It was after a particularly unpleasant visit from Colin. He'd got his sticky paws on it, the book, I mean, and I... Well, after that, I kept it in the safe. I was looking at it one day, and I turned to the back, as he had done—and there it was." I cleared my throat. "I'm ashamed to say I'd dropped the book the first day my grandfather lent it to me. The jolt must have unstuck what was left of the old glue. I thought it was what Colin was after, but it wasn't. We even checked it for pencil marks—you know, in case there was a code or something."

He lifted his brows and nodded. He was reading it again. Then with a smile, he carefully refolded it and gave it back to me. "As you say, there are no clues. He must have been very frightened. Bombs have a habit of falling indiscriminately sometimes. Well, well. Thank you for showing me."

I said: "Mr Landeck—Helmut—before you go, there're one or two more things. If my grandfather has to be told, my parents will have to know as well." I gestured slightly to my and Huw's marks of battle. "With your permission, of course. I don't think I'll be able to keep it from them, and I'd rather their knowing had official backing. I mean, they're involved anyway, because of the break-in. Is it all right?"

He was silent for quite some time. Then he nodded slowly. "Yes, I agree; they will have to know. Very well, you may tell them." He gave me a charming grin. "And you, as my colleague, will escort the Homer back to Britain for me, together with this piece about the bombing, and there you will deliver it to your grandfather, so that I may do this thing properly. I will need his signature for it, and he must have a receipt."

My dismay grew throughout this, but I tried to conceal it. "Very well," I said without enthusiasm. "As long as you don't want me to go down any more wells. That I do draw the line at."

"It will not be necessary. And the other things you wished to ask?"

"I wondered whether we might go and visit Colin in hospital. Do you think that might be possible?"

Helmut looked round enquiringly at Luigi.

"I will tell the hospital to expect you," said Luigi. "Both of you?"

"Not me, at least not just yet," said Huw. "I must go back to work."

"I'll go," I said. "But there are things I'd like to know first."

"Such as?" Luigi was putting his notebook back in the spotless white saddlebag at his right hip, and as he buckled the flap, he subjected me to the same considering look he had given Helmut.

"Medical bills, if any. I don't suppose he'll have thought of insurance, he came out in such a hurry. Does he have family, for example?"

"Why do you care?"

The question was honestly put, and I tried to answer honestly. "I'm not sure I do, exactly, but we can't just leave him. I know we're in no sense responsible for him, but he only did what he did because he was desperate."

Luigi pulled down the corners of his mouth and lifted one shoulder. "I will ask my divisional superior if I can accompany you. There, I shall ask all the questions you require to have answered. *Va bene?*"

I said gratefully: "*Va molto bene* indeed, if that's the correct Italian. Thank you very much."

"I wonder what *de nada* is in Etruscan?" mused Huw, drinking coffee. Luigi and I laughed.

"*Also gut.*" In his only example of stereotypical German behaviour, Helmut Landeck clicked his heels together, bowed over my hand and turned to leave. Then something seemed to occur to him. "Now, before I forget, it is my turn to ask a question, Huw, if you please. In what way, in your opinion, is Germany repeating her mistakes?"

I gave a little gasp, but Huw didn't hesitate. He put down his cup and saucer.

"The best way I can put it is to say that one size doesn't fit all: it fits nobody."

Helmut considered this. "You would have me understand that Germany's approach is not...suitable for other E.U. countries?"

"Not only is it not suitable, it's looking positively dangerous. Look at Greece, or Spain. The way to make any necessary amends is to support your allies as far as possible in a way that suits them, not yourself. That doesn't only apply to Germany, by the way."

Helmut's mouth thinned a little. "There is no coercion," he said stiffly.

"I beg your pardon, but there is: financial coercion. It may not be at the muzzle of a Sten gun anymore, it's more subtle than that. Too subtle for most people to do more than feel, and resent without knowing why. That's dangerous— just as dangerous as...as the other way."

"Too much nanny-state, eh?"

"Far too much. Only the infirm need a crutch. The rest of us just need the occasional helping hand. And that we can provide for ourselves and each other, for the most part. Would you give tuppence for an organisation whose own auditors have refused for the best part of two decades to sign off its accounts properly? Or whose elected Parliament is a parliament in name only? No, thanks."

Luigi said from the door: "In my country, we are desperate to regain our differences, our individualities. Here, it is only the government that likes centralisation. Centralisation is power. I spit on it, and on greedy little men who print money to make themselves yet more powerful."

"Bankers!" said Helmut with a comprehensive gesture that made us smile and lessened the tension that had crept in.

Huw said with a tinge of apology: "You did ask."

"Indeed yes. Your answer is brave, and honest—and very probably shows us the way forward."

"That, from you?"

"But yes, why not? I happen to agree with you. So do many in Germany—and probably all over the Continent. I have one more question. Cassie, please, why the Pozzo?"

"Oh, dear," I said, beginning to laugh. "I thought it was a public lavatory. I'm so sorry, Luigi, I don't intend the least insult. I had some idea of locking myself in. When I saw it wasn't... Well, by then it was too late. I couldn't go back, so I had to go on."

A pleased smile widened Helmut Landeck's mouth. "Ding dong bell, Cassie's in the well," he said surprisingly.

"Don't," I said.

"*Alles verstanden.* Good morning."

He was chuckling to himself as he left.

Luigi said: "He knows everything, that one. Everything. I too go and make my report. I will ring here with a time for the hospital." He shouted something to his aunt, who called something back that made him laugh, and he strode off. We heard the front door bang again.

Huw sighed into the silence. "I don't even know what day of the week it is. I suppose I must go back to work. I would love to go sightseeing, but I don't dare. I'm going to be in enough trouble as it is, explaining away the state I'm in."

"I shouldn't think Colin's left you any money to go sightseeing with," I said.

"I haven't got my wallet back yet, but that is more than likely. All the more reason to go and earn some."

"*Does* he have family?" I asked.

"I have no idea. If not, I expect the Italian police will know who to inform. I should have offered to tell the Dean. Someone's going to have to."

"Yes." I let out a long breath. "I could tell Luigi this afternoon that you're going to find out, if you like."

"Thank you."

I said, somewhat confusedly: "It seems so…lonely."

"He is lonely." He took my hands and folded them between his own. "Perhaps it's better this way, darling. I mean, if his brain does turn out to be damaged. Once someone gets the gambling bug badly, he's a target for every parasite. I swear they can smell people like Colin from five hundred paces. Where would it have ended?"

"That man, the journalist, was murdered," I said.

"Yes?"

"Well, with Colin out of the way, aren't we still in danger?"

"Sweetheart, no. How can we be?"

"I've still got the Homer."

"But the lists aren't in it. Both sides know that now."

"N…no. I mean, yes."

"And if Colin couldn't put his hands on them to photocopy them, or whatever, with his *entrée* to the Greatrex family, how is anybody else going to?"

I hadn't anything to say in reply to this, but the illogical feeling persisted. I said discontentedly: "I suppose I'd better go and see about the Panda. I wish I'd thought of it before Luigi left. I could have gone with him."

"We'll go together."

"Oh, crumbs, of course, there's your car, as well. Thank goodness one of us has some money."

So we went together (in a taxi, which Giovanna called for us), and Huw picked up his keys and his (empty) wallet, and I paid two huge fines, for Huw's car, which he promised faithfully to retrieve later on, and to get the Panda out of the pound. We piled thankfully into the Panda, then we couldn't drive it anywhere because the battery was flat, so a police car came along and got it started, and we crept away on our best behaviour, but we didn't get further than a few yards because I'd forgotten we'd run out of petrol.

And there we stayed, weak with laughter, until Luigi was sent to find out why we were sitting there and blocking the entrance. He put in a litre for us and told us he would pay for it himself. He bent through the driver's window to give me directions to the closest petrol station.

"And visiting begins this afternoon, sixteen hundred hours. I will meet you there."

I agreed to this, my laughter quenched. We thanked him and drove decorously out of the gates.

"The police station's another place we daren't show our faces, and now I'm going to make myself notorious at the hospital by arriving with a police escort," I said.

"I'll tell you another still, and that's the museum. Will you walk with me?"

"Of course...but have you got time for lunch first? A proper sit-down lunch? You can always say you've spent the morning with the police—and that's the truth."

Huw hesitated, and I hurried into speech again. "I'm sorry; of course you want to get back to work. Will you get into trouble? We'll go now. Never mind about lunch."

"It's not that. I haven't got any money."

"I know you haven't. But I have." As he still seemed to be hesitating, I said: "Huw, this is the twenty-first century."

He looked surprised. "It's not that. It's just that I would have liked to treat you, that's all. There's a place nearby where all Orvieto eats—and that's the best recommendation."

I was touched, and a little ashamed. "I'm sorry. I didn't mean to come the heavy-handed feminist. I suppose I'm so used to my parents regarding me as though I'm not all there."

"Do they? That wasn't the impression they gave me. Are you sure it's not really you who thinks you mightn't be 'all there'?"

I was astounded, and could find no answer.

"People tend to take one at one's own estimation, I find," he went on. "Besides, if you knew what academic hares you've started in my brain, you'd be jolly proud of yourself."

"W…would I?"

"Indeed yes. There's such a thing as being too specialised; too close to a subject."

"Not seeing the wood for the trees?"

"Exactly. Thanks to a chance remark you made, I'm halfway out of the valley and seeing both wood and trees far more clearly."

"Really?"

"Really. Don't ask me to tell you what I'm talking about. I'd rather put some work in on a new theory first. Then I'll tell you, and, what's more, I'll credit you properly."

"If you think I'd understand more than two words," I replied, baffled but game. "Come on, where's this restaurant of yours?"

We parked the Panda properly this time (and paid for it), then dawdled up the Corso Cavour, looking in all the shops. We had a proper sit-down lunch in a shady little street; and after

I had waved Huw off to work, I sat for a bit over my coffee. Now, in the time I had before visiting Colin, would have been the perfect opportunity for a little gentle sightseeing round the charms of Orvieto. I might even have explored the inviting flight of paved steps I had glimpsed, that curved gently up between the old houses. As it was…

I sighed, and lowering my expectations, regarded the Duomo thoughtfully.

The blue-and-white stripes theme was continued inside, and it was blissfully cool. Draping my cardigan round my shoulders, I found my way to a side chapel and sat down to contemplate some frescoes depicting the Apocalypse.

Nearby was a middle-aged couple, also apprehensively surveying the writhing, tormented figures. I think something must have shown on my face, because the woman, seeing me, slid into the next seat but one to mine and put a hand on my arm.

"Are you all right?"

She spoke English; indeed, she was English. "Feeling the heat?"

I certainly wasn't up to explaining, so I smiled and nodded.

"We're not used to it, coming from England. You are English? Yes, I thought so. I was just saying to my husband, wasn't I, Ron? Very shick, but still English."

She said this as though it were a compliment, which indeed it was. She had one of those ironed-out North Country voices that make you long to say 'do I 'eck as like' or 'ee bah goom' or 'I'll go to the foot of our stairs' to get her to speak more naturally.

"You want to try the guided tour of the caves if you're sightseeing—get you out of the sun. Nice and cool down there. We did it yesterday."

"Caves?" I echoed. "Underground...caves?"

She eyed me slightly askance. "Well, yes, they usually are." She tittered. "Hewn out of the tufa, they said. Funny word. There's all sorts, wait a moment, I've got some info somewhere..." She fished in the pocket of her nylon rucksack. Producing a sheaf of papers printed off the internet, she rapidly scanned it. "Yes, here we are; this is it: ...*tunnels, galleries, wells, stairs, quarr*—"

"Wells?"

"Yes, that's right. Where was I? *Quarries...*"

I cleared my throat. "And—stairs, I think you said?"

"Yes... Yes, that's right, stairs." The tone was definitely doubtful now, and she glanced down as though to check that the Orvieto Tourist Board had not wilfully misled her.

"No stairs today, thank you," I said firmly, as though she were trying to sell me some.

"No? It says that the Pozzo di San Pa—"

"No!" I caught at myself. "No wells, either, thank you. No wells at all."

"Oh." She surveyed me critically. "That's a nasty cut on your face. Did you fall down or something?"

"Something like that," I said.

She stood up, looking over her shoulder for her husband, and hastily stuffing the sheaf of papers into the wrong pocket. "Well, if you're quite sure," she began. She was backing away from me.

"Quite sure," I said, nodding firmly. "Absolutely, utterly, completely, one hundred per cent sure. Thank you."

I took another taxi to the hospital.

Luigi was there, chaffing a couple of shiny-eyed nurses. As I clambered slowly out and stood contemplating the steps up to the hospital entrance, they tore their adoring collective gaze away from the undeniably handsome Luigi, and looked at me. I had done what I could to remove yesterday's mascara, and I had put on lipstick, but like the policewoman last night, they combined a businesslike efficiency with effortless, specifically Italian elegance. I couldn't slink by in the dark this time, so I had to brazen it out; but it's difficult to brazen anything out when you haul yourself up the wheelchair ramp gripping the railing as though you were eighty-two instead of twenty-two. My grandfather would have put up a far better show.

"There is a lift," said Luigi, grinning. "No stairs."

"Thank God for that," I said.

Colin was barely recognisable. He lay straight and silent in his high hospital bed, still with the orange neck brace on. I turned a shocked face to the nurse who had accompanied us, and Luigi translated her explanation for me.

"It is a precaution. It has not yet been possible to assess him properly."

The nurse's gaze flickered to me, then to Luigi, and she began talking in rapid Italian. Luigi listened intently, his head bowed, and occasionally nodding. When she had finished, he said to me: "You are thinking I understood all of that. I did not." He smiled at the nurse. "I think she was telling me exactly what's wrong with him."

"Oh. Please say that I do not understand medical matters, and could we have that again very, very simply? Will he recover, or not?"

Luigi rendered this in Italian, and the nurse replied with a shrug.

"They will not know until the physical condition stabilises and they can do some tests."

The nurse threw me a perfunctory smile and tapped her head. I think she meant Colin's condition rather than her assessment of my intellect.

"Ask her, please, if they have any details of his family."

Luigi relayed this. The answer was short and rather horrifying.

"None. He came from a children's home. His next of kin is somebody at Oxford University—somebody called Dean. There is another name. Wait, I make a note…"

The *Dean*? "No, don't worry—the Dean is the person in charge of his college. Luigi, that's *awful*. Nobody at all?"

Luigi shrugged, and forgetting my hurts, I found my own shoulders rising in sympathy. I winced as the muscles creaked in protest, and reflected that at least the hospital would relieve Huw of the responsibility of informing the Dean.

"In that case," I said, "I would like to make myself financially responsible for him while he's here, if necessary, and ultimately for his—repatriation. Is that the word?"

Apparently it was. Both the nurse and Luigi opened their eyes at me. Luigi protested that repatriation meant financial ruin, and I tried, with limited success, to explain that it wouldn't mean financial ruin to me.

"I'll have to discuss it with Dean—with the Dean," I said, "but when Colin wakes up, it won't do him any good to—I mean, it'll be better if he wakes up in familiar surroundings. You know, on home turf."

Feeling I could have put this better, I turned gingerly—I was beginning to feel rather wobbly, and I still had to get back to Assisi—and looked again at the silent figure.

Poor, orphaned, addicted Colin, seeing his one bargaining counter slip time and again from under his desperate gambler's fingers, thanks to one Cassie Greatrex. This definitely came into my father's third category; and while there could be no enjoyment, there could certainly be satisfaction, and perhaps even—yes, even reparation, if that wasn't too strong a word.

They were both watching me.

"You are quite sure about this?" This was the nurse, through Luigi.

"Oh, yes, quite sure," I said.

"There will be forms to fill in," said Luigi, in the tone of one who warns of a rampaging and incurable disease.

"I am sure there will be forms," I replied darkly. "There always are."

SEVENTEEN

But for themselves…they went into polished baths,
and were cleansed…

Book X, *ibid.*

I DON'T REMEMBER the journey back. I must have reached the
hotel safely and simply thrown myself on the bed and gone
out like the proverbial light, for when I did at last rouse from
deep sleep into daylight and pain, I was still fully dressed,
and prone, arms and legs anyhow.

I groaned and squinted at my watch. Nearly six.
Turning cautiously into the recovery position, I grazed
my bad ankle on something sharp, hard and unyielding,
with a strangely soft covering. My bag. With Homer still
in it.

This brought me fully awake. With a few choice
expressions from my father's vocabulary, I got myself
upright and sitting on the edge of the bed.

"Right, Mr Homer," I said, pulling the bag towards me
and opening the neck. "This relationship is *so* over." I hauled
him out and dumped him on the bed. "You," I said to him,

"are going to Germany soon, whether you like it or not, so put that on your needles and knit it."

Then I tried standing up. This was not, initially, a great success, nor was taking my clothes off much fun, but finally I got myself into the bathroom to examine the damage.

My left shoulder was bruised blue and violet, and there was a horrible long scrape up the inside of my left shin. The ankle was also bruised and swollen, and had bled through the plaster. I had collected other bruises along the way, including a raw and swollen scratch across my forehead that looked like a sabre cut. At least it wasn't a black eye. No wonder the woman in the Duomo had eyed me askance. I surveyed Giovanna's dressings and decided that they probably wouldn't survive a bath, but a bath I had to have.

I lay back, groaning partly in pain, partly in pleasure, and soaked for half an hour. When the rich, creamy vanilla-scented oils had done their work of removing all traces of that beastly well from my body, I got out, wrapped myself in an enormous towel, and padded carefully back into the bedroom.

There was a voicemail from my father. Two words only: "Mission accomplished."

"Oh, well *done*, Daddy," I exclaimed in delight. And a text message from Huw:

Yr Unc Wm and I Assisi tomorrow stop will you dine stop H

Mummy and I were both fluent users of textspeak, but it gave me an idiotic amount of pleasure to see that Huw, like my father, favoured Victorian telegram language. However, he didn't go quite as far as my father, who punctuated everything properly, including shopping lists. I texted back:

Yes pls c u then. Bring the caterpillar. C

What a pity, I thought as I pressed 'send', that you couldn't keep texts in the pigeonhole of a desk.

I didn't bother to dress, except in a clean nightgown, and I ordered dinner and a large glass of wine in my room.

*

The next morning I felt and looked, if anything, worse than ever. The bruises were darkening impressively, the muscles in my thighs had locked solid, and the romantic sabre-slash looked today exactly like the bad scratch it was, but I made myself dress and go down to breakfast. When I say 'go down', I didn't use the lift, either: I made myself take the stairs. I tried not to count them. When I reached my table, I crept unseen into my shady seat and put on my sunglasses.

Mummy and I had found a super hair and beauty salon when we were last in Assisi, and after breakfast I booked an appointment for a massage and to have my hair and nails done. The massage was torture but necessary, although I wasn't sure how to explain the mess my body was in. "I fell down some steps," I said through gritted teeth, and left it at that.

With my hair newly washed and styled and my nails redone, I began to feel more human, and as I didn't feel like sightseeing, I bought half a dozen postcards and took them back to the hotel, and wrote the same thing to my parents, Dinah and Ginny, Grandpa, and a few chosen friends. I couldn't pretend I was anyone interesting, on account of the bruises, but it felt pleasantly retro to be sitting there writing postcards on the terrace.

Later, I decided to brave the stares of the other guests, and changed—carefully—into a bikini. Then I went along to the pool and slept and swam and sunbathed, and thought a lot about Huw. I didn't think about Homer once.

I took the lift to my room, to change for dinner.

A long, lazy, holiday day; exactly as it should be.

I met them in the small square above the Basilica.

I had stopped at the Soliano's reception desk to tell the concierge that I would be out to dinner, then bade him a good evening and left the hotel.

The table I had sat at on the first evening was free. I pulled out a chair and sat down with my back to the restaurant so that I could see over the benign bulk of the Basilica as well as keep an eye on arriving cars. I rather felt the need of the happy normality that the aimlessly milling tourists, the flocks of nuns, and the earnest pilgrims provided with their comings and goings. Call it delayed reaction if you like, but I ordered *grappa* and sat swirling the cocoa bean and was content to watch the setting sun deepen and darken the flushed purple and rose of the Basilica towards night, which it did with that Mediterranean speed that always takes one by surprise. The air was soft and warm on my bruised flesh, and I sat back and sipped my drink and let the sounds and sights of Assisi wash over me, soaking away the experiences of yesterday.

A squabble, conducted in increasing frustration by a couple of young hikers as to the respective merits of maps and satellite navigation, began to absorb me, and I listened unashamedly.

"…I mean, look at that rag. Old-fashioned, or what? It's soaking wet, *and* you've torn it—and yesterday it nearly blew away altogether! Where would we have been then?"

"Exactly where we are now. As for that fancy gadget you spent the electricity money on, you couldn't raise a signal for love or money when we were doing the Via Flaminia! *And* the battery was flat after an hour! Call that smart? I don't! Let me tell you…"

Halogen lights sliced pink and blue past me and over the ancient holy walls with the cold sweep of a scimitar's blade, wiping the smile from my face. As they took the hairpin at the bottom and flooded the Piazza below I saw that one sidelight was out. Instantly my diaphragm tightened with fear, and my breath was stopped altogether. The couple moved away, still arguing, but I had forgotten them. I think I was even half out of my seat as the lights were quenched under the corrugated iron roof of the parking places. Then a door slammed, and another, and Huw and Uncle Will came into view and mounted the hill towards me.

I swallowed painfully, my heart jumping in my throat, and sank back onto my seat. That something was visible in my face was evident from the answering expression of alarm on Huw's. He quickened his pace and took the hand I instinctively put out to him.

"What's the matter, Cassie? Are you ill? Tell me!"

I shook my head. My lips were trembling, and the returning breaths came quick and shallow. "It was the lights. So silly. I should have remembered it was your car. I keep thinking it's his. I thought I'd sit and wait for you, then I just saw the lights, and—"

"Damn," said Huw forcefully. "I'm so sorry, darling. I should have thought—should have warned you." He sat down next to me, still holding my hand, and Uncle Will took the other chair. "Better now?"

I nodded, and smiled a little tremulously.

"Good girl. What's this, on the bottle already? How sensible. You should eat the cocoa bean. Caffeine's supposed to be good for shock. Let's have some more."

He glanced enquiringly at my uncle, who was staring at the tablecloth and paid no attention. Huw lifted a hand. My waiter stopped on his way past as though Huw had tugged at a string round his middle. He backed gracefully up to the table and bent to us.

"*Signor?*"

"Three more of these, please, and the menu."

"*Prego.*"

While the ordering was in progress, and minds were changed and changed back again, I recovered my composure and smiled a bit nervously at my uncle. I had no idea what to say to him, but I need not have worried: after one brief, rather puzzled glance at me, he paid us no further attention. Having made what looked like a supreme effort and chosen something to eat, he was now holding the menu upside down and staring past it with an unfocussed gaze. A little smile kept pulling at the corner of his mouth, and at one point a small squeak of what could have been excitement escaped him. I bit my lip and looked away. Huw and I drank our *grappa* and talked desultorily about his day at the museum, and threw the odd conversational gambit in my uncle's direction in case he should come back to earth (which he didn't). This uneven state of affairs lasted until our first course arrived and the waiter placed a bottle of something that gleamed like butter in front of him. Then he came to himself with a start, said loudly: "Well? What are we waiting for? Drink up! Drink up! I've got work to do!" and fell on his plate.

With my mother's social example in mind, I tried hard to weave my uncle into such conversation as Huw and I were able to have, given that we were not alone, but it wasn't until we were halfway through our *pollo alla prosciutto* that I ventured to address him directly. "Is everything all right, Uncle Will? You seem a little distracted."

He lifted his attention to me with some effort. "Oh, yes…thank you. Do I? Yes, probably. I'm sorry, I'm a poor companion this evening. No, I've had some news, that's what it is. Wonderful news." He looked like a schoolboy whose birthday is imminent.

"That's good," I said, nudging Huw's knee with my own under the table. "Are you going to tell us, or is it private?"

He drew in a deep breath and sat with his mouth open for a moment or two. "I, er, I've had a… There's been a… That is, someone's made a donation to the dig—an *enormous* donation. No, I haven't a clue who: it was anonymous. And my licence has been renewed, heaven alone knows how: I've been nagging at them since I got out here. They've given me six months. I hardly know if I'm coming or going. Yes, that's it. D'you see?"

We made conventional and hearty noises of congratulation, but he had burst into speech again.

"Of course, it's not enough, not nearly long enough, but it's better than six weeks. I cannot imagine who's responsible, or how to begin to thank them."

There was a touch of accusation in his tone, and I thought he had a very good idea who was responsible.

"That's tremendous, Uncle Will," I said innocently. "It's the best possible news. I'm so glad for you."

He peered at me over the top of what he called his eating spectacles. I smiled deprecatingly back.

"If I find—" he began.

"If you find what, Uncle Will?"

He did not answer, but ate for a little while in

concentrated silence. Lifting a forkful of chicken, he pointed it at Huw and drew a deep breath as though something had occurred to him. Then he must have changed his mind, for the fork went into his mouth. He chewed slowly and absently.

"What?" I said. Beside me, Huw chuckled.

"It doesn't matter," replied my uncle somewhat indistinctly.

"You were going to say something."

"No, no, not at all."

"You were!"

He dropped the fork. "If you must know, I was wondering whether this dig will possibly prove the sort of connection between Etruscan and other languages that Huw has been promulgating with such tiresome assiduity. It won't, of course, but I shall be most careful to keep an eye out nevertheless. I'm quite coming round to some of his arguments. But it already looks as though it's pre-Roman, and that's enough to be going on with. Oh, believe me, yes! My goodness!" His gaze sharpened on me for the first time that evening. "Look at you, Cassie! Has someone hurt you? That's a bad cut on your forehead."

"No one's hurt me, Uncle Will, I promise," I said soothingly, rescuing Huw, who had begun to stammer some sort of explanation. "I fell down some stairs. It was very clumsy of me. Er—did Huw tell you anything?"

"No: we were talking about the dig. Now, cough up, young woman. Good heavens, you look as though you've been in a fight!—and Huw doesn't look much better! What have you been up to?"

This aspect of yesterday's dramas had not occurred to either of us. Like lightning, I decided on a hazy version of the truth.

"It wasn't as bad as that," I said, with a light, rather false laugh. "You know the Pozzo di San Patrizio? Someone—some Italian—started making a nuisance of himself, and I sort of found myself in the Pozzo, you know, to get away from him. I thought it was the ladies, you see—and it wasn't. Huw rescued me, but not before I'd fallen down. I…I'm not badly hurt, just a bit shaken."

"I see. What happened to the nuisance?"

"I…er…"

"He got away," said Huw smoothly.

"As well for you. Neither of you seems to have been much of a match for him," said my uncle, and lost interest.

Later, we wandered down to the Piazza and stood under the shadow of the great bulk of the cathedral. Here we idly watched my uncle, who had spotted a colleague, and, hailing him, had sprung up from the table and accompanied him down the hill, trailing his napkin with him. They were now talking energetically, to the evident and patient boredom of the colleague's wife, who stood by, her eyes going from one to the other like someone watching a lacklustre and third-class tennis match.

Huw folded me into his arms and rested his chin on the top of my head. My uncle had turned his colleague round, spread the napkin over his back, and was drawing something on it with the same quick, nervous economy of effort that I had seen Huw use in the museum. Then, draping the napkin over the boot of someone else's car, he turned the colleague round again and began, with gusto and in detail, to explain his drawing. He had completely forgotten us.

"That was an impressive spot of quick thinking," murmured Huw over my head. I could feel the vibrations of his voice through the crown of my head. "The subject didn't come up on the way here—he was extremely technical, most of the time, until he suddenly fell asleep. I nearly jumped out of my skin."

"I know, I felt you. I didn't think of it. I rather wanted not to, if anything. Do you think he bought it?"

"I think so. I know him pretty well, and he's not really interested in anything that isn't in Oscan, or Umbrian, or younger than about two and a half thousand years old."

"You're absolutely right. Half the time you'd think we were nothing to do with him, Mummy says, for all the attention he pays, but he does surprise you sometimes. Oh, goodness me, look at him, and that poor woman, she looks fit to murder the pair of them. I bet that's his precious villa all over the restaurant's best damask. We might be here until midnight unless you prise him away and physically put him in the car. Oh, well." I yawned and stretched luxuriously in his embrace.

"Mm. I expect they can spare one napkin. Wish I could stay with you." He bent until his cheek was next to mine. "That reminds me. My course comes to an end tomorrow. Shall we make an arrangement to meet in London, or Oxford, or somewhere?"

"We can do better than that," I said, turning in his arms. "Come home with me."

"I won't be able to change my ticket. You know what airlines are like."

With a slight grimace that I hoped he didn't see, I took my courage in both hands and told him about the JetWorld hours. "So all you need do is meet me at Perugia," I finished, a little uncertainly. "We can go whenever you're ready. It doesn't even have to be tomorrow, unless you need it to be." I watched him with a touch of anxiety. It was suddenly immensely important that he accept me, riches and all. "It's my world, Huw. It's my gift to you," I finished priggishly, then could have kicked myself.

But he didn't make the mistake of taking it the way ninety-nine people out of a hundred would have done. His face was thoughtful, even grave, in the gentle dark, and a warm breeze stirred the crisp curls. A pair of lovers— another pair of lovers—strolled past us, embraced in each other, in step, silent, indivisible. Huw glanced at them, and smiled, then looked down at me again. "Thank you, Cassie. I accept your gift—and your offer. You can't imagine what a treat it will be."

I was so relieved. "I know what it is," I told him solemnly, "to fly economy class. Don't you dare snort at me like that: it's true!"

"Huh," he said with derision. "Choice—or necessity? Come on, confess!"

"Oh, all right then: it was choice," I replied defensively. "But at least I know what it's like!"

"Chicken-feed. You wait until you've queued until two in the morning for a stand-by seat, and had the flight cancelled under your nose at the last minute. Come on, let's go and remove your uncle. That poor woman needs rescuing."

*

We said very little when we met at the airport the next day, and not much more once we were airborne. Huw did observe that he was sure he was developing a split personality as we took our seats in the little aeroplane.

I looked up from fastening my seatbelt. "Why?"

"Yesterday, I was sitting on a blue plastic stackable chair

with a hole in the back, at a wobbly table covered with coffee-stains and obscene graffiti in indelible marker. And now, look at me." He patted the cream leather upholstery appreciatively.

"Good heavens, where was that?"

"One of the offices at the museum. The high life it's not."

"Evidently," I said.

Some little while after that, I think I heard him mutter something about historians, but I might have been mistaken, as his eyes were shut at the time.

I followed his example and gave myself up to the luxurious embrace of my comfortable reclining armchair.

*

It was degrees colder at home. Huw was going straight back to Oxford to render up an account of his field course and other activities to his Dean, and I was going back to London. It had been decided that Colin would have to be flown to Brize Norton since he was a witness in a case of international importance, and be taken straight to the John Radcliffe. There the Dean, as Colin's next of kin and the one responsible for his welfare while he was still a member of the college, would be able to keep an eye on him. Mr Landeck knew where to find us; and Uncle Will's affairs were taken care of; which left only me. I was already missing Huw as we passed through customs, counting the seconds until our parting. In consequence, I was bright, and so positive that Huw began to look a bit worried, and might have missed his connection if I hadn't pushed him away.

"No, go on," I urged him. "You've got a serious career ahead of you: go and smooth your Dean's ruffled feathers. I only hope he hasn't been following our capers in the press. Away! We'll see each other soon—won't we? After all, we must go and visit Colin."

"Yes, we must. I'll ring you. I've told my mother I'm bringing you to stay, so we could do the John Radcliffe and the Dean in the morning, and go on from there, if you like."

"Oh, I'd love that. I'll drive to Oxford and pick you up. Look, hadn't you better go?"

"Yes. Hold on, I've forgotten something. Two things, actually. What's the date?"

"What, today? I haven't a clue. Is it important?"

"Rather. If it's the end of term, I have to be out of my set."

I hesitated, on the brink of offering him something I wasn't quite ready to offer. "Oh," I said lamely, at length. "What shall we do, then?"

He stared gravely at me for some time, and I waited in expectation. "I'll ring you," he produced finally.

"You said that already."

"Then I'd better keep my word, hadn't I?"

I gave him a little push. "You're hopeless. What was the other thing? Is that important as well?"

"Yes, very." He was rummaging in his rucksack and now brought out a paper bag. "Wait 'til I've gone before you look, promise?"

"Promise," I said, with a break in my voice. I took the bag and cradled it. "Go!"

He kissed me, hard, and went.

I waved after him. At least, I hope it was him; I was half-laughing and half-crying, and I couldn't see very well through the tears. Which was silly, I told myself severely, wiping my eyes. What had I to cry about?

He had gone. It was some moments before I could turn my attention to the bag. There was something cold and hard inside. I opened it, and felt, and brought out the contents carefully.

It was a large green china caterpillar. It had painted blue whiskers and a wide smile. I loved it immediately.

I closed my hand over its smooth, cold curves, and stood there gazing at it, seeing neither it nor anything else.

EIGHTEEN

...I felt a curious little thrill go through me—the inevitable
response [...] to the age-old device of fable; the dead man...
the mysterious paper...the frayed and faded clue leading
through the hills of a strange land...

Mary Stewart: *My Brother Michael*

WITH OUR ASSORTED parents in mind I thought I might as
well ring mine and confess straight away. Besides, I wanted
to know something on my own account.

My father answered. "Your mother's here. Do you want
a word?"

"Yes, please, in a moment. Daddy, do you know how I
can fund a...a certain line of research for an undergraduate?"

"This isn't the Bardsey fellow, is it?"

"Of course not!" I was horrified and affronted.

My father began to sound more hopeful. "Is it the other
one?"

I sighed. Honestly, parents. "Yes, it is, as a matter of fact."

"You could offer to pay his expenses," suggested my
father.

"Is that the only way?"

"Not necessarily. You could always endow a research establishment for him. The outlay would depend on his discipline, of course." My father chuckled at his own wit.

"A research establishment..." I gave a little gasp, my thoughts taking wing. What, be able to *pay* people who thought along Huw's lines—*help* him to amass the supporting evidence he needed to substantiate his theories?

My father, no doubt reading my mind, said quite sharply: "I was joking, by the way. I suppose he's proud, this undergraduate of yours?"

I dragged my mind away from a gleaming new building twice the size of the National Archives. Was Huw proud? Yes, but in a good way.

"Yes," I said, "but in a good way."

My father's resigned sigh came over loud and clear. "I haven't the faintest idea what you're talking about."

"Darling old Daddy," I said, fondly tolerant. "Can I have Mummy, please? There's something you both need to know, so be prepared."

"Oh, God, you're engaged to a penniless chemist, and you're going to set him up in a research establishment. It needed only this," said my father with deep foreboding, and surrendered the receiver.

"Hallo, Cassie, sweetheart," came my mother's voice. "Did you have a nice time? What did you get up to?"

"That's just it," I said, thinking quickly, and not so sure as Huw had been of my uncle's distance from family matters. "Has Uncle Will rung you?"

"No, darling, of course not. Why?"

I breathed a sigh of relief and crossed my fingers. "Well, there's something you and Daddy ought to know that Uncle Will needn't know, if you see what I mean."

She said acutely: "It's not the penniless chemist, then?"

"Mummy, no! Not yet, anyway. And he's not a chemist, he's a linguist."

"Ah, that one. Forewarned is forearmed, I suppose. You'd better tell me. Wait a moment—I'm going to sit down."

To begin with, I don't think she believed a word of it. But whether it was the reiteration of Helmut Landeck's name, or the information that the German and Russian governments were involved, or that I would have to go up to Oxford at the first opportunity to see how Colin was, she stopped disbelieving me and listened in silence to the rather disjointed account from which I edited a certain amount. Possibly as a result of this, she did not, as I had feared, insist on my coming home immediately. I think she said something about coming up to London, but I was so relieved at having brushed through it that I didn't pay much attention. "So you see, Grandpa's going to need our support," I finished. "I mean, who knows what memories this is going to stir up? Helmut said he wanted to contact him as soon as possible, but he agreed to let me tell you first."

There was a little silence before my mother spoke again. "Where is the Homer?"

"Well, it's here, but it's going to Germany soon. Helmut needs Grandpa's permission—and I think he wants to ask him some questions."

"I see why we're needed. At least it won't be anywhere near you. And you're absolutely sure you're all right?"

"Absolutely. A bit part-worn, and rather bruised, but fine. Promise." I could tell by the quality of the sound that my mother had put the conversation on speaker so that my father could hear. He had been silent throughout, but he spoke at last.

"So that little tick invited himself down to my house to finish off the job, is that it?"

"Just about, Daddy."

"And now he's in hospital?"

My heart was thumping. "That's right."

"And you're going to visit him."

"Yes, on the way down to Cambridgeshire to see Huw's mother."

My father growled, but all he said was: "Category Three, I take it? You're a good, brave girl, Cassie—and kind. I'm proud of you."

My throat tightened with sudden tears. My "Thank you, Daddy" came out sounding flat, as though I were unmoved. But my father knows me better. He said briskly, to give me time: "Anything else you need us to do?"

I expect he could hear the smile—and the tears. "No, thank you, that's all: just look after Grandpa. Helmut's a very nice German, but I don't know how Grandpa will feel about it."

"Don't worry about him. His generation knows how to respect a brave and honourable enemy—and most of them were, you know."

"I know." I told him what Helmut had said about forgiveness so that all the sacrifices should not be wasted. "He said we could be friends for our grandfathers' sakes, too. I…I rather like him."

"I'll ask him for his banking details," said my father, "and transfer a large capital sum to him straight away."

"Oh, very funny. Give Grandpa all my love, and tell him I'm really sorry I can't tell him myself, but I've got to go to Oxford. And for goodness' sake, tell him his precious Homer will be quite safe!"

"We will. Here's your mother again."

"I only wanted to know if you'd managed to see anything of Orvieto. I've always wanted to visit it."

I began to laugh. "Not really—unless you count some tombs, several car parks, a spell in Purgatory, a police station, the inside of a hospital—oh, and some scenes from the Apocalypse."

"As long as you enjoyed yourself," responded my mother imperturbably.

With that under my belt, I started to prowl restlessly round the house. Now was as good a moment as any to think about curtains and carpets. I am my mother's daughter, after all. Because if Huw and I... Biting this one off as definitely coming into the chicken-counting category, I carried on unpacking and looking critically round my bedroom. Really, the curtains were awfully girly. I straightened, a pile of underwear in my hands, debating whether to go and get a tape measure. Then it struck me. Hadn't I already been round the house taking measurements and writing them all down? I'd done it methodically, too, on a separate sheet for each room, jotting down ideas for colour schemes. I certainly didn't want to do it again.

I frowned in an effort of memory. What had I done with them? I tried to go over my movements. Which room had I been in last? The sitting-room came straight to mind, but for some reason I was almost sure I'd done that first. So, where had I left them?

I incline more to tidiness than otherwise, but I do have my moments. I put the handful of underwear I was holding into the laundry basket and once more swept my bedroom with a glance, then giggled as I remembered that it was somebody's notion of housework; I couldn't think whose. I scuffled among the usual clutter on my dressing-table, then opened some drawers. Nothing. I looked in the other two bedrooms and both bathrooms. Still nothing. I came out onto the landing and looked over the banisters. The sitting-room door was standing invitingly open. I heaved a sigh and trailed downstairs. I knew perfectly well that I had done this room first. They wouldn't be here, therefore. Had I left them in the kitchen, perhaps?

Once in the kitchen I looked round in dismay. It wasn't that it was untidy—my daily saw to that—but there was an awful lot of places to look. I opened the refrigerator, with a vague memory of my father's once having found his car keys there. No lists of measurements; but my eye fell on a box of miniature chocolate éclairs, and I took one and munched it as my gaze roved round. Nothing like an éclair for grounding a person in reality. There was no little sheaf of notes on the glass shelves.

Then, out of nowhere, a sudden memory, vivid as a flash of lightning, conjured up by heaven knows what, of the ghastly *crack* as Colin's temple hit the stone sill. He was sliding down the wall into the waiting water…

I shook my head violently and slammed the refrigerator door on the horrible little picture, and stood there for a few moments, breathing deeply, fingers clenched round the handle. He was going to be all right. *All right.* They had said so at the hospital. There was nothing to worry about… nothing at all.

After a bit, I resumed my search, lifting the breadboard and knitting my brows at the row of cookery books sitting smug and innocent. Not there. Finally, more and more aware of a teasing sense of *déjà vu*, I wandered discontentedly back to the sitting-room, licking my fingers.

Granny's desk. Of course. I ran to it and opened it. Huw's letters were there in their pigeonhole, and I put out a tender hand to the caterpillar, undulating across the top, but otherwise nothing, nor in the drawers.

"Oh, *warts*," I said aloud in disgust. Anyway, it didn't matter. Huw would have to have a say now. Perhaps I could get him to do the measurements again. I'd ask him the very next time I saw him. In the meantime, I would go to Christopher Wray's Lighting Emporium to see if I could find some table lamps for the desk.

I found a pair, Wedgwood creamware, with pleated silk lampshades. The assistant, assessing me with the same insulting ease as had the waiter in Assisi, himself fitted the plug, popped two light bulbs into the carrier bag, and saw me into a cab with an indulgent smile. My *amour propre* was salved when my telephone went, and I could pretend it was a call I was expecting.

It was Huw, in a hurry. There was a slight change of plan; he was on his way; would be with me as soon as possible. "Wait there," I said. "I'll be as quick as I can."

He brought his luggage with him—all of it. It spilled down the steps and over the pavement. He hastened to open the door for me, and I stepped carefully over a tennis racquet, a carrier bag from which some grass-stained cricket flannels billowed, and a box of books.

"I'm really sorry about all this. I had to bring it; nowhere to leave it. I'm assuming nothing, by the way, but if you don't object, I'll play watchdog and sleep on the doormat."

"I have a spare room," I said. "You'd better bring that lot in."

"There's something else."

A tiny flutter of fear, somewhere deep. I said with foreboding: "What?"

"This." He indicated the rolled-up paper sticking out of the rucksack at my feet. He didn't need to elaborate: I saw the crudely coloured cartoon-work straight away.

This time, it was far worse. The tone of *To be continued…* was nastier and more personal, and talked of the abuse of family connections to jump the queue on to important digs over the heads of those better qualified; the evils of nepotism and public schools; and a lot more in the same toxic vein.

"Oh, etc., etc.," said Huw. "I wonder how Colin found out. He must have talked to someone at the dig and emailed this before the accident. Fast worker." He flung it onto the coffee table. "I'm sorry to introduce such a sour note, but I thought you ought to see it."

"You did the right thing," I said. "But when did he get the time? He must have done it before that Russian man got nasty. I don't exactly see him standing his ground in the face of fire. In any case, they're my family connections, not yours."

"They've never allowed niceties like the truth, factual accuracy, that sort of thing, to get in their way."

"It doesn't actually mention my uncle," I said rather miserably.

"It doesn't need to. *Pre-Roman villa found near Orvieto; race against time*, blah, blah."

"What did he hope to gain?"

"Perhaps he was trying to scupper my career before it begins."

"Wait a moment." I picked it up again and found the article.

"What are you looking for?"

"It would have been easy for him to find you'd gone up to Uncle Will's dig, wouldn't it?"

"As winking. He only had to ring the museum. Why?"

"Only that with all the research he's been doing into my family, he could have found that William Maskell was my uncle and just taken it from there. In fact," I added even more miserably, "I damn' well told him myself. He probably did this before he left."

Huw shrugged. "Can't be helped. Let's hope the chip-shop paper didn't also get wind of my extra-curricular British studies courtesy of our Colin, or I'll be out on my ear." He shook his head. "That's an appalling state of affairs."

I tossed *Town & Gown?* back onto the table. "I suppose these will stop now that...now that he..."

"I sincerely hope so." He was by the window, and I regarded his profile fondly. He had an appealingly beaky nose. "We were right, by the way. It was gambling, but online poker, not fruit machines. The Dean told me."

I forgot about his nose. "Online poker! You mean sitting crouched over a computer for hours on end, getting into debt?"

"Hooked like any fish, more and more addicted, falling prey to anybody who cares to take advantage of you. Hence the loan shark." A muscle flickered along the lean jaw. "Colin borrowed £500. The compound interest worked out at over 80,000%. The police found the chit."

I was horrified. "But that's—*nearly half a million pounds!* That's utterly monstrous! Goodness knows I can't stand him, but what an awful fate! No wonder he was so desperate! What about the loan shark?"

"They've got him already."

"Fast work! If Colin's brain is damaged, Huw..."

"I know. He'll be beyond the reach of the predators. I find that quite a comfort." He abandoned the window and went to my bookshelves.

"Yes," I said. "And if it isn't?"

"I haven't a clue. The Dean will keep an eye on him, even though he's over the age of eighteen. I could try and keep tabs on him, but he hates my guts… We've got an appointment to see the Dean tomorrow, by the way. I thought we might as well bite on the bullet and go to the John Radcliffe afterwards."

"All right," I said, without enthusiasm.

He was running his eye over the titles. "What have we got here?"

"Now don't," I warned him, "say anything at all—*at all*—about my taste in literature."

"Light relief is essential to the human condition. Ask Shakespeare." He pulled out a biography.

"I haven't looked at that for ages," I said, and went to stand beside him. "And I'd hardly call it light relief." He smelt delicious. I inhaled deeply. "Historical," I said.

He slanted a glance at me. "Who, me? I had a shower this morning, let me tell you. I don't think I've kissed you yet, have I?"

"No," I said, the ready colour suffusing my cheeks.

"Then I'd better," he said, and did.

It was a while—quite a long while—before we surfaced.

"In the best thrillers," he said against my hair, "important bits of paper are always hidden in books. They're used as bookmarks, or—"

"Or left on buses. More often than not, they're crumpled up and used to light the fire," I objected.

He shook his head and let me go. "That's whole manuscripts, at least in the best books."

As one, we turned to look at the grate. It was empty. We turned back to the shelves. He ran one thoughtful finger along, and I sat down on the arm of the chair to see him better.

"If you're checking for dust—" I began, but he interrupted me.

"Aha, here's something. My mother will approve: Mary Stewart is her favourite author. I love the way your mouth turns down at the corners when you smile." He pulled down *My Brother Michael*, turned it spine upwards, and shook it ruthlessly. Some papers fell to the carpet.

After a stunned second, he put *My Brother Michael* down as carefully as if it had been Homer's first draft. We stared at the floor.

"Laundry lists," I said at last.

Huw swallowed. "Washing machines."

"Yes. You're quite right."

After a bit, he said: "Will you? They were in your book."

"N…no. You do it. You're the word-man round here. You look like all the best heroes when you lift one eyebrow like that."

His face, as he bent and picked up the papers and examined them, can best be described as expressionless. I waited, my breath suspended with excitement. It was a moment before he could bring himself to speak. When he did, his tone was non-committal. "'Spare room: 12' 5" x 14' 3". Possibly navy blue and buff scheme, walls pale buff with gold leaf on beading, navy blue bed covers ottoman silk piped in buff, north-facing, or too cool?…'"

"The measurements!" I sprang up.

"Too cool for words, and obviously important, but not, I think, of interest to our Helmut."

I fairly snatched them from him. "I didn't mean that sort of cool, fathead! I mislaid these ages ago—I was looking for them again this morning. I couldn't think where I'd left them. Oh, well, it was a nice try."

"Your books are too tight on this shelf," he observed. "May I?" He put one hand down behind them to ease one or two out.

I was already glancing through the schemes and criticising or approving my own taste, and I said something vague in reply, so although I didn't see what caused him to utter the exclamation, there was a quality in his tone that made me look up in some surprise.

He was holding a book in one hand, and something else in the other.

"You've found an original Magna Carta," I said placidly. "I was wondering where it was. We'll go halves on the proceeds, and you can fund all your—" Then I saw his face. "What is it? What have you found?"

"It's them," he said hoarsely. He cleared his throat and held a small sheaf of papers out to me.

I stayed where I was, holding his shocked gaze, not taking them. "It's not," I said at last. "It can't be. It's just not possible."

"Look. It is."

I reached out a strangely reluctant hand.

It was the same handwriting. My grandfather's, on the same furred, war-issue paper. I knew it instantly. With careful, unsteady fingers, I unfolded the sheaf. Somehow I was on my feet, though I don't remember standing up. Huw came to my side, and together, hardly breathing, we looked.

There were three pages, divided into columns of closely written names, addresses and telephone numbers. In the last column were itemised artefacts. I scanned them, my eyes popping as names such as Raphael and Tintoretto flashed past like the Taurid Shower in the night sky. Breughel's name was there, too, and Pinturicchio's; and in the first column, others: German names made notorious by their wartime associations. Household names of horror.

"Jackpot." Huw's voice was not quite steady. He pointed with a forefinger that trembled a little. "Will you look at this!"

It was in the third column. *Dagon, by Lenormant and de Witte*; and in the column of addresses, a Russian name all too familiar to us today from the present administration.

"Dagon is another name for Oannes. The Etruscan amphora from which this painting was made used to be in the Royal Museum of Berlin."

"Used to be?" My heart was thudding.

"I might be wrong, but I think it disappeared during the war. Nobody has seen it since."

I refolded the pages with hasty care, cradling them. "Dear God Almighty," I whispered.

Huw said with difficulty: "But—*how*? How on earth do they come to be here?"

I could only shake my head, but even as I did so, a memory sparked. "The first evening I had the Homer," I said slowly, "I knocked it off the arm of the chair. They must have fallen out then—do you remember I told Helmut? The jolt must have broken the old glue somehow. I know I picked up something else at the same time, but I didn't pay any attention. I thought it was the measurements—if I thought at all. I just shoved it—*these*—onto the bookshelf. I was more concerned with the book—I thought I'd damaged it."

"So they were here all along."

"Well—yes. In the Homer."

"Until you dropped it, by the mercy of heaven, and they fell out."

I didn't get the meaning of his tone straight away. "God—yes," I croaked then, my skin prickling with remembered fear. "If I hadn't—if Colin had found them after all..."

"But he didn't. They were safe."

"Yes, thank God. *Thank God.* Think of it, all those years—until now." I fell silent and closed my eyes.

With sudden excitement flaring in his voice, Huw said: "Now what the hell do we do? We can't possibly take these to Oxford with us."

"N…no—of course we can't. I suppose we'd better—"

I stopped abruptly. A woman's voice had sounded from the front door, calling my name.

"Oh, *hell*! It's Mrs Mitchell!" I mouthed frantically. "What are we going to do?"

"You keep asking me that—I haven't a clue!" hissed Huw.

"Cassie, dear, are you there? Your front door's open again, and there's luggage all down your steps! Goodness me, I thought you were leaving the country! I've just come to see if you were all right. We don't want any repetitions of the last time, do we?"

I clutched the precious pages, and we goggled at each other. I don't think I could have moved if I tried. Mrs Mitchell came into the sitting-room on a wave of *Calèche*.

"My, don't you look nice and brown! Have you been somewhere gorgeous? But what have you done to your face?"

Yet again I stammered something, and it seemed to satisfy her. Her gaze fell on Huw, who turned his head slowly and gazed at her as though she were a fabulous beast, stepped out of the pages of *Le Morte d'Arthur*.

"Well," she said, "you don't need rescuing from this one! How do you do!"

"How do you do," echoed Huw blankly. "I'm so sorry about all the luggage."

"It's yours?"

"Yes, I've—"

"Italy," I said vaguely. "That is, we've just come back. At least, we didn't take it all out there—and it's not mine anyway."

Mrs Mitchell gave me a kindly, indulgent smile that perfectly expressed her opinion of this. I pulled myself together and gave the lists to Huw as casually as I could. "This is Huw Trefor, Mrs Mitchell. Mrs Mitchell is my next-door neighbour."

She began to look amused, and came further in to shake hands. I was trying to think of some tactful way of getting rid of her when her amusement vanished abruptly. She exclaimed: "Why, how extraordinary to see that again!"

This threw me. "Wh...what? See what again?"

"That dreadful gutter newspaper. My poor husband had such trouble with them, oh, years ago, now."

We gaped at each other, at her, and then at the table.

I said wonderingly: "You don't mean *Town & Gown?*, do you? I wouldn't have thought you'd even heard of it."

She picked it up as though she had a dead rat by the tail, and flicked over the pages. "I wish I hadn't. We threw a very expensive firm of lawyers at them when they insinuated that my husband was evading tax, and that the chair he'd endowed at Oxford was backed by dirty money. How depressing; it's exactly the same: cheap gossip, insinuation, and spite. Disgusting."

Huw was holding the precious sheaf much as Galahad might have held the Grail, but at this he focussed on her properly. "A—chair? At *Oxford*? Which one?"

"No, I'm wrong there, not a chair. A bursary, or something. Funds for the deserving, anyway."

I said: "For what, Mrs Mitchell? I'm so sorry, my wits have gone begging. Please do sit down."

"That's all right, dear, I won't stay. It was to teach people art history detection. My granddaughter graduated in it. She was one of the first."

Huw said: "The Philip Mitchell bursary? That was your *husband*? Good God!"

I was stunned. "But that's an extraordinary coincidence!"

I don't think she heard me. She was smiling rather mistily at Huw.

"You know about it? That's nice. Seems dreadful, doesn't it? Seventy years ago, and we're still living with the consequences. Old sins have long shadows." She shook her immaculate head. "Well, I can see I've come at the wrong moment, so I'll leave you. Do stop leaving your door open! Anyone would think you want half the world wandering in! You'll have people thinking you don't want all that stuff you've brought, and if you don't watch it, it'll vanish, you mark my words. I know this is a nice district, but some people will pinch anything, anywhere."

Huw and I stopped staring at Mrs Mitchell and stared at each other again. It seemed as though some wordless agreement passed between us. I put my hand out to her. "Don't go, Mrs Mitchell. You might be exactly the person we need."

We told her everything. She interrupted us only once, and that was to ask if we'd had lunch. When I said we hadn't, she used my telephone to ring her cook and order lunch for three. As soon as she had hung up, we continued our tale, with many omissions and amendments. When we showed her what we had just found, she clapped both hands to her mouth to stifle a squeak.

"Are those them? May I see? Why one's grammar always deserts one in moments of great excitement, I simply can't imagine…" Her voice died away as Huw put them into her hands, the hands that Dinah had manicured many times. Automatically, I noticed that she needed to make another appointment. She looked at the lists in complete silence, then put them on her knee. Her hands were flat on them; protective, art-lover's hands. Not like Colin's. I looked away.

She lifted her head, and her eyes had tears in them. "Oh, my dears, how *amazingly* lucky. And you have no idea at all how they got behind those books? None at all?"

"We have a vague idea," I said. Mrs Mitchell listened intently as I limped to the end of yet another explanation. Then she drew a deep breath, said "*Well!*" a couple of times, gave them back to Huw and rose, tiny, immaculately groomed, resolute.

"Come along, and bring those with you. I know exactly what to do with them. I don't know what Concita will have drummed up for us, but let's go and eat it this minute. Nobody can expect to stand all this drama on an empty stomach."

I was too stunned and anxious to enjoy what Concita had drummed up, or even to remember much of it, but by the time we were settled in Mrs Mitchell's drawing-room over coffee and *petits fours* and discussing what to do, I felt much better and more confident.

Her strategy was simple. It was that we should relinquish the lists to her and she would put them in her safe-deposit box at her bank that very day. "Then we concoct a letter to your Mr Landeck and tell him they are in safe custody."

Huw was looking doubtful. "I don't like the idea of involving you, Mrs Mitchell. A man has died for these."

"Two men," I said.

She gave me a quick, enquiring glance.

"Colin's great-uncle," I explained. "Not to mention his family."

"And millions like them," said Huw. "Poor, weedy little bloke."

"Yes," I said. "I shall always be glad that he died before...
before he was found."

"One of the lucky ones," said Mrs Mitchell stoutly.
"Now, my bank's not far, and there can be no valid objection
to my taking a hand. Nobody's going to know, not if we
move quickly."

"I suppose not," I said, liking it as little as Huw. "Isn't
there some other way? What about my safe?"

"Absolutely not," said Huw with an air of finality. "I
suppose I could ask the Dean..."

"Oh, no, you don't," I said. "The fewer people who know
about this, the better, even if he is Colin's next of kin."

"You're right. The effect on Colin, if he ever—"

"Don't!" I said, quite sharply.

"Sorry. All right. It does seem the best solution—on the
condition that we come to the bank with you," agreed Huw.
"And an email would reach Helmut quicker than a letter."

"Good idea," approved Mrs Mitchell. "May I leave the
electronics to you? That's a relief. I'll try and ring Rachael
as well. She went straight out to Germany, to help restore
people's treasures to their rightful owners. It's quite likely
she'll know all about your Homer's secrets, even if she's not
working on it herself. She did tell me the name of her boss,
but I can't recall it."

"That's settled, then," I said, greatly relieved.

She twinkled at Huw. "I think there's something else. Tell
me to mind my own business if you will, but I assume that
that mountain of luggage means your term has ended?"

"Er, yes, I..."

She nodded in satisfaction. "I thought so. I said to myself
when I saw it, that looks definitely end-of-term-ish. Am I to
understand from the startled and rather harassed expressions
you're both wearing that this arrival is unexpected?"

"It's not unexpected," I said loudly, "it's just that—"

"As a matter of fact, we were just discussing it. I'm—"

"I've got a spare room," I interpolated, for some reason anxious that she should apprehend the matter to the full.

Huw said smoothly: "Please don't worry about me, Mrs Mitchell. I'm supposed to be taking Cassie to stay with my mother, but that'll have to wait until this is sorted out. About the only clear thought I've got is that we have an appointment with the Dean tomorrow, but Cassie said she'd drive us up, so at least there's one problem taken care of—"

I cut in guiltily, glad of the diversion. "I'm afraid it isn't taken care of."

"Isn't it? Why not?"

"I haven't got a car."

"Oh? But you said—"

"I know. I was thinking of the MG. It's my father's. I sort of thought it might be rather fun to tootle up the Oxford Road, like Harriet Vane did."

"But if it's your father's, isn't it in Surrey?"

"Yes. That's the whole point."

"Oh."

Mrs Mitchell, who was no fool, said firmly: "You can make this your London base for as long as you like. Until you two sweethearts sort yourselves out."

She hadn't meant anything, but I know I was blushing furiously, and I put the backs of my hands to my hot cheeks. Huw's colour was high, too, as he tried to thank her.

"You can have a key, and come and go as you please. No, don't thank me again. You're a brave young man, and it'll do my house good to have you here. It'll make Cassie feel more comfortable, too."

"I don't deny..." I began.

"It's very kind of you, Mrs Mitchell, particularly considering that all Cassie offered me was her doormat," said Huw blandly.

Mrs Mitchell cut off my laughing protest. "Of course, if you learnt to shut your front door... No, I won't tease you anymore." She sounded arch. "You'd better have a car for tomorrow, I think."

"Well, yes," I said, "but—"

"You can have mine—and my driver. It'll give him something to do."

She cut short our fervent thanks, and while she telephoned her bank, Huw sent an email to Helmut Landeck. Mrs Mitchell's driver then took the three of us to her branch, a private one in Prince George of Denmark's Row with its own car park. He escorted her in while we waited. This was also her idea; she didn't think it was a good plan to have either of our faces recorded by the cameras. So we sat in the luxurious leather-upholstered back, investigating rather nosily, and stroking the varnished burr walnut. Huw said he was rapidly becoming accustomed to this mode of living, and we started to sing *The Good Life* together, until Huw said that that wouldn't do at all; he wasn't feeling in the least bit sad. "We'll sing 'gladness' instead," he said firmly. So we did, and it was fine, so we changed all the words, and laughed a lot, and I thought, not for the first time, that here was a man who would change anything for the better.

He looked down at me. "Cassie."

"Yes?"

"There was one good bit about the *Town & Gown?* piece."

"What?"

"Family connections."

"All that's yours is mine, and all that's mine's me own, do you mean?" I responded, with a quizzical lift of one brow.

"Eh?"

"Family quotation. You might as well get used to it."

"Is that a proposal?"

I was horrified. At least, that is what I told myself my reaction was. "No!" I stammered. "That is—"

"*I* see. You were waiting for me to do the deed."

"*No!* I mean…"

He stretched luxuriously. "You sweet, old-fashioned thing," he murmured, mimicking me. There was a wicked glint in his eye. "Will you marry me?"

"Well, of course I will," I protested.

He said: "I can't afford to buy you a ring."

My head was comfortably on his shoulder, and my eyes were shut. "'Tisn't a problem. I'll buy one."

"You will not. We haven't even slept together yet."

I lifted my head and squinted at him. "Huh? How does that follow?"

"It doesn't. It's just an observation. Since we're on the subject, I'll wait if you will. I seem to have surrendered to a superior force in the form of Mrs Mitchell anyway."

"It's a deal. No, it's not, it's a *non sequitur.*"

"You'll probably have to spend half your life up to the knees in mud," he warned.

"I'll buy some waders. If I'm going to be financing your digs, I'll need more than… Here she comes."

"We'd better tell our parents first," said Huw.

"That's all right," I said lazily. "If your mother's anything like mine, she'll know already."

NINETEEN

"The Proctor would like to speak to you, sir,"
said the Bull-dog, grimly.

Dorothy L. Sayers: *Gaudy Night*

I DON'T KNOW what I expected a Dean to look like. The
only Dean I had ever read about was a female one in a
book written about eighty years ago. This Dean was smartly
dressed, even dapper. I detected an expensive but not elegant
aftershave; and he had a strong Glaswegian accent, which I
shall not attempt to reproduce here. I will only say that the
news bulletin I had once seen, in which a Glaswegian was
interviewed, had been entirely justified in using subtitles. And
I discovered his name, which was O'Leary. Patrick O'Leary.
Call me prejudiced, but I prepared to dislike him on sight.

He came forward to shake hands, and waved us to the
armchairs by his fireplace. This, I was disappointed to see,
was tiled over and had one of those unconvincing electric
stoves on the hearth. Vaguely impressed by the ancient,
carved stone, the worn flags, and solid, silvery-grey oak
doors of Huw's college, I was disappointed not to see

hurrying figures in black gowns. I took my seat suffused with the sort of feeling one has in a museum or a cathedral; sort of best behaviour-ish and rather small-girl, and looked about me while the Dean clinked glasses at an impressively laden table. There might not be a proper coal fire, but there was sherry. This seems to have fallen out of favour with our age group, but my father has never allowed fashion a look-in where good wine is concerned, and would never allow me to do likewise, so I accepted a glass. It was good sherry, too. Mr O'Leary dragged a chair up and sat down between us, and while we exchanged a few commonplaces, I sipped with pleasure and began to relax.

"Well now, I'm not sure where to start," he said. "It seems Colin and I owe you two a great deal."

"It was Helmut Landeck who saved him from drowning," Huw said.

"Yes, so you told me. The whole thing is even less believable in daylight."

I sat back. There was something about the *Colin and I* that was warming and encouraging. After all, the poor man couldn't help his Christian name. After a bit more sherry, I found I could even forgive him that.

"Yes, yes indeed," he was saying. "A sad business. To think that one of our undergraduates…" His voice tailed off, and he stared out of the window. "You can actually see the John Radcliffe from this room. There it is: the Lego-like building."

We both looked. It was exactly like an intelligent five-year-old's efforts with a box of Lego bricks, and blinding white in the sun that bathed Headington Hill. I could picture the Dean at his desk, looking over towards the hospital, there in spirit with Colin; his student, his ward, his responsibility. Not so lonely after all.

"We're going to see him later," said Huw. "As I told you yesterday, Cassie's the one who—"

"Yes," broke in Mr O'Leary. He sounded rather curt, which surprised me, but perhaps it was only the usual sort of emotional constipation that afflicts some people in the presence of the very rich indeed. It seemed that my diagnosis was correct, for he swirled his sherry rather too vigorously and said: "I personally am very grateful to you, er, Cassie. I could never have... That is, I'm afraid I was hardly in a position to... We are not a *rich* college."

He drank deeply, and I thought of what Huw had said about cheeseparing. Glowering at his glass, he went on: "I should have noticed, of course. There is no excuse."

"Forgive me, but I think there is," I said after a tentative glance at Huw. "It's well known that gamblers and other addicts are very secretive. You might be his next of kin, but you can't be his keeper all the time."

"No," agreed Huw. "And he's of age."

"True, true. But still. Still." He thrust out his lower lip, giving him the look of a disgruntled baby. "I don't like the publicity for the college. I don't like it at all."

"Has there been any?" asked Huw in some surprise. "I thought it had been buried pretty well. There was nothing in the papers yesterday, and nothing today. We...er...we feared there might be."

"No, but people *talk*."

I had the impression that the national papers were of less importance to him than the possibility of people talking more locally, and I wondered whether he was thinking of *Town & Gown?*. The next moment, my suspicion was confirmed.

"Of course," he said, pulling at his lip, "now that that unfortunate journalist is out of the way...and with Colin safely tucked up in a hospital bed… Not, of course, that he'll be there for ever, but I have made it a condition of his staying on here that there'll be no more truck with peddlers of the sort of fly-blown gossip that…" His voice trailed off again, and he upended his empty glass hopefully.

"I'm awfully glad you're keeping him," said Huw nobly, if insincerely. "He's got a good brain."

"*Direction!*" shouted Mr O'Leary suddenly, making me jump. He set down his glass with a snap. "You must have direction in life! This place is purely and simply the means to an end these days! And don't run away with the notion that I think that's necessarily a good thing, because it isn't, and I don't." He stabbed a well-kept finger at Huw. "Take him! We're hoping for good things from him next year, despite his great age. If he would but keep to a more orthodox path in his researches…"

"Think what I'm told to think, you mean? I'll see hell freeze over first," replied Huw gently. "I go where the records take me. And in any case, haven't we already agreed that I'm going to be careful? I know better than to try and batter closed minds apart. It does far too much damage, to both sides. It's enough at the moment to know that you haven't put a spoke in my wheel."

"And nor do I intend to. Softlee softlee catchee monkee. When you're dealing with a false psyche, whether it's of a person or a whole nation—well. And I am not a psychiatrist," added the Dean austerely, looking at me over the top of his lilac-rimmed spectacles.

"The time is about right for beginning to present the truth, and I'll tread very carefully," said Huw mildly. "Once I've safely graduated, though—watch out, that's all. In any case, I would never do anything to jeopardise your position—while I'm still here." He bared his teeth.

"Poor Colin," said Mr O'Leary, flinching a little; "yes." He shook his head sorrowfully, and I began positively to like the man. He brightened. "I expect you'll like to know that Colin's doing well, much better than expected. There's no damage to the brain, and the neck was merely strained. He's had a thoroughgoing shock, and there's no lasting harm done. In fact, with help— Well, never mind. Who's to say, after all?" He slapped his beautifully pressed knees. "This man, Landeck, you know he came to see me? No? He wanted to question Colin, but the hospital wouldn't let him just then. I expect he'll be back." He rounded on me. "And I gather," he exclaimed, with a bewildering change of subject, "that William Maskell's your uncle!"

"Yes, that's so."

"He lectures here—but I expect you know that. He was telling me," pursued Mr O'Leary in some disapproval, "that since his licence has been extended, and a large donation made to the dig, he won't be available for the next six months."

"Yes, he told us that too. He seemed to think it was a very good thing." Feeling absurdly guilty, I tried for a winning smile. "I'm sorry about the lectures."

"I should coco," said Mr O'Leary with deep feeling. "If I can't find some left-over Emeritus to lecture in his stead, I'll have to take them myself. I'd ask old Purvis—he's the least unreliable—but he's taken his great-niece to Uzbekistan, and we all know what *that* means. Great-niece, my left foot!"

I choked over my sherry, and Huw gave a shout of laughter.

Mr O'Leary smiled with a touch of apology. "Who knows what he mightn't unearth? Your uncle, I mean. He's not your great-uncle, is he? Good, good. Afraid I'd put my left foot in it, ha, ha! It's all very well, but *I'm* not going to lose any sleep over the Romans, and I wouldn't expect William to, either. I wonder if I might be able to wangle a visit to see how he's getting on? I doubt if the budget will… Well, we'll have to see, that's all."

From which I gathered that his disapproval was not disapproval at all, but good old-fashioned envy. I wondered whether my father would know how to endow a chair at an Oxford college.

"What a *lovely* lot of stairs."

Huw grinned at me. "You didn't want to wait for the lift," he reminded me.

"I was wrong," I said. "We'll wait for it if I have to grow a beard waiting."

"I'm sure Dinah will know what to do."

I didn't quite have time to grow a beard, and soon the battered lift, which we shared with two tired nurses going off duty; a patient, pale and thin as a thread, who pushed herself and her drip slowly into the lift on a walking frame; and a harassed-looking shirt-sleeved young medico with an ink-stained breast pocket where his ballpoint had leaked, disgorged us onto a landing. We examined the huge signposts to the various wards. I spotted Colin's ward number, and pointed.

"There we are," I said. "Left, left, left again, and all around the houses. I hate these places."

We set off, and after only two wrong turnings, found our way into a quiet corridor. We identified Colin's ward easily, since there was a policeman sitting stolidly outside the door. Before we could enter, we had to give him our names, and he checked us on his list and opened the door for us.

We found ourselves in a small ward with four beds. Two were unoccupied. In the far bed was a bandaged and deathly still figure, with drips, and a monitor of some sort beeping quietly and regularly. In the bed closer to the door was Colin.

He was sitting up—and talking to a girl perched by his feet. I regarded her in surprise, and with interest. She did not look like a nurse, despite an immediately apparent air of professional competence. Some sort of consultant? Beside me, Huw stiffened at the sight of her, and I thought I heard him mutter something.

Colin's face, which had been quite animated, went blank and shuttered as we came in. I was unpleasantly reminded of the way he had stood at the corner of More Street and the King's Road, the wind lifting the fair hair, but the purpose I had sensed so strongly then had gone out of him. I detected aggression and wariness, but he looked defenceless in his pyjamas, and there was a substantial bandage over his left eye.

The girl had risen, looking as though she was prepared to fight his or anybody else's corner. Goodness knows I had not been looking forward to this, but her pugnacious attitude was distinctly off-putting. We stopped about six feet from the bed.

"Hallo, Colin," I said nervously. "If we're not welcome, just say so. We only wanted to see how you were."

He responded with a sullen twitch of one shoulder. I glanced at Huw. We approached a little closer until we stood a pace or two away, opposite the girl.

"I didn't bring anything," I blurted out foolishly.

"What, no expensive box of artisan chocolates?" There was the suggestion of a jeer in Colin's voice. "Or did you forget the wreath? Well, I'm not dead yet."

Huw sighed.

I said quickly: "Goodness, I don't know. It's customary."

He clicked his tongue in weary scorn. "Whatever."

The girl, a wiry little thing in leggings under a woollen dress, flat ankle-boots, and a knitted hat over feathery dark waves of soft hair, looked belligerently from one to the other of us. "Who are you?"

"Oh, let *me*," said Colin with exaggerated, sarcastic courtesy. "*Miss* Greatrex, and *Mr*—or is it Professor, now?—Trefor."

"Don't be an idiot, Colin," said Huw mildly. "This is Cassie. I'm Huw; same college as Colin. And who—"

"Friend or foe?" asked Colin, flashing a bright, meaningless smile.

"And who are you?" asked Huw of the girl, ignoring this.

"I don't think it would mean anything to you if I told you," she replied with an irritatingly excluding air.

"It might. Try me," suggested Huw, declining, with just the faintest suggestion of gritted teeth, to be excluded.

The knitted hat tossed impatiently. "I'm Rachael Levinson."

"Are you a consultant?" I asked. She wasn't dressed like one, but then, that's no guide these days. I wondered suddenly, and with sudden, rather shame-faced compassion, if she were the help the Dean had mentioned. I didn't think he had specified anyone, but somehow the name was familiar.

"No! I'm a friend. A university friend. Not Colin's college. You could say we met through work."

"Work," repeated Huw with palpable derision, his lip curling.

I said hurriedly: "Are you an historian, too?"

"Yes. Look,"—she reached out to Colin—"I'll come back."

"No, don't go." Colin abandoned his aggression and put out a supplicating hand in response to hers. "These are the people who..." His face convulsed with sudden pain, not physical. "Cassie paid for me to be flown home."

The girl's eyes flew to me, their expression hard to read. She said nothing.

"And Huw... Huw probably saved my life."

"Eh?" Huw had been pulling up a chair for me, but at this he cast a look of surprise at the figure in the bed. "How do you work that out?"

Colin was plucking at the blanket. "You made me see what a bloody idiot I was." The words were mumbled, even ungracious. Despite their confessional nature, there was a glint in the sideways glance at us that I didn't like; almost as though he was seeing how we were taking this.

"Well, there's something," said Huw. The Welsh lilt was faintly there, cool, and welcome as a shower of rain in the overheated room, and the tone of his voice had been pacific enough, but for all that, I wondered if he were working at it. There was something about Colin Bardsey that lit Huw's blue touchpaper. And something about all this brave owning-up that didn't—quite—ring true.

The girl said to me: "You live next door to my grandmother, don't you?"

A light went on. "Of course! You're Mrs Mitchell's Rachael! I thought I'd heard your name before. Isn't that the most amazing coincidence? However do you come to be here?"

"It isn't really a coincidence at all," said Rachael repressively. "There are very few people who do what I do, and I have been working with Helmut Landeck since I graduated. With my connections at Oxford, and in London, he thought I would be the right choice."

It wasn't said smugly, but with an academic's precision. The right choice...to do what? To befriend the young man who had so nearly died? Remembering how Helmut had handled him, it fitted in well with what I knew of the German's large charity. And just perhaps it was to pick up any stray snippets of information Colin might let fall... It came to me that of all the assorted academics and clever people I'd met lately, Rachael was the only one who made me feel inadequate.

On Colin, however, her precision had a different effect. I saw him look briefly at her, then down again, and the expression in his eyes was one of admiration. Not entirely academic admiration, either, I thought. Good for Helmut.

"Your grandfather," Rachael was saying, "will be told how useful his forethought is going to be to us. There are many families who will have cause to bless him when we are able to return their rightful property to them."

We had only sent the email the day before, and I didn't know if there had yet been a reply. Without Helmut's go-ahead, we had no right at all even to hint that the inventories were found. Safely in Mrs Mitchell's bank or not, they burned a hole in my mind. I murmured some conventional reply, wincing a little at the expression on Colin's face. He went on plucking at the blanket, not looking at any of us.

Rachael said: "I am looking forward to seeing *The Iliad*. It is quite an adventure story. There's a lot to do."

"Rachael and I have something in common," said Colin, addressing the mound that was his feet. He left off defacing N.H.S. property and gave Huw a fleeting, defiant glance. "She's Jewish, like me."

"So it's personal," I said, trying for a smile.

"You could say so," said Colin.

"Of course not," said Rachael at the same time. "We must never allow the personal to interfere with our professionalism."

This sounded pompous, like something she had picked up in a lecture-hall, or from a textbook, and since I could find nothing tactful to say in reply, I kept quiet.

Huw, less reticent, and his disbelief patent, said: "If you're able to do that, you're more than human."

I couldn't help myself then. I said: "If there's no personal element, what drew you to such a field at all? Didn't your grandfather endow the bursary in the first place? He'd be awfully proud of you, I'm sure."

I'm sorry to say that it pleased me to see how pink she went. It stripped her of her academic veneer and made her look a lot more human.

"That's quite true: he did," she said stiffly. She shot a glance at Colin, and all at once I thought I knew just where the personal was obtruding itself into her life.

"The personal makes a good guide," Huw was saying, "as long as you keep it on a light rein."

"Or a chain," said Colin. He jerked his chin at the girl. "She's going to help me stay clean."

This made Rachael blush hotly, as though the naked revelation of her humanity were something to be ashamed of. I took pity on her, and sat down on the chair Huw had set for me. It was a blue plastic one, with a hole in the back. I was very careful not to look at him.

"I gather," I said to Colin, and choosing my words, "that you're going to make a full recovery."

"Yup."

I tried again. "Have you thought what you're going to do when you get out of here?"

"Yup," said Colin again, annoyingly. The hazel eyes gleamed. "I'm going out to Germany for the rest of the summer, and I'm going to get a job or something. Then I'm going to go back to Oxford next Michaelmas term, and I'm going to switch courses."

I called down silent blessings on the Dean's head. "To do what?"

"Art History Detection," he said. His tone was even, and he directed a look of faint challenge at Huw.

"That's a wonderful idea," I said, more warmly.

"I think so. Do the thing properly. No more stalking people, and...trying to steal their books."

For the first time since he had walked into Dinah's salon, I liked him again. He gave me a ghost of his charming smile, as though he hadn't used it for a while.

"Two wrongs not making a right?"

"Yup, that's about it. And it's a new-ish discipline, so I'd be in demand. There'd be lots of money in it."

Liking withered rapidly. I dropped my gaze, but not before I had seen the gleam of disapproval on Rachael's face. If Colin thought he was going to have this new path all his own way, he had another think coming.

"And I expect all this has the Dean's blessing?" asked Huw, as though he had read my thoughts—and as though we hadn't left the Dean's rooms an hour since.

I shifted my chair noisily so I shouldn't have to hear Colin say *Yup* again, and so lost his reply. But in any case, a nurse came in just then, and Rachael, Huw, and I were excluded in a professional competence of nylon curtain and thermometers. We murmured our goodbyes, and found ourselves out in the corridor. The stolid policeman watched us closely without getting up from his chair.

"Rachael," I said.

She lifted her brows coldly at me.

"We're both very glad Colin has you to be his friend." I spoke hurriedly, not sure how the words were going to sound. "You must believe me when I say that I—that neither Huw nor I wanted for a single second—I mean, we both…"

"I know what you mean," she said, surprisingly gentle. "He told me what a complete tit he made of himself. He said he thought you were very brave."

"I don't know about that," I said awkwardly. "I do know that I have two loving parents, which Colin hasn't, and that—makes a difference. Heavens, I can't begin to say what I mean. What I mean is, I think, that he actually has us as well as you, even if he doesn't want to think so." I let this piece of ineptitude die quietly. She said:

"That's kind of you. He's had a horrid time. Don't be offended, but I shouldn't think he'll want to see either of you ever again. Too many bad memories. But it's still nice to know, and I'll make sure he does."

And with that, she cast a final glance through the glass panel in the door, nodded the knitted hat curtly to us, and went.

As the diminutive and undeniably trim woollen back-view disappeared into the throng of worried visitors, hurrying medical personnel, porters, trolleys, and all the other paraphernalia of a busy teaching hospital, Huw murmured something.

"Say that again? I missed it."

He obligingly repeated it. "'I grow old, I grow old; I shall wear the bottoms of my trousers rolled.'"

"*What?*"

"Sorry. Comes of being a poet's son and not being able to write poetry: I quote a lot. Doesn't that sound like an online gambling den?"

"Or a comic-strip Grail knight. Er—was that a sample of your father's poetry?" I tried not to sound dismayed.

"Certainly not. It was Eliot, the incomparable Eliot, of the T. S. variety. I don't actually like my father's poetry much," he added, "only please don't tell my mother I said so. T. S. Eliot also ran as far as she's concerned."

"I wouldn't dream of it. *Don't* you?"

"No. All blank verse, sandals, seventies political angst, and no metre. Concrete Corbusierism, great indigestible slabs of it."

"Dear me," I said politely.

"Quite. Me, I'm a hopeless romantic. I like my verse to go with a pentametric swing, and preferably rhyme a bit. Well, quite a lot."

"I'll hold you to the romantic bit," I said. "Talking of which, lunch?"

"Yes…" He said it absently, but there was a gleam in his eye that put me on my guard. "Can you bear to wait for a bit? I've some rather important things I've still to say to our delightful Mr Bardsey, and I wasn't banking on an audience. I hope the nurse won't be much longer… Ah." This as the nurse emerged into the corridor and walked briskly away without acknowledging us.

Huw patted his pockets as though looking for something. "I'm sorry," he said blandly to the policeman, "but I've left my notebook in there. May we?"

I didn't quite trust that gleam, and was expecting—hoping—that the policeman would refuse us without hesitation, so it was somewhat to my dismay that he waved us in without a murmur. In fact, I think he even smiled.

TWENTY

Dog, thou art now again escaped from death; yet came ill
very nigh thee: but now hath Phoebus Apollo saved thee...

Book XI: *ibid*

"OH, PLEASE, NOT again," protested Colin. "What do you
want now? Hey, what the hell are you doing?"

"Ensuring that we won't be disturbed," replied Huw,
pulling the curtain round the bed.

Colin shrank back against his pillows. His eyes went to
the red alarm button lying beside him.

"Don't worry," said Huw, sitting down. "You won't need
that." He was grinning, not nicely.

"I don't want to talk to you," said Colin truculently.

"I don't much want to talk to you, either, but the sooner
you tell us what we want to know, the sooner we can get out
of here. I just about exhausted my stock of consideration for
you by not speaking out in front of your woolly watchdog
just now."

I had resumed my seat of earlier. The flimsy nylon
curtain enclosed the three of us in an uneasy intimacy, and

I pushed the chair a little further back from the bed. I had no idea what questions he wanted to ask Colin, so I stayed silent, very aware of the rhythmic beeping from the opposite corner of the ward.

Huw said: "I'll begin by reminding you that you owe me £300. It took me three months of bar-work to save it up. When are you going to pay me back?"

The colour washed into Colin's face. He muttered something, and was silent. He looked as shifty as Huw had accused him of being.

Huw sighed. "When you go out to Germany and get a job, you can save it up and pay me back. Is it a deal?"

"S'pose so." The hazel gaze still lay on the alarm. Huw leant forward, picked it up, and sat back, holding it in his lap, just out of Colin's reach.

"Now, you listen very carefully to me. I've got some very unpleasant things to say to you, and I hope they hurt. We're all very sorry for you, being an orphan and all that, but I have no father, and I haven't allowed it to sap me of resolve. My mother hasn't allowed widowhood and poverty to get the better of her. Cassie could have coasted through life, but she hasn't allowed her money to drain her of character and purpose. Why on earth should you be allowed to carry on as though the world owes you a living?"

No answer. Colin, scarlet, glared at his knees.

After a moment, Huw went on: "For some unfathomable reason, you've got several people prepared to give you their support. Don't you think the least you can do is to pull your finger out and make an effort? And before you jump in with one of your excuses, I heard all you said about looking for work in Germany and changing courses, and that. It's a start, and a good one, but I'm not talking about the academic stuff: this is about how you continually duck out of real life."

There was a silence. Colin didn't attempt to reply.

I said gently: "Colin, you owe it most of all to yourself. We all have trials in life, obstacles to overcome, weaknesses. You should be fighting yours. Don't waste time and energy fighting us. We're on your side."

"Even him?" The tone was bitter.

"Yes," said Huw. "Even me. You said so yourself, remember? I know you've got a good brain: I said as much to the Dean. That's a huge asset. You didn't crib Cassie's father's work because you aren't able to think for yourself, did you?"

A shrug and a sullen mutter, which Huw seemed to be able to interpret easily.

"Exactly. You did it in a hurry, for mon…for other reasons. If you apply your energies to your advantage, instead of—what did you say?"

"I *said*, I don't know how to. All I learnt at school was what you dismiss as *academic stuff*. I don't know any…" His voice trailed away.

I spoke for him. "Life skills? Is that what you mean?"

Another weary lift of the shoulder.

I put a hand on the bed. "When you said Rachael was going to help you get clean, what did you mean?"

No answer.

I persevered. "You couldn't do yourself a better favour than to talk to Rachael—and listen to her advice." If I was sure of anything, it was that Rachael Levinson had enough life skills for two.

"I've told her stuff already."

"That's fantastic," I said warmly. It had come grudgingly, but at least it had come. "There's something else you can do for yourself, and that's join a group that'll help you battle the gambling. I'm sure there'll be one in Oxford. You never know, it might not be in your blood: it might just have become a habit."

"Is there a difference?"

I was startled. "Well, yes, of course there is."

"I don't see it, myself."

"That's only because you're not used to questioning your motives. Heredity has to be lived with—coped with—strategised. But bad habits can be broken, and good ones formed in their stead—*if* you're prepared to put in the effort."

The words sounded familiar, and I realised that that was another thing my father had taught me. I hadn't known that it had even gone home, never mind stayed with me. That this was indeed foreign territory to Colin was evident from the scornful disbelief on his face.

I said: "There is one thing I'd like to know."

"Well, what?"

"What made you jump for the window like that, down there in the well?"

The colour ebbed swiftly, leaving him pale and wary. "I didn't think. I heard the footsteps. I thought Saratov was after me. I just wanted to get away."

Huw said incredulously: "You've actually *met* Saratov?"

"I told you. Well, I told the German."

"Oh, that. You call that meeting him?"

Colin shifted in the narrow bed. "We weren't exactly introduced socially," he said with a sneer.

"Oh, dump the chip off your shoulder before you hurt yourself," recommended Huw, losing patience. "My background's as undistinguished as yours, for what it matters. And whoever said that good manners are reserved for middles and uppers? Is that any way to honour your parents, whether you knew them or not?"

"I've had just about enough of you," muttered Colin angrily.

"What did he say to frighten you so badly?" I pursued. "We guessed that's why you came out to Italy in such a rush. You might as well tell us the whole story."

The hazel eyes glinted suddenly, and the bandaged head turned away. "He got past the porter somehow," he said unsteadily. "It was a hot day; my door was open. He just walked in. I'd got my head into an essay, and—there he was. He didn't beat about the bush. He said that if Russia didn't get to those lists before Germany, he'd have to dispose of me. That's how he put it: 'dispose of me'. He…he told me what had happened to Kevin, and that he knew all about our plans. Actually, he put the blame on Helmut. You can imagine I wasn't any too chuffed to find him on my tail as well."

"I don't see how it would help to murder you too— although on second thoughts—" Huw began, but I spoke quickly across him.

"I expect it was just a threat. But down in the well you said you'd seen Helmut leave."

He clicked his tongue in a kind of weary scorn at my stupidity. "I only *said* that."

"You saw nothing? All right." I left it. "So you took fright, and came out after Huw."

"Sort of, and sort of after you."

"After me? But how did you know I had the Homer with me?"

"I didn't. I thought you and he"—a jerk of his chin at Huw—"were holding out on me. The diary said the lists were in the back of the Homer, and I suppose I refused to believe they weren't there. I mean, they *had* to be there. They…they were worth a huge sum to me."

"Which you would have dribbled away on your virtual poker games," said Huw.

"Whatever. If you don't like the answers, don't ask the questions. O'Leary said you had taken your Fitzgerald out to Italy—he actually thought it was quite funny, so I thought I'd take a—" He stopped.

Huw said cuttingly: "Don't tell me. You thought you'd take a gamble on it."

Colin, pointedly ignoring Huw, said to me in sudden, urgent excitement: "I got lucky in that last game: it paid off, and how! I only needed to draw one to get the fifth for the flush, and there it was—*there it was*: the pot was mine! Just like that! I mean, it was insane!"

"Yes," I said shortly. It was the first spark of animation he had displayed, aside from anger, resentment, and all the rest of the dreary catalogue of chronic victimhood, and it dismayed me. I wondered just what his chances would be once he got out of hospital.

He cast me a sulky look. "I was on a lucky streak that time. It got me out to Athens—and then finding your dad there, large as life, just when I needed him. How could I lose? Then, as soon as I saw all the scribbles your boyfriend had done in his Fitzgerald, I thought, what was the point of that, unless you'd brought your granddad's out with you to compare it with? Gave me a laugh, that did. Scribbling all that crap in the wrong sodding translation! Codes!"

"It gave us a laugh, too," replied Huw evenly. "Where did you get the money to fly out to Italy? Another successful bout of gambling?"

Colin said nothing.

"What, surely not silent in seven languages? Did you nick it?"

"Huw," I said warningly.

"Did you?"

"Bloody hell, *no!*"

"Then where? Go on, you evasive little wart, *where?*"

The questions pounded remorselessly, like a huge, incoming tide on the sand, and Colin suddenly gave way.

"Oh, all *right!* Saratov gave me the money, okay? I told him I hadn't got the lists, but I knew where they were. At least, I wasn't sure, obviously—but I had to tell him something. He—he frightened me, just standing there, looking at me. He said I'd better get a move on, hadn't I, and find them. There would be more when I handed them safely over to him—much more. And he—"

"He what?" Huw's voice was dangerously light.

"He said if I didn't find them, he'd do so himself."

My feet were cold. My hands were gripped tightly together in my lap. I didn't want to ask, but I had to know. "Did he—I mean, does Saratov still think the lists are in the Homer?"

"He must do." There was a faint surprise in Colin's voice. "Otherwise, why send me after you?"

Huw said: "And does he know that you haven't found them?"

A shrug. "Who knows? I'm safe enough here, aren't I?"

"You miserable little... You seem to forget you're not the only one concerned in this!" The steely note was back in Huw's voice.

I stirred on my uncomfortable seat. "Am I to take it that your delightful Russian friend *knew* I had the Homer on me?"

"Well, of course."

"How?" Huw was leaning forward.

"God knows," said Colin warily, shrinking away. "He didn't give me chapter and verse. He's been watching you, I should think. He watched Kevin, and me. He probably searched your house. He's very good—you'd never have known he'd been there." He shivered suddenly. "Now I think I've had enough of you two badgering me, so go away, will you?" With a surprisingly swift movement, he shot out a hand to snatch the alarm button, but Huw was too quick for him.

"All in good time. We want to know what made you think you could turn over Mr Greatrex's study and get away with it, and how you got onto Cassie's father in the first place."

Colin sank back on his pillows with a gusty, resentful sigh. I was glad to remain silent, to digest the uncomfortable knowledge that my every movement must have been under surveillance for some time. My every movement... I looked down at my hands in my lap, conscious, now, only of a slightly accelerated heartbeat, and, behind it, a thin black weft of disgust threading through the familiar fear. The idea that that man—that murderer—had been within twenty miles of me, never mind in my house...going through my things. But why hadn't he found the papers? Had he *planted* them? But what on earth for? How would incriminating me help him? Where had he found them? Had they been in Russian hands all along? Were we now mere pawns in some intricate and deadly political game of Grandmother's Footsteps? Would we be—how had Colin put it—*disposed of* when we had outlived our usefulness, as the wretched Kevin Dunston had outlived his? I wrenched my cringing mind away. Listen to Colin. Anything's better than wondering and worrying. And then: *Helmut.* He would know. I must speak to Helmut...

"It was in Athens, at the museum, if you must know," Colin was saying. "He was examining the Lemnos stele with the curator, and talking nineteen to the dozen about it. I heard the curator address him by name, that's all."

319

I looked up at that, eyes narrowing in anger and disbelief. "*All?* Is that what you call it? How dare you?"

Huw made a sudden movement, and Colin jumped. "Don't touch me! I'm not well!"

"I wouldn't soil my hands, you dirty little beast, even if I am in the mood to rip your lying head off your shoulders and play football with it. Now, give!"

Still with that air of injured resentment, Colin gave at last.

It seemed he had waited only for my father to leave, then approached the curator, and, with some story of knowing my family, learnt that my father's next move was to visit Lemnos itself before flying home a couple of days later. Colin, seeing only that the coast would be clear, and with money to burn from a successful game, went straight to the airport and changed his ticket to an earlier flight. Arriving at Heathrow he had taken the bus and a taxi to my parents' house, and just as Mummy and I had thought, watched the house on the off-chance of an opportunity. As soon as we had left that morning to go and collect the eggs, he slipped through the unlocked doors of the study and began a hurried and unavailing search through my father's things. That he had found nothing was, I gathered with a wry, inward smile, not so much due to there being nothing to find as to the prevailing state of chaos. Not daring to stay any longer, he had lingered only to make a note of my address in London and my place of work before slipping away as furtively as he had arrived, over the gate at the back of the garden. In Oxford once more he had gone to ground, and with Kevin Dunston's help, thought up his plan of campaign. Then he located me at Dinah's salon and set to work.

"Are you aware," I said into the silence that succeeded this squalid little tale, "that you left your fingerprints all over the study?"

He came away from his pillows with a jerk, and a wince that the sudden movement cost him. *"Fingerprints?* God, I never thought... Oh, well, it doesn't matter. I'm not on anybody's records. They won't find a match." The confident, cocky note was back. He leant back again and smiled at us.

Huw lifted his lip and said, with a good deal of meaning: "Your prints are on the records now, though, even if you're not. Better make sure nobody finds a match in the future, eh?" His eye fell on the bedside table. "It would be quite easy," he added mildly, picking up the clear plastic beaker that stood there and holding it up to the light, out of Colin's reach, "to make absolutely sure of that, if you follow me." He scrutinised the beaker. "Smashing: a perfect set. All I have to do is put this in my pocket and take it away with me. Oh, no, you don't! Helmut will know exactly what to do with this."

I said: "I expect the Italian police would be glad of a set, too."

Colin, confidence shattered, said sharply: "Give that back! It's mine!"

Huw got up and stood for a moment, looking down at the quivering, groping figure. "No," he said finally. "I don't think so. This is our insurance policy." He put the beaker in an inside pocket, and tossed the alarm button contemptuously onto the bed. "Come on, Cassie. Let's get out of here. I need some fresh air."

"Huw."

"Mm?"

"Colin said—he said that Saratov had been watching us. Do you...do you think he still is?"

"Pretty unlikely." His deep voice was lazy, peaceable, and immeasurably reassuring. "Where would be the point? If I were Saratov, the person I'd be keeping an eye on is Helmut Landeck. I'm willing to bet he's gone haring off to Bonn in Helmut's wake. National pride at stake, and all that. I expect the German government will have taken the Russian government aside and murmured something in its collective ear to the effect that Saratov's services are somewhat redundant, and could they please remove him from duty."

"Oh. That's...that's good."

Silence reigned for some miles.

"Huw?"

"Yes?"

"Did you really say we were engaged?"

"Not in so many words, but I do vaguely recall making a proposal of marriage to someone. Was that you?"

"Because if you did, if you really mean it, we need Champagne. I refuse to let Colin Bardsey deprive me of my celebration."

He patted a few pockets. "Quite right: I approve of your approach. I don't seem to have any on me."

"Money, or Champagne?"

"Either."

"I do call that thoughtless." I rummaged in my bag. "We'll have to raid the petty cash. Here you are. Shall we go together?"

"Not on your life. You can get the glasses ready."

Mrs Mitchell came out to greet me as soon as she saw her car. She was, understandably, anxious to hear how we had got on, and delighted that we had met Rachael. It was some time before I got away, and then only by saying I had promised to go and meet Huw.

"Haven't you given him a key yet? Poor boy!"

I escaped without answering this.

And now I was fussing about the sitting-room, plumping cushions and tidying aimlessly; which was why I paid no attention to the taxi idling under the window. When the doorbell rang, I ran to answer it, expecting to see him. But it wasn't Huw. It was my family. Their taxi pulled away, leaving me alone with them.

"What, only three of you?" I asked, dismayed, as they converged upon me. "Couldn't you find Uncle Will, or my cousins, to make up the numbers? What are you doing in London, anyway? Not that I'm not delighted to see you, I am—particularly since there's something important I—"

"I told you to expect us, darling," said my mother. "May we come in?" she asked, coming in. I backed up, compelled, quite literally, by *force majeure*, into the sitting-room.

"We have just been confessing, vicariously, to your grandfather," said my father, pacing up and down as far as the limited floor space would allow, "and he insisted on coming to see you for himself."

"Most certainly," struck in my grandfather. "I want to hear this preposterous story from your own lips. Your nice German friend gave it me over the telephone from his side—but he seems to think his government needs my *Iliad* more than I do. I want to know all about it from your side. I could barely make head or tail of your parents' story, except something about your falling down a well. Which," he added, scrutinising me, "looks more likely than I gave it credit for."

"And when you've finished that," said my mother, with her arms folded, "you can tell me exactly what possessed you to pour a lot of nonsense into my little brother's ears. He believed every word of it—until he got back to Orvieto and found it humming. That's how he put it to me—after we'd faithfully told your grandfather, too! So I gave him your version, and he didn't believe a word of that, either. Now I don't know what to believe, and you, my dear, are going to tell me."

"Phew," I protested, privately cursing my uncle. "Can you arrange among yourselves who's going to get their answer first?"

My family all began to talk at once, but my mother comfortably won the day, and I was obliged to give in.

"Look, let's sit down, shall we?" I suggested. "It was difficult to know what to tell Uncle Will—he'd just got the news of the donation, and his mind was on other things. But I certainly told you the truth, Mummy, or most of it." I smiled a little uncertainly at my seething grandfather. "When you brought your *Iliad* home in 1945, Grandpa, you also, whether you knew it or not, brought home your inventories of people whose works of art had been looted. It's priceless information—and we simply found ourselves in the way of some rather nasty bandits who'd stick at nothing to use those lists for their own purposes."

"Simply!" echoed my mother.

"You know what I mean. There's nothing else to tell. I'll apologise to Uncle Will, but you know what he's like." I turned to my grandfather again. "Huw and I wondered if you'd perhaps been hit in the head, Grandpa, and forgotten that you'd stuck them into the back?"

My grandfather shrugged helplessly. "I must have done, darling. I had no idea at all. But I've still got my old Record of Service somewhere: any wounds I sustained will be in there. I certainly remember compiling the inventories—although I thought I'd burnt everything. That is," he corrected himself, "I *assumed* I'd burnt them. Better that, than they should fall into the wrong hands." He gave my mother a strange look. "If I'd had the slightest idea, Moira, I would never have lent the book to her."

My mother put a hand to his arm. "Of course not, Hector; not for one moment. We've told you that."

"Where are the inventories now?" asked my father.

"In the bank."

"Your bank?"

"Well, sort of. I mean, we deposited them at Goldhanger & Newbold's all right, but in Prince of Denmark's Row."

"That's not your branch," objected my father.

"It's Mrs Mitchell's branch. It was her suggestion—and it was brilliant, as it turns out, because her granddaughter is an Art History Detective, and we actually met her today. She's going to be working on your *Iliad*, Grandpa. They had some idea of reconstructing the lists from the ink-stains. We sent Helmut an email from Mrs Mitchell's house telling him they were found, the inventories, I mean, but I'm not sure if Helmut has already taken them back to Germany." I glanced at the time. "Which I don't think he can have yet, because it's not tomorrow, and the bank's shut now, anyway. Oh, dear, I'm not explaining this very well."

"I can shed some light," said my grandfather. "He wants me to meet him at the bank and formally identify them as mine. Thing is, we can't do that without your Mrs Mitchell, and he has no way of getting in touch with her."

I said: "Crumbs, we didn't think of that. But it's all right, Huw can send him another email."

At the exact moment that my grandfather asked: "Who is Mrs Mitchell?" my father spoke as well.

"Where is *The Iliad*, after all the excitement?"

I said, distractedly, because the doorbell had just rung, "It's—she's my— That must be Huw. Hold on a second." I ran to the door. "You've been ages! Why, hallo again, Mrs Mitchell."

"Cassie, dear, I wanted to tell you that Rachael's just rung to ask me for…" She stopped. My family had broken *en masse* into vociferous speech again, and were plainly audible from the hall. "I'm sorry, I wouldn't have bothered you if I'd known you'd company. I'll make myself scarce. Come round when you can."

"No, please come and join us. You are—once again—the very person we need. If Huw comes back with the shopping, and brings his mother, and possibly the Dean as well, we can have a proper celebration. Perhaps a street party? No, well, never mind. Everybody, *this* is Mrs Mitchell, my exceedingly kind next-door neighbour, and repository of top secret documents. My mother and father, and my grandfather. They're all in the know, Mrs Mitchell, so you needn't worry. Grandpa's got to go and identify his handwriting, Helmut says, which he can't do without you, and he doesn't know where you are anyway, Helmut, I mean, and I'm being grilled to a crisp by my loving parents, so all in all I'm jolly glad you've…"

This petered out. She wasn't listening to me, or exchanging conventional salutations with my mother and father, both of whom had stepped forward with hands politely held out. Under the expensive *maquillage* she had gone quite white. Bemused, I looked from her to my grandfather, and saw that he had gone equally pale. He was staring at her unblinkingly. Greetings died on everybody's lips. The room was, suddenly, very quiet.

She spoke then, in a strangled whisper.

"But—I know you! You're the man in Berlin! The English officer who helped me escape from the Russians!"

TWENTY-ONE

Where sportive ladies leave their doors ajar.

Browning: *Fra Lippo Lippi 6*

SHE CAME FORWARD to him. "I would know you anywhere! You're alive! It is a miracle!" Another wavering step; her hands went out, as it were of their own accord.

My parents' eyes and mine went from her to my grandfather like homing bees to the hive.

"Inge?" It came out hoarsely, almost a boy's croak. "*Ingelore?*"

"Yes, I am Inge! But you! I never knew your name! There was not time!"

She spared my parents and me a fleeting, comprehensive glance, and said, with a little frown: "Greatrex...it must be. Is it so? It is? After all this time, I find out your name! My brave Englishman! So young! Never have I forgotten you, never!"

His hands, veined and strong, took both of hers and closed over them. "You're safe," he said in a low voice. A smile began to tremble at the corners of his mouth. "I am so glad. In good health? comfortable circumstances? You look—marvellous."

"Yes, yes, both! I have been so lucky! Please tell me your Christian name!"

"It's Hector," said my grandfather; and suddenly I could see the twenty-year-old Second Lieutenant, the young man who had written so dramatically about the Lancasters while the very bombs were dropping and there was gold to be guarded with his life. I didn't want to stare, but I couldn't have dragged my gaze away from them if I'd tried. Tears had welled in Mrs Mitchell's eyes and were beginning to fall. She blinked them away, and stood back a little so that she could look him up and down.

"You look so strong, still! so fit and—and manly!"

"I run a gymnasium," said my grandfather without taking his rapturous gaze off her, "here, in Chelsea. You are—just as you were. I knew you instantly. They asked if I had lost my memory," he said, "and it's true: for some things, I had. But you? I never forgot you, you brave girl. I remember how you shook your fist at the Russians! I felt if it was the last thing I did, I would get you safely away from them." He dropped one of her hands, brought out a handkerchief, and himself dried her radiant cheeks. For some reason this made them both break into tremulous laughter, and seemed to bring them back to some sense of their surroundings. My grandfather closed her fingers over his handkerchief when she would have had him take it back, and kept her hand in his own. He cleared his throat.

"You'll no doubt have gathered by now," he said, in our general direction, and keeping the irony light, "that I...that we've..." Despite himself, his voice tailed off, and his eyes went straight back to her.

I pulled myself together. "That you've already met? Yes, I think you could say so. It's—I don't know what to say. It's like a miracle!"

"I was fifteen," said Mrs Mitchell, now blushing pink. "I will not tell you what a fate he rescued me from. Both my parents were dead, killed in the bombing. Women all over Berlin committed suicide to escape what the Russians would do to them. Ach, all these years, and my English begins to escape me! I am a girl again! Hector! It is a beautiful name!"

"Thank you," said both my male relations in unison. This made us all laugh, and dispelled a little more of the tension.

"And so you are Cassie's grandfather? I find it ludicrous that you should be anybody's grandfather. I think I had better sit down."

"I'm so sorry," I said hastily, "I think we've all been hit for six. Mummy, let's go and do some tea, or something."

"I rather think *or something* is called for," said my father firmly. "This needs celebrating!"

"There's a bottle of Prosecco in the refrigerator." I offered this doubtfully—this was my father, after all. "But Huw will have got some Champagne. He went to the supermarket. He's been ages. You see, there's something we want to tell you—"

"That's my girl. You might as well bring what you've got. It'll do to be going on with. Will he mind if we start without him? Where do you keep your glasses?"

"In the cupboard," I replied, "and I'm sure he won't mind. You see, we—"

"Come on, Pa! Why have you not said a word about any of this? I want to know everything!"

It was understandable, I suppose, that nobody had the least attention to spare for anything else. I fetched the bottle and gave it to my father, and he took it and opened it, the while pelting my grandfather and Mrs Mitchell with questions over his shoulder. My mother drew Mrs Mitchell to the sofa, and everybody settled down to hear the tale.

I accepted a glass, but I stood a little apart. It wasn't that I didn't want to hear—of course I did. But I had just got engaged, and my feelings were a bit confused. Not about Huw—never that. No, it was that for the first time I had a life apart from my family. It was the same lonely feeling as I'd had at the dinner-party—and yet not quite the same. I drank, and watched their animated faces, and listened. And gradually I realised that I would not, after all, be apart from them. The focus had shifted slightly, that was all. Relationships change over time. And they would always be my family, no matter what. I sipped a bit more, considering this; allowing the new certainty to take root. I began to feel better. I even smiled as I watched them, now all talking at once.

There would be little hope for quite some time of breaking our news. I would slip out and see if I could intercept Huw on his way back and prepare him. Perhaps by the time we got back, the initial buzz would have settled down, and we could announce our engagement and really have a party.

I left the door wide just in case I missed him. I did tug at my mother's sleeve to tell her, and she said, "Of course, darling," warmly, but I knew she hadn't heard me. It was funny, but it didn't really matter.

There was no one in the street. When I reached the corner where the plane tree is, three houses along, I turned and looked back past it—I'm not sure why, unless it was to confirm me in my new sense of independence. The light was streaming through the window and out of the open door, lying in hospitable welcome across the pavement. There was laughter; and eager voices raised themselves in question and answer. I smiled, and was about to go on my way, when a man detached himself from the shadowed doorway of a house opposite mine and stood at the top of the steps looking across the road. For a moment, I thought it must be Huw, and was puzzled. Why was he coming from that direction? He could hardly have got lost. And where was the shopping? Had he put it down under the portico, perhaps reluctant to announce himself amid a brightly lit and noisy family get-together? My foot went out to step into the road and go to him before it was barely formed in my mind to wonder why he had not hailed me immediately.

He moved then, and I saw two things straight away. He was carrying a coat of some sort over his right arm; and he was a stranger.

Disappointed, and still no more than beginning to be wary, I brought the foot back—and then, all at once, was glad that I had done so. He glanced keenly, and—as I thought— straight at me. From instinct, I melted behind the trunk's solid shelter. He looked tough, and hard, and dangerous, and suddenly I was frightened. This was no Colin Bardsey to be faced down with a doorstop in my hands. I tried to think back, but it was like bringing a jibbing horse under control. Had he heard me? My shoes were rubber-soled and made no noise on the flags. He must have seen me leave, then. My clothes were dark; perhaps he would think I was already long gone. I kept mouse-still. Checking swiftly to left and right, he extended the arm with the coat slung over it, almost as though to shake hands with someone, and crossed the road. He gained the pavement. He was coming... The thoughts crashed about chaotically. I knew I would never get away— the tree was too smooth to climb—he would catch me before I could run to safety. I was done for, as Kevin Dunston had been done for... The scream rose in my throat. I was going to die, and Huw was nowhere.

He bypassed me altogether, took the steps two at a time, and disappeared into the house. I distinctly heard the *clunk* of the spring lock as he shut the door—my door—behind him.

Where any of the heroines I enjoy reading about would have leapt bravely into action, I just stood there behind my tree with one hand flat on the smooth plane of its bark and the other trembling over my open mouth. Then fear for myself drained abruptly, pushed out by fear for my family. I think I took a pace or two into the empty air where a moment ago there had been an open door and nobody on the steps, but at the same time I didn't believe what I had just seen. The fear alchemised to indignation. Soon I would be angry; and that might help.

"Hey!" I protested, futilely enough. My voice sounded silly, and small; vulnerable in the open air; and still the anger did not come. I had the strongest impression that this was not a casual snatch-and-grab. Whether he had seen me or not, he had seen me make things easy for him, and had seized his chance. In short, the man had a purpose in mind. But still I stood there, gaping uselessly, for about five seconds, when a faint scream—more a gasp of shocked surprise—from the house finally brought me back to reality and the need for action. The gasp was instantly followed by a forceful question from my father, and I moved then as though the pavement were red-hot.

The sitting-room window was open several inches at the bottom. Whether it had been my mother or Mrs Mitchell who had let out that frightened gasp I had no idea, but as I reached the railings, I heard a man speak, in a cringe-making echo of Colin.

"You will give me the lists now, and there will be no trouble."

Oh, God, no, not again. Not another one. At least Colin had said 'please'.... Then the mad inconsequence of this yielded to an icy thrill up the marrow of my spine as it came to me.

He had spoken in a Russian accent.

I clutched the railings and craned to see.

The tough man was standing not ten feet away from me, between the sofa and the window. His back, head-to-toe in black, was half-turned to me, and his fingers drummed, not quite idly, on the bottom of the sash.

My palms, cold and sweating, slipped on the slender iron bars still faintly warm from the day's sun. Shrinking away from the betraying pool of light, I crept up the steps on the other side and sat down abruptly, taking the warm iron again in a convulsive hold.

I'm glad, now, that shock momentarily drove out of my mind the name of Kevin Dunston's murderer. For I had no doubt that that's who it was, holding my family hostage. Why, I had known even while I was hiding under the plane tree... I think if I had remembered, I might have screamed there and then and sent them all to their deaths. As it was, I knew one thing only, and it blundered uselessly about in my brain like a wild animal in a trap: the Russian murderer, the so-called negotiator who had been watching me, was in my sitting-room, and I could do nothing until Huw came. All I had to do was wait for him. He would know what to do. Why on earth was he taking so long? I hardly dared move my eyes to search the darkened street for him.

Just above my head and to my right, my family's and Mrs Mitchell's voices were joined in angry protest. I distinctly heard my father begin to speak, but his words were obliterated entirely by a motorbike which roared into life just then, revving its engine noisily. It sounded shockingly close. It shot past me far too fast and spewing blue exhaust. In its wake, I heard the same voice say, presumably in reply to my father: "This is rubbish."

The Russian accent was strong, harsh and guttural; a wholly alien sound to be emanating from my house. Now the words came all too clear.

"Come, I followed the old one to the bank with the two young ones, and I followed home again. Where are they?"

"If you mean my daughter," came my father's voice, "she has gone to meet her boyfriend. We are expecting them back at any moment, and you will not be welcome."

"Be silent," said the Russian. He sounded both curt and bored, and I thought: *This must be chicken feed to him. He'll hardly have to break sweat...* "Do not waste my time. I have been watching this house; and you, old one, have my government's property. You will now give me those lists."

"Not at this time of the evening, I won't!"

Mrs Mitchell did not sound calm at all. I wanted to shout out to her, to beg her to be reasonable—to conciliate him.

"Then we sit here all night until you give them," said the implacable foreign voice. "It is all one to me."

Whether it was all one to my family and my neighbour, I didn't hear. A party of what Mummy would instantly have recognised as the latest generation of Sloanes had tumbled out of the pub on the corner—the corner where Colin had stood—and were weaving their way up the street towards me with much upper-crust joshing and laughter. They made so much noise that I couldn't hear what was being said, and I sat on my step, cursing them as they went past, thanking God when they did not see me. Then I forgot them as the sitting-room sash came down hard into the frame, making me jump, and cutting off all sound. Panic-levels soaring, I peered into the dark, willing Huw to appear; to come to the rescue for the second time...

The Sloanes had gone. The night was empty. No sound from my sitting-room, and no sign of Huw…

The plane tree became two; and there was a figure coming towards me…a strong, purposeful-looking man with a long stride…and a bulging carrier bag in each hand. I uttered a tiny whimper, half of terror, half of relief, and flew to him.

Even from a hundred yards' distance he must have spotted something was wrong, for no sooner had he caught sight of me than he broke into a run, rather hampered by the heavy shopping.

It's practically impossible to sprint with a finger pressed desperately to your lips for urgent silence. I abandoned the attempt, and flung myself at him. "Thank God, thank *God*," I panted, trying to keep my voice low. "The Russian man's in the house. I'm sure it's the one who murdered that journalist. My parents—my grandfather—Mrs Mitchell's there too. He's after those pestilential *bloody* lists, Huw—I'm so afraid—what on earth are we going to do?"

"*Saratov? Here?* Christ Almighty!"

"For God's sake, keep your voice down! He's standing right by the window!"

"Is he, indeed? So much for his having followed Helmut. What on earth does he hope to gain, I wonder?"

He put the two carrier bags he was holding roughly down on the pavement, and put an arm round me. It was incredibly comforting. "Perhaps he has followed him—here." My teeth were chattering, and I snuggled to him, hoping for both arms.

"What do you mean?"

"Of course—you don't know what my grandfather said." I told him, trying to hug him close, before becoming aware that he was not, as I had feared, pushing me away, but was looking for something. "*And* he—Saratov—said he'd followed us to the bank! What are you doing?"

"Trying to get my telephone out," he replied, tugging. "These jeans... Ah."

I stared down at the little black instrument in his hand, then up at him. "Who are you going to call? Huw, you can't! He might hear you, and shoot Mummy, or Grandpa or somebody! He might shoot all of them! Don't, please don't!"

He squeezed me briefly to him. "I'm only going to text Helmut. If anybody can help, he can, okay? And Saratov's not going to shoot anyone. One shot from him and we'd be six deep in armed Met. officers before you can say Achæan naval commanders. Did you see a gun, by the way?"

My smile was a sorry affair, but at least I tried. "No. Sorry: I've got you by the jumper again." I deliberately relaxed my grip. "I didn't even know Helmut was back in London."

"Yes. He said in his email."

"Well, that's something. But what the hell do we *do*?"

"Wait a moment. I don't normally like predictive text, but there are times... What about this? *Saratov holding C's family and neighbour hostage More Street, Chelsea.* What's the number?"

I told him, and he typed it. I watched doubtfully. The whole thing smacked of unreality, and seemed, somehow, to be supremely irrelevant. He pressed 'send', and put the thing back in his pocket.

"Now, while we're waiting, how would it be if you tell me exactly what happened?"

I gulped. Tears were not far away. "Okay. I'll do my best." I told him as quickly and lucidly as I could. It steadied me a little, which was a good thing, because halfway through, Huw's telephone uttered a mournful bleep. I knew what that meant. My heart sank. He hauled it out, not that he needed to: he knew as well as I did.

"*Message not sent.*"

"Oh, God..."

"It'll keep trying. Carry on."

"Where was I? Oh, yes, I'd just got to the bit where he said he'd followed us to the bank. Colin was right. He must have been watching us for ages." My voice broke on a sob and I gestured to the other side of the road. "That's the doorway, there. He must have been there while I was alone in the house—must have seen my family arrive and Mrs Mitchell go in." I shuddered. "Didn't I say...didn't I *say* it wasn't over?" The scalding tears sprang, stinging my eyes. "I can't *bear* it, Huw! It's too much, after what we've all been through! And Grandpa and Mrs Mitchell have only just found each other again—he helped her escape from Berlin—she was only fifteen, and they knew each other straight away— you should have seen how they looked at each other..."

I don't know if you've ever given way to a fit of sobbing without making any noise, but the only way I could do it was to jam my face against Huw's chest. It seemed to work; perhaps it was the lack of air. He held me close until I had quietened a little.

"Thank God you aren't in there with them. Why aren't you, by the way?"

"I was coming to meet you." I sniffed, and wiped my eyes on my sleeve. "You said you wouldn't be long, but you've been ages! What on earth kept you?"

"Busy evening; the place was packed."

"Oh. I didn't think of that." I sniffed again. "Daddy told him I was going to meet you. He was very clever, the way he put it. That man could have taken it any way he chose. I mean, he made it sound as though I was meeting you at King's Cross, or something."

For a second only, the arm went rigid round my shoulders. He relaxed it immediately, but some tiny change in him had already communicated itself to me so fast it might have been by telepathy. "What's the matter? Have you thought of something?"

He didn't answer, at least not directly. "But we are expected back."

I didn't understand to begin with. "Well—yes, of course. Why?" Then I saw. I began to shiver. "You mean—we've got to go back? Back in there, of our own free will?" My voice rose. "What, just stroll in and pretend we don't know he's there?"

He put a finger to my lips. "Just that. We've got to walk in as though we don't have a care in the world."

For a moment, I couldn't say a word. I just stared at him while the tears rolled unheeded down my cheeks. I think it was the worst few seconds of the whole terrifying business. It makes me hot with shame to think of it now, but the first thing I said, in a tiny, sulky voice, was: "I don't want to."

"Would you prefer to stay out here?"

I wiped my face angrily. "*No!*"

"Darling. Listen to me. If we don't, he might suspect something, and…and get a bit nasty."

I started to stammer something, heaven knows what, but he cut remorselessly across. "If by some remote chance he is armed, he'll have a heck of a job keeping six of us covered." His mouth twisted a little ruefully. "The other thing is, I'm a boxing blue, for what it's worth."

"Wh…what's that?" My jaws were set fast, and I spoke through my teeth.

"Sort of college prize-fighter, only guess what, no prizes."

"Bully for you." Too late, I heard the sneer in my voice.

He took me by the shoulders, bending his knees a little so we were eye to eye. "Don't you see?" he said gently. "It means I could be pretty useful—if necessary." He straightened and looked down at me.

There was a long, long moment of utter silence while

I battled with myself. Like any civilian, I was used to being bombarded with official exhortations not to meddle; to walk by on the other side; not to get involved. Unfortunately for officialdom, Mummy is a good, practical Christian, which means that she does things that need to be done, instead of waiting for other people to do them, and she does them straight away. She had impressed it upon me from an early age to do likewise. And I could hear my father's voice, too: "You don't keep a child safe by keeping it away from danger. You keep it safe by teaching it to handle danger safely." I had been brought up on these principles. But acting on those same principles is another matter altogether. I thought of another moment, in the Piazzale Cahen, when I had run away. I had left Huw then. Was I going to leave him again to face the music on his own?

I swallowed so convulsively that it hurt my throat, and dried my face on the back of my hands. "What will Helmut do when he gets the message?"

He hugged me, hard. "Goodness knows, but you can bet your last pot of nail varnish it'll be something efficient."

"Do you think," I said cravenly, "that we could ring 999 and say the house is being burgled? It's just an idea."

He gave a soft laugh. "It's not a bad one, but somehow I'd rather have Helmut and M.I.5 than the local constabulary, however well-intentioned. Did you notice if Saratov was carrying anything?"

"No, why? Oh, God, you don't think he really was armed? He wasn't toting an AK-47, if that's what you mean."

"Did he have a jacket on of some sort? I'm sorry to do this to you, but it might be important."

"I know." I closed my eyes. "No," I said after a moment. "No. Dark jumper, or fleece, and—black jeans, I think. Quite tight-fitting, anyway. Does that help?"

"It certainly does. It means he's not wearing a holster, so he can't be carrying anything larger than a small pistol, and if he had jeans on, he might not even be carrying that."

I gave a rather uncertain giggle. "He put his hand out, with the coat over his arm, just as he went inside. I thought for one idiotic moment he was going to shake hands with someone. It looked so odd."

Huw took this more seriously than I thought it warranted. "You know, that could have been an almighty bluff."

"You mean he was *pretending* to carry a gun under the coat? Why should he bluff? He didn't mind toting a gun round Oxford—or using it!" In my mind's eye I saw the slim, tough figure again. I conceded it with reluctance, and only partially. "He could have had a knife on him, I suppose."

"Look at it this way. While you don't want to be caught carrying small arms round London these days, he'd find it impossible to stab all of us one after the other. He might have thought he'd find just you and your mother, perhaps, or, God forbid, you on your own. He'd have been pretty certain of being able to deal with two untrained women—and I don't suppose he'll have bargained on finding two old soldiers in your sitting-room, and both of them still fighting fit. Hence the bluff. See?"

I saw—and I think I wanted to believe it, but I said obstinately: "The curtains aren't drawn—and he only just shut the window himself a few moments ago. If he couldn't actually see Daddy and Grandpa from his hiding-place, he'll have been able to hear their voices. And even if he did see me go, and it is a bluff, he'll still have to be jolly sure of himself."

Huw turned his head and looked. He seemed a lot taller than I was, and I saw a pulse going under his jaw. Then he put his mouth to my ear.

"Stay here a moment. I'm going to see if I can see anything."

"Huw, don't!" I hissed. "What if it isn't a bluff after all?"

"Then it's a double-bluff, which is confusing, so let's not go there. Look after the Champagne and don't drink it all. I'll be back in a sec."

He shrugged off the coat and gave it to me, "in case I rustle", dropped a kiss on the top of my head, and melted silently into the night in a wide curve that took him out of the direct line of sight of the window. I folded the heavy Barbour tightly in my arms, not taking my eyes off him.

He approached the railings from the opposite direction, ran lightly up the steps and leant as close to the window as he dared. It began to dawn on me that someone might be hurt—might, even, not be alive at the end of this ghastly business... My hands were like ice. I shifted the burdensome mass of waxed cotton under one arm and dug my fingers in my pockets. They touched metal. My house key. I dragged it out. I hadn't known I'd brought it with me.

In a few moments, Huw was beside me again.

"I couldn't see much, just Saratov sitting on the back of the sofa with the coat just as you described. But I saw your parents, and heard your grandfather and Mrs Mitchell, so everybody's alive and kicking." His mobile bleeped again then with the same unhelpful message. He checked it, made a gesture of impatience, then silenced it and put it back in his pocket. "I wonder if he's made provision for a quick getaway." He looked round, as though for a likely vehicle, but cars were parked all along the side of the road. "I can't see anybody double-parked, engine running." He turned back to me. "What have you got there?"

"My house key. I didn't know I had it on me," I whispered. My teeth were clenched to control the chattering. "It sort of—settles it, doesn't it? I looked at him doubtfully. One corner of his mouth was lifting in an odd little smile, and I realised with a jolt that he wasn't afraid. Surely with Huw I would be safe…and Daddy and Grandpa were both there. They would know what to do. Despite myself and my fear, I could feel my blood beginning to tingle with a kind of what-the-hell recklessness. Any action was better than standing here doing nothing. And Huw was looking wolfish again. I thrust his Barbour at him. "Some academic you are," I said more confidently. "You should have been in the S.A.S. yourself. Now what are you looking for?"

He was searching in one of the carrier bags, and tenderly brought out a noble, gold-shouldered bottle.

"It'll make a fine weapon," he said, hefting it. "Well, Cassie mine? He's expecting us, so we'd better turn up. Are you game?"

"Do I have to answer that?" I added, rather hollowly: "You will remember that I can't act for toffee, won't you."

"I can, though. I've been the leading light of O.U.D.S. since I went up."

"All that and boxing too? I'm impressed."

"Don't be." He put the bottle in the poacher's pocket of his ancient Barbour. The waxed cotton was so rubbed and baggy from all his textbooks that it vanished without trace.

"What are you going to do with it?" I asked, with a good deal of suspicion.

"You never know: bottles of Champagne might catch on as a weapon. Bag your man and drink the contents to celebrate, two for the price of one. I'll put it to Helmut." He must have seen my face then, because he wiped the grin off his own. "It'll be quite safe," he said rather lamely. "You watch."

"Huh. Just don't bring lilies to my funeral, that's all."

Assuming the mien of an innocent civilian with nothing more dangerous on his mind than a celebratory evening with friends and soon-to-be family, he picked up the supermarket carrier bags, and we walked back along the pavement like any pair of young lovers. My heart was certainly racing, but it was not, this time, from passion.

I didn't dare look in at the sitting-room window as we passed it; and the half-dozen steps were far worse than anything St Patrick could dream up. I could hardly force my shaking hand to find the lock. As the key grated in, I distinctly heard the harsh voice grate out: "Nobody move!"

I should have been terrified, but I barely turned a hair. I simply opened the door. I think I even laughed softly; the way a girl does with her lover.

TWENTY-TWO

Another man could scarce have lifted the cup from the table,
when it was full, but Nestor the Old raised it easily.

Book IX: *ibid*

THE STRANGE THING was, nothing had changed. I don't know
whether I expected the hall to have turned scarlet, or the
furniture to have sprouted scales, or my entire family to have
been abducted aboard a U.F.O., leaving only scorch marks
on the floor, but it all looked exactly as it had when I had
left—could it really only have been about ten minutes since?
My ears were on stalks, but all I could hear from the sitting-
room was a kind of watchful silence.

We glanced at each other—and I remembered something
that turned me to stone.

"Huw?"

"Mm?"

"It's on the dining-table."

I willed him to understand me; I didn't dare say more.
His jaw dropped, but only for a second. Quick thinker that
he was, he rustled one of the carrier bags over the threshold,

saying under cover of the small noise: "Too bad. We'll have to brazen it out."

Following his lead, I squared my shoulders and said clearly enough to be overheard: "No, look, it's there—at the bottom."

As though on our way to the kitchen to put Huw's purchases away, we stopped by the sitting-room, and—I must be a better actress than I thought—put our heads in. I heard myself say perfectly normally: "Hallo, everybody, we're back."

My father was on his feet. He was pale, and looked every bit as dangerous as the stranger I had deliberately not yet looked at; not like my father at all. "Cassie…"

I didn't dare look at the dining-table, but I did allow myself to see the man behind the sofa. He had slid to his feet the moment we appeared. He was well-muscled, not tall; with a square face, expressionless green eyes, and a flat, thick, cruel mouth with lips at once sensuous and compressed. The hair and brows were pale brown, and sparse. My gaze swept swiftly over these attributes and went to the coated right arm like a pin to a magnet. *Was* he bluffing? From his vantage point he could keep all six of us covered with ease— or appear to. I was suddenly less sure, and fear clawed at me anew.

"Who are you?" My voice was flat, betraying nothing, and my lips were stiff. Behind me, Huw moved so that a bag bumped against my leg. I knew that both bags, with the supermarket's name in bright orange, were plainly visible to the man by the window. I let my gaze rove round the members of my family, allowing myself to become aware that something was badly wrong, and my voice warm into righteous indignation. "What are you doing in my house? What the hell's going on?"

He spoke then. "You be quiet. I ask questions." The coat jerked in my father's direction. "You! Sit!"

I held my breath. Part of me wanted my father to defy him, to do something spectacular that Bond might have been proud of; but I only know that when he sat down, slowly and deliberately, after one long look at the man in black, I was never more relieved in my life.

Close to, the harsh Russian accent sounded shockingly strange and threatening, and far too real. Mrs Mitchell's eyes were closed: the man's face was only three feet or so above her head. My grandfather's hand was over hers, and I saw that it was trembling. He looked cowed, and frightened, and—old. It was unsettling, and it should have taken any last spark of fight out of me, but it didn't. Never before had I seen my grandfather old and afraid, and at last my anger rose. My father's jaw was set hard and his mouth thin; my mother's face was shuttered; white; afraid. What this thug had done to my family gave me courage. I came a step or two further into the room, concealing the table from his view. "This is my house," I said, my voice high and loud, "and I don't know you from Adam. I don't know what the hell you're doing here, but I want you to leave, please. Now!"

My mother uttered the faintest of protests as Saratov interrupted.

"When I have what belongs, I leave."

He might have been talking of catching the next train. He lifted the shrouded hand at Huw. "Sit, you. Leave the bags. You have mobile? Put it on the table."

I only just managed to control the electric shock of alarm that live-wired through me. What if Helmut should text back...or, worse, ring?

Huw, looking alarmed and wary, rested the bags on the floor, and placing his mobile face down on the smooth wood of the coffee-table, shuffled sideways to the chair by the fireplace, looking the picture of fright and affronted shock. From it, I realised, he could watch Saratov's every movement. I perched on the arm of Mummy's end of the other sofa, opposite Grandpa and Mrs Mitchell, and put my arm protectively round her shoulders. Her hand clutched mine painfully, and I kissed her.

"Now," said Yuri Saratov, hitching his hip onto the back of the sofa, and lowering the coated arm so that it rested across his knee. He looked horribly at home. "Now, we wait until you give what is mine."

Oh, God. A battle of wills. I closed my eyes for one despairing moment—and opened them again at Mrs Mitchell's wail of protest. She half-turned so that she could look up at the figure so close behind her, and actually wagged an admonitory forefinger at him.

"Now listen to me, young man! If you imagine that at my age my bladder will survive another half-hour of this...this outrageous nonsense, you can think again!"

He glanced down with a kind of pitying indifference, assessing her harmlessness, then shrugged. "You have five minutes. I know exactly where the toilet is in this house, so no funny business, or the boyfriend dies."

Hard on the heels of the disgust and fear that this roused in me came surprise to see my grandfather's brows twitch together and his eyes begin to burn with a suddenly kindled anger. This was at puzzling variance with his general air of senile decay, and it was only slowly that it dawned on me that the latter might be assumed. In another second I was sure of it. Seeing me watching him anxiously, his expression cleared, and his left eyelid slowly dropped in what I can only describe as a wink. Keeping my face straight, I let him see that I had taken the hint. Mummy and

Huw—and I—were not the only ones who could act a part, it seemed. I even managed to look concerned as he made one or two attempts to rise, as though to pay Mrs Mitchell a charming, olde-worlde courtesy. Falling back, defeated, he put a shaking hand on her arm.

"I'm sorry, dear," he said in a reedy old voice. "I can't get up without aid."

"Don't give it another thought, Hector," she said calmly, patting him. She cocked a challenging sideways glance at Saratov.

The Russian's eyes gleamed green, chips of Arctic ice, giving nothing. They flicked from her to the back of my grandfather's head. And then to Huw's mobile. And then to my father, my mother, me—and back to Mrs Mitchell... but not behind me. Not to *The Iliad*, lying gleaming dimly in the darkened dining-room. Why the bloody hell hadn't we taken it to the bank with the all-important lists? Of all the stupid... But that wouldn't help. I consoled myself that Huw and I had been right about one thing: he had his work cut out for him, covering the six of us at once. As if in confirmation of this, the coat twitched with just the faintest hint of indecision before he jerked the shrouded hand at me.

"You. Turn it over."

"What?"

"The mobile. Turn it over. Do it!"

I bent, as slowly as I dared, and minding more that in so doing I was leaving a clear line of sight for him straight into the dining-room. The mobile, now face upwards, showed a blank screen. I slid back onto my perch, my heart thumping. He had followed my every move.

The eyes skimmed to Mrs Mitchell again. "Five minutes!"

"*Halt's maul, Arschgesicht,*" she answered with a sweet smile, and left the room, her head high.

Saratov's pale brows twitched as he watched her go, and for just a second he looked baffled. As though this had given my mother an idea, she looked across at Huw and said: "*As-tu trouvé quelque chose à manger, mon cher Huw?*"

"No talking," said Saratov automatically.

"I'm sorry," said my mother placatingly. "My daughter's boyfriend is French. He doesn't speak any English."

Huw cast one sullen, furious look at Saratov, and shrugged.

I was thinking furiously. Had he said anything—anything at all—since we entered the sitting-room? No, I was sure he hadn't. And no one would ever guess that he and my mother had only once before set eyes on each other. I could only guess at what my mother might have in mind. I was looking at Saratov throughout this short exchange, and I saw the green eyes narrow and his gaze dart uncomprehendingly from my mother to Huw and back. I was certain then, as certain as if he had told me so himself, that he spoke neither German nor French. My own grasp of the latter tended (naturally) to the dinner-ordering variety, but I understood it better than I could speak it. Grandpa, I knew, spoke fluent French, and my father's was competent. If necessary, then, we could communicate without Saratov's understanding a word. Helmut had called him a fellow negotiator, I recalled, but I didn't think much of a negotiator who couldn't speak any languages. Perhaps he was, after all, the contract killer I had called him; an ignorant thug who could be outwitted. I gave Mummy's shoulders a covert squeeze of congratulation. If only the mobile didn't give us away... That was bad enough, but I tried to think about that rather than the thing that was beginning to nag at me. If Saratov had followed us to the bank, why was he here at all?

Mrs Mitchell reappeared in the quiet room and took her place beside my grandfather. I felt a surge of admiration for her; she actually picked up her glass and drank a little as though she were at a cocktail party. Then she put it down with a defiant click on the table and sat back. My grandfather took her hand, and she patted his in a motherly fashion.

Silence, crackling with menace. I sensed that my father, though leaning back in his seat with one knee crossed over the other, was acutely alert. I was passionately grateful for his and my grandfather's presence. I didn't dare look directly at Huw, but my peripheral vision told me he was sitting slackly, slumped as though already vanquished. Saratov, on the other hand, was at his ease, half-seated on the back of the sofa; relaxed, alert, and looking fully capable of keeping us up all night.

The thought horrified me. *Surely* help would come soon, not leave us here with this…this trained and determined man, this murderer who shot people in the back. If only Helmut would just turn up, and not bother to reply to the text, not think about replying…

I realised that my attention was concentrated fiercely— had been for some time—on the arm that lay so lightly along Saratov's right thigh, and I must have made some small noise because when I looked up, he was smiling at me. It was not a nice smile. I looked away coldly. The edge of the sofa began to feel hard beneath me, and my leg had gone numb, but the only other place to sit was opposite Huw, and I couldn't risk Saratov's seeing that book. Besides, I was only an arm's length from the door, and that might be useful. I stayed where I was.

Nobody moved or spoke.

The silence stretched on: leaden, tightening, breathing with threat and fear. People passed along the pavement outside, laughing and talking. A taxi pulled up; doors slammed; footsteps sounded. Another door—someone's front door—

shut. The taxi pulled away. From the Embankment, a siren wailed, and, somewhere, a dog barked excitedly.

The carriage clock ticked on. It sounded hectic and far too loud. I remember being afraid for it in case Saratov became impatient with it for talking. I turned my cheek to Mummy's hair, and she leant against me.

Was there a gun under the coat? Was there? And again: *Why the hell hadn't I put that book in the safe? Why didn't we take it to the bank? Why?*

I shifted on the sofa-arm and nearly cried aloud as pins and needles stabbed my leg with a million tiny stings. I would have to move soon.

But not yet.

It took me some moments to realise that from this slightly altered position, I could see under the loosely lying folds of the coat. That dim gleam of flesh was his hand. I shaded my eyes, as though the light distressed me, and looked as closely as I dared, but it was impossible to discern whether the curled fingers lay naturally, as a hand will, or whether they were curled round the butt of a pistol.

I looked away, at Granny's desk, and tried to think coherently.

Surely the man must have put two and two together and made at least four. He knew, because he had followed us, that we had taken the lists to the bank. He must therefore have gathered that they were tucked away in Mrs Mitchell's safe-deposit box. And Huw and I, instead of keeping the keen-eyed lookout he might have expected, had been nosing about our luxurious transport and singing our heads off. Which brought me back to my original question. What was he doing here? Was he hoping to frighten her into signing for them and releasing them into his control? But he hadn't said anything that indicated it. I thought back. No, he had only said that we would sit here until he had them. Which must mean that for some reason he thought they were here in the house. Which meant that even if he saw the book, his need of it might not be so urgent. Might not be. It was not, however, a risk I was prepared to take. I was the one—once again—who had left the book out: I would do whatever was necessary to protect it.

Yet it didn't make sense. I was more and more convinced that he would never have been fool enough to show himself to all of us unless it had been monumentally important, and he completely sure of his facts and himself.

It came to me only gradually. He simply couldn't know the lists were in a safe-deposit box. He must have thought it was just an ordinary trip to the bank that for some reason involved Huw and me as well as Mrs Mitchell. I frowned to myself. Didn't the man know about these boxes? He can't have done. It was the only possible answer. It occurred to me then that if, like most people, he did his banking online he would never have come into contact with the concept—and I knew from Dinah, whose account was with a High Street clearing bank (which ours were not), that few banks had safe-deposit boxes any more. Whatever the answer, I was now sure that we had something over this thug in that we knew where the lists were—*and he did not*. I kept my eyes lowered, hugging this knowledge to myself.

It must have been about half an hour later when Mrs Mitchell stood up—without Saratov's leave—and challenged him. "Now I must go again."

Saratov grunted, and watched her, but did not attempt to prevent her. Once again she left the room; once again she returned a few minutes later. Naturally, I had no idea whether she really had bladder trouble, but if not, it was another damn' fine piece of acting which might give my father a possible opening. Soon I would have to go to the loo myself. And I didn't know if I had Mrs Mitchell's courage. If only Helmut would come...

We waited.

*

Mrs Mitchell had paid another visit, and the clock told me that we had survived through a mere two hours of our vigil. The tension was stretched taut as a steel hawser, and I could wait no longer. I looked Saratov straight in the face and said very clearly: "You know, you're barking up the wrong tree."

My father moved uncontrollably. My mother gasped: "Cassie, don't!" and put a pleading hand on my arm. Saratov looked at me, deadpan. I darted a glance at Huw and almost laughed aloud. The peat-brown eyes sparkled and were immediately veiled; and I knew that he had come to the same conclusion. In the same second, I realised that the Russian had not understood my slang any more than he had understood German or French. He said, with silky insolence, in confirmation of this: "What are you talking about?"

My mother whispered: "Cassie, darling, don't, oh, please don't."

I hugged her but kept my defiant gaze on the still figure opposite. "The lists are not here." I spoke slowly and clearly.

The swathed arm twitched. "Of course they are here," said Saratov, just a fraction too late.

"No, they are not. They are in a safe-deposit box at the bank you followed us to."

Silence. He said roughly: "You shut up. We wait."

Content to have rattled him, and tremulous with nerves at my own daring, I subsided.

My grandfather spoke then, from the other sofa. What he said made me start and blink at him.

"I think it's about time for a spot of backgammon. What do you say, Hector, my boy?"

This was accompanied by a smile every bit as predatory as Huw's. He saw my startled gaze on him, and winked at me. Of course, Saratov saw none of this, and for a moment I was thoroughly confused. Then the thin smile vanished, and resuming his cowed, senile demeanour, he cast a deprecating glance behind him as though seeking the Russian's approval. I looked quickly at my father, and was almost sure that the answering flash in his eyes was of grim, satisfied agreement. By the time Saratov had caught up, however, it had gone, and my father's face was wiped of expression.

I stared. The extraordinary irrelevance of this strange suggestion, following on from my revelation, and coupled with my grandfather's unusually saturnine grin, seemed somehow to season the tension with a dash of Looking Glass surreality. I believe it would not have surprised me if Saratov had obligingly pulled a travelling games set there and then out of the black, woven folds of stuff and settled down to a match with one or the other of them. *Surely he wouldn't hold it so casually if...*

"Have we a board?" asked my father. His face was as unreadable as though he were playing poker—or Russian roulette. And, which was odd, he addressed himself to my grandfather when—surely—he should have been asking me. Not that I had a backgammon board. I was just wondering, rather wildly, whether I should say I didn't possess one, and didn't play anyway, when my grandfather spoke again.

"We've got the floor: that'll do for a board." He flexed his hands. They were strong hands, weight-bearing hands.

The floor? What was wrong with the table? What on earth was wrong with the two of them?

Mrs Mitchell was giving nothing away, but the sideways glance she gave him showed an endearingly schoolgirlish worship shot through with surprise and faint alarm.

"Good thinking, Pa," said my father, still poker-faced. "It won't be for the first time, will it? Tell you what, I'll move the table."

Move the table? I looked huntedly from one to the other of them, now completely baffled.

My father directed a mildly enquiring glance at Saratov, who, after the faintest pause, shrugged nonchalantly. The thought crossed my mind that he was, indeed, just a little bit out of his depth. Run-of-the-mill thuggery and political murder were one thing; three different languages and an incomprehensible conversation about boxes and tables were quite another. This at least was immensely cheering, bluff or no bluff, and I dared another modest change of position to ease the pins and needles.

I was still looking from one to the other of them in bewilderment, trying to make up my mind whether this was the height of foolishness, or a genuine attempt to divert us, when the discussion, if I can call it that, took a further, and dramatic, turn for the bizarre.

"An excellent idea," my grandfather was saying approvingly. "We don't want to break it."

I know my mouth fell open. I stopped surreptitiously rubbing my leg. Beside me, my mother quivered as my father leant forward to shift the heavy table from the middle of the floor to between his end of the sofa and Huw's seat. I was thinking confusedly that he must be very strong, he seemed to move it so easily; when suddenly it struck me that in moving it, he had also moved the mobile out of the range of those glacial green eyes. Was *this* his motive? But why all the business about backgammon?

I believe I had even begun to frame some sort of question when several things happened within lightning seconds of each other, and the tense, sweating night burst apart like a fireworks display.

Huw's mobile pinged; and Saratov stood up and made a sudden, involuntary movement towards it. In the same moment, his gaze narrowed past me, behind me, on the other room. Whether he had seen the book or not, I will never know, for my grandfather seemed suddenly to swell to twice his already impressive size as though at a signal he had been waiting for. He gave vent to a primæval sound, midway between a grunt and a yell, that froze Mrs Mitchell, Mummy, and me solid in sheer, atavistic fright. Heedless of Saratov, I sprang to my feet, pins and needles forgotten, the hair furring up on my body.

Gone was the frightened old man. My cosy grandfather lifted his powerful arms, and catching Saratov round the neck in a suffocating grip, brought him flailing down over the sofa and onto the floor, just where the table had been.

Mrs Mitchell let out a little scream and clapped both hands to her mouth. At the same time, Huw, with breathtaking speed, leapt to his feet and grabbed the coat as Saratov fell, and, whisking it out of reach, snatched up the mobile at the same time. Next moment, the Russian was thrashing, prone, on the carpet, both arms locked at the wrists under one of my grandfather's knees and his head forced back by a ruthless hand; and my father was doing something military and efficient to his ankles that made him scream.

No gun had gone flying from Saratov's hand. I drew a deep and very shaky breath from sheer relief. Colin himself could not have gambled more successfully.

Mrs Mitchell quickly recovered herself. "Oh, Hector, well *done!*" she cried, clapping her hands together.

My grandfather shot an approving grin at me. "Thank Cassie: she pushed the brute right off balance; gave me my chance. Good work, granddaughter. Have you thought of joining the Army?" He reached up his spare hand to me, and we shook, brothers-in-arms.

"Have you got any rope by any chance, Cassie?" My father might have been asking for a box of matches for all the emotion he displayed.

It took me one coruscating moment to review the contents of the odds-and-ends drawer in the kitchen and shake my head. "No, I haven't." I added helpfully: "But there is some string."

"Damn. You lie still, you," he said roughly to Saratov, and began with his free hand to unbuckle his belt. He whipped it out of the loops and flung it round Saratov's ankles, pulling the free end through the buckle tight enough to elicit another yell of pain. Then he wrapped the rest of the belt's length round and secured the pin of the buckle through the tightest hole. After that, he sat on the ankles, and he and my grandfather, exchanging boyish grins of pure pleasure, shook hands over the body writhing on the floor. Neither of them looked a day over twenty.

"Nice work, Pa!" said my father happily. "Good for you, Cassie!"

"Good heavens," said my mother at last, faintly.

"The benefits of encouraging your enemy to under-estimate you," said my grandfather with great satisfaction. "Life in the old dog yet. I'll give you *boyfriend*, sonny. Lie quiet now, or I'll have to hurt you. I don't want to do that, not with ladies present. Not nice."

I cleared my throat and uttered the first thing that occurred to me. "I'm enormously impressed, don't think

I'm not—but how on *earth* does backgammon come into it?"

"Oh—turning the tables," said my grandfather. "It's a regimental thing. Code. Very useful. Taught your father. M'father taught me. Haven't used it myself since... What? Oh, thank you, Moira. Just the thing." He took the long silk Hermès scarf—her new one—that my mother was silently holding out, and tied up the Russian's wrists, on which he was still kneeling as negligently as though he were making up the fire. He offered the ends to my father, who did something efficient with scarf and belt that bent Saratov backwards in a fiendish sort of yoga pose, and dragged out of him a hoarse and fluent stream of abuse.

"That'll keep him quiet for a bit. At least—Cassie, darling, can you find a kitchen cloth, or something? And bring the string, please. We'd better gag our uninvited guest. He's spoiling our party. It's just as well none of us knows any Russian, eh?"

"I do," said Mrs Mitchell on a spurt of laughter.

"Don't listen, Inge," said my grandfather over his shoulder. He sounded shocked, and for some reason I found this funny.

"You *bet*," I said, on a choke of laughter, and sprinted off to the kitchen.

I came back with the cloth and the string, and my grandfather efficiently gagged the trussed Russian with a damp J-cloth. Then we all sat back and watched him squirming on the floor.

"*Well*," said Mrs Mitchell, her eyes shining. "*Well!* You were absolutely *splendid*, Cassie! I never even thought of the safe-deposit boxes! I hope that J-cloth is *soaked* in detergent!"

"It was worth a try—it just seemed so odd. But you deserve some acclaim, as well. Just what did you say to him when you left the room first of all?"

"I only told him to…er…to hold his tongue, in gutter German," she replied innocently. "I'm afraid I decided to find out if he knew any. I couldn't resist. It's a very vulgar thing to say—*and* I was rude about his looks, too. If he had known any German, he'd have reacted to that for certain. But he didn't. One thing, though: he knows lots and *lots* of Russian. Quite vernacular, as you might say."

"Attagirl!" I said in delight. "Up the Greatrex family and friends!"

"He doesn't know any French, either," said my mother. Mrs Mitchell looked questioningly at her, so I quickly told her what had happened while she was out of the room. Then we all congratulated each other, loud and voluble with relief; and Huw spoke for the first time since we had entered the sitting-room.

"I say."

We stopped talking and turned our heads to look at him. He was still holding Saratov's coat, and his face was white, the fine mouth slightly open in a kind of vague horror.

"What?" I said, suddenly frightened again. "What is it?"

For answer, he fumbled in a pocket and brought something out. We all craned to see. It was a small and wicked-looking gun, blunt and ugly.

"Oh, God," I said weakly, and sat down.

"Good lord, is that a Stechkin OTs-38?" enquired my father in tones of professional interest. "Very handy. I've always wanted to see one of those close up. They succeeded the PSS, you know," he added for our general information. "I understand they have the advantage of not leaving shell casings about. So untidy if you're on a secret job. May I?"

He held out his hand. Wordlessly, with his eyes on me, Huw gave it to him, and he and my grandfather plunged into an animated technical discussion involving such mysteries as single-stage pistons, full-moon clips, minimised muzzle rise, and integral laser sights, of which Huw and I, staring aghast at one another, took in hardly a word; and to which Mrs Mitchell and my mother, still congratulating and comforting each other, paid no attention at all.

"In the pocket of his coat all the time," said Huw at last.

I considered this, and identified a caveat. "Close to hand, but—but not actually *in* his hand. Don't you think that makes it better?"

"I'm not sure, but at least we were right."

"Only sort of. I thought we'd decided he was bluffing." My voice sounded hollow in my own ears, and I felt a little faint.

Huw swallowed. "You're quite right: we did. Don't *ever* let me talk you into *anything, ever again*," he said, quite fiercely. "I should be *flayed* for encouraging you to walk into such danger."

That pulled me together. "Hogwash," I said more robustly. "It was my idea, remember?"

"No, it wasn't. In any case, it ought not—*must* not—involve a *blatant* misreading of a highly dangerous— Oh, heavens, what now?"

The sound of engines outside in the street; immediately swallowed in a theatrical squeal of brakes. For a split second I wondered if someone were watching a television programme with the volume turned up too high, then light winked blue, swept round my civilised sitting-room. Doors slammed; orders were shouted. A metallic-sounding voice, deafeningly close—despite the shut window—and every bit as alien an intrusion as the man on the floor, spoke far too loudly and almost in my ear. The accent was clipped.

"Yuri Saratov! The house is surrounded! Give yourself up!"

"God, it's Helmut!" gasped Huw, fumbling for his telephone. "I'd forgotten all about him!" He looked at the screen, then raised one agonised eyebrow and looked away. He held it out to me.

On way with armed police back-up. ON NO ACCOUNT PLACE YOURSELVES IN ANY DANGER. *Helmut.*

"Oh, dear," I said unsteadily, laughter bubbling anew. I clapped a hand to my mouth, and we both turned and stared round-eyed at Saratov, who, hearing his name, had begun to squirm frantically and make choking noises through the kitchen cloth. The megaphone blared again.

"Yuri Saratov, come out with your hands up! The house is surrounded!"

"But he can't," I said on a surge of mirth that threatened to overcome me. Little bursts of hysteria prickled through my bloodstream like pins and needles.

My grandfather put one foot on the small of Saratov's back, not in any indecently triumphant spirit, but more as a reminder to him of his lowly status as our prisoner. "Quiet, please," he said, quite kindly. Then to me: "Cassie, darling, it's your house. How do you feel about answering the door to that nice Mr Landeck?"

"The more the merrier," I said.

"Are you mad, Hector?" demanded my mother, electrified at last into speech. "The place is swarming with armed police! Cassie, on no account are you to answer the door!"

I'm afraid this made me give way to the giggles that had been threatening to consume me. I picked up my mother's barely touched glass, and stepping carefully over the thrashing Saratov, went to the window with it. Throwing up the sash,

I put my head out and waved the glass gaily, spilling some of the wine.

"Helmut, is that you? You got here quickly! It's all right, he's quite safe: we've tied him up. He's all yours. Bloody hell! What's all this?"

Three police cars were drawn up, all winking bright blue, and now sported several officers crouching behind them and pointing whatever armed police point over the roofs of their vehicles. I learnt later that they had cordoned off both ends of More Street; a helicopter, with an armed detachment, had been detailed if needed; and Sky News had pipped the B.B.C. at the post for a juicy breaking story.

But I knew none of this at the time, so, infected (I think) by the general air of drama and excitement, I perched carelessly on the window-sill, squinted against the roving searchlights, and toasted the armed officers in Prosecco. "Helmut, where are you? Oh, you're there! Good health!"

His familiar face was a picture as he lowered the megaphone and called up to me from the pavement. "How do you mean, safe—tied up? Are you serious? Has he hurt any of you? Tell me! There is an ambulance on stand-by."

The rimless spectacles were flashing blue: on, off, on, off. It made it difficult to take any of it seriously. I gave another snort of laughter, probably from sheer relief, and out of the corner of my eye I saw a couple of the officers straighten up and lower their weapons. One of them began to look rather cross, and I don't blame him. "No, we're all quite undamaged. You'd better come in and have something to drink. We've finished the Prosecco, but Huw's got a bottle of Champagne. He was going to hit him over the head with it, but he didn't get the chance, so we'd better drink it. I promise you, he's quite harmless. Saratov, I mean, not Huw. My grandfather did it, with Daddy's help. It was simply brilliant! I wish you'd seen it." I hopped down. "Come and join us—but I warn you, there're already seven of us in here, and I don't think there'll be room for all your friends!"

Helmut called something curtly to them, and took the steps two at a time. One of the officers detached himself from behind a car and followed briskly. I ran to let them in.

The sitting-room, already crowded, now resembled the Black Hole of Calcutta. Helmut's keen gaze went straight to the trussed figure on the carpet, quiet now and staring up with hatred. Keenness vanished in the blankest bewilderment, and I realised that the German had only half-believed me. He said weakly: "Saratov? This? Here? How?"

"All yours, Landeck," said my grandfather politely.

The Russian gave vent to another stream of what but for the gag would have been the rankest abuse, and my grandfather stirred him with a lazy foot. "Manners, young man, manners," he said.

My father stood up. "If you're Helmut Landeck, you'd better have this."

Helmut looked at it, set his teeth, and said something soft in German under his breath that made Mrs Mitchell gurgle again. He took the Stechkin and handed it to the officer, who pushed it into a plastic bag and pocketed it without a word.

"Fingerprints!" exclaimed Huw. "Mine—Mr Greatrex's—they'll be all over it!"

"We will sort them out," said Helmut.

"The beaker!" I cried.

"Oh, God, yes! What did I do with it?"

"In your pocket!"

He found it and held it out. "It's got Colin's prints on it. Told him you would know what to do. I took it from the hospital. Sort of insurance—you know, if he ever decides to take up burglary as a career. It'll have mine on it, too."

"And the nurse's," I said.

"And Rachael's."

"And now mine. There is also the DnA..." Helmut closed his eyes for a second, then handed the beaker to the officer. He cleared his throat and visibly pulled himself together. "You have done my job for me," he remarked, running a professional eye over Saratov's bonds. "A silk scarf and a leather belt. Highly effective. In time, I should like to know how this was done."

"Silk's very strong," offered my mother, quite as though she were talking to a friend over lunch at the Savoy.

At this point the police officer, huge in his armoured vest, and crackling with radio-ed information, left the room. He must have called for back-up, for he returned a moment later with another silent, armoured giant, and the room shrank still further. Between them, they replaced the scarf and belt with handcuffs. Saratov was hauled, none too gently, to his feet, and marched forcibly out of my sitting-room. Mrs Mitchell, her pretty, gentle face suddenly distorted with hatred, sent a stream of fluent German after him which caused Helmut's eyes to widen. He shut the door hastily behind him.

My grandfather put an arm round her shoulders, and she leant against him, and was silent.

"Oh, *Hector!*" With a small, strangled sob, my mother walked straight into my father's arms. I turned my face to Huw's shoulder.

Then Helmut came back, and the police with him.

*

It was long before we got to bed that night. We had to give statements, and it didn't need Huw's warning glance for me to guard my tongue. I said only that I had gone out to meet him and help him with the shopping, and that Saratov must have slipped in behind me. I had seen nothing. I had met Huw, and we had walked into a room full of hostages. Yes, very unnerving, to say the least of it. No, of course, we would never have done so if we had had the slightest idea. No. No, certainly not. Highly dangerous, and not to be thought of. Yes, indeed; most unwise. Of course, that was it: the aftermath of the business in Italy. Yes, my family knew about that. Very unfortunate. Highly sensitive. Public interest. Yes, of course I would be vigilant about my front door from now on. Fingerprints? DnA samples? Of course; anything that might help... My mother caused a slight sensation at this point by announcing that hers and mine were already on file, and explained, blandly, and without appearing to notice the effect her words had produced, about the break-in.

So she and I were released, as it were, and my grandfather explained his part in turning the tables, with my father co-opted; and Huw related how he had found the gun. I thought Helmut's voice was more edged as he asked if any of us had known he was armed, but Huw said no; once in the situation and unable to get out, we assumed he was bluffing, with the coat over his arm. We had thought it perfectly safe. Which was true, I reflected. As long as it didn't occur to Helmut to ask if we'd sent the text before or after entering the house...

After Helmut and the officers had gone, and the blue lights had faded, my grandfather spoke into the silence they left behind them.

"Inge, I am going to see you home. And tomorrow I shall come and pick you up and escort you to the bank."

"We will go in my car."

"Very good." He looked round, frowning a little. "Ah, there's my *Iliad*. I'll take it with me, shall I?"

He picked it up from the dining-table, and, with his back to us, didn't see the effect that this produced on Huw and me. Mrs Mitchell nodded her immaculately coiffed head, and put a hand to my cheek.

"That's what comes of leaving your door open," she said, not without satisfaction—and not unnaturally assuming that my expression of horror was a natural consequence of the evening's events. "Don't do it again."

"I shan't," I said fervently.

"Oh, and Huw?"

"Yes?"

"I take it you won't be needing my key? No? Well, goodnight, everybody. Congratulations. Yes, that's it: congratulations."

With just the four of us left, my sitting-room began to reassume its proper proportions. My father was staring at the sofa where Grandpa had sat, and shaking his head, and my mother had wound her scarf round her neck again and was rhythmically pulling the ends through her hands. The table was back in its proper place. The whole thing might never have happened.

"I feel about a hundred," she said. "To think of Hector...! At his age! What a manœuvre! I know he's in good health, but really!"

"Damn' good, wasn't it?" agreed my father. "Clever old devil. Eighty-eight next birthday." There was a tinge of something in the unmistakeable pride that made me look twice at him.

"Daddy," I said accusingly, "I do believe you're jealous!"

"Of course I am," said my father impatiently. "What a performance! I might even start going to his gym myself!"

"Hats," said my mother, half to herself.

I giggled.

"Eh? How do hats come into it? I'd better put my belt back on."

"Two new hats, I should think," she went on as though my father hadn't spoken. I knew perfectly well what she was talking about, and began to blush. She said: "It's just as well we've got a big house with a flat lawn, isn't it? And the field at the back will do very well for parking."

"I haven't the faintest idea what you're talking about," said my father.

"I'll explain on the way home."

"Please do. By the way, I haven't said how brilliant you were, Moira. I spotted what you were up to. It was inspired."

"It wouldn't have worked if Huw hadn't responded so magnificently. How nice to see you again, by the way, Huw."

"And both of you too," grinned Huw, solemnly shaking hands with my parents.

"Your Mrs Mitchell put the idea into my head," continued my mother, looking pleased and a bit embarrassed. "I thought it might come in useful to be able to communicate without our uninvited guest eavesdropping, but my thunder was well and truly stolen by my aged father-in-law." She straightened. "Now, Cassie—"

"Cassie's fine, darling. You leave her be."

"But—"

"No. Huw will look after her."

"But I— Oh! Yes, of course. Well, goodnight, darling. Goodnight, Huw. Quite one of the family already." Even then she hesitated. "Hector, are you sure—?"

"Quite sure. Come on, Moira."

This exchange took them down the hall and out into the street. Which, since my grandfather had disappeared into the night with his past, left the two of us alone. The room felt as large as a saloon at Buckingham Palace.

Huw said diffidently: "Since we're engaged…"

I turned my head to consider him intently. "So we are. But we still haven't managed to tell anybody."

"We've told each other. Won't that do to be going on with?"

"There's something else we're going to keep between ourselves."

"*The Iliad* in full view of Saratov throughout? I should say so. In some ways, we really haven't shone all that much, have we?" His turn to consider me. I don't know what he saw in my face, but he smiled and said: "Ah, now I understand about hats. Your mother knows already."

"Not from me," I said. "None of them gave me a chance. She's just being a mother."

"My mother knew, too," said Huw. "She'll want a new hat. She loves hats. She'll probably knit one."

"That's another 'I told you so'. Talking of hats, I should think Mrs Mitchell will go and buy another soon."

We both looked at the empty sofa. The memories would fade in time; of course they would.

"Wasn't your grandfather wonderful?" There was nothing in Huw's voice but admiration.

"Yes," I said. "They both were. And Mummy. And you, you moved like lightning." I thought I had infused the right degree of bright warmth into my voice, but Huw knows me better than that.

"Nothing but good has come out of this, you know," he said, putting both arms round me. Since this was what I was hoping he would tell me, I looked eagerly up at him.

"I know we've both been frightened, and you've been hurt, but we can be happier about Colin than I ever thought would be possible. Lots of damaged families will have their property restored to them at long last, and your grandfather has found love. And then…"

"And then there's us." I took the spark of courage he was offering. For a long, breathing moment, we stood close, not talking. His heart was hammering against my breast.

"Do you think you can manage the stairs?" he asked, on a sigh that stirred my hair.

"Any number of them. I'd even do the Pozzo again, with you."

"You realise all my luggage is next door."

"I've got a new toothbrush, and you can borrow my razor and shaving foam. Do you mind smelling of vanilla?"

"For better, for worse. Let's lock the front door first, shall we?"

So we did; and then we climbed the stairs together, and went to bed.

EPILOGUE

And let the rest pledge friendship and sure oaths;
so may ye dwell in deep-soiled Troy...

Book IX, *ibid.*

"I CAME HERE after Gwilym died," said Glesni Trefor. "I found Wales too..." She stopped, bending her head. "My sister lives not far away, in a village near Cambridge." The shadows from the chestnut tree danced over the thick curly hair, so like Huw's, that she had confined at the nape of her neck with a pink velvet bow. The Welsh accent was stronger than his; spoken music, an intoxicating lilt.

"My Aunt Catrin lives in a house much like this one," remarked Huw. He had been trying to make a mint julep, on the score that he had never had one before, which seemed an excellent reason; and he was stirring the doubtful-looking concoction with a sprig of mint from the garden. "You'll be thrilled to learn that the road is called Priam's Way." He shot me a brief, unsmiling glance from under the untidy hair, but his eyes were alight.

I laughed, declining the bait. "You'll be relieved to know,

Mrs Trefor, that I haven't brought old Homer with me. By now, he'll be safely in Germany being minutely examined for his secrets. My grandfather has been invited to be the guest of the German government for some ceremony or other, and the German Chancellor wants to thank him personally."

"And how," observed Huw, with a good deal of feeling.

Helmut had gone with my grandfather, Homer, and Mrs Mitchell in style to Goldhanger & Newbold to retrieve the precious lists, subsequently escorting the whole boiling back to Bonn. At the last minute, he had said lugubriously to us, and looking like anything rather than a man who has brought off a successful mission: "By the way, I should inform you that the major part of the Treasures of Troy have been located." Aware that he had stricken us to a dumbfounded silence, he had permitted himself a small, cold smile. "They have been at the Pushkin Museum in Moscow since 1993. Goodbye."

We were still wondering whether this was a representative sample of the famous German sense of humour.

For the rest of it, Saratov was safely behind bars; and Colin, his place on the Art History Detection course confirmed, was due to leave hospital soon. My parents had joined my grandfather and Mrs Mitchell in Germany; and amid the excitement, I had managed to speak to Dinah and hand in my notice. Ginny would be delighted, she said, and murmured something about hats.

We were sitting in the shade on the terrace of Glesni Trefor's house. This was a pleasant, airy sixties building, which had immediately reminded me, when we arrived the previous evening, of *Bewitched*. We had cleared away a late breakfast, having talked far into the night; and now, conversation having lapsed into the merely desultory, I was conscious of a languor and inner peace both new to me.

Huw's grandmother's engagement ring glowed on my finger, and with a kind of lazy delight, I turned my hand this way and that, absorbed in the play of green fire kindled in the emerald by the dappled sun. The ring had fitted perfectly; and my nails—all of them—were a demure pale pink.

I looked the other way, over the palings, where a river meandered through water-meadows under the kissing trails of willow. Calves gambolled, and dignified cows grazed, tails swishing. We hardly needed Homer: this was *Iliad* country in itself. In such a country, one should only talk of comforting things. In this rich land of Troy we dwell in peace.

Reality has its own methods of grounding us. I said to Glesni Trefor on a sudden upsurge of recollection: "Huw told me you designed knitwear. I'd love to have a look."

"Would you?" Her wary, unsmiling gaze slid sideways to me, as it had done several times already. She had been just as tense last night—but I had told myself that that was understandable. It was less understandable on this gorgeous summer's late morning. Not for the first time, I wondered how much—and what—Huw had told his mother of me. Putting this to him on the journey down, he had replied reasonably, if unhelpfully: "Oh, you can do all that personal stuff yourselves."

Now he looked from one to the other of us, and sucked one of the mint leaves in a way that told me he knew precisely what was passing through my mind. "Yuck. This doesn't taste nearly as good as it smells." He dropped it on the grass and grinned reassuringly, as a father might encourage unwilling children.

"So like his father," sighed Glesni. "Well, if you're really interested… "

As soon as she vanished into the house, I pounced. "What on earth did you say? She doesn't seem to like me much!"

He cast me a look of affectionate scorn and said he had at least told her my name. "Your circumstances are your business, though."

"And my hurdle, evidently!"

"Money doesn't make you any more of a human being."

"Or less," I retorted, with spirit.

A gleam of acknowledgment from the peat-brown eyes. Stippled noonday sunlight played over the strong features. "You'll love her designs."

I should have known better. I gave up. "I'm sure I will."

And I did love them. Her taste marched with mine so exactly that another link in the chain was forged there and then at the wooden picnic table under the chestnut tree as she spread out her drawings.

"I do what I can with the internet," she said, "but I don't enjoy using it, and I actually find it pretty limiting. I know, I know, everybody sneers when I say that, but I find it kills the creative process to have to think the way a computer does."

I put down a drawing of a mini-dress in blocks of cream crochet and lilac suede. I desperately wanted to say something but wasn't sure how to put it.

"You don't agree," said Glesni Trefor, misinterpreting my silence.

"I do, I do," I protested. "I was only wondering how on earth to put something rather important to you. We've only just met, and the last thing I want is to offend you."

"Try me," she said, with Huw's reasonableness.

It was strange but the words came to me easily. "All right: I'll ask you outright. What would you say is holding you back from expanding?"

"Having to do the admin.," she replied immediately. "I loathe it. I resent every second spent on spreadsheets and navigating my way round the internet's sclerotic arteries when I could be drawing."

Over the hurdle... I took a deep breath and told her about Dinah and the salon. "And she's doing so well, too. That's it, really. I could be useful to you as well, if you like."

I had spoken my piece diffidently. She hadn't said a word throughout. I saw her glance at Huw with a strange expression, almost as though she was seeing him for the first time, then brought her attention back to me with something of an effort.

"How?"

"Pay an assistant's wages for you."

"And how do I pay you back?"

...And into the straight. "Anyway you want. Anyway that doesn't leave you short. A small share of the profits if you really want to be formal about it, once you begin to make some. That's what Dinah did. And if you want,"—I touched the cream-and-lilac drawing—"I could model for you. Please? I'm beginning to feel I might do something dreadful if I can't wear your clothes immediately. Or preferably sooner."

She gave a reluctant laugh. "How would your modelling help me?"

I made a little *moue* of distaste. "I'm what they call a Frower. I'm supposed to have contacts." I heard the embarrassment in my voice, and was annoyed. "That's silly. I do have contacts in the business. I know I'm not tall, but I have strutted my stuff on the catwalk in my time. Think Kate Moss." I smiled rather sheepishly. "I keep telling myself that being rich is nothing to be ashamed of. I'm even beginning to believe it."

"Good girl," said Huw. "What do you Frow, particularly?"

"Horrible tantrums," I said, "particularly if I don't get my own way about clothes."

Glesni Trefor looked at me suspiciously. "What's a Frower?" She sounded very Welsh.

"Must I say? It's someone who sits in the front row for fashion displays."

"Well, there's interesting. Not like the Nuclear Wintour, I hope?"

I laughed. "No fear. But if I go to, say, the next Katranzou show, and I'm photographed sitting next to Tory Burch and wearing one of your creations... Well, you can picture what happens next, I think."

She was looking owlish and solemn, and didn't offer any response to this for a moment. Then she said: "Who chooses the assistant?"

"You do," I said. "If you have someone in mind, that is. If not, I'll give you a hand."

"Know someone in the recruitment business, as well, I suppose?" Her tone was polite, and I hoped she wasn't humouring me.

"As it happens, yes. Will you think it over? Please don't be offended with me for offering. It seems that money can do such a lot of good if it's allowed to." My involuntary glance at Huw was beseeching, but he was smiling into his glass like a haruspex whose prophecy has at last been fulfilled.

"What I don't understand," she said, puzzled, and a bit cynical, "is what's in it for you. This is a lot of money we're talking about."

"I can see that I shall have to confess the rest." As succinctly as I could, I told her about the trust fund, and Daddy's categories. "And I've found that sometimes I can even combine business with pleasure. Which is what this would be." I fell silent. The ball was in her court now.

She didn't reject my offer. She wasn't looking at me. Her eyes were shadowed, and a small private smile played on her mouth. So had Uncle Will looked at the restaurant above the Piazza in Assisi. I held my breath, and waited. Huw finished his mint julep and put the empty highball glass down.

The clunk of glass on wood seemed to be a deciding factor. Glesni Trefor came back to the present with a start and said: "It'll be a proper arrangement."

"Of course. You can do a business plan if you really want, all costed, projections, the lot. Not that I'll stick out for one, you understand: I'm just there as a backer." I gave her a rather doubtful, hopeful smile. "It's a lot more flexible than a bank, and you'll be getting a backer who understands your field. Mr Mainwaring I'm not. Take all the time you need to think it over."

She gulped, as though she were about to dive from the top board, and said tensely: "Don't need to. I'll do it. I'll accept your offer."

Huw exclaimed: "That's the way to go, Mum!" and gave her a bear-hug.

Neck and neck past the post. I wanted to hug her, too. "I'm more glad than I can begin to say. I'm desperate to wear your clothes. I don't know when I've ever seen anything more gorgeous. Do you wear them yourself?"

She sighed. She seemed younger, gentler, as though the decision had released something in her. "I used to, but I refuse to show you any photographs of a younger me, in case it makes me cry." She looked down ruefully at her curves. "I design the clothes I'd wear myself if I had the figure. As it is, you can only go boho when you look like a stack of old tyres. I was always the sturdy one. Sensible legs, my sister Catrin says. She, of course, has gorgeous legs, completely lacking in any sensible qualities. And she's younger than me. Huw, now, he gets his build from his father."

"Not to mention his wardrobe," observed Huw. "Oh, look, there's a caterpillar. I wonder if he'd like this mint."

We were trying to explain why this was funny when I gradually became aware of a sound. It would be truer to say that I sensed it first in my bones, the way one senses the deepest organ-stop on a mighty organ in a grand cathedral before the decibels swell and flower into music. Almost before I had registered it, I knew what it was, though to my certain knowledge I had only ever heard it on film before.

An Avro Lancaster. And the music was her four Rolls-Royce Merlin engines.

She was coming fast, if not quite at her top speed of nearly two hundred and ninety miles an hour. The majestic, mighty roar filled the sky from horizon to horizon as she approached from the south-east. I don't remember springing up from my seat and running out onto the sunny lawn, but then Huw and his mother were with me and the three of us shaded our eyes as she passed solitary and proud right over our heads. I do know that we were waving frantically, as though she had just returned safely from Berlin. I know, too, that as her distinctive cocked tail-fins receded, taking that glorious, bulldog-belligerent growl with them, I was laughing and crying at the same time.

"She's part of the Battle of Britain Flight," said Huw. He had an arm round each of us, and though he kept his voice casual, his eyes were shining like a schoolboy's. "She'll be on her way home to Duxford. I wonder where she's been on her own."

I could only gasp: "Oh, how *utterly* wonderful! I'm *beyond* thrilled to have seen that! I'll remember it for the rest of my life, I know I will! Oh, how jealous Daddy will be! Hell, I haven't got a handkerchief! I must tell my grandfather!" I wiped tears and mascara over the shoulder of Huw's father's writing-jumper.

He looked at his watch by dint of hugging me closer to his side so that he could see his wrist. "You'd better," he said.

"Well, I will," I said. I was still hungrily watching the empty sky, but the casual tone was now shot through with an electric undercurrent of something I couldn't identify. I raised my eyes to his face. "Why, particularly?"

"Look," he said in a strange voice.

I looked.

It was twenty past.